ON THE
SUBJECT
OF
GRIFFONS

LINDSEY BYRD

RIPTIDE
PUBLISHING

Riptide Publishing
PO Box 1537
Burnsville, NC 28714
www.riptidepublishing.com

On the Subject of Griffons
Copyright © 2019 by Lindsey Byrd

Cover art: L.C. Chase, lcchase.com/design-portfolio.html
Editors: Carole-ann Galloway, May Peterson
Layout: L.C. Chase, lcchase.com

ISBN: 978-1-62649-883-9

First edition
May, 2019

Also available in ebook:
ISBN: 978-1-62649-882-2

ON THE
SUBJECT
OF
GRIFFONS

LINDSEY BYRD

RIPTIDE
PUBLISHING

*To Justine, for inspiring me to write this story,
and to Tommy for being wonderful exactly as you are.*

TABLE OF
CONTENTS

CHAPTER ONE

K era sat with her hands folded in her lap. Her father, on her left, negotiated with the bankers, while her sister, Ciara, silently offered support from Kera's right. Kera would have preferred to have this conversation without them, but the bankers had come by no less than four times this week. They weren't interested in speaking to *her*, and listening to them spin the same horrid story as they waited for her to find proper representation grew more exhausting by the hour.

Each morning she woke to them knocking on her door, refusing to leave until she let them in. She'd tried ignoring them. She'd made every effort to block them from her mind. But her children had started to look nervous whenever there was a knock on the door, a trend she had no interest in continuing or encouraging if she could help it.

So she let the bankers in. She was talked at. And at some point, she'd memorized their spiel enough to recite it by heart. They always started with their shows of sympathy: *"You must understand ... a lady such as yourself is just not equipped to manage such things."* And they always concluded by asking her to sell her home.

Ciara had been incensed when Kera described the meetings, insisting that they call their father to intervene. It took two weeks before Kera managed to overcome the guilt and despair of not being able to handle the bankers herself. Giving in felt like giving up, and Kera loathed how despondent it made her.

Still, her father had conducted business between the banks of Ship's Landing and Alexandria for years, advising the Travers banking institution from the comfort of his home at Crystal Point. He wasn't quite the legend that Kera's husband, Morpheus, had been, but he was respected enough to mean more to these men than her.

The bankers always came in pairs. Their hair was held back with dark ribbons, black tricorn hats tucked low over their eyes, and their pocket watches clicked far too loud for her liking. Even though there were different representatives each day, they were always from the *same* bank, with the *same* pocket watches, always clipped to the *same* button on their waistcoats.

Her father barely batted an eye at their pocket watches or their coats. He seemed impervious to the nuisance presented before her eyes. He told the bankers in small, simple words that the Ivory Gate was his daughter's home. Kera and her children would not be moved from it. The debts would be paid, but considering her husband's death . . . she needed time to restructure them. In any case, she hadn't missed a single payment yet, so their concern, while appreciated, was unnecessary.

Appreciated. Kera squeezed her fingers in her lap. She could not imagine something she appreciated *less.*

"We're concerned for Widow Montgomery," one of the bankers insisted. "Being a widow of a trait—"

"My husband was *not* a traitor," Kera said. Ciara's fingers snatched at Kera's palm and squeezed tight. Pain blossomed around fragile bones not used to such strength. The bankers nodded their heads, placating and somber; one even reached out to pat her knee.

"We understand it's been a trying time for you, madam. But your husband's attempt on our esteemed Overseer Wild's life was quite apparent . . . I imagine discovering you were wed to an assassin must be rather difficult."

"And yet it's my husband who's dead and not the overseer."

Ciara's grip was near bruising. Even Father sighed and shook his head.

"You must forgive my daughter. As you said, it's been a trying time." He cut her a sharp glance from the corner of his eye. He'd been terrifying in her youth. One look could send demons into her heart and mind, promising a lifetime of torment should she not obey. Even so far into her maturity, with children well on their way to adulthood of their own, he could cow her with a frown. Kera's limbs turned loose and awkward beneath his expression. She tilted her head toward her chest and she squeezed her sister's fingers in return. "Though I will say, the reasons for Montgomery's actions were never understood. As assassination carries a more political lean . . . It's entirely possible that he acted from more personal strife."

Heat rushed to Kera's cheeks. She could feel the men casting looks about themselves, nodding and smiling and nudging their elbows in a way that made her skin crawl. Her tongue affixed itself firmly to the bottom of her mouth even as one of the bankers dared to say, "Ah yes, the Aurora Sinclair affair. Wasn't too long ago now was it? Such burdens the gentleman placed on his family."

"Yes. Indeed."

"Perhaps we should move on?" Ciara suggested airily, fingers still tight around Kera's palm.

The bankers cleared their throats. "Yes, ah, of course. Ahem. Well, you see we've calculated her income. As we said, from our understanding the Widow Montgomery will not be able to continue payments for much longer. Agreeing to this sale will be a preemptive measure to ensure she will not be taken advantage of in the future."

The other banker reached for the tea that Kera had served them twenty minutes ago. It had cooled, but he didn't appear to mind. "And with the plague in the city and all these children . . . holding on to this house may not be in the widow's best interest."

Father hummed low, running a hand over his chin as he inspected the documents the bankers were quick to offer. Each one showed line item after line item of projected expenses and return on investments. Kera had looked them over each time they came calling, and they always seemed the same.

Her shoulders sagged, falling out of their forced posture. After two hours of negotiations, through most of which she had been ignored, Kera was finished. She could not fathom why her presence would be required any longer. "Excuse me, gentlemen." She pushed from the pale green couch her husband had purchased during her first pregnancy and strode from the room.

Ciara followed behind, keeping careful pace with her. Not so close as to risk stepping on the hem of her dress, but still close enough that Kera could feel her walking through the slight tremble of the floor. "They're not trying to be disrespectful," Ciara informed Kera, each word clipped and pointed.

Kera nodded. She knew that all too well. In fact, when they came tomorrow, she could hear them tell it to her face again. *"We're just concerned for you, Widow Montgomery."* And then they would request that she sell her home and all her belongings once more. Just yesterday, they'd taken it upon themselves to instill their opinions on her current state of being. *"A woman such as yourself, widowed so . . . unfortunately, should be taken care of by a proper gentleman. One who will not act so brashly."*

"You realize they hate me only because my husband put their patriarch in jail. Henry Travers was guilty on all charges, but that bank has been nothing but horrid to our family ever since."

"They don't *hate* you, Kera; they're conducting a good faith service for their business. It's in their interest for you to sell. It isn't personal."

"Of course it's personal," she murmured, letting her eyes travel over the dusty webs on her ceiling. "Everything is personal." Dust had accumulated on all the surfaces, and though she'd known she had to clean for a while, she hadn't managed to quite bring herself to do it. The servants had been sent away not long after Mori's death. She hadn't been reckless with her finances; she did know they were finite.

But now the house was unwashed. There was a faint smell of something rotting in the floor, lurking in the cellar, and she hadn't yet mustered the energy to find it. It was one thing too many, and she wasn't interested in tracking down every flaw in the world. There were too many to number.

Ciara had started herding Kera's children into industriousness not long ago. Kera had heard them singing songs as they cleaned their rooms and tidied the kitchen. The older ones had been helpful, minding their siblings even as they attempted to put things right.

"It's been a year," Ciara reminded her.

"Has it?" That couldn't be true. There had been no celebrations for the start and end of winter. No feast days. She couldn't recall the name-day gatherings. They hadn't celebrated her union day. She folded her hands together and rubbed at the ring she still wore: two bands folded together in an endless loop.

"I don't suppose you have a destination in mind?" Ciara asked.

Kera stopped short, feet skidding to a halt. They had been walking in circles, looping up and around the Ivory Gate's second floor without so much as a pause to float between rooms. Dropping her hands back to her sides, she pressed her lips together.

Ciara sighed. She stepped closer to Kera and said in her kindest voice: "It's all right to grieve."

Kera laughed.

No, it wasn't.

She hadn't been permitted the luxury of grieving without condemnation since the day following Mori's funeral. She was reminded that she had eight—*seven* children, and that it was her responsibility to find them a father who would raise them *properly*. Whatever that meant. Some people were kind enough not to mention how Mori's influence had already led one of her children down the path of dueling and debauchery. Some were not. She had heard the whispers in the streets, the vile things said at the market. *"At least the young one won't have any of* his *influence."* As if little Aiden not knowing his father were a good thing.

"Can you imagine what Mori would have said to our guests downstairs?" she asked Ciara instead.

Ciara allowed the change of topic, stepping closer to loop her arm around Kera's. "I imagine Morpheus would have given them quite the lecture on proper banking and financing while they sat upon the couch taking notes the whole time, charmed by his nature and awed by his genius."

Kera could envision how he would look. His slight body dressed in his favorite green coat, arguing with words she doubted even ten percent of the population knew the definition of. She smiled at the thought of it.

"Kera?" Ciara asked, gently. Always gently. Kera's smile slipped away. Ciara was waiting for an actual response, but words shriveled and died on Kera's tongue.

She clawed desperately at the folds of her brain and managed to say, "He'd have been furious with the plague."

Her sister was not impressed. "If only he'd managed to put his temper toward something productive before he passed."

Something wet pricked at Kera's eyes. She turned her head so her sister couldn't see, feigning an adjustment to trail her sleeve across her lashes and catch tears before they fell. Ciara, however, was not so easily convinced. She pressed on, determined. "Would it be so bad to sell the Gate? There haven't always been . . . the *best* memories here."

The words were a betrayal—wrapping around her throat with a cloying hand that strangled even as it pretended to help. "And which memories would those be?" Kera asked so quietly she wasn't even sure her sister would hear her.

But she had. She touched Kera's shoulder, saying her name in full like it would somehow ease the blow. "Kerryn—"

"No." Kera shook her head. "No. This is my home, Ciara. And I'm not going to leave it just because . . . I'm not going to leave it."

"I couldn't live in a house where my husband died," Ciara said. "Where my *son* died."

Kera twisted back, away from her sister. She shook her head, brought one hand to her mouth.

"Kera, even before that, with Mori's *affair* and the blackmail—"

"He *never* brought her here," she snapped. "He promised. He never brought her here."

Ciara said nothing. Her fingers fiddled with a loose hair ribbon at her front. She wrapped it around her palm forward and backward, tightening and loosening as she gave Kera what must have been the most pitying look in her arsenal.

"It doesn't matter either way. Good or bad, Ciara . . . This is our home." Kera swallowed hard. "Mori promised me forever in this home, and I'll not lose it just so some bankers can add it to their collection."

One of her hands slipped to the locket she'd worn since the day she was married. Her husband had presented it to her when no one was around to see, shy even though they'd already exchanged their vows. He was scheduled to return to the war in the morning, but they'd made no mention of it that night. He'd placed the locket in her palm and requested that she keep him in her heart. He had whispered, *"My beloved Kera, I wish you all the happiness in the world,"* in her ear, and she'd held it close always. She ran her fingers over the locket's sides and edges, thumbed at the clasp with a nail in need of snipping.

Ciara bit her lip, then started talking, even as Kera's thumb found the clasp. "There is a lot of debt that is in need of . . . restructuring."

Her concern was sisterly and fond, but Kera would not be swayed. She popped the locket open, then snapped it shut without even looking at it, repeating the action a few more times as she replied. "I will not take my children from the home their father built for them."

Ciara folded her hands in front of her, a delicate gesture of calm. She nodded her head, even bent her knees a little—the slightest curtsy Kera had ever seen—serving as an apology and polite acceptance in one. "I am worried for you, my Kerryn."

"Well you need not be." Kera's hand fell back to her side. Even if her father ceased his support, even if her sister refused to give her aid, she would not be moved from this house. She would not leave her home. The gods themselves couldn't move her from this building, so let the bankers try.

Tipping her head toward her sister, she asked for a few moments of privacy. Ciara didn't seem surprised by the request. It was one that Kera had asked for countless times over the past few months. Ciara did seem resigned, however—resigned and despondent even as she smiled and kissed Kera's cheek. She told Kera that she would attend to the children, wherever they might be, and departed without another word.

Kera stumbled to her room, closing the door behind her. She slid down the hard wood surface, and drew her knees up to her chest. Her dress pooled around her, fabric bunching along the boards. Then, with no one around to see her and her brow resting on her knees, Kera let herself cry.

She tried to overcome the swell of hysteria, but the tears came without consideration to her efforts. The damnable headache that *always* came in tandem with her tears arrived in prompt fashion, as if to say *well you're already in pain, what's a bit more? You can take it!*

As foolish and as ignorant as the bankers might think her, Kera was aware of her predicament. For all his wonderful talents, Mori had borrowed too much in order to see this house built. He had promised her the world, and ignored the cost, desperate to give her a life she thought she wanted.

But she had never wanted this.

She had just wanted him with her. She had wanted him when he was a penniless soldier fighting in the revolution against Trent, when he'd been desperate and eager to please. She wished she could turn back the clocks. She wished she had asked him to leave the war behind for her. Or, barring that, she wished she had asked him not to follow General Zakaria into politics. He could have worked as a lawyer, and they could have had a quiet and comfortable life.

There would have been no dreams of Ivory Gates or glory, but neither would there have been pistols at dawn and death that ruined everything they had ever planned.

Kera allowed herself a moment to laugh, holding the locket tight, tears staining her knees. She laughed. Mori would never have settled for anything less than what he had done. He had never been capable of sitting still. Such a quiet life would have brought him unimaginable misery. He would have become something wicked and cruel: a chained beast that snarled and snapped at any who passed. Their marriage would no longer have been a thing he treasured, but a thing he endured.

He'd had one affair during a time when their relationship was already filled with bliss. She couldn't imagine what would have happened if he'd been miserable at home.

Something shattered downstairs. The echoes of glass hitting the floor reverberated through the house even as Kera heard her sister scream. Lifting her head, Kera pushed herself to her feet. Ciara shouted, "Aiden!" over and over, and each recitation of her son's name drove Kera's heart faster and faster.

She rushed out, tripping on her skirt hem in her haste. She jerked at the fabric to pull it up and out of the way. When she reached the ground floor, she saw them all together. The bankers, her father, Ciara, her children—all seven—assembled in the parlor, door to the cellar cracked open just a little. The children liked to play down there from time to time, but their play had been interrupted. Aiden was on the floor, shaking, limbs thrashing. His dark eyes were rolled back in his head and his mouth was frothing.

Kera pressed her hand to her lips, and she leaned against the doorway. *No. Not little Aiden . . .*

But it was too late. The plague had come to the Ivory Gate, and for the second time in as many years, she felt helpless.

As Kera stood immobile, her father ordered her children to collect their things and leave the Ivory Gate. Ciara rushed out to find a physician as Kera knelt on the floor with her four-year-old son nestled in her arms and stroked her fingers through his hair. The bankers fled. They covered their mouths and rushed out without concluding their negotiations. Kera couldn't be bothered to find out where the talks had left off. It didn't matter.

Her son was dying.

Kera listened as her father made plans. He spoke and made decisions. He determined the safest place for her other children would be up north in Alexandria, nestled in the Leona family estate of Crystal Point. He told her she should go too, and she had stared at him until he backed down. A strategy that worked well on parents, but did nothing at all to assuage the fears of children as they were ordered toward the door.

Cirri, Kera's eldest, had the good sense to wait until her grandfather had left the room before approaching. She was already bundled in her traveling cloak, her hair pulled back in a tight braid at the nape of her neck. Everyone always said she looked like Kera, but when Cirri asked, "Is Aiden going to die?" Kera could only see her husband in her daughter's face.

"I don't know."

Cirri's jaw set. She peered over Kera's shoulder toward the closed door her brother lay behind. "Can I see him before we go?"

"No." Kera shook her head before Cirri could argue. "You know that if you . . . if you contract his illness. You *know* you won't be allowed past the quarantine. Even as it is, your grandfather is going to have to sneak you out of the city. There's enough risk at the moment, we can't add more to it."

One of the kids dropped something, and there was an argument starting in the parlour. Junior snapped at all of them until the shouts stopped.

"Will you look after them for me? Until we can return?"

"I'd rather stay here."

"At the Gate?"

"If you're taking Aiden away, then there's no contagion *here*. I can finish my classes and—"

"Cirri. Are you honestly arguing to stay behind in an empty home, abandoning your siblings to the care of your aging grandfather for the sole purpose of attending university?"

"She wants to stay behind because she's convinced she's *found her one*," Junior announced, entering the room.

Cirri let out a noise—half screech, half howl—and thrust a furious elbow at her younger brother, but he sidestepped it deftly, dancing out of its way. She blushed furiously, stumbling around her words as she babbled another excuse.

Pressure built behind Kera's eyes. She rubbed at the bridge of her nose, mind whirling and stalling whenever she felt close to finding an appropriate response. Cirri and Junior had started bickering, though, and it quickly drowned out any calm reaction she could have maintained. "Enough."

"Mama—"

"Your brother is *dying* of a plague, Cirri." Her hand dropped to her side. "I need you to take care of your siblings. I need Junior to escort you all, and my father, safely to the Point. And I need to trust you both can manage this maturely without purposefully instigating one another. If you've *found* someone, then they will be here for you when this is over."

They both had the good grace to look chastised. "Auggie and John are old enough to understand," Junior said quietly, "but Marcus and Kerryn . . . what are we supposed to tell them? They don't even really remember when our older brother died . . ."

"They're scared," Cirri muttered, as though she hadn't wanted to admit it. As though, if she'd ignored it long enough, it wouldn't actually be true. It wouldn't actually be something she'd need to face.

"I am too." Kera placed her hands on their cheeks, cradling them as gently as she could. "And Aiden . . . he's scared as well. But, we can't let fear keep us from moving forward. Or from protecting the ones we love. I'm going to be there for him, but I can't be there for you or them. I need to know I can depend on you both."

"You can ..." they said, worry still firmly affixed on their faces.

"But ..." Junior glanced toward the door once more. "Will ... will he survive?"

The papers had written about little else in the past few months except for the plague. They'd described it as an all-encompassing illness, though one that acted erratically with no known explanation. Some victims fell ill and died within the day. Others held on to life for weeks before giving up the ghost. Kera couldn't tell her children which version Aiden would have. She couldn't even assuage their fears by telling them it didn't seem so bad. She, like the physicians and healers with their useless tinctures and equally worthless advice, could not even begin to predict how this would continue to manifest.

"I hope so," she whispered to them both. Then, kissing their brows, she drew them into fierce hugs. "Please, please look after your siblings."

They promised, and then they were gone. They left with one brother or sister held in each hand, walking tall as they climbed into a carriage heading north. Kera waited until they'd left for good, and took a moment to pray for their safe travels.

Then she turned and opened the door to her youngest son's room. Ciara was there with a physician she'd summoned. He was still examining Aiden. The man wasn't anyone Kera recognized, but he moved Aiden's limbs this way and that, applying his concoctions with practiced ease that spoke of experience. Yet despite various liquids being poured down Aiden's throat, her son did not wake.

"Is there truly no cure?" Ciara asked. She wrapped an arm around Kera's shoulders as the physician finished drawing a blanket up to Aiden's chin.

The man straightened himself up to his full height and peered down his nose at them. "You are . . . the Widow Montgomery, correct?" he asked in return, as though he didn't already know the answer to his question. As though this house hadn't been marred and mocked, praised and held up as the pinnacle of town gossip.

Kera entertained the idea of climbing to the top of a table, glaring down at the physician and asking why her name or status should mean a thing. Her son lay ill on her bed while he wished to exchange pleasantries. Or more likely, he wished to see what he could extort from her. Instead, she dipped her head. "I am," she replied, finding her voice because of necessity alone. She could serve as a proper widow for his inspection, just as she could serve as a proper wife and mother.

The man rubbed his beard. "There is no cure."

Kera's breath stuttered twice in her throat before finding egress. She turned her back on the scene, ignoring how Ciara kept whispering soft prayers at the boy still lying in an unmoving heap in the same place her firstborn and her husband had died. Maybe Ciara was right. Maybe this house did have too many bad memories.

"However," the physician continued, flicking his eyes toward Ciara, as if he knew the next words he spoke would be foul and wrong. "A woman of your . . . financial security"—Kera longed to laugh at that—"may find other ways to alleviate your son's ailments."

"You charlatan *hack*!" Ciara hissed. She strode across the room with one hand rising in fury. Sensing his imminent doom, the man stepped back, bowing his head to avoid the blow.

"I mean no offense, my lady, but money does have influence in the world."

"You would hold my sister's child hostage? His health a prisoner to your greed? You would rule yourself through avarice, you disgrace?" Ciara never had shied away from speaking her mind, nor flinched from high society and all its imperfections. Kera envied her strength of will, her fortitude.

Little Aiden let out a mewling sound, and Kera faltered. She tore her eyes from the physician and Ciara so she could sit at his side. Her fingers touched his damp hair. *It's too much. Please. It's too much.*

The physician was making excuses. Spit left his mouth as he sputtered and attempted to explain, but Ciara refused to listen. She badgered him onward, insulting him and threatening him with legal action when his protests continued. "As you said, she is the Widow Montgomery, and if you believe that we will not take this to the overseer himself . . ." Ciara trailed off. Ciara *clearly* had far more faith in their overseer than Kera did. The mere thought that Overseer Wild would grant Kera an audience after everything with Mori was absurd. Any chance he'd had at executing some form of professionalism had vanished when he'd refused to respond to her letters regarding her husband's missing pension payments. A clerk had needed to write to her eventually, saying that she was lucky she hadn't been evicted from her home and all assets seized under suspicion of treason. No. There'd be no help there.

The physician looked between the sisters with clear uncertainty before clearing his throat. "I meant only that the cost for such medicine is high, not that I would defraud the good lady."

Kera wanted to speak up and ask him to state his intentions, but her throat seemed to swell closed. Words refused to leave her mouth. Her sister needed to intercede on her behalf, mustering her fury in Kera's stead.

"You will inform us forthwith, or I will call for the soldiers to come."

"Griffons, my lady," the physician squeaked. "Griffons are said to shed feathers that can cure blindness, grow talons that can cure any illness. Should the lady have the funds for such an expedition, these tokens could save the boy's life."

Aiden's brown eyes moved beneath his lids. His lashes opened just enough for her to see them. They were wet and tragic, glistening and fever sick. Kera tried to smile for her boy. She tried to encourage him, and tell him that he was going to be all right. However, Aiden's eyes closed too quick for that, and his breathing sounded more ragged by the moment.

Acting as Kera's spokesperson, Ciara was undaunted and undeterred. She plowed forward, snarling, "Griffons haven't lived in these parts for hundreds of years. The closest we've had are tourist trinkets sold in the streets."

The physician swallowed, looking too disquieted to continue. But as he squirmed, Kera thought back to what *she* knew of the creatures . . . "Mori rode into one during the war," Kera whispered aloud, recalling how he used to pace the house during thunderstorms, rubbing at three deep scars that ran from shoulder to elbow on his left arm. "He said they migrate north from time to time . . ."

Seemingly emboldened, the physician nodded briskly. "There aren't usually any in the north . . . but there are nests in the south. And there are permanent nests near the Long Lakes."

Ciara scoffed loudly, snapping that "The Long Lakes are hundreds of miles away!" while Kera envisioned the journey. A map formed in her mind, plotting the most strategic course even as the physician continued to argue with her sister.

"It is the only possible cure that I can imagine for this ailment, madam!"

"Yes, and the fact you could turn quite the profit on griffon talons means nothing to you," Ciara hissed in reply, sharp as a viper. "You are free to leave, good sir. We shan't trouble you any longer. Be gone!" The man had the audacity to huff as he walked from Kera's home. He slammed the doors to the Ivory Gate so violently that a stern rebuke was given to him by someone on the road. Kera could hear the chastisement through the bedroom window.

Holding her son's hand, Kera looked down at his well-loved face. She traced her thumb along the back of his knuckles. She tried to think, but her thoughts kept circling. They kept returning to a question that had haunted her since her husband's death: *What would Mori do?*

He was gone now, and she was the leader of this household. She was the Widow Montgomery, and she needed to make this decision. The world expected her to behave as her husband would, and she couldn't fathom how that might be.

Her sister sat on the other side of Aiden, bed dipping beneath her. Although her presence was calming, Kera couldn't help but consider the fact that Ciara should not be here. Ciara had children of her own, and a husband besides. A family that needed her and would be devastated by her loss. Aiden only had Kera. There was no one else for him but her. "You should be wary not to catch it as well," Kera warned. Ciara ignored her.

She stroked her fingers through her nephew's black hair, watching as he coughed. Kera met her sister's eyes. Decision already made. Ciara knew it too, her face twisting into a scowl that looked so close to their mother's it was eerie. "I can have John go," Ciara said.

"Your husband deferred from the war effort and can barely ride a steed." Kera said, slow and kind. In all the time Kera had known him, John Barker had simpered and quaked in the face of his far more boisterous and well-spoken wife. Ciara managed him like Mori managed politics: sometimes with skillful words and temperance, and most other times with raging fits of passion that forced his opponents to behave. The idea of him serving as a brave champion riding south to do battle with the griffons was laughable in its own right.

And in any case . . . even if her brother-by-law managed to acquire the goods, he would not be able to return in time to save Aiden. Her son would have expired, and the trip would have been for naught. John would need to take Aiden with him, and Kera would never be able to see her son go and not attend as well. She had to be there with him, so that if he took his last breath, she could be there to give him one last moment of love. She had sat at her husband's and firstborn's sides when they died, she would do the same for her youngest.

She would not allow him to die without knowing he was loved. "It should be me," she said. "I'm his mother. It will be me."

Ciara stared at her. She looked frozen in time, watching as Kera walked to her closet and retrieved a satchel. Kera knew she would need food and water to start her journey, as well as riding clothes for both her and Aiden, warm blankets, and money to replenish their supplies with.

Her mind whirled. *Is this what Mori felt?* she wondered as she collected her things. *When his brain conjured notions all else considered strange? When he saw the path to his future, and took it?* Kera begged his forgiveness. A year after his death and she was understanding parts of the man she loved that she had never understood before.

"You cannot mean to travel to this nest on your own?" Ciara asked. The clarification did nothing but bolster Kera's intentions. She lifted her arms and unbuttoned her dress, letting it slide from her body and onto the floor, while she secured a pair of rarely worn leggings from her bureau. One of Mori's blouses and a wool coat went next. By now, Ciara was on her feet. "Kerryn, my dear sister, you—"

"I will save my son's life," Kera said. She turned, drawing her back up straight. She was a Montgomery. She would *always be* a Montgomery, and she would not bend. "I will save my son's life, and I will secure my home, and my children and I will live here as we are meant to live here, and *no one else* is going to die." Not so long as her chest drew air.

She would not lose one more thing she cherished. She *refused*.

"You have other children," Ciara reminded her, as if she didn't already know that. The words slapped across her face with the same brutal force as a physical blow, and Kera clenched her teeth against them. She glared at her sister until Ciara recoiled. Ciara stammered an apology, saying, "I meant only that you have other children under your care. Ones who equally need their mother."

"Ones," Kera reminded right back, "who will survive quite well under their beloved aunt's care." She was a tree. Unbent. Unbroken. Unmovable. "Ones who even now are traveling north to Crystal Point to escape illness. I shan't see them even if I stay here with Aiden. And . . . should I stay with Aiden, I am not long for this world either. I will catch the plague same as he. I can either die here in this home having done nothing, or I can find the griffons and save my son."

Ciara didn't seem to know what to say to that, so Kera said it for her. "So long as there is breath in my body, I will not allow another to dictate my life story." Then, drawing herself up as high as she could go, Kera said, "I am the Widow Montgomery, and I will not allow tragedy to rule my life. Aiden will not die."

For the first time in her life, Kera had rendered Ciara speechless.

It was the only good part of the day.

CHAPTER TWO

Kera attacked the issues surrounding her departure with clinical precision. She drew up two lists, cataloging each item she would need for her journey, and then sent her sister to collect the materials. Food, medicinal herbs, and additional clothing were placed on the table in the drawing room for future organization. Kera found her husband's old saddlebags and readied them for packing, all the while thinking about the most important means she had for the journey: her horse. Or rather, her husband's old warhorse, a tall chestnut mare named Holly.

Holly was calm and dedicated, with a fearless demeanor. She'd carried Mori into battle after battle, from camp to camp, without faltering or questioning his resolve. Raised in a warzone, Holly never flinched at the sound of gunfire. Kera had heard stories from multiple sources that said Holly was an anomaly in the field. She never reared up or misbehaved, and she followed Mori around like a lost dog.

For his part, Mori used to treat her with all the tender care of a family member. He'd rubbed her down each night, checked and cleaned her saddle, addressed any and all sore spots, and rested her when she went lame. He'd written letters to Kera whenever he had a moment during the war. In each, he would include a passage about Holly. They'd never failed to make Kera smile, and she'd found herself wishing both Holly and him well as they continued to fight for their country's liberation from Trent.

Mori had introduced them after the war. He'd been rather giddy about it. He'd taken Kera by the hand and babbled as he brought her to the stable. He'd told stories as Kera stroked Holly's dark mane, and Kera nodded her head as she listened to each one. When her husband had fallen silent, Kera'd taken Holly's face between her hands and thanked her for her service. She knew full well that her husband would have died without a dependable mount, and Holly had saved his life more than once. Scars lined Holly's flanks. Mori'd rarely spoken about how they happened, but Kera knew that each one served as a record of her husband's tenuous grasp on life.

The horse, unaware of Kera's heartfelt gratitude, had spread her lips and whinnied in Kera's face until she produced a sugar loaf for consumption. She was, and always had been, a spoiled beast.

After the first war had ended, someone in the Overwatch had commissioned a portrait series for war heroes to be displayed in the new capital. General Zakaria had insisted Mori submit himself for the production, and he (grudgingly) did as he was commanded. The painter had expressed interest in creating a masterpiece displaying Morpheus Montgomery the Great and Triumphant War Hero Returning From Battle. Mori brought Holly to the studio; he was informed that a stallion could be provided for the final product.

Mori responded the way he always did when he took offense: He refused. Unless Holly was in the painting, he would not take part in the commission. *"She's the best horse you will ever know,"* Mori insisted. *"I shan't dismiss her merely because she's turned old. We all age, and I'd have accomplished nothing without her by my side."* The general had to intercede on his behalf, and the painting was completed in due time. Holly had been the only horse to have her portrait done for the capital series. But as far as Kera and Mori were concerned, she'd more than earned her place in their nation's history.

Holly was old now. She'd fought through two wars and outlived her brave soldier in the end. She deserved to live out her retirement in peace as a proud member of an elite rank of equine. She didn't deserve a final journey in her twilight years.

But she was the last horse in Kera's possession. The children's ponies and her own mare had been sold long ago. All of their tack and riding apparel had been traded for food and supplies, leaving only Mori's old war things. Despite her impressive résumé, Holly would never have fetched a good price at market; she was too old for that. But that hadn't been what stayed Kera's hand in the end. Holly was family. She was one of the last remaining parts of Mori's life that Kera had left.

She would never be sold.

The mare huffed when Kera entered the stable. She walked toward her with slow, measured steps. "Hello, my dear," Kera greeted as she rested her hand on Holly's muzzle. Holly lowered her head for a scratch along her nose. She was as mild-mannered and steady on her feet as she always had been. She didn't sway or shift about. She stood still and awaited her inspection.

There was a comfortable routine for this. Mori taught Kera it long ago, and she fell into the pattern with great ease. She checked Holly's legs and back; she pressed her hands along Holly's spine. Holly twisted her head to watch Kera, but didn't complain even when Kera came to rest by the scars on Holly's flank. "Morpheus tore his arm beating that griffon from you," she murmured, tracing her hand along Holly's rump.

Holly whinnied at her and puffed hot air from her nostrils. Her hooves stomped against the ground, forcing Kera to smile. Petting the mare's neck with a firm hand, Kera took a deep breath. She trailed her fingers along Holly's throat until she could cup Holly's face between her palms. The stomping stopped. Holly lowered her head so she could look into Kera's eyes. "My son is ill," Kera informed the mare. "I know you are old, and you deserve your retirement. I know I am not Morpheus, but I need your help. You're all I have . . . all I can afford . . . and I need to get to the Long Lakes. There's a griffon nest that may have the cure to Aiden's illness. Will you help me?"

Holly puffed air into Kera's face. Her bangs ruffled from their place above her eyes. Kera blinked as Holly whinnied. Then, she smiled.

Good enough.

Kera reached for a halter and secured it on Holly's head, then she attached the lead rope and led her out to the crossties at the center of the stable. Mori always brushed Holly down before a long ride, and so Kera started now. Considering how empty the stable was, it took longer than necessary to find the appropriate tools, but Kera was dedicated to doing it right. She found everything, then set to rubbing her hand in small circles to knock the dirt off with a currycomb.

Holly's head hung low, and she dozed while Kera worked, too geriatric and content to bother being alert. Kera didn't mind. She used the time to consider her plan and reject the errant thoughts that kept telling her how foolish she was being.

Ciara had spent the better portion of the past hour attempting to talk her out of this. She'd suggested that they hire a team, perhaps someone with military training, or expertise, or *anyone* else. But Kera held fast. She consulted Mori's *Bestiary* and committed herself to her argument.

Griffons would attack any party of more than five who entered the outskirts of their territory. Soldiers and hunters alike were torn down by exhibiting the intent to kill or disrupt their territory. They scented fear and they were brutal against those who bothered them. Mori only managed to survive his encounter because he'd stumbled upon them. They hadn't known he was there, and *he* hadn't known he was there, until they were all on top of each other in a panicked mess.

A team of reckless soldiers would no doubt be destroyed by the griffons, and she could not allow her own terror to obscure her intentions. She didn't need to kill the griffon. She just needed to get close enough to collect a few feathers or find some talon shavings near its scratching trees. She could use both castoffs to help Aiden.

"I won't even be in any danger," she reminded herself for the twelfth time that day. Perhaps she wouldn't even *see* the beast. Perhaps she would find the nest while it was out hunting.

Holly snorted herself awake, shaking all over as she decided if consciousness was right for her. Dust rose through the air, causing Kera to cough and lament her poor care of this horse. When Holly glanced at Kera, her expression seemed almost wry.

"You're right," Kera sighed, resting her head on Holly's flank. "I didn't think it would be that easy either." Luck, she had learned, was rarely on her side.

Fetching her husband's saddle, Kera attempted to hoist it from its rack. Her arms quaked under the great weight, pushing her down into the earth. She heaved, hoisting with all her strength. "I've," she gritted out, "carried . . . *eight* children . . . you . . . terrible . . . *thing.*" Up it went, dislodging from its peg and sending her stumbling a few steps backward. Regaining her footing, she approached Holly.

"And I—" she lifted as high as her arms could lift, Mori's saddle hanging awful and heavy from her fingers "—*can* carry you."

She grunted and struggled to get it up. Just a little more . . . *just* a little—

Holly's hooves danced, irritation flickering in her expressive brown eyes as she twisted her head toward Kera. The saddle was *on* Holly's back, but so was a stirrup. It had gotten caught on the throw and now lay on Holly's spine beneath the weight of the obscene saddle. "Just stay still," Kera ordered the mare, walking around her and fixing it on the other side.

No. Wait. She had missed a step. With the stirrup in place, the whole image came complete, leaving Kera blinking at the saddle sitting on Holly's naked back. She'd forgotten the saddle blanket. Kera ran a hand across her brow and took a deep breath. "Right," she mumbled. "All right."

Reaching up, she pulled the saddle off Holly's body. She grunted loudly as it slipped from her fingers and struck the ground. Dirt splattered the leather paneling, and Kera glared at it. She fought the temptation to yell at the awful thing or kick it out of spite. Marching back to the sparse tack room, she snatched the blanket meant to protect Holly's back from the rough rubbing of the saddle.

Laying it along Holly's body, she almost felt Holly's approval. The horse was all but snickering at her as she went to retrieve the saddle from the ground. "You laugh, but you must bear it," Kera warned. Holly was impervious to her threats, pretending as she was to be invested in Kera's ministrations.

Bending her knees, Kera drew in a deep breath. She got her hands into position, this time ensuring that the far stirrup was hooked over the pommel for when it went over the horse's back, and *lifted*. Her thighs burned as she hoisted the saddle upward, but she carried the momentum with her. Gasping as she lifted the saddle up, up, up—and it was over. The horrible contraption settled onto Holly's back, looking far too innocent considering the trouble she'd had getting it in place.

Sweat slipped down her nose. She rubbed her face on her sleeve. It was impolite and indecent, but she knew full well that there was no time for propriety while they were on the road.

As quick as she could, she buckled the saddle into position and looped the leather lines where they should be. When she went to cinch the strap beneath Holly's belly she tugged up, waited several moments for Holly to exhale, then tugged again. The horse had mastered the art of expanding its chest until the cinching was over, and then releasing its breath so the saddle was far too loose. Even if Kera hadn't ridden in some time, she remembered Holly's trickery. Holly let out an unamused huff as Kera cinched the saddle tight.

"Foiled again," Kera informed her without the slightest bit of remorse. Holly's tail flicked in annoyance, and Kera rolled her eyes. She pat her neck a few times, soothing the horse with some broad strokes along Holly's throat. She needed to leave soon. Ciara was working on getting her traveling gear prepared, and Kera needed to go in to check on her.

But just for a moment, with no one around to see, Kera rested her head on Holly's shoulder. She wrapped one arm around Holly's wide neck. "I don't know how to do this," she whispered.

Holly's head dropped. It was almost an embrace. Kera leaned into it, pulling back only when she felt Holly's lips mouthing at the pockets of her clothes, searching for the treats she always used to keep on hand.

"Priorities, eh old girl?" She nudged the mare's head back so she could step away safely. "Just have to keep my priorities straight."

Then she turned, and walked back inside.

Ciara was pacing when Kera stepped in through the front door. Kera's bags were already packed. They just needed to loop it over Holly's rump and they would be ready to travel. Aiden could settle in front of Kera as they rode. His small body would fit with Kera's in Mori's saddle. It would be a tight squeeze, but it would work.

"Don't do this," Ciara requested again. "Please, there are other ways. This is a rash decision, and you have no idea what's out there."

"I'll be bringing *The Absalonian Bestiary* and *Herbalism* with me." She lifted both books as evidence, then slid them into the top of her satchel.

Ciara scowled at her, her lips pressed together. "You will die, you understand that, don't you?"

"I will die no matter what. And when I do, I shall join my Morpheus." Kera knew the words would break her sister's heart. She knew that they hurt Ciara in a way that was unfair and unkind. Ciara lifted her fingers to her mouth and took half a step back. But Kera held fast. It was the only excuse that would work with Ciara. "Kiss me goodbye, sister. For either I will die here with Aiden from plague, or I will die trying to save him. But I will not survive this illness unless he does."

Ciara rushed forward. She wrapped her arms around Kera's body and held her close. She pressed a hand to the back of Kera's head and sobbed loud and un-ladylike. "I have just lost my dear brother-by-law, and now you shall rid me of you as well? You horrible child!"

Kera eyes started to burn, but it did nothing to weaken her resolve. Her mind was already made up. "Will you pray for me, Ciara?" she asked instead. Ciara promised she would. "And the childr—"

"Shall want for nothing. You must promise to send me updates when you can. Post them to Crystal Point, we'll stay there until the worst of this is over."

"I promise." If Mori could manage to pen letters in the midst of two wars, Kera could manage on a safe (she kept reminding herself that it was safe) ride to the Long Lakes. The threats were the various types of nightwalkers that haunted the nights and a griffon she likely wouldn't see. The former was resolved by staying in a town at night, the latter was irrelevant. She was going regardless of whether she'd encounter a griffon or not.

Food and lodging were Kera's key concerns. Aiden's health was fragile, and who knew who else he could infect on their journey. No one could know that he was ill. The governor had already put a ban on travel for the infirm. Some cities had even locked their doors to travelers in hopes of keeping the plague at bay. She needed to stay in a city to avoid a night outside, but the logistics . . . were complicated.

Kera would manage, though. Somehow, some way, she would manage. "Do not sell my home."

"It will stay with the Montgomerys until they choose for it to leave their hands," Ciara agreed.

Kera tried to think of what else needed to be done. Mori had made her promise to update her will after his death, and she'd done so not long after the funeral. She'd sat in front of a solicitor and had spelled out her affairs. She'd used Mori's old paperwork as a template and divided the estate as best she could. Aside from the limited financial sums each of the children would receive, she'd ensured there were dresses for Cirri and Kerri, Mori's war uniform would go to Junior, and all of them would have equal ownership of their vast library.

Kera's affairs were, fortuitously, already in order. She had nothing more to fear.

Kissing Ciara's cheek, she walked to the couch and lifted her young son into her arms. His fevered brow pressed against her chest. He nuzzled her in his sleep as she listened to Ciara collecting the saddlebags. There was a brief passing game as Ciara finished with the saddlebags, took Aiden from Kera, waited for Kera to mount Holly, then passed Aiden back. All the while, Ciara kept her comments brief and perfunctory. Her displeasure was a tangible thing clawing at Kera's back, but Kera distracted herself with wrapping her arms tight around her son and adjusting her position in Mori's saddle. Her feet felt awkward in the stirrups, but it was manageable. She breathed deep. *I can do this. I am the leader of my household. I can do this.*

Kera memorized her sister's jawline, her eyes, her dark skin, and black curly hair. Ciara was a beautiful woman. She hoped she'd see her again.

"We *will* see each other again," Ciara said, as though reading Kera's mind. Her wise eyes sternly focused on Kera's face. "Even if it's in the next life, we will see each other again, my wonderful sister."

The temptation to stay threatened to rear up again, so Kera tore her eyes from her sister's face. She took a deep breath clicked her tongue.

Mori's great warhorse gave a mighty fart, tail lifting as she passed gas, and then slowly walked out of the stable.

Holly was a smooth walker. She kept her head down and moved her legs one right after another. Kera held one arm around Aiden's body and kept him steady as she guided Holly with her other hand. He was still asleep, but his limbs continued twitching despite that.

The plague had haunted the streets of Ship's Landing for over a year, starting just before Morpheus's death and increasing in strength afterward. No one knew how the ill were infected, but once they succumbed, it was already too late. Kera remembered seeing the wailers in the street. Friends she'd had for ages, screaming in mourning as their loved ones were carted away.

Initially, physicians had flocked to Ship's Landing in an effort to help the victims. But as the plague spread, more medical professionals began to contract it as well. Fewer and fewer new arrivals came, and those that did bickered for months as they tried to find the cause of the sickness. But for all their efforts, no one understood why some lives ended like a shattered glass of wine, while others were barrels with a crack at their base, slowly letting one drop of life slip out a moment at a time.

Kera tried to remember what Aiden had been doing the last time she'd seen him well. Playing with his siblings. Cirri and Junior had helped the little ones dress for the day. Then they'd taken them down to lessons. When she was home from university, Cirri had been leading "classes" on needlepoint in the drawing room. Kera remembered seeing Aiden sitting on Cirri's lap once. His little hands latched around Cirri's as she made fine stitches in the shape of flowers and letters. When the bankers came, the children had left to occupy themselves elsewhere, Aiden skipping after the others. Perhaps they'd been searching for monsters in the cellar. They all loved to play pretend.

He'd been in perfect health . . . and then he hadn't been.

Kera bent her head and kissed her son's hair. She urged Holly onward. They lived almost eight hundred miles from the Long Lakes. To get there, first she would need to cross the river to Tymber. They would need to travel along the ocean for almost two weeks past Doleystown and Kytesberg until they were well into the deep south.

Holly's slow steps plodded along. "You must think me mad," Kera murmured. Holly's ears flicked back to listen to her. One swiveled so it faced her while the other returned to the front, Holly's attention divided between the road and Kera's voice. "I'm not mad." She was talking to a horse while riding with her dying child to a griffon's nest on the off chance that they would survive the journey and not be killed by a plague in the meantime, but she *was not* mad.

Holly continued walking, immune to Kera's growing anxiety. "You've probably seen enough to know I'm not mad." Holly had seen more wondrous things than she ever had. Kera used to be enamored with the war stories Mori would tell. He and his soldiers sounded gallant and brave as they rode about with their guns firing and swords raised in the air. Mori's friend, a True Lord from Ruug named Amit, had told Kera that her husband had been the bravest of them all for facing the nightwalkers.

"Was the griffon large?" Kera asked Holly. Holly huffed in response, taking a long stride as if to present her rump for evidence. The scars were hidden by the saddlebags, but Kera knew them well enough. She'd seen paintings of griffons in city hall next to images of salamanders, sirens, and vipers. But unlike the sirens, renowned for pulling sad sailors to their graves, or selkies making off with hapless children, the griffons had merely been celestial creatures flying high above the rest of them.

"You know, considering the likelihood of encountering a griffon in the first place, I have to admit I'm *amazed* you even met one. There are hundreds of different nightwalkers you could have run into that night." Holly huffed loudly, throwing her head up and down just enough so the reins didn't pull too much in Kera's hands. "But you didn't run into a wraith or a specter or even a death march, no you ran into a *griffon*. I saw a death march once, did you know that?"

Holly did not respond. Her ears wiggled to and fro, but despite being told since she was a child that meant the horse was listening, Kera strongly suspected Holly was more interested in the food in her saddlebags than the words coming from Kera's mouth.

"My father took my siblings and me out to see one. They're horrifying, did you know that? All the spirits rise up and reenact their final moments leading up to their death, and I'm sure you know just how many battlefields there are now after the war." Battlefields that Kera would be unable to completely avoid on her ride to the Long

Lakes. She shivered atop Holly, hugging Aiden closer and adjusting her seat.

Holly pushed forward, heedless of Kera's diatribe. They made good time crossing the river. The road wasn't busy, and the lack of traffic encouraged her to move a touch faster than Holly would have preferred. Even at their accelerated pace, though, some travelers paused to watch her ride by. They seemed incredulous as their eyes wandered across her clothes and overall appearance.

Kera didn't give herself permission to feel embarrassed. She knew how she appeared with all her adornments and baubles left behind her: ragged and plain. She'd spent each day of the past year wearing a mourning dress. Plain though it had been, her show of grief was far more acceptable than trousers and a traveling coat. She hated how that made her feel. She guided Holly off the main road and kept to the quiet trails leading south, doing what she could to avoid the dumbfounded stares of the casual civilian traveler.

Her brain felt like an ouroboros, endless and cannibalistic. It chewed on its own tail in a desire to sustain its own quest for knowledge. Her thoughts circled, each one hurting worse than the one that came before.

Clouds began to turn the sky overcast, when Aiden woke. He mewled at her chest. His dark-brown eyes opened and stared up at her, fevered and delirious.

"It's all right, Aiden," she cooed. "It's all right."

He cried out, though. Limbs shaking as he thrashed in her arms.

Holly slowed to a stop. Her head turning to look back at them. Air huffed from her nostrils and she shifted restlessly. She didn't know what to do, and Kera didn't either. She knotted her reins as best she could, and *woah*ed Holly unconsciously as she adjusted her hold on Aiden. Aiden's limbs didn't flail so much as stiffen and seize in place. She wasn't sure if she'd have preferred the alternative or not.

General Zakaria's wife, Najah Zakaria, had once spoken to Kera about the shaking illness. Her daughter Amani had suffered from tremors, and they worried Amani would bite her tongue and drown in her own blood. If Kera remembered, they used to put a cloth in her mouth to stop the fear. Kera fetched one now, pulling a stretch of fabric from her pocket to slide between her son's teeth. He gurgled and choked as he shook, but she could hear him breathing through his nose. "You're going to be all right," she repeated to him. "You're going to be all right."

Holly shifted, unhappy with the wriggling weight upon her back. Through it all, Aiden continued to cry. He lifted his tiny hands to his mouth, and Kera held them back to keep them from his face. "Hush . . . hush . . . baby . . . hush . . . it's all right. It's all right," Kera whispered. She tried to keep calm, to not sound desperate or frantic. She wasn't sure she was succeeding.

Holly whinnied.

It felt as though Kera were trying to juggle and cook all at once. Keeping Holly content and Aiden safe seemed like an insurmountable task. Panic blossomed in her chest as she realized that she had no idea what she was doing in the first place.

I shouldn't have left. The thought circled about on repeat. It wrapped around her brain and slid down her back, taking root deep in her body until she recoiled in order to free herself from the self-defeating madness. "It's barely been ten miles," she hissed out loud. "I've hardly started." She squeezed her son. "I can't stop now."

The shaking stopped, and Kera sobbed in relief.

She rested her head against his small shoulder and breathed against his back. She retook her reins and urged Holly onward. Aiden was asleep again, and showed no signs of waking. *My son is going to die.* She knew then and there. "It's either here or at home," she spoke out loud. Giving the terror a voice felt almost like signing his death warrant, but she let spite motivate her anyway.

She would not let Aiden die without a fight, and if that meant she forced herself through an eight-hundred-mile journey on her own, she would do it. Kera urged Holly to walk on.

The sun started to dip beyond the horizon as Kera reached a small tavern. She stopped Holly before they approached the stable. Aiden was warm against her chest. His head lolled against her shoulder, little legs jerking very subtly every now and then, almost as if he were simply kicking in his sleep. Holly turned her head. One big brown eye stared up at Kera, as if to say, *Are you ready?*

"They could get sick," Kera whispered. Holly's eye kept watching her. Waiting. Her son jerked a little more. "They could all get sick and die." It would be her fault, too.

Risking a glance over her shoulder, Kera stared out into the dark. Already, it felt as though the shadows were moving. Nightwalkers seeping backward into existence. The hair on the back of her neck stood on end. Her breath felt chill in her breast. A shadow, or a black cloak, flickered on the edge of her vision, and her heels kicked on impulse. Holly's head swiveled around and her great hooves clacked on the stones beneath them.

A boy approached as they neared the stable. Turning Aiden so his face wasn't directed at the child, Kera cleared her throat. "Please . . . and how much for board for the horse?"

"A copper piece, miss," the stable boy told her as he rested a hand on the reins just under Holly's chin. Fishing a coin from her pocket, Kera handed it to the boy. Adjusting her hold on Aiden, she leaned forward and then swung a leg over the saddle and Holly's rump. Her knees almost crumpled beneath her as she half fell, half stumbled off the horse. The boy caught her back with a startled yelp, bracing her so she didn't fall to the ground.

She clung tight to Aiden, anxiety sparking along her senses. *It's all right*, she reminded herself. *It's all going to be all right.* Then she caught sight of her saddlebags, and realized that between her son and her things—she could only carry one.

"If . . . you don't mind waiting, miss," the stable boy offered. "I can help assist you with your bags?"

Some of the anxiety lessened at that, and she nodded. "Please." She tried not to think about how she was risking this poor boy's health by letting him interact with them. Still, the boy was quick about his work. He hurried to move Holly into a stall and saw to her care. Kera even had a moment where she could stroke Holly's muzzle and remove a stray leaf from her mane. "Thank you," she whispered as Holly snuggled into her touch. They wouldn't have made it this far without her.

Once finished, the boy retrieved Kera's bags and led her into the tavern. He called for the owner to come meet them, and a portly man did just that. The gentleman wiped his hands on a small towel as he approached, eyeing Kera up and down. "What can I do you for, missus?"

"Just a room for the night, and lodging for my horse. I'll be gone by morning."

The man nodded, still rubbing at his hands. "Don't have any free rooms, missus, but there's a couple open beds if you don't mind sharing. One's . . . with a gentleman, and another's with a lady and her young lass."

Kera hesitated. Logic dictated the safer option was, of course, the room with the woman. However, with Aiden's illness . . . she would be horrified if he infected a child and mother.

The innkeep jutted his chin toward the man in the corner. "There's one boarder." Following his gaze, Kera tried to hold back her distaste. The man in question was leering her way, licking his lips. Food and drink had tangled his beard, coating it in a greasy finish. Flinching away from the mere thought of spending a night in close quarters with such a man, she forced a smile, anxiety swimming through her as she imagined someone else coughing and writhing in the throes of a fit that no one could stop. Her voice sounded far stronger than she felt when she managed to say, "The lady, if you please," at long last.

Without even batting an eye, the innkeeper nodded and barked at the stable boy to lead her to the room she requested. The sun disappeared behind the hills, and the night howls of the dead began to start. Aiden didn't wake. He remained unconscious against her shoulder, looking to all the world like any other child made tired from a long journey.

The stable boy chattered as he led her up a staircase to a room with a well-worn door. He needed to adjust the saddlebags in order to free a hand to knock, but he did so with surprising grace. Two raps, then a pause earned them a reply. "Come in," they were beckoned, and the boy pushed the door open for Kera to enter.

"Begging your pardon, miss," the boy announced for the present occupant, "but you've a roommate for tonight. S'another lady 'n' her bairn."

"That's . . . fine," the woman in question intoned. With that acceptance, Kera rounded the bend and entered the room. Aiden slipped a little, but she managed to catch him in time. She kept him from falling from her bloodless fingers. The boy didn't notice.

He shuffled in and placed her things on the ground before bidding them a good evening. He shut the door behind himself as he left.

For her part, Kera was struggling to understand how her life had come to this. She stared at the woman sitting across from her on one of the two beds. Horror painted Kera's skin, her *soul*, with a thick miasmic lacquer.

This, she thought as she tried not to cry, *is a joke. A cruel joke.*

Perhaps their family really *was* cursed.

For there, sitting across from her, resting with her back against the headboard of the farthest bed in the room, was her husband's mistress, Aurora Sinclair.

CHAPTER THREE

M ori used to write Kera the most beautiful letters. He rhapsodized on his love for her. He called her the sweetest names. He wished her every happiness in the world. Once, he wrote her an entire letter dedicated to the feeling of her arms around him. How he yearned for such an embrace while he fought his wars, he wrote. He cursed his new position in the Overwatch for keeping them apart. It was unfair that he was expected to toil day after day, when the gods knew his place was at her side.

In each and every one of those letters, Mori failed to mention that he had also had an affair with a twenty-three-year-old girl named Aurora Sinclair.

She must be . . . what . . . thirty-seven now? She was a woman in her own right, as was the girl beside her. Kera *had* known Aurora had a daughter near Cirri's age, but Kera'd rejected such knowledge as unnecessary. She had done much the same for all else Aurora-related. She didn't care about Aurora's family. She didn't care about her relatives. She. Didn't. *Care.*

Forced to examine the woman who'd caused immeasurable discord to her marriage, Kera supposed Aurora had aged . . . well. Her black curls were pulled back in a tight wrap, and there were lines under her eyes. Her cheekbones protruded from her face, though her nose was acceptable. Kera wished she could find fault in Aurora's appearance, either too pretty or too hideous, but Aurora was a plain woman with a normal appearance.

Kera hugged Aiden closer. She should go.

". . . Mrs. Montgomery," Aurora intoned. She placed her feet on the floor by her bed and stood. Her pace was geriatric, weathered, and exhausted. She rubbed her palms on her thighs as though she needed to force stiff muscles into position. Kera's eyes flicked over Aurora's clothes. The dark trousers were of poor quality, and just as inappropriate as Kera's own. Wonders never ceased.

Kera didn't make any move to approach or go near. She was eager to keep distance between them both and shuffled through tutor cards of conversation starters in her mind. *Words.* How hard could it be to form *words?* "Mrs. Sinclair," she managed, glancing toward the door. Perhaps she and Aiden could risk the night. Holly was used to traveling in the dark. Mori had rhapsodized about *that* too. No one else on General Zakaria's staff ever volunteered to traverse the wicked space between dusk and dawn.

"Lawrence," her unwelcome interloper corrected. She attempted to form a smile. It was the same half-somber grin the bankers liked to wear. It made Kera's nose twitch. "Or, eh, if it pleases you . . . just Aurora. Don't go by Sinclair anymore." She slurred some of the words together, her *you* was too short, and her words dangled as if she meant to say something more but cut herself off at the last moment.

"Ah. I had heard of your divorce from Mr. Sinclair. A pity." She was being nasty. Aurora's plain features sank a touch under her eyes. Her flesh darkened in splotches, lips twisting into a grimace. Kera took a deep breath. Let it out. *Stop being so rude.* "I apologize . . . my tone is . . . not the best." After the day she'd had, and the urgency with which she'd left her home, the last person she wanted to see was Aurora Sinclair.

No. That wasn't true.

She was quite certain that all of her good manners and well-behaved habits would be set to the side in the face of Brennan Wild. She might even take up her husband's pistol and fire the shot he *should* have fired into Wild's side the year before. Unlike Mori, she wouldn't miss.

Aiden whined a high-pitched keening noise that distracted her from Aurora and thoughts of murder. She took a few steps back until her boots clicked against the wall. Aiden squirmed against her body, and Aurora's eyes never left Kera's face. She was assessing and judging them in equal measure. "He's sick," Aurora deduced.

"I can leave." Kera was already mapping out their exit. She was already factoring in how many hours she could stay awake and how much stress Holly could take.

But Aurora shook her head and walked to a satchel of sorts that was lying near the end of her bed. "No. No, it's fine. Faith . . ." She glanced at her daughter, still sleeping and not at all aware of the confrontation that was brewing. "Faith is as well."

Kera couldn't help feeling a swell of grief rising up within her. This was the world that they lived in. A world where mothers watched their children die as their husbands abandoned them through death or disloyalty. She curled around her son, breathing in the smell of his body.

Fever heat warmed her brow as her son's wet breath ghosted across her cheek. She tried to hold back a sob. She would *not* cry in front of the woman her husband found more desirable than her. Swallowing back every vile thought, every cry for vengeance, every emotion that was not pure and good, Kera thanked Aurora Sinclair.

Aurora did not need to let them stay. She did not need to let them share her space. She could have protested, and Kera would have had nothing. "I . . . appreciate your kindness," Kera gritted out.

Aurora looked for all the world like she would rather swallow her tongue than continue this conversation one moment longer. Still, she forced another banker's smile and retrieved whatever it was that she intended to grab from her bag. Walking toward Kera, Aurora handed her a folded strip of fabric that smelled of something fruity and sweet. Kera had no idea what she was meant to do with it. She held the cloth between them and blinked at Aurora until Aurora deigned to provide instruction. "The smell . . . it makes the shaking not as bad."

Confusion filled Kera's body, but she lowered the cloth to her son's face. Aurora didn't say anything more. She turned her back on Kera and Aiden, while Kera felt more imbecilic with each passing second. Then, to her very great surprise, the boy *did* start to settle. His whining ceased, and he returned to dozing once again.

"Thank you," Kera repeated. This time, she meant it far more than she had before.

Folding her hands in her lap, Aurora inspected Kera as one would a piece of meat. Spoiled? Unspoiled? Fit for consumption? "If you'll forgive me," Aurora began, and even with Aurora's kindness tonight, *that* was the one thing Kera was incapable of doing. Forgiveness was not in her nature. "Where're you going?" Aurora raised a brow as though she knew where Kera's mind had gone. She all but dared Kera to voice her opinion here and now.

Kera scowled, unused to her thoughts being so plain to read. Only her husband had managed to do that, and it was a familiarity she had no intention of sharing with his mistress. A part of her longed to make up some falsehood that would make Aurora regret starting this conversation to begin with, but . . . Kera's eyes traveled to Faith. Faith was young and blameless for her mother's actions. "The physicians suggested that . . . griffons could cure my son."

Aurora looked almost pensive as she nodded, accepting that response. "And . . . where are your . . . escorts, Mrs. Montgomery?"

She continued to call Kera that. *Mrs. Montgomery.* How long had it been since someone called her *Mrs*? How long had it been since someone deferred to her by the name she had expected would be *hers* all her life, rather than the dark and dreary reminder of failures long since passed? She had been *Widow Montgomery* for over a year now.

Why was it that the first one to call her by her true name was *Aurora*?

Why did it feel like it was less polite intentions, and more a stab? *Mrs.* Montgomery. The wife of the man she'd slept with. Mrs. Montgomery. The wife that had to smile in public as her husband bared his guilty soul to the world. *"Yes,"* he had said. *"I did this awful thing, but being an adulterer does not invalidate my many other accomplishments!"*

"My name is Kera," she snapped, desperate to be free of any reminders of Morpheus's sin. "I have a name."

Aurora pursed her lips. Her jaw clenched. "I . . . I meant no offense." It was not quite an apology.

For the first time in years, Kera wondered if Aurora even knew who she was. They had never spoken or interacted before. The most they had shared were a few strained glances across the street before neighbors would surround Kera and inform her all the ways she should be managing her household.

The countless stream of busybodies had overwhelmed Kera to the point where she had made it her priority to never speak with Aurora at all. She didn't want to hear the rumors that would follow. She didn't want to hear the excuses that would echo in her ears. She wanted silence. A silence that she never received when her peers took it upon themselves to offer their words of support or dismay as she struggled to sort the wreckage of her life.

Kera had been raised to not speak out against them. She had been taught that her place was to remain firm and calm amidst the storm. It was her duty to be a pillar of support her children could flock around, offering them all the stability their father had tried his best to destroy.

Silence could only mask pain until the turmoil reached a maelstrom of inescapable ruin. Right now, Kera was too angry to sit across from this woman, after *everything else*, and stay *silent*. "When you and my Mori—when you and *my husband* were together. Did you know my name?"

Did Aurora know that Kera had been pregnant at the time? With her fifth child, John? Did she know that after Mori finished with *her*, he came home to Kera and tended to her aching feet? Her sore back? Did she know that he brought her food and bought her dresses? That he kissed her in the morning and right before bed? That he had been there and delivered the child he conceived with *her* while he also was spending time with Aurora? Did she *know*?

"I knew," Aurora whispered. She looked faintly ill. Kera wondered if she had made Aurora uncomfortable. If she had given her even a *fraction* of the pain that Kera felt since the moment Brennan Wild decided to tell the world about her husband's affair. Her husband hadn't bothered to inform her until she had read about it in the morning paper. Then and only then had he tried to explain. She hadn't wanted to listen. She still didn't.

But now that she had been given the smallest hint of awareness from Aurora, Kera's mind flooded with questions. Did Aurora know that aside from his affair, Kera and Mori had never known conflict? Had always been the best of friends? Hand in hand in all things. Blessed with beautiful children. Granted such great fortune with their affairs. Surrounded by good men and women. Did she know that once the affair became known, the façade crumbled?

Kera's world fell to ruin, with one tragedy after another. First, Brennan Wild took it upon himself to destroy Mori's reputation, then General Zakaria died, her eldest son died, *he* died. He died just as she had forgiven him. Just as she had found it in her heart to set all the pain to the side. Just as she had determined that with their son's death, she could not handle the heartbreak. The loss of one more member of her family.

Did Aurora know that she had sat at her husband's deathbed, holding him close and begging him to stay? Begging him for more time. Begging him not to leave her because they had lost so much already. Time she lost because of *her*?

"I'm sorry," Aurora told Kera.

It was not good enough. Two simple words did not erase the pain and dismay of having her world shattered like stained glass in the sun.

Kera tucked her head to Aiden's cheek. She breathed in. She breathed out. She tried to remain calm, and convince herself that even with all of her turmoil, a room with Aurora was *still* safer than anything else.

"I don't expect you to forgive me," Aurora continued. "But... but I *can* make rep-rations?"

She stumbled so badly that Kera wanted to take delight in it. But a much larger part of her was dismayed. Comparisons were drawing up in her mind. *Was this what he liked about her? Was this what I did wrong?* "Rep-*ar*-ations," Kera corrected anyway. She even tried not to sound mocking as she asked, "How could you possibly make reparations to *me*?"

Aurora did not back down. If anything, Kera's scathing words seemed to embolden her more. She straightened her back, tilted her chin up. "You're traveling to the griffons, right? Ehm. Well... we are too? I... I can help you get there."

Kera *did* laugh at that. It was hard not to. Aurora looked like she believed Kera would accept that offer. It was as if she expected Kera to spend her time with the woman who destroyed her relationship with Mori. But despite Kera's *obvious* amusement at the comment, Aurora held firm. She seemed undaunted by Kera's reaction, remaining steady and calm, as if determined to succeed.

"You are traveling alone, are you not?" she asked. Kera's laughter stopped. "No woman has her bags dropped off by the boy downstairs when she got a guard or servant to do it for her." The observation was frustratingly astute.

Kera scowled. Her nostrils flared with her temper. "You mean to extort *both* Montgomerys?"

Aurora flinched. It was not a subtle thing, but a whole body affair. Her limbs jerked like Aiden's during his fits. She averted her eyes, hands clenching down so tight that Kera could hear them crack from across the room. "I *mean* to make . . . make amends to the woman I wronged."

Kera tried not to feel guilt. She struggled not to snap back and argue her point, giving voice to some indeterminable feeling that was both wrong and unnecessary. But the guilt came anyway, and shame came soon after.

Aiden is dying, she reminded herself. Aiden was dying, and Aurora's Faith was dying, and *they* were more important than the pain that their unique pasts wrought. "How do you know of the griffons?" Kera asked.

"Been working for the Travers family since my divorce. They talked about griffons before. And when Faith fell ill . . . they told me where I could go to find them." She walked back over to her bag and withdrew a sheet of parchment. This too she offered to Kera for review.

Taking it, Kera let her eyes roam over the page. It was a map. "Before my husband put Henry in jail, the Traverses were good people . . . I'm glad at least the rest of their family hasn't turned sour."

"Yes . . . they've been very kind. Henry's still dead and they're still tryna make do. But they've been good to me and Faith . . . they never did much like your family though. Heard them talking about you sometimes."

"Yes. They're trying to get my house from me."

"At least you have a house for them to try to take."

"At least." Kera swallowed back an unnatural urge to be violent. She hadn't struck anyone or anything in years, but the feeling was growing to an alarming point the longer this conversation dragged on.

"Look . . . I'm not trying to start anything, Lady, but I know where I'm going. I have the map to the den. And it's safer to travel in groups. We . . . we *should* work together on this. It'd be safer for all of us."

"I don't have an escort," Kera confirmed.

Aurora pointed toward a small squiggle at the far end of the map. Her dirty nail aimed right at a tight scrawl reading *The Long Lakes*. "Unlike *you*, my lady, I've never traveled in a carriage to and fro. I've never had the, um, *luxury* of your dresses and pearls." She wrung her hands at that. "I know *this* world . . . and I know how to navigate it. I can bring you to the griffons."

"Just to make *amends*?" Kera spat. She returned the map over and adjusted her hold on Aiden as she tried to understand what could motivate a woman like Aurora to want to help *her* in any way, shape, or form. Nothing positive crossed her imagination. All explanations were mind-boggling. Kera couldn't follow the thread of this conversation, nor weave it into a narrative she could understand.

"No," Aurora admitted. "Woulda done it even if I didn't know you any." Was this what Mori saw in Aurora? Was this what he wanted all along? Someone strong and brave and fearless? Someone who took a map and raced off into the world, confident she would be fine?

"I can take care of myself," Kera told Aurora. She had the *Bestiary*. She had *Herbalism*. She could manage. Somehow, some way, she would manage. She could do this too.

Aurora, however, remained unconvinced. She bit her lip and shifted her feet as she tried to find the words she longed to say. Whether it was another chastisement on Kera's privileged status, or another method of irritating her further, Kera was not in the mood. She—

"I won't force you to travel with me if you don't wanna," Aurora cut in. "Gods know it's . . . best . . . that you and I not speak to each other at all, all things considered. I just . . . We are going to the same place. And it's safer . . . and I'd not forgive myself should anything happen to you Mrs.—Kera."

"You forgave *yourself* for sleeping with my husband," Kera said before her brain could catch up with her. Aurora scowled, face always in motion. She *clearly* never learned how to mask her emotions, nor how to play the charming lady, capable of controlling the room at a glance.

She was a commoner, a simple woman who lived a simple life. And she was also a *clever* woman who'd seduced a brilliant man from a loving marriage. A vixen. A harpy. Kera conjured names and disparagements as easy as could be. Each term came to mind with greater speed and fluency. She needed to bite her tongue to keep from giving them life.

Aiden whined again. He squirmed in Kera's arms and distracted her from Aurora once more. She looked down at her son, and let out a startled gasp. His eyes were open, and he was staring up at her with such stunned confusion. Pulling the cloth back from his face, she managed a smile.

"Mama . . .?" he asked, sweet voice breaking and cracking in the air.

"Darling," she greeted in turn. "How are you feeling?"

Aiden looked around the room without answering, far more interested in investigating. "Where . . . are we?"

"You should feed him while he's awake," Aurora lectured Kera. "He'll sleep again soon, and if you can get him to eat and drink now, it will make your journey easier."

She was right. Kera *knew* she was right, but just hearing the advice made Kera want to spurn it. Made her want to reject it and every other word in that sentence, because *Aurora* was the one who spoke them. *That's unfair*, she forced herself to remember. *That's unfair, and it's cruel.* And it didn't help Aiden.

Reaching for her saddlebag, she opened it and retrieved the small folded napkin that held Aiden's premade dinner secure. It was a simple thing, just some bread and cheese that Ciara had cut in their kitchen back at the Ivory Gate. She lowered herself to the ground so Aiden could sit upright and eat it on her lap. Cross-legged and woozy, Aiden leaned against her. His coordination wasn't strong, but what toddler *had* good coordination when ill?

Handing the first mouthful of bread to her son, she watched him eat. She followed the motions of his hands as he brought the demi-baguette to his mouth. He chewed with small teeth in careful little bites. Aurora watched them the whole time.

Occasionally she looked toward Faith, but Faith was still asleep. She hadn't moved an inch. Kera tried not to think about her daughter, Cirri, lying in Faith's position. It was hard not to. With Aiden already weak and shaking in her arms, imagining one more child in a precarious position was not difficult.

"I fear that *my* faith may not be strong enough to forgive you, Aurora," Kera told her husband's former mistress.

She had forgiven Mori. In the seven years before his death, they had worked on fixing the damage from his affair. Mori had pledged himself to correcting his errors every day. Had fought for her forgiveness, and earned it when she deemed herself capable of *feeling* again.

Aurora had never earned it. She had never shown Kera any interest in apologizing for her behavior, nor reached out before this day to speak. To be fair, Kera doubted she would have even granted Aurora an audience had she asked for one. But Aurora had never asked in the first place, so Kera didn't allow the thought to linger too long in her head.

"You have hurt me too severely for me to forgive you for what you've done," Kera said.

Aurora nodded, implacable. "I don't expect you to forgive me. I made the choices I made. I fucked your husband." Kera flinched both at the word and the admission. Seven years, and the admission still struck home. Hearing someone else confirm what she had known all this time still made her heart beat too fast, her lungs seize, and her head spin.

Why didn't he tell me?

"But your boy don't deserve *this*," Aurora continued, "and so I'll take you to the griffons. Please, ma'am. Please let me take you to the griffons. Morpheus Montgomery's son don't deserve to die because you and I are arguing over our foolishness."

Kera expected to feel pain at the sound of her husband's name. She expected to feel something other than a slow and steady resignation, but she knew Aurora was telling the truth. Aurora was sincere in her wishes and beliefs, and Kera could even understand Aurora's intentions.

Faith was still lying on the bed, skin waxy and limbs. Just as Aiden had been all day. "I apologize for damaging your family like I have," Aurora went on. "I truly am sorry. But your husband was a good man. And he loved you all dearly. Please . . . please allow me this one chance to make it up to you. I don't know how else to make it better."

Aiden chewed his cheese in slow bites with his jaw moving left and right like a goat, his fingers dusted with grain from the meal. Kera knew full well that the plague would wrap its way around him once more, pulling him back to the depths of despair far too soon. He would become immobile; he would seize. He would take one step closer to death, just as Aurora and she invariably would.

Someday soon, they would both fall as ill as their children. Their only hope was to reach the Long Lakes in time. *Think of Aiden.*

"Show me the way," Kera whispered.

Aurora, to her credit, didn't smile or try to make any false promises. She just nodded and said, "I'll do my best, Lady Kera. Promise."

And her best, Kera supposed, would have to do.

CHAPTER FOUR

I t was still dark out when Kera woke to the sound of Faith mumbling in her sleep. Aurora tried to settle her daughter, but it took time. Kera watched as Faith's limbs twisted. Her neck strained. Her hands opened and closed at her sides. The image was too familiar to ignore. Though Aiden remained still at Kera's side, enjoying a temporary peace, Faith's struggling tugged at her heart.

Faith mewled and reached for her mother. She was awake, coughing and clawing at her own neck. Kera imagined ants in her throat. Running about beneath the flesh. She imagined Faith trying to dig them out one by one, even as Aurora pulled her hands back.

"'S'all right," Aurora soothed. "'S'all right." Faith didn't seem to believe that.

Kera wanted to ask how long Faith had been suffering from the plague, but considering how her and Aurora's last conversation had gone, she doubted it would be acceptable to pose the question. She'd allowed her personal grievances to blind her earlier, and *now* it wasn't the time. All she could do was watch Aurora tend to her daughter and hope that Aiden didn't join Faith in her agony.

With strong hands, Aurora propped Faith up on the headboard. She then left to fetch water from a pitcher by the window. Faith curled forward, but remained upright. Though her limbs continued to jerk, and one hand still clawed at her throat, Faith didn't appear to worsen. Instead, she seemed determined to lift her head and get a better look at Kera. "You—you're—you're—"

"The Widow Montgomery," Kera supplied. She reached for the cloth Aurora had given her for Aiden earlier. She held it for Aurora to take as the woman passed by with the water.

"Call her Kera," Aurora corrected, laying the fabric on her lap. She braced the back of Faith's head with a firm grip, then lifted the cup to her lips. "Her son . . ." Aurora hesitated, looking at Aiden, then Kera in quick succession.

"Aiden," Kera drawled out as slowly as she could, relishing perversely at how Aurora stumbled over the information.

"Her son, um, *Aiden* is also ill. So, ah, we'll be traveling to the griffons together." Kera had never seen incredulity on the face of a dying woman before. Faith managed it, somehow, with startling skill. Kera needed to hide a smile behind her hand at the expression. She would never have dared give such a look to her mother when she was Faith's age. But Aurora didn't seem put out by her daughter's cheek. She just shrugged one shoulder and stroked the sweat from Faith's brow. It was a gesture that made Kera's heart ache. She busied herself with checking on her own son.

Watching felt far too voyeuristic.

"It's for safety," Kera said. Both women failed to react in any way. Kera grimaced. She felt even more like a fool than she had before. "It's mutually beneficial."

Aurora helped Faith finish drinking, then held the cloth beneath her nose. The girl jerked her head back. She whined, complaining without words as she snatched the cloth from her mother. Spasms traveled down her arm, but she affected another glare of disobedience that Aurora ignored once more. Faith was holding the cloth to her face.

She's good at this, Kera thought as she watched Aurora pitter-patter about the room. She anticipated her daughter's needs. No second-guessing for Aurora Sinclair. When she decided to do something, she did it. She fetched a bucket for Faith to relieve herself in and stood over her daughter until Faith scooched to the edge of the bed.

Kera averted her eyes. If when *she* was seventeen, Kera's mother had to help her with her bodily functions, Kera was almost certain she would have died from embarrassment, plague be damned. At least Aiden was small enough that some assistance could be accepted and anticipated. But Faith was well on her way toward being considered an adult. Kera could hear the echoes of her own mother's disparaging remarks now. Painted in oil and made permanent in her mind. *Hurry up, can't you go faster? This is entirely indecent.*

Faith plunked her *unmentionables*, as Kera's mother liked to call it, into the bucket without so much as a complaint from her parent.

"Do you need it?" Aurora asked Kera when she finished getting Faith back on the bed.

"No . . . thank you."

Kera took stock of her energy. Her exhaustion seemed to have slipped away in the night, and she felt little out of place. Consciousness beat its drum against Kera's skull. *Up, up, up, up, up!* She wasn't going to fall back to sleep. Sighing, Kera stepped away from her son. She glanced about for a tinderbox and found one by Aurora's abandoned pitcher.

Her match lit on the first strike. Shadows climbed like demons up the walls. Lowering the flame to a lanterned candle, she watched as warm light waged war against the demons. It slashed at the monsters with phoenix talons. Fire held no fear of the dark. Lantern held aloft, Kera fumbled through her bags until she found Mori's books. She pulled them out one by one, resting them on her knees until she could slither an arm beneath them. Then she stood and brought them both to her bed.

It seemed as though they survived the journey so far. A cursory glance over the covers revealed no foxing around the edges. Of course, it had only been a single day. Less than that, if she were being honest with herself. Still, it made her feel good to know that they remained in proper order. Settling back down next to Aiden, Kera opened the book on herbalism and started to read.

Herbalism is the study of plant life for use in medicinal purposes. In Absalon, there is no shortage of such flora, and much of these flora are the essential ingredients to many of the most basic treatments of today's ailments. A mixture of—

"Is that Mori's?" Aurora asked. Kera flinched. She glared at the woman, her previous revulsion returning full force. She had no desire whatsoever to speak about Morpheus with *her*. No desire to share his books with her. These were her last tie to him, and she would not ruin them by sharing them with Aurora. "He taught me my letters," Aurora revealed, ignorant of Kera's feelings. Kera's fingers tightened around her book. "I knew them before, mind you . . . but I couldn't really spell, couldn't really write."

Kera knew that. She'd seen the letters Aurora sent Mori, filled with scrawling words that were no better than chicken scratch. Each of the sentences had terrible diction and awkward attempts at fluidity that splattered on the page. Until one day the wording began to improve and the lines stopped wiggling like they'd been written while lost at sea. It hurt more, knowing that Mori had spent time with her outside of their carnal pleasures. He had talked to her. He had educated her. He had tried to make her a lady. *His* lady.

Except, he already had one.

And even if he came back to her, even if he was faithful from that moment onward. *Even if.* He had still strayed. For two years, he had strayed. And Kera didn't understand why.

"I do not want to hear you speak of him," she told Aurora. The other woman bit her lip and returned her attention to her daughter. She didn't look back.

Struggling to keep herself from growing more agitated, Kera opened her book once more. This late at night (early in the morning?), she found that her eyes strained when making out the letters. They blurred and she needed to blink hard in order to draw them into focus. Still, she scanned the introduction and flipped through the next couple of pages until she came to the first plant.

As with most of Mori's books, he had penned notes into the margins. Kera traced a finger over the small drawing he'd made beside the header. It was a five-pointed leaf with a spiral stem, tucked in and around where the author had typed *Angelica* in bold font. Beneath the drawing was a shorthand message that Kera didn't understand, some combination of letters and punctuation she assumed made sense to her husband, and then instructions. *Ground into a powder. Good for the heart and rheumatism.*

She turned the pages, glanced along the notes more than anything else. *Anise - diuretic.* On the next page, the words *anti-vascular-constrictor* were circled. *Grapefruit seed extract* had *Anti-fungal* written in bold letters, with a humorous aside beneath it: *Worked quite effectively on John's feet.* That made her smile. The note was too old to have been about their son or her brother-by-law, worn and faded as it was. He must have been referring to John *Sarren*, then, his best friend during the first war.

A few pages later and she found one for a laxative. *Amit was satisfied.* This time, she did laugh. Considering their circumstances, it was an inappropriate thing to do, but Kera couldn't help it. She was embarrassed to note that she had drawn both Aurora's and Faith's attention back her way. She flushed, not sure what to say or how to explain. Faith was sick and unwell, Aurora had just received a scolding, and Kera was laughing.

She laughed again, nervous ants skittering beneath her skin. She struggled to silence it as soon as she could. "It's . . . I'm sorry," she apologized once she managed to swallow the noise that kept trying to rise up within her.

"Laughter's good for the soul," Faith muttered, leaning her head back against the wall.

Perhaps that was true, but Kera had already proved that she was not ready to heal her soul. She held the book to her chest and looked out the window, watching as the flickering lights of the guarding fires burned, and listened to the creatures of the night.

Just before the sun rose, Kera woke her boy while Aurora and Faith prepared for the day. The room was still dark as she pressed her hand to Aiden's brow, feeling the fever that had taken hold on his body. But his dark eyes blinked up at her with groggy curiosity, and he asked, "Where . . .?" as he turned his head this way and that.

"You're very ill, Aiden. I'm taking you south to get you better."

"Why?" he rasped around the word, coughing up into her face. Turning her head, Kera pressed her nose tight against her shoulder, shivering as her hands tightened around Aiden's shoulders. She took a deep breath, then looked back.

"We're going to see the griffons, would you like that, dear? They're very good at helping little boys and girls who are sick."

"Who's the griffstons?"

"*Griffons*, and . . . they're . . . well they're beasts. They're magic. Like stories Junior tells you before bed. They're like . . . well, they look like birds and cats put together I suppose. It has the head of a bird, I think, and the body of a cat."

Aiden coughed again, long and hard. He twitched badly enough that Kera let up on his arms, letting him roll to his side and curl up into a miserable ball. He rubbed at his face, fat tears sliding across his cheeks as he tried to steady his breathing. "Ducks?" he asked.

"Ducks?" She tried to imagine it. A great duck monster with cat paws. She grinned as she gently swept her thumb along Aiden's cheek. "No dear, I don't think they're ducks."

That settled that. Aiden frowned and tugged his arms over his head, decreeing, "Not goin'," in his most authoritative voice, as though no amount of poking, prodding, or cajoling would pull him out of his despair.

"Aiden? Aiden, that's enough. Aiden, we need to eat and then leave. We have to go. Aiden. *Aiden*." His shoulders hitched, and he coughed and wheezed around his tears. Glancing over her shoulder, Kera wasn't the least bit surprised to see both Faith and Aurora staring at her. Shame burned through her as she lifted Aiden up and carried him to her pack. He squirmed and sobbed harder, hacking against her neck. "That's enough," she ordered him as she sat down and retrieved the food Ciara had prepared for them. "You need to eat, and then we're leaving."

She pressed some bread into his hand and he sniffled loudly, shaking his head. He shoved it at her. She pushed it back in turn. "Don't wanna," he said.

"You need to eat so we can leave."

"No."

"Aiden—"

He pushed the bread at her, then coughed loud and long. His tears stopped. He coughed harder and harder, breath straining on each inhale. Thrusting the bread to the side, Kera rolled him onto his stomach over her left arm, letting him dangle downward as she struck his back hard. Dark phlegm spat up from between his lip, staining the floor in a goop that grew bigger with each swat. It took five strikes before his choking ceased. He sagged against her body, tantrum and fit subsiding in unison.

"Not hungry," he whispered.

"I'll set it aside for later."

"Okay."

She stroked her son's spine for a few moments, then kissed his hair. Standing, she carried him back to the bed and dedicated herself to cleaning. No trace of illness could remain. Even if it meant she needed to clean the rancid *unmentionables* bucket herself, she would. No one else would get sick from them. *No one.*

Aurora watched her without saying a word. Kera supposed she was grateful Aurora hadn't intervened prior, but now the younger woman was pulling her daughter to her feet and showing no inclinations toward helping Kera in the least. With an arm around her daughter's back, she was able to carry her things with her other hand without any assistance. "I'll meet you outside," she said, marching out before Kera could even blink.

Frustration crashed against the rocks of Kera's complacency at high tide. Faith at least had the excuse of being frail and infirm, but there was no reason why her mother couldn't have helped Kera with *their* bedding, bucket, and remains. Trying to contain the illness so no one else would be affected took time. Aurora had made the choice to lodge in a tavern, same as her, the least she could do was try to keep others from getting sick. By the time Kera finished, that furious tide was full on preparing to flood the town and everyone in it. Sweat slipped down her nose. Her muscles ached. Her teeth felt like murderous things eager to tear into flesh and leave nothing remaining. Still, she was very polite when she asked the stable boy to return to assist her with her bag. It wasn't his fault that Aurora was a lazy lout.

The boy was just as helpful as he had been the day before, carrying her things downstairs as she balanced a far-more-subdued-Aiden on her hip. Her son's arms wrapped around her neck and he buried his head against her shoulder, quiet and still like the grave. Holly's bridle and saddle were already in place by the time Kera arrived. It caught her by surprise, and she went to thank the stable boy, but he told her it was Aurora's doing.

"Thank you," she muttered in her new traveling companions' direction. The tide balked. Was it supposed to thank the evil townspeople it wanted to drown? She didn't get a response. *Yes, it was.*

Aurora was focused on helping her daughter up onto a dapple-gray gelding, steadying her when she swayed. "I can hold him when you get up too," she told Kera when the stable boy finished attaching the saddlebags to Holly.

The tide said *No.* The tide said *I'd rather die.* The tide said every foul word that Kera's mother made her kneel on rice for even *thinking,* and Kera's knees still hurt at the thought years later.

But Aiden wasn't the tide, and he reached toward Aurora with the sleepy innocence of a child who just wanted to be done moving about, *thank you very much.* He didn't notice or care about the tension between his mother and Aurora. With as much dignity as she could muster, Kera placed her son in Aurora's care. She held him as long as she could. The transfer was smoother than she would have liked. Easy and without conflict. Aurora didn't struggle at the transition nor the weight, and Kera wondered if she was used to wrangling children on her own.

"Is Faith your only...?"

"I cared for the Travers children, and others," Aurora replied. A nanny, then. She had been a nanny to wealthy families. The tide wanted to ask Aurora if the wives of her employers found it difficult to trust a known adulteress near their husbands. The tide must be ignored at all costs.

The stable boy folded his hands and let her step onto the cup he made. With a little hop and a quick boost, Kera swung her leg over Holly's rump. A rather successful mounting all things considered. "Thank you, sir," she said as she handed him another coin. He smiled and blushed, thanking her right back.

Aurora passed Aiden to Kera without comment. The stable boy prepared to hoist her up too, but she required no assistance. One foot slid into the stirrup and she was settled on her gelding in moments. Faith's hands were clasped over her mother's, serving as a balancing point to make sure her grip didn't fail. Aurora was not much taller than her daughter, and the inconvenience meant that once she was in position, Faith had to slouch so Aurora could see. Faith tucked herself low and out of the way, and Aurora's chin rested over her daughter's shoulder.

The pale morning light grew more yellow with each passing second. If they wanted to make good time before nightfall, they should leave now. Meeting Aurora's eyes, Kera waited until she saw her nod slowly. Then she clicked her tongue and urged Holly forward. Aurora and her gelding followed without a single word passed between them.

In previous years, whenever Kera traveled with company, she spent her journeys talking to them. Or, more accurately, she spent her journeys listening to them. Her sisters and children enjoyed gossiping endlessly with one another. Mori loved telling tales. None of them ever struggled to find the words they wanted, and their eloquence had always been the cause of great envy in Kera.

Riding beside Aurora, Kera wished she had Mori's wit, her children's innocence, her older sister's poise, or her younger sister's gumption. As it was, she had no idea what she was meant to say to Aurora, nor any notion on how to start a conversation that wouldn't develop into another conflict between them.

They rode from town side by side, and good manners compelled Kera to make conversation; however, all the good manners in the world couldn't compel her brain to think. She didn't *need* to talk, of course. There was no rule or regulation requiring them to speak, and she hadn't anticipated having a riding partner during this journey. Considering the fact she had resigned herself to solitude when she left the city, what needed to be said?

Aiden wriggled a bit in front of her. He was awake for now, though he seemed hazy and uncertain. It defied any logic in illness she had ever known and every sickness she had ever seen. There had been no slow buildup, nor occasional coughing in the night, nor sores on his skin. There had been nothing to suggest that he had been unwell, until all of a sudden his body failed and the shaking started with no sense behind its existence.

"I don't understand," she whispered against her son's head.

Aurora's head swiveled to look back at them. Lips pressed in a thin line. "The . . . *plague?*"

Kera needed to bite back her first thought. Her words had not been for Aurora. They had not been Aurora's to warp or shift about. Kera had spoken to Aiden, and yet her words were stolen from them and redirected anyway.

"Yes," she agreed. Then, because it *had* bothered her, and the tide could only be ignored for so long, "You did not wrap the bedding."

"I wouldn't," Aurora replied. She seemed uncomfortable for a moment, but then urged her gelding so they were walking closer together. Holly didn't notice or care. Continued moving forward. "Faith's not gonna get nobody sick. She's not con-conta . . ." Kera watched as Aurora's tongue peeked out between her lips. Teeth biting down on the tip. As if by the action alone she could latch on to the word that was lost to her.

"Contagious," Kera supplied. Aurora nodded and repeated it slowly, but not correctly. Kera shook her head. "Con-*tay*-jis."

Aurora narrowed her focus on each syllable. "Con . . . *tay* . . . jis?"

"Yes. Good."

A pretty smile formed on Aurora's face, and she nodded again. "Contagious. Faith's not contagious."

"The plague is *highly* contagious," Kera countered. "All of the physicians who came to investigate the plague contracted the illness, and whole families died by the household just on my street alone."

"Maybe," Aurora shrugged.

"*Maybe?*"

"Just find it strange is all. You fancy rich folk never get sick as much as the rest of us. But now it seems you're all—eh . . . well . . . at least *more* of you're getting sick than we are." Kera blinked, hesitating as she considered her answer. Aurora pressed on, "The poor always die first. So why's it not affecting the gutter?"

"It *is* affecting you," Kera pointed out, motioning toward Faith with her chin.

"But I work for the rich. I'm the Traverses' laundress." Oh. Not a nanny, then. "I'm always with 'em. Mopping their floors and cleaning their beds."

Kera didn't know what to say to that, but Aurora wasn't wrong. Before his death, Mori had commented how strange the plague was and how unusually it behaved. He had written letters to Amit, asking his medical advice. He had flipped through the pages of *Herbalism* in hopes of finding the answer to the problem too, but as far as Kera knew, he'd never found one. Every impossible thing had a scientific answer in Mori's mind. Each problem could be quantified. And yet, he hadn't quantified this. Sometimes, a plague was just a plague. Sometimes there was no cure.

Still, Kera did feel a tingle of uncertainty rippling in the back of her mind. "By your logic," she said slowly, "any laundress or servant who came in contact with the plague in a rich family's household would have contracted it."

"But they haven't."

"*You* have, your daughter, at least, has. That on its own says it's contagious."

"Maybe we're just unlucky. Don't know, do I? All I know is that it doesn't feel right, and it don't act like any sickness I've ever seen. Can't be treated none either."

Thinking back to the night before and the scented cloth that Aurora had given her for Aiden to use, Kera shook her head. "It can be managed . . . What was that odor?" It had been familiar. Something spicy yet sweet. An aloe plant of some sort, perhaps.

Aurora took her time replying, grimacing as she focused on the road. "I'm not too good at the word. It's . . . you-ka . . . you-kalee?"

Oh! "Eucalyptus!"

Aurora nodded, and Kera nodded right back. The scent was familiar now, triggering memories she'd half forgotten. She groped through the murky fog of her mind and pulled up the sight of her husband bringing bottles of the oil home after he'd been traveling. He always purchased some before leaving on long journeys too.

Kera turned in her saddle, holding Aiden steady as she rummaged through the saddlebags. It was awkward and her back twinged as she twisted too much, but she found Mori's book and turned forward once more. Holly huffed at her in annoyance, and Kera winced when she realized how tight she had pulled the reins. She gave some more slack and apologized to the good girl before fumbling to open the book.

It wasn't easy. Between balancing the reins, her son, and the book, it took a long time to find the page on eucalyptus. Once she did, though, she read it out loud. "'The health benefits of eucalyptus oil are well-known and wide-ranging.'" Aurora leaned toward her a little, so Kera raised her voice. *Be polite!* she reminded herself. "'Its properties include anti-inflammatory, antispasmodic, decongestant, deodorant, antiseptic, antibacterial, stimulating, and other medicinal qualities. Eucalyptus essential oil is colorless and has a distinctive taste and odor.'"

There were more notes on the sides of the pages, but one in particular caught her eye. It was tucked in the corner and circled twice. "'Very effective against bed-bugs.'" She paused, blinked twice at the words, then looked up. Aurora met her eyes.

This time, they both laughed. And this time, Kera didn't stop for fear of bothering the other woman.

CHAPTER FIVE

They reached Doleystown by the end of the day. Dark shadows had started stretching out across the land, shrouding the tops of the buildings with a cloak seeped in the dusky night. Faith was more or less conscious when they arrived, rolling off the gelding. Aurora helped her down, asking her quick questions, trying to see if she was all right. Faith, feverish and warm, pointed at Aiden and asked, "How's . . ."

"He's still alive," Kera murmured as she dismounted with Aiden. He'd slept for most of the day, but on occasion he'd wake enough for them to stop and feed him. Kera even congratulated herself on getting him to swallow almost a full canteen of water at one point. He'd sicked up some, but he'd kept most of it down. She was even able to wash his skin with the eucalyptus that Aurora offered. They would need more soon. Aurora hadn't expected to share, and Kera knew they needed to be careful using it until they found a fresh supply. Still, Aurora hadn't said anything as Kera used what little she had. It was . . . kind of her.

Faith's eyes fluttered as she swayed on her feet. Her skin took on an unhealthy pallor. She looked ready to vomit, and Kera felt like a useless voyeur. Off in the distance, the night howls started. They needed to get inside immediately if they wanted to be safe. Old rhymes she used to sing as a child started to twist about her mind. She hated how nervous it made her. *First come the wraiths, black as night. Then come the ghosts, with skin like ice. The specter joins the dark. The ghoul is in the park. Run, run, run, or they'll tear you all apart.*

Each noise drew her ear. She twisted her head and searched her surroundings, trying to see if the figures were starting to rise from the ground. Fire kept the monsters at bay, and the townsmen were lighting torches, but wraiths could hide in the shadows. They could cross the threshold if the line wasn't secure. Ship's Landing always made sure the guarding fire lines never broke, but perhaps these smaller towns and cities weren't as safe.

Kera's heart thundered. She flinched when Aurora called her name, startling her out of her reverie even though she knew she ought to be paying attention to them and them alone. This group was her priority, and yet—

"We need a room for the night," Aurora told Kera. Yes, she knew that. "Faith is too sick, they'll turn her away at the door." She was right, of course. Aiden could be passed off as a sleeping child, but someone was sure to notice how unbalanced Faith was. They would question her, then turn them away for fear of their families catching the plague. Kera couldn't even blame them for that. "You need to get the room for us. Something on the ground floor."

Kera stared. "I—" She glanced toward the inn. It seemed so far away.

"Please," Aurora begged her, arms around Faith. Faith was starting to shake harder; if they didn't get inside soon, the whole town was bound to find out. Aiden was sitting on a barrel nearby, knees drawn up to his chest, waiting like the good boy he was. "I can wat—"

"*No.*" Kera straightened and squeezed her reins even harder. She glared at Aurora. How dare Aurora even suggest such a thing? She was not leaving her son with Aurora *Sinclair.* Whether she called herself Lawrence or not. She was not going to allow her child to be anywhere near her. Aurora blackmailed Mori for years because of their affair. What she could do with Kera's son . . . Kera had no interest in finding out. "Take the horses."

Aurora glanced about the stable. No one was here, everyone was off lighting torches and ensuring the fire line stayed in place. Settling Faith down on some hay, Aurora took the reins. She was trembling and perhaps more than a little frightened. If Kera took too long, someone would find Faith and Aurora both and . . .

"I'll be back as soon as I can," Kera promised. Reaching down, she pulled Aiden to her chest. Her muscles ached. Each tendon strained and filed a complaint with the manager. "As soon as I can," Kera swore once more. Aurora didn't say anything in return. Just watched her go with wide eyes.

They were running out of time.

Kera hurried to the inn. She flattened out her hair as she went, adjusting Aiden so he was curled around her body. His little arms hung by her sides, and his brow burned hot through the cotton of her shirt. She needed water for a bath. She had to wash him and try to cool him down as best she could. Riding in the sun had done neither him nor Faith any favors, but it wasn't as if they could pen a letter to the griffons and ask them for their aid.

Yes, hello, please send us feather posthaste. Your obedient servants, Kerryn Montgomery and her husband's mistress.

Pressing open the door to the inn, Kera smiled at the woman behind the counter. "A room for the night, if you please," she asked. The woman looked from her to Aiden.

"Just the two of you?"

"My sister and niece as well," she lied. "The poor girl is ill from sun-heat. We've been traveling all day."

"Aye, the sun's been quite hot today. Whatchu traveling 'round dressed like that for?"

"We don't have the coin for a carriage, but my fool brother is determined to marry. Says it's the love of his life, though he's waited half of it to find her."

The woman laughed and reached for a mug, wiping it with a filthy cloth before jutting her chin toward the left. "Got one room there, so long as you have the coinage for *that*."

Kera did. She pulled out the fee, thanked the woman, then arranged for water and food.

Key in hand, she rushed back to Aurora and Faith.

They were just where she left them. Aurora relaxed when she saw Kera, though. *Isn't that a surprise?*

"Tie the horses to the peg," Kera explained. "You'll need to come back for them. Let's just get Faith inside first." Stepping forward, she retrieved Holly's reins and looped them several times around a post one-handed as Aurora did the same to her gelding.

Pulling Faith to her feet, they stumbled forward, Kera still balancing her son on her hip while she used her other arm to assist

Faith. It was painful. Pressure descended on her body and her chest felt tight the farther they walked, but they reached the room just as the torches finished being lit. Aurora helped Faith fall onto the bed. There, Faith's limbs thrashed. Her joints went akimbo, back arching like a man in the throes of lockjaw.

Kera slammed the door shut and drew the curtains. "You need to go tell the stable boys about the horses," Kera told Aurora.

The woman looked at her, incredulous. "You can't be ser—"

"I am entirely serious. I cannot leave Aiden alone, but I can tend to Faith. It must be you."

"He wouldn't be alone! He'd be with me!"

"I can't *leave* him."

"Would you leave *your* child in a fit?" Aurora asked her sweetly, face twisting into a vicious snarl.

No. She would not. But . . . "I cannot carry the bags. Not with Aiden. The eucalyptus and the books . . ."

Aurora hesitated, then flew into motion. "You'll not harm her," she demanded. Kera swore she wouldn't. Then Aurora whisked out of the room faster than she had entered. A feat in and of itself.

Kera shut the door behind her and went to Faith's bedside. Aiden was settled not far away, but he wasn't the priority at the moment. Not now. The poor girl was gasping for air, hands clawing at her throat. The ants were crawling once more. Hoisting her upright, Kera felt the muscles in her arms burn as she slid into position behind her. The complaints sent from her body were being triplicated, and the frenzied manager kept commanding the employees back in line. They didn't have the luxury of a break. "Breathe, Faith, breathe. There's a good girl. There's a good girl. Breathe."

As with Aiden earlier, Kera reorganized Faith's body, trying to get her into the perfect position to enable air to flow to the lungs. She struck Faith's back a few times, whenever something lodged deep in her throat, listening intently to the sound of Faith's breathing until she settled.

Aurora whirled back inside. She dropped the first set of bags, then rushed out for the rest, door slamming once more behind her. Kera kept her focus on Faith. Aiden watched them the whole time, hands over his ears, and he cried. She couldn't go to him. Not now.

Rubbing Faith's back, she kept her mind on her and her alone. "Breathe, Faith," she instructed. "You're doing so well. Breathe."

A good breath got through, and Faith stabilized her hitching lungs. Deep breath in. Deep breath out. There was sweat pouring from her face. Her hair was a tangled mess. But! She was breathing.

Aurora returned. She stumbled to Faith's bedside. Kera changed her position so Aurora could hold her daughter.

"I'm sorry," Aurora whispered in Faith's ear. "I'm sorry I left you. I'm sorry. I won't ever. Never. I'm sorry."

"She was unharmed in your absence, Ms. Lawrence," Kera said.

Aurora didn't respond. She sat at her daughter's side, shoulders tense. Kera knew full well that she had hurt the other woman. Kera even knew that she had made a mistake. Aiden was safe the whole time while Faith struggled in terror. Kera should have left to secure the horses. She *could* have carried the bags and left Aiden with Aurora. Aiden would have been fine.

"I'm sorry."

The lines of Aurora's back constricted even more, a viper ready to strike. She sat poised for one timeless moment as if considering her prey as it offered up pitiable excuses.

"I . . . didn't mean to cause offense."

The viper sprang forward.

"Cause *offense?*" Aurora seethed. Kera's chest tightened. Her lungs struggled to draw air. There was no helpful hand knocking breath back into her chest. No assistance from the cosmos as her brain searched for the correct words to say. The manager gave all its employees free rein to evacuate the premises, and she fell in a boneless heap before Aurora's gaze. "*Cause offense!* Lady Montgomery, how could someone like *me* possibly be offended by someone like *you?*"

Kera flinched. She glanced toward Aiden, who stared in *awe* at the viper. He had never seen someone raise their voice to her before. Even feverish and weak, he was boggling at the sight. Sliding from the bed, Aurora strode toward Kera. She towered over her. "What'd you think I'd do?" she growled, making no attempt to hide her wrath.

Kera's breath stuttered in her chest. Her mother's voice overlaying Aurora's words in a heated rush (*If you're not going to act like ladies, you don't get to dress like ladies!*)

Head down.

Hands in lap.

Smile at everything.

"Tell me!" Aurora shouted.

Kera flinched. *(Don't raise your voice!)* She raised a hand to her trembling lips. The words were paralyzed within her throat, never reaching her tongue. She couldn't form their shape or breathe her intentions. Tears pressed against her eyes. *(Ladies do not cry in public.)* She should excuse herself, but there was nowhere to go. She was in a Doleystown inn, and night had risen. The howls of the dark had already started, and she dared not step outside.

Better the monsters within than the monsters unknown.

"I'm sorry," she managed to say, her words wet and garbled. Frightened and dismayed, disgusted and horrified, she repeated it again, "I'm sorry."

Aurora still stood over her, sneering, "You're *sorry*."

Kera's nose clogged. She wiped at her eyes, desperate to be rid of the indecent affliction. Words. Words. She just needed to find the right words. Something Aurora, for all her limited education, seemed to have no trouble doing.

"You being *sorry* doesn't fucking matter," Aurora hissed.

Kera wondered if this was how duels started, if this was how it felt to face the wrath of one so slighted. To be incapable of mitigating that disaster, until the tempest took hold and lifted you up, high into the air, wrapping its winds around you before crashing you to the ground. *By my honor. Count to ten.* Mori and her first son had both given their apologies as they lay bleeding to death at her home.

A noise was produced in the back of Kera's throat. Her mother would be appalled. Father would be horrified. Unladylike. Unbecoming. She pressed her hands to her eyes.

"Stop crying," Aurora ordered. Kera didn't. "Stop crying!" Rough hands wrapped around Kera's arms.

She gasped as she was drawn to her feet. Her back pressed against the wall.

"You don't trust me," Aurora continued. Kera was frozen. The change in position shocking her into immobility. "*Learn to*," Aurora commanded.

She released Kera then, leaving her to stumble and catch her balance.

Aurora sat by Faith's side. One arm wrapped around Faith's shoulders, the other resting on Faith's hand.

Kera sank down to the floor. She didn't know what else to do.

The words never came in time.

They must not have been important.

CHAPTER SIX

K era's younger sister, Gale, had been a spitfire from the moment she'd drawn first breath. She'd belonged in the same world as their older brothers, but while they'd never complained about her chasing after them with a stick she pretended was a sword, their mother took it upon herself to mold Gale into the clay doll she expected all her daughters to emulate. Their mother punished Gale whenever she acted out, which was far too often to be considered acceptable. Gale spent a week shoveling manure in the stables at Crystal Point, months de-weeding the cobblestone walkway, and she had been given the grueling task of tending to the chimney each day for no other reason than to teach her humility. It never caught on. Kera had watched all of this in open wonder, never understanding why consequences never seemed to matter to her sister. Gale had just kept running from one disaster to the next, heedless of warnings, and eyes always set on the horizon.

While not *pleased* to hear of Gale's death, Kera couldn't help but feel an almost natural acceptance. Of course Gale would catch a chill running about as she did. Of course she had taken with fever acting as she did. Of course. Of course. Of course.

Sitting on the floor of an inn, tears staining her cheeks, wearing clothes inappropriate for a lady of her stature, Kera couldn't help but wonder why she hadn't taken advantage of learning more from Gale while she'd had the chance. Jealousy, perhaps. Jealousy that while Gale never ceased to combat their parents and society whenever she could, Kera had never been brave enough nor talented enough to try.

Not the social marvel of Ciara, not the fearless harpy of Gale, Kera loitered in stagnation between them both. Two days of traveling had left her muscles sore and aching, overworked and misused. She was filthy and reeked of the road. Her hair was tangled, and there was dirt beneath her nails. She could taste the salt of her tears as she licked her lips.

Gale wouldn't have been afraid to argue with Aurora. Ciara would have stood her ground. Kera hadn't, and Aurora ignored her. Aurora's focus was fixed on the reason she was here: Faith. Kera was here, acting out of class far too late in life, because her child was dying too. And because she was hysterical. Couldn't forget about that.

She had run out of her home without sparing a second thought, and she was surprised Ciara hadn't sent some men after her. She half expected John Barker to burst through the door of the inn and demand that Kera go home. He would take it from here.

The door remained shut. John Barker didn't appear.

He wouldn't. The only ones on this journey were her and her son, and Aurora with her girl. Only there was no Ivory Gate waiting for Aurora at her journey's end. She had no funds to finance her journey. She only had her daughter, a teenage girl who was cumbersome to manage. Faith didn't have the luxury of being carried by her mother. Despite fever and exhaustion, shaking and pain, Faith needed to stand and mount a horse each day. They were stronger women than Kera would ever be. Stronger, perhaps, than even Gale had been. At least Gale had the benefit of knowing she had wealth and privilege to defend her. Aurora had nothing, but like Gale, the prospect of pain didn't stop her from standing up and fighting for what she wanted. No matter the cost.

And because Kera was so keen on torturing herself, she whispered one question into the night, "Why did my husband go to you?" and closed her eyes so she wouldn't have to see Aurora as she provided her answer.

Aiden was asleep now, Faith too. They were as alone as they could be considering the circumstances. Aurora let out a long breath of frustrated air. "You told me not to talk to you about your husband," she reminded, tone still tart. The viper had gone away, turning into a python instead. Squeezing her victim as slow as she could so Kera could suffer longer.

Kera should wait until the tension between them cooled, but she just wanted it to be over. She was tired of preparing herself for the next blow; she just wanted it to land. "Please," she whispered. "I . . . would like to know." Aurora had every right to refuse. She could brush Kera to the side. Ignore her. Laugh in the face of her desperation.

She didn't. Even with her eyes closed, Kera could sense Aurora watching her. Could imagine the look on the other woman's face. Swallowing, Kera dared herself to look back. The anger was gone. The fire had been doused. It was replaced by a blank mask that Kera knew all too well.

She saw it each morning when she looked in the mirror. She felt it each night when she lay down for sleep, convincing herself she had done well and telling herself the day had been a success.

"Your husband loved you," Aurora said. It was not the answer Kera wanted, not the knowledge she wanted to hear. She tried to bite back on her frustration, ignore the feelings of inadequacy that multiplied with each passing second. A loving husband did not conduct an affair with a married woman. "Maybe it'll shock you, but we didn't . . . sleep with one another each time we met."

It didn't make her feel better. It wasn't even a shock. Mori had spent hours awake at night, staring out the windows and waiting for the dawn. Words would possess him and drive him to write. They would have driven him mad if he hadn't followed their commands. He'd had moods where his thoughts seemed incapable of stopping and he would have to pace from one side of the house to the other to calm his mind. He even had a habit of walking the length of the city if the house felt too constraining. He walked until he was too exhausted to move or think or do anything at all except sleep. Kera couldn't imagine Mori going to Aurora for sexual release, and then saying nothing at all afterward.

"The first time . . . you'd left," Aurora continued. "Gone to your father's for a holiday, I think, along with the kids."

"It's not my fault," Kera whispered like it was a prayer. A recitation of words she had chanted again and again and again. The defense was all she had against the insipid thoughts that haunted her in a death march of their own. *If you'd been a better wife, if you'd been what he'd wanted, if you'd stayed . . .*

Ciara would have affirmed her. *It's not your fault. He was the one who made that choice. It was his fault. His fault.* Aurora didn't. She kept the blank mask affixed, undaunted by her protestations. "The truth is, *Lady*, I needed money."

"We had no money—"

"You had *plenty* of money to someone like me." It was true. Kera knew that. Knew her standards and beliefs were far different from Aurora's. But the silks and the dresses didn't amount to prosperity, though Mori worked tirelessly to afford them. He never stopped trying to make enough to care for her and their children. He had been uninterested in giving her a life she might not be able to enjoy in luxury.

She had attempted, once, to tell him that they didn't need money. She didn't care about that. She'd just wished he spent more time with them. He had looked at her like he hadn't understood a word she'd said. Like she had blathered on about a topic and been so incomprehensible, he couldn't readjust to her worldview at all. *Of course we need money*, he had started to say, before shaking his head and leaving the topic unfinished and mangled in the air.

Mori had kept them in comfort, and he'd done it with a frugality that ran counter to his generosity. Their charity made them who they were far more than their avarice. They had money. The very idea they could think of things such as *charity* spoke to their wealth, however insignificant it might have been compared to that of their peers.

"The night we met—" Aurora sighed "—he'd been . . . out of his head. I came up on him as he wandered 'bout the city alone, talking to himself." Kera had heard this story before. She knew all the intricate pieces. "I came to him in bruises. Told him I needed aid, and your husband . . . he was a good man. He gave me aid."

Except for that. Kera hadn't known that. "Bruises," Kera repeated.

"Jacob . . . my husband? He thought Morpheus would be distracted by 'em." For a brief moment in time, Kera couldn't help but wonder if she had known anything about the affair at all. She hadn't read a single letter Mori had sent her on the subject. Whenever he'd tried to explain Aurora, she turned a deaf ear. She listened to him beg her for forgiveness and nothing else.

And she *had* forgiven him.

When their first Aiden had died, she had been desperate for salvation. Desperate for companionship and friendship, and he had been there. He had held her and whispered his own heartbreak into the void, joining his voice with hers. Neither of them capable of being alone one day more. Not for anything.

She had taken him back into her heart, been his friend and confidante once more. He'd treated her like she was the most important thing in his life, and she wanted to be the most important thing in someone's life again. She'd told herself she could ignore his affair, so long as he stayed with her. So long as he didn't leave.

Bruises.

It was a strange thought. Mori had never lifted a hand to her. Never raised his voice. Kera was not unaware that such men did exist. Young women (*twenty-three*, she reminded herself, *Aurora was twenty-three at the time*) were not always privileged enough to be with a kind husband.

"I told your husband I'd been beaten," Aurora continued. "Abandoned. That my daughter and I just needed some money to get out. He said he didn't have any on him."

He never did. He always kept it at home. Unless he planned to spend money, he left it at home. He wrote checks more often than not. He liked keeping his ledger in good order with receipts and marked transactions.

Aurora said, "I didn't think he'd come. But he did. So I told him that I needed to repay him. He refused." Discomfort swelled within Kera. "He was the first man to refuse." Aurora's features softened. Her eyes drooped some. Her lips tilted upward in a nigh unnoticeable smile. But Kera *did* notice it, and she found it fond. Aurora had been fond of Mori's refusal. "Your husband tended to my wounds. He brought that book"—she pointed toward *Absalon Herbalism*—"and he created a salve that he rubbed onto my scars. He looked in on Faith, and he made me promise to tell him if Jacob came back."

"You didn't sleep with him?" Kera asked. It felt like a lie.

"Not that night," Aurora replied. "He came to my home, at first, in kindness. And each night I offered to sleep with him. Thanked him in as many ways I knew how. He seemed . . . there's a word. Not confused. More than. It has a *b* I think?"

"Bewildered?" Kera offered. She recalled the moments when Mori was bewildered, and they usually came when he received a kind gesture or an act of familial decency. It was as if he'd never been aware such things existed.

Aurora nodded. "Be-wil-dered. And each day more out of sorts than the day before." She made a noise. Disgust. "I do believe those men at the Overwatch meant to torture him until he lost his mind."

Kera didn't miss the deadlines or furious pace. The frantic way Mori jumped from one mess to another. Who knew winning independence from Trent required so much paperwork? General Zakaria trusted Mori to lead the charge as he always did. Come up and conceptualize an entire country's laws and regulations? For Morpheus Montgomery, such things should have been easy. He worked and worked. He wrote and wrote. He compiled endless calculations and philosophical theories to help paint a portrait of Absalon's future. He deserved so much more.

"When he came to see me, he seemed in a fit of terror. That he hadn't finished on time. That he needed to work harder. Faster. He started crying, so I held him."

It's not my fault, Kera reminded herself. *But I should have never left.*

Aurora went on, "When we did sleep together, I . . . I think he just wanted to stop thinking about everything else. He wanted comfort. Kindness."

"You blackmailed him," Kera reminded this *tender-hearted soul* who offered her husband something as blasé as kindness.

"It was the reason I even spoke to him," Aurora confirmed. "Jacob wanted the money he felt your husband had. And he knew how devoted to you Morpheus was. With proof Morpheus had indeed been unfaithful, he knew he could make Morpheus pay him." Biting her lip, Aurora almost looked guilty for what she'd done. She *almost* looked hurt by the words she was telling Kera now. "Don' think I'll ever forget his face when he came to our home, letter in hand."

Kera could imagine it. Morpheus simply wasn't built for betrayal. He had only two close friendships aside from Kera, but John Sarren had died in the war and True Lord Amit had returned to Ruug. He never attempted to grow close to anyone else. Instead, he seemed to believe that if he had no one to lose, he wouldn't have to suffer their departure.

Aurora's letter would have torn him apart.

"Jacob beat me the night he sent the letter," Aurora revealed softly. She reached for the laces on her blouse, untying them and sliding the shoulders back. There was a jagged scar running from the base of Aurora's neck down across her collarbone, splintered like cracked glass. "I remember kneeling on the floor at Jacob's feet. His hand in my hair, as your husband stood in the doorway. Jacob said he knew what your husband did. 'Pay me, or I'll tell your wife.'" Aurora grimaced. Redid her laces. "So he did. He told Jacob not to touch me again, and Jacob said a whore was a whore and he would do what he wanted with me if it meant he got what he wanted. Morpheus told Jacob he wanted his *whore* untouched, and paid Jacob to keep me that way. And he did. Jacob beat me less, he left Faith alone. Morpheus came, and offered *salvation* by making Jacob rich."

Kindness, Kera presumed, had always been her husband's greatest flaw.

"It was almost two years later, when he got me and Faith alone. Gave us a good sum of money, and a choice. Take the money and leave Jacob, or don't. But he no longer would line Jacob's pockets. He put me in touch with Mr. Wild and he helped arrange my divorce."

"*Brennan Wild* helped you divorce your husband?" Kera very nearly yelled. Aurora didn't seem the least bit surprised by her reaction.

"It was how he knew of the affair in the first place, and why he had the information to go to the papers during the overseer election."

Kera's rage flooded her senses. She needed to look away from Aurora's face, needed to take a few moments to steady her breathing enough to regain control of her emotions, to build levies strong enough to block the tide from drowning her completely.

"Jacob," Aurora continued once Kera managed to uncurl her hands from fists, "found himself in and out of prison, struggling to stay ahead of the law Mori moved around him. Wasn't hard after so long for him to find other ways Jacob was breaking the law."

Aurora ended her narrative with a forced smile. A *there you have it* expression that left Kera feeling as though someone has scraped away at her insides with a trowel, digging through her soul and leaving her bare and barren.

She lifted a hand to cover her eyes. Rubbed at them with her thumb and forefinger. "Mori didn't need to *respond* though. After Wild published it in the papers, he didn't need to confirm it. He could have just kept it quiet. He didn't have to name you or say . . . just how he deceived me."

"Suppose he didn't, but for someone like me? It don't ruin my reputation any. So what if I'm hated? So what if no one likes me? Fine. Let them mock. It don't matter. And . . . if nothing else, I was the woman who lead Morpheus Montgomery astray." Kera flinched, and Aurora softened her tone. "I'm sorry."

"No . . . no, it's . . . it's fine. It's true."

"Just because something is true doesn't mean it doesn't hurt to hear it said. Regardless of the political motivations he may have had . . . he made a poor choice."

"He likely saved your life," Kera said, struggling to understand how Aurora could possibly say such a thing considering all the intricacies of the tale. "You believe it was a poor choice?"

"I feel my own guilt over those years," Aurora replied. "I think on how many years I took from him? How much stress and horror I inflicted when I followed my husband's wishes. For my place in the act." She took a long breath. "But . . . at the end of the day, when I embraced him that first night? When he allowed me to sleep with him? Even for the comfort he so desperately wanted? *He made that choice.* And for him? For you? For all the years you lost together? It was a poor choice. And . . . I'm sorry for my place in it."

Kera stared at Aurora, and she nodded. She believed her.

CHAPTER SEVEN

Kera couldn't sleep.

Aurora and Faith slept soundly, but sleep didn't come for Kera. Instead, she lay awake listening to the sound of the night. Aiden was curled up at her side. One of his hands clung to the sheet like a preferred blanket, and she kept an arm around his back to secure him. He was breathing badly. Each inhale was ragged and worn. But at least he inhaled. At least he exhaled too. As he breathed, Kera's thoughts tormented her brain like flies to foul meat. Biting and tearing at her until she scratched open another sore and let that fester too. The more she tried to ignore them, the more they stung. It was impossible to get any rest.

Hours passed. Aiden's fever raged, and his breathing was shallow. She watched his limbs twitch for hours, but she felt his heartbeat against her side. It was still strong, and perhaps over time his brow *wasn't* as hot as it once was.

Birds chirped the first few notes of morning. Doors opened as townsfolk began their day. She kissed Aiden's brow and settled him on the pillow before standing to dress. Glancing over toward Faith, Kera was glad to see the girl was doing better than before. Her face was still damp with sweat, and she twitched just like Aiden, but she'd made it through the night. It felt like an accomplishment.

Kera knelt beside her saddlebags and pulled out the laundry that she and Aiden had accumulated. She did the same for Aurora and Faith, though there wasn't much. She used a sheet to tie the bundle together, then hesitated. Aiden was on the bed. Aurora was not far away.

It won't take long to go to the river. We have to wash to stay healthy.
Mori had always insisted on cleanliness when they were ill. Wounds
were battlefields filled with soldiers. If the enemy troops infested the
land, the defending army couldn't rebuild their decimated villages.
The wound needed to be scoured and the excrement removed. Kera
wouldn't have time to wait for the sun to burn off the excess water
once she finished, but there was a fire pit in their room. She could set
the clothes out to dry there, and if she did it soon enough, they should
be ready for when they left. But . . . she looked at Aiden.

Looked back at Aurora.

Biting her lip, she knelt at Aurora's bedside and placed a hand on
her arm. Aurora came to with a start. She jolted back and blinked at
Kera like a lighthouse keeper catching sight of a ship-killing storm
on the horizon. *Clean the wicks and replenish the fuel, there be nasty
weather ahead. Even the gods be afeared of this storm. The tide alone
will kill them all.*

"I apologize," Kera whispered. "I did not mean to cause you
fright."

"You speak too fancy so early in the morning, Lady." She sat up,
glancing toward Faith immediately.

Feeling her cheeks burn, Kera tried to keep from ducking her head
in embarrassment. "Apologies," she mumbled, before rallying. "I'm
going to wash some clothes by the stream. Can you watch Aiden?"

Aurora frowned. She blinked a few times, clearing the sleep from
her eyes as she focused on Kera's face. It wasn't a storm, it was an
absence of water in the first place. The whole ocean had drawn back
leaving nothing but sand and dead crabs in its wake. "I shouldn't have
put my hands on you," Aurora murmured. "You don't need to do this."

There were so many excuses Kera wished she could say. So many
reasons why of course she shouldn't need to do this. Of course she
should just wait for them all to join her. Each excuse felt empty in
Kera's mind; each thought seemed half-formed at best. They were
useless excuses, there to obfuscate her discomfort, fear, and prejudice.

"That's not why . . . Apology accepted, but I want to . . . I need
to . . . Please?" she asked, praying that Aurora would take her apology
for what it was. If she was rejected again, Kera didn't think she would
be able to go through with it. She'd stay here and the laundry wouldn't

be done. It would sit and reek and they would all die from filthy soldiers laying waste to fertile ground.

The younger woman hesitated. She stared at Kera long enough for Kera to feel like she should just forget everything. Two days wasn't long enough to require a cleaning. It wasn't *necessary*—

Aurora reached out and touched Kera's hand. "I'll look after him," she swore.

A rush of relief flooded Kera's body. She thought she said, "Thank you," but she didn't know for sure. Her lips felt like they moved. Her throat couldn't recall the feeling of words spoken. The chords questioned one another. Did they give voice to her gratitude? Who knew.

Kera stepped back and collected their things. She clutched the bundle to her chest. Her lungs remembered to breathe at the door. They expanded her chest. They filled her with sweet air. Sweet strength. Trembling fingers reached for the handle on the door. She opened it. She stepped out and closed it. Her son was behind her, with the woman she swore she'd never forget. It was all right.

He was safe.

Her lungs continued working. Her eyes examined the terrain. It wasn't quite morning yet, the birds were little liars, but neither was it proper night. The sound of the nightwalkers had faded with the bulk of the shadows. They must have scattered back into the shadows of the underworld until sundown tonight. A cool silvery glow shimmered over Doleystown. Somewhere, the sun was starting to rise once more.

Heaving her load, Kera walked toward the riverbank. She kept one foot moving in front of the other. Like Holly, she moved without conscious thought. Doleystown wasn't very large, and it seemed peaceful. She shouldn't have feared the security of the fire lines. They were still lit along the perimeter. She plodded forward.

And she hopped over the line.

The river ran parallel to Doleystown. It was a winding thing that spilled into the west bank of the Great Sea. Its depth was deceiving as the water was clear enough to see the bottom, and someone drowned every year trying to touch it. Even up in Ship's Landing, reports on the drownings were common. Some even blamed sirens or selkies for it. There had to be some reason people kept braving the water.

Crouching on the shoreline, Kera found no such compunction. She didn't want to swim, or to touch the stones in the river bed. She wanted to wash her clothes. With no washboard, she utilized a few smooth rocks that were of acceptable quality. Her nails dug them up from the mud. She cleansed them in the water, then settled them into proper formation.

There was something calming about laundry. Soak the shirt. Lay it flat on the rock. Rub at it until the dirt and stains come up. She lacked the surfactant that helped maintain the color and remove the grime, but she could manage without such luxuries. She kneaded her knuckles into the fabric and winced when she pressed too hard and scraped one along the rock.

Blood trickled down one of her fingers. She watched as it dripped into the river, disappearing like it never existed. Kera brought it to her mouth. Copper and dirt embraced her tongue. She sucked and swallowed, checking intermittently until the bleeding stopped. Then she continued washing. She didn't have time to dawdle.

By now, the sun had started to peek up along the horizon. Gray light took flight, crossing the sky with a sweet stain. It coated the clouds in shadows and shades, blues and silvers tilting toward gold.

She let her mind wander toward Aiden. Was he awake? Was he scared without her there at his side? Had he started to fit? It took all of her willpower not to allow her fear and self-doubt to rule her mind. She took hold of the next shirt and dunked it into the water.

The river stung her hands. It was icy cold, and her skin wailed unhappily. Her cut shriveled and shrieked. It didn't matter. She was determined. She let the chill ground her as she glared at a black stain on the back of Faith's shirt. She had no idea how she got it. It was spoiled and stank of rot. She didn't even know how they could have missed it. "Just wash, you," she commanded the blight, rubbing harder and harder. The stain wouldn't rise. Scowling, she reached for a sharp stone. She scratched as hard as she dared, not willing to tear the thread, but *quite* eager to remove its malevolent stain.

"Having trouble?"

Kera jumped. She tugged the shirt up like a shield, holding it in front of her as if it could ward off any threat. It couldn't. *I'm an idiot*, Kera decided.

The woman who interrupted her was old and frail. She was just as wrinkled as the shirt Kera had been attacking. Crevasses and divots lined her cheeks and brow. Her skin bunched up and stretched thin in a simultaneous amalgamation. She was an ellipsis tagged onto the end of time, continuing when the sentence had long since met its end.

Each crest and valley told a story. Each pockmark on her shriveled flesh bore a memory. Blue veins slithered up the woman's throat and down into her wrists. Her hands were gnarled and twisted, each joint a swollen creaking knob. Dark spots kissed the skin beneath her chin. Her hair frizzled in the early morning air. Kera didn't think she'd ever seen someone so old.

Nor had she ever seen someone more beautiful.

With clothes, worn and ragged, draped unflattering about her portly frame, the woman smiled at Kera as though they had been friends all their lives. "Begging your pardon, ma'am, but are you all right?" Her voice was comfort. It was warm. It was gentle and as frail as a newborn's first breath.

Kera pulled the shirt she'd been mangling beneath the water, and set it out to the side. She tucked a loose strand of hair behind her ear and smiled. "Yes, madam. I apologize, have I disturbed you?"

The woman laughed like a tree bending deep in the wood with the wind rustling its branches and pushing it more . . . more . . . more. "Can't disturb me none. I've seen and heard all there is to know already. But only, you looked so upset, ma'am."

"It's this mark," Kera replied, holding the cloth up as evidence. "I fear it's bested me. I've never quite had a talent for this, though I do try."

Wrinkles pulled back, arching around the spread of the woman's lips. A smile that had been shared amongst thousands of people in her lifetime. The woman reached for the shirt. Kera passed it to her. Weathered hands squeezed the cloth. Wrinkles seemed to meld together, sliding from the fabric to her flesh without hesitation. "Quite a bother, innit always?" She scratched at the mark with her nail. It didn't clean. "I used to wash all the clothes in town."

"You were a laundress?" Kera asked.

"Once," the woman hummed. She ambled a final few steps closer, and when she did, Kera caught the briefest flicker of light. It was so fast that she might have imagined it, but for a moment Kera could have been certain the stranger *vanished* and reappeared right before her eyes. *Ghost*, her mind supplied.

The chill from the river water bit deep into her hands. It ran along the veins of her wrists, up and down her spinal column, and latched to the back of her brain. She felt the cold gripping her like a visceral thing. Wrapping about her body and refusing to let her go. Kera breathed out, and her breath fogged before her face.

It was not cold enough for that.

The ghost knelt at Kera's side. Her fingers creaked and echoed. She groaned, as though her bones still ached. As though the pain lingered on despite no longer existing. She flickered just a little more, and Kera's attention flitted toward the horizon. The sun was rising higher, and before too long the woman would be cast back into the shadows of night. Usually spirits disappeared well before now. They didn't dare risk the light.

"I've never seen one of you out so late before," Kera murmured to herself, watching as the woman bent to the water and tried to clean the stain. "Or early, I expect the case may be."

"Oh I come each day, ma'am. The folks in town don't visit like they used to. Jealous, I think." The woman rubbed at the dark mark as she spoke, and Kera watched in awe. She took note of the surety in the ghost's motions. It seemed so easy for the woman to push and pull at the cloth, bending it to her will while still caring for its fragile nature.

Mori had always told her that the ghosts they interacted with during the wars rarely meant them harm. They seemed to prefer continuing the tasks they had left off on their death, longing for validation and a sense of accomplishment.

Sometimes Kera wondered if that meant she, too, was a ghost.

With the sun rising, there was little threat here. This woman was calm and tired. She moved with languid precision. Kera wondered how long ago it had been since she passed. Her clothes did not seem too dated, perhaps her death was recent. Perhaps she was a new acquisition to Doleystown that the night guard had not yet frightened off or cast away.

Feeling impolite to not reply, Kera urged the ghost to continue speaking. Prompting her with a curious, "What are they jealous of?" as she settled in to listen.

"Of my many good years," the woman teased. "When they do see me they shout and yell. They hurt so much now though . . ."

"I'm sorry to hear that, madam."

The woman shrugged and held up the shirt for inspection. The spot was gone. Removed from existence like it had never been there before. Unable to help herself, Kera clapped her hands in delight. "Oh, *thank* you! Thank you kindly, truly you've a gift for the impossible," she praised, retrieving the shirt and marveling at its fresh appearance. "Please madam, may I know the name of my savior?"

She must have startled the ghost, for the woman was looking at her with wide eyes. But, slowly, the aged face was split by a tremendous smile. It reminded Kera of her grandmother, who at seventy-three years of age determined she had no time for bothersome things like manners and appropriate behavior. If, at seventy-three, she wasn't going to be allowed to fart at the dinner table, then well, *when was she going to have the chance*? Her parents had called her grandmother dotty and hidden her away from polite company, and Kera had spent every day of her childhood dreaming of the day she could be the dotty old grandmother sitting in the closet plotting when to fart.

"My name is Rachel, ma'am," the ghost said.

"Kera," she introduced right back. "If it pleases you, I'd be most gratified for your tutelage. I fear I must move on soon. I've a long way to travel. But I'd appreciate your assistance in the meanwhile. Though . . . I have not much to pay you for your time."

Kera winced as she finished, wondering if she somehow caused offense. She didn't know what could offend a ghost. She'd never crossed the firewall before. She never had the chance to meet specters, wraiths, ghouls, or phantoms. Their hauntings were loud enough outside the city that she avoided it at all costs. Even now, she couldn't quite place what it was that inspired her to leave before the sun was up. Just a feeling. A feeling that everything would be all right.

Years of living in terror had prepared her for something more than . . . this, more than beautiful Rachel with her glorious smile and clever fingers. And Rachel *wasn't* offended by her request. In fact, she smiled. She reached for the next item in Kera's pile, and together they tended to the clothes. Rachel told Kera about her life in Doleystown, flickering every so often as the sun rose more and more. Kera listened and nodded along while they cleaned.

She asked if Rachel knew much about the people here or their stores and where she could find medicines for her children, and Rachel directed her to a Mr. Davis over by West Way. He had an apothecary there and Kera was told she might just find what she was looking for amongst the items on his shelf.

"Are yer bairns sick, then?"

"Aye, my little boy and . . . and a girl, a . . . an acquaintance's girl. They're both sick."

"Sunshine and fresh air. That'll do 'em both some good. Don't you be hiding them in the dark now, it's the sun that'll heal 'em. You mark my words."

It was kind advice, kindly met. Kera smiled and said, "Yes, madam," before listening to Rachel tell her a story about the time yellow fever came to Doleystown many years ago.

The longer she spoke, the more *that* day's sun yawned over the horizon. It pushed back against the final remaining silvers and grays of night, shifting the sky darker and lighter in turns. Reds and golds combatted a brilliant blue that soon reached out across the sky. Kera and Rachel both watched as a golden beam traversed the ground toward them.

"Thank you, Miss Kera," Rachel said just before the light touched her. Kera reached for the shirt in Rachel's hand, letting her fingers touch Rachel's just one last time.

"May you find peace, my dear Rachel," she prayed. "And find a good rest when you are able." Rachel's smile was brilliant. Her eyes glittered with tears, but she thanked Kera again. When the sun touched her body, the wrinkled and aged woman faded from view as though she had never been there at all.

The shirt fell limp in Kera's hand. She held it steady for a moment, waiting in case Rachel reappeared, but as the seconds passed and the minutes gained, she lowered the shirt to the rest of her pile and wrung them out one final time. She watched in silence as the droplets fell into the river, missing her new friend already.

Then, task complete, Kera collected the clothes in a heap and walked back toward town. The fire line was being turned down, and some members of the town's night guard spied her as she approached. One even called her over. "Please, ma'am, did you go down to the river?"

"Yes?"

"Only, did you not see the phantom there?"

Kera hesitated. She was not very good at recalling the differences between ghosts and phantoms and specters. The subtleties confused her, and they seemed so minute it had never crossed her mind. But if they believe the woman to be a phantom, she was not going to argue with them. Though she asked, "Ms. Rachel, you mean?" in case she was wrong.

"You *spoke* to her?" the guard was loud enough that his colleagues arrived as well. They exited the guard house, all fresh-faced young soldiers who spoke in hushed tones with furtive glances. "However did you survive?"

"I'm not certain I understand?" Rachel had never shown any signs of violence. In all the time they'd spoken, she hadn't threatened Kera once.

"We've been trying to be rid of the thing for years. Keeps coming back."

"And she's violent?"

The guards looked a touch confused by her question. "Well, she's a phantom innit she? Why'd'ya wan' one o' them around for?"

Kera had no notion of how to respond and forced her expression to turn agreeable so as not to cause *them* offense. Thanking them for their good service, she passed them by. They stared after her and muttered to themselves about her behavior loud enough for her to hear. It should have bothered her. She was rather surprised that it didn't. In fact, she was tempted to ask them what they expected her to do when Rachel appeared. Brandish Faith's shirt at her like a sword? If it made a poor shield, it made a worse weapon. *Honestly*, she huffed. *Soldiers.*

Pressing open the door to her room, Kera found Aiden sitting with Aurora and Faith on their bed. Mori's *Bestiary* was spread open on

Aurora's lap and it was clear she was trying to read it to them, though she stopped sounding out the words when Kera stepped inside.

Closing the door, Kera brought their damp clothes to the fire. Aurora had stoked it after Kera left. It was plenty hot enough to dry their garments. "You left before the sun rose," Aurora chastised, low voice filling the room with an unhappy timber.

"I wanted to care for the clothing and have them done by the time we leave."

Aiden coughed and Kera turned to address it. She needn't have bothered. Aurora had already lifted him up with a confident hand, placing him on her knee and folding him forward so the phlegm could leave his throat.

"There're monsters in the dark," Faith whispered, eyes trailing toward the *Bestiary*. Kera couldn't help but wonder if that had been an appropriate book to read while they all considered her chances of returning unscathed.

"They're not so scary," Kera assured as she laid out the shirts and trousers, draping the socks as close as they would go. It was quick and busy work, and when it was done, she cut up some fruit and cheese for their breakfast.

Before they left town, they would need to resupply. The coinage in Kera's pocket was becoming lighter by the day, but she should have enough to afford their journey south. In two days' time, they would arrive at Absalon's future capital, and if they pushed on just a little longer from there—Mount Maladh. Najah Zakaria had once told her that she and the children were more than welcome at the Zakaria estate whenever they wished. It was an offer that Kera was all too eager to accept.

The sooner she could place the capital from her memory, the happier she would be. If they could avoid staying there altogether, she would much prefer it.

She had no desire to be anywhere near that detestable city and all of its unkept promises. Brennan Wild wanted to make that city his home, and considering her present mood, she was liable to do something she would regret if she needed to confront the man.

"You all right?" Aurora asked. The question startled her, and she looked back over her shoulder. All three of them were staring: Faith with awkward uncertainty, Aiden with eyes so wide, and Aurora seemed to expect Kera to admit she'd been tortured by some horrible beast whilst she had been gone.

"I'm fine," she replied. "It's going to be a long day."

They had a lot of ground to cover, but when she looked back at the clothing by the fire, every single shirt and strip of cloth was already dry. Kera blinked. She reached out to touch them. It wasn't some illusion.

"Kera?" Aurora pressed.

The fire must have been warmer than she'd thought. Shrugging, Kera smiled at her three traveling companions. "It's going to be a long day," she repeated. "But . . . a good one. What do you think, Aiden; shall today be a good day?"

"Will there be ducks?"

"I shall help you look for them as we travel if you like."

"Promise?"

"Promise."

Then he smiled as big as he did before all the illness came and threatened to take him away, and for now, that was good enough for her.

CHAPTER EIGHT

T*he Absalonian Bestiary* wasn't a large tome. If anything, Kera
believed it should be larger. There were whole sections missing,
particularly on phantoms, ghosts, and other nightwalkers. She
flipped through the pages while Aurora and the children dressed, but
it seemed as if the *Bestiary* was far more interested in the creatures of
the day than the spooks that haunted the evening hours.

Frustrated, she instead turned to the entry on griffons. Of all
the notes accumulated throughout the book, it was the one that
had the most detail. Mori's careful scrawl was scattered throughout
the chapter. However, and far more interestingly, there was another
pen dotting the page as well, often contradicting the main body of the
text as it added details on eating habits, mating rituals, and personality
traits.

Where the text of the book fixated on what the griffons looked
like and what their range was, the additional notes were far more
comprehensive. Every so often, the researcher sketched a detailed
picture to accentuate their point: the long hooked curve of the griffon
talon, the pad of the griffon's back paws, the particular curve of the
beak, and the eyes, which *can see up to seven hundred yards with perfect
clarity*, the researcher reported.

She turned the page and smiled at the charming sketch of baby
griffons hatching from their eggs under the last paragraph. The book
had gone into the basic mating rituals of griffons, but the notes all
but filled up the page around the downy-feathered image of cat-birds
in eggs. *Although it is true that griffons mate for life, should a griffon's
partner die, they do form intimate bonds with other widow(er)s, forming
unconventional family units that thrive despite the lack of a true mated*

pair. Further, griffons appear not to be concerned with matters of gender and will mate with both sexes. They have been known to adopt abandoned or lost eggs should the parents of such eggs be proven dead.

Mori had drawn a line from the notes and added one word: *Fascinating.*

The other notetaker responded: *Don't be a putz.*

The familiarity was charming in its own way. They went back and forth with their extraneous observations like a game. Mori wrote: *The front talons can tear and shred as swiftly as any large bird. And their back paws provide the thrust needed to take flight.*

And he circled a line from the original author: *Tokens given by griffons are considered to bring good fortune,* while underlining the unknown researcher's added context: *Gifts alone. Stolen goods will bring discord instead.*

Aurora leaned over Kera's shoulder to look at the pages. She was dressed and ready to embark. She'd even washed her face in the small basin they'd received the night before. Her pale wrap tied her curls into submission and not a lock was out of place as she bent closer to the page Kera was reading. "Soldiers used to carry 'em. Feathers. Do you remember that?" Aurora asked, pointing at the words.

Aurora would still have been a child during the first war. Sitting on her parents' knees— *No.* She'd have been working alongside her parents. Watching the soldiers on parade, then cleaning up after them when they had gone.

But during the second she would have been an adult. Trent hadn't wanted to give them their independence. But they'd had the taste of freedom after the revolution, and they weren't going to give it up no matter what the cost.

"Did you know anyone who fought?" Kera closed the book and stood.

"A few. My father volunteered for a few months, was over at Hark's Point." She huffed then, shaking her head and picking up their saddlebags, throwing one over each shoulder. Faith was sitting upright, shivering despite the blanket wrapped around her shoulders. She wasn't fitting yet, but there was no need to tempt fate. She should get mounted before she lost too much energy. Without Faith's help, Kera doubted they'd be able to get her up.

Aiden coughed under his breath at his mother's side. She ran her fingers through his hair. "That was a long winter."

"You know, the winter wasn't the hardest bit."

She did know that. The papers had entertained themselves with writing about how frigid the weather had been. The politicians had recused themselves with talk of how they could not control the weather.

And yet, it hadn't been the weather that'd led to so many deaths. It hadn't been the weather that'd caused hundreds of men to starve. The shelters had been put up. The fires had burned well enough, but the supplies had never come. The help had never arrived. The men and women at Hark's Point had died of starvation, not cold.

"Mori once said the taste of bark became so common, he'd rather see Trent retake all of Absalon than bear one more meal of it." It was not a comment that looked good on paper. For years, his detractors used it as an excuse to call him a Trent sympathizer in disguise.

Aurora huffed, shaking her head and rolling her eyes to the ceiling. "Sometimes I wonder if Morpheus knew how much trouble he made himself."

Likely not.

In any case, Kera stood and stretched her back as straight as it would go. "There's an apothecary not far from here, they may be able to provide us with some more eucalyptus."

Aurora pitched her voice so it was high and airy, mocking with each word. "Why, Lady Montgomery—"

"You do have my permission to speak my name, you understand?" Kera cut in. Aurora nodded like a bored school child, unimpressed and unmotivated to change.

"*Lady* Montgomery," she continued, "shall you lead the way?"

It was a dangerous thing, moving the children through the town. While Aurora's theory on the contagion had seemed accurate thus far, it wouldn't matter to people living here. All they'd know is that the plague had reached their town. At best, she and the others would be barred from traveling any further. At worst, Kera imagined both Aiden and Faith killed and burned to keep the illness from spreading.

Neither was an option that Kera had any desire to think on for long.

Aurora managed to distract the stable boy and blessed Faith summoned all of her strength so she could climb up onto the horse. Her left foot slipped off the stirrup while she was swinging her right leg over the gelding's rump, but Kera caught her. She held her steady as Faith finished mounting, both of them gasping for breath as their muscles burned. Aiden clung to Kera's leg the whole time, far too close to the gelding's hooves. Aurora plucked him up though. Cooing at him as Kera mounted.

"Hard on the horses to ride double all the time," the very helpful stable boy informed them.

"You don't say?" Aurora snapped back. Kera's cheeks flushed at the harsh retort. It wasn't his fault. He was just trying to be helpful. Besides, Holly's nose was hanging low; she was weary after so many days in the field. The poor girl deserved a nice pasture to graze at her leisure, not another endless trek through the Absalonian countryside. Kera made to apologize for Aurora's behavior, but snapped her mouth shut once she caught Aurora scowling at her. Perhaps she didn't need to add her commentary just yet.

The apothecary was on the opposite end of town. They kept to a side street that traveled along the back of the store fronts rather than the main road. It kept peering eyes from looking too close at their children, but it also meant they passed the shop they wanted twice by accident. They needed to keep turning around, until Kera spotted a few sprigs of herbs that just *had* to be a sign.

Aurora took Holly's reins for Kera as she dismounted. Half asleep as she was, Holly wouldn't have gone anywhere even if Kera left the reins about her neck. But the illusion of safekeeping helped put Kera's mind at ease. Routines were safe. They were calming. Aiden already disliked the break in routine that tugged him from the horse he had just gotten settled on. He whined and kicked Kera's stomach as she pulled him down. He didn't even apologize. She was too exhausted to care.

Tapping her purse at her side, Kera ran through some mental arithmetic to calculate how much she had left on her person, and how much she could spare. Then she walked around the building to the shop's front and stepped inside. An elderly man looked up at her from behind his work station. A mortar and pestle were set in front of him, and a grindstone not far away. "And you are?" he asked.

"Kera," she replied. "My son and niece are ill. I'd hoped for some medicine."

The man leaned over his counter to squint at Aiden.

"They both suffer from the same . . . he burns with fever," she admitted. "And their appetite—"

"Yarrow and peppermint for fever, peppermint for the food too. You'll be wanting some ginger and fennel seed as well."

"And eucalyptus, if you please," Kera continued.

The man grunted at her, scooping up her supplies and dropping them into small pouches on the counter. "That won't do much for your fever."

Eyeing the product, Kera thanked him. "I'm aware of its properties . . . but the eucalyptus is not for the fever."

He squinted at her, then back at her son. "That's no ordinary illness, is it . . . *Kera*." His fingers tapped against the counter as Aiden squirmed. His head pressed against her throat, and his cheeks set fire to her soul.

"We'll be out of your town shortly," Kera replied. "But I need that eucalyptus."

"Where you off to, then?" He pulled a jar from the shelf and carried it to a set of vials. He poured slowly, filling the vials one by one.

"The griffons."

"*Griffons!*" He threw his head back, laughing loud enough that Aiden made a noise of protest against her neck. "*You* mean to fight the griffons?"

Fighting was not exactly what Kera had in mind. If she could avoid them she would. Kera knew full well that she was no warrior and had no weapons. She wasn't capable of fighting a monster like a griffon.

Refusing to be cowed or bullied by the man, she adjusted Aiden once more. Squaring her shoulders. "I wish to save my son and niece."

"Yes and while you're worried about them, those menaces will tear you apart. They are violent and horrid beasts. They'll smell you before you ever enter their territory. Kill you the moment you think you'll be rid of them. Did you know no army has ever managed to best the creature? And you want to go alone. Who's going to protect you? Him?" He pointed at Aiden with one of the vials. "Their skin is thicker than armor. Their beaks can tear through the trunk of a tree. Feathers that cure blindness. Ha! Why do you think there are those still blind? Talons that cure all illnesses. Turn wraiths back into ghosts. Put ghosts to rest. Ha! And the people are still ill. Wraiths still exist. Ghosts still walk this land. You're wasting your time."

"How much for your wares?"

"Why bother? That child is as good as dead—"

"How much for your supplies, sir, so that you may be rid of the dead once more?"

"Twelve coppers."

Kera's breath caught in her throat. *Twelve?* "That's more than three nights at the inn."

"You won't need your money for long. What's it matter to you? Five more days with your son? Hmm? Give or take? How much is that worth?"

"You're a horrid man," she gritted out, reaching for her purse. She dropped half of her coins onto the table. He counted them with a twisted expression, tongue poked out between his lips, and eucalyptus still in his palm. "Give me the vials," she demanded. He laughed again.

"You're a fool."

"Give me the vials I've paid for." He waved them before her face, jerking it back when she reached for it, then settled them with the pouches on the counter. The tide crashed against the levies. Rage boiled beneath Kera's skin. She scooped up her wares. She forced herself to breathe. She kept her back straight. Her son never slipped off her hip.

She was a lady.

She managed.

Then he said, "The ghost of Morpheus Montgomery thanks you," and she froze.

Her limbs stiffened. Her fingers cracked along the joints. They locked tight about the vials and the herbs. Aiden's head lifted up from where he'd hidden it. Her feet were rooted down. Digging deep into the earth. Securing her stature. Enhancing her stability. The tide pulled back.

Not to passivity, but to form a tsunami.

After Mori's death, Wild had done his very best to ruin her husband's reputation. They had never liked each other in life, and now that he wasn't there to defend it, Mori's good name had swiftly transformed into a synonym for corruption. Kera wasn't dumb. She wasn't blind or ignorant. She knew the rumors. She'd lived through the publicity following her husband's affair and understood full well what people thought of the man she loved.

Smile, her mother's voice reminded her. *Agree.*

No.

Not this time.

"*What* did you say?" Kera asked. It startled the man. Startled him enough that it wiped the cruel grin right off his features. "No. No, I am quite certain I heard what you said," Kera pressed on. Undaunted. "'The ghost of Morpheus Montgomery thanks *me*,'" she quoted, sliding her voice up and down his graveling accent.

"I—"

"Since you *clearly* have no notion who I am, I shall tell you." Leaning forward, glaring at him with every ounce of energy she held in her body, she spelled it out as viciously as she could. "My name is *Kerryn Leona Montgomery*, Morpheus was my husband, and the medicines that you have provided for such an *exorbitant* rate are an insult to him and all he worked for."

The apothecary's face turned impossibly white. He sputtered. Searching for words. She would not listen. "My husband fought for this country from the moment he stepped foot on her soil. He was Isra Zakaria's most trusted advisor. He built the financial system that you've so *clearly* perverted for your own personal gain. He put down rebellions, he championed for good human rights, and has always had the best interests of the *people* and this country at heart. He secured this country's credit, negotiated treaties, and was the founder of its international trade system. He stabilized Absalon's economy after its freedom from Trent, and *you think he'd be grateful you swindled from me twelve coins*? When your goods are worth two at most?"

She was breathing hard. Her heart hammered in her chest. The town was flooding, the people drowning. The water choked the life out of good sense and sensibility. She gritted her teeth and she leaned forward even more. "Your avarice is a mockery of everything my husband worked so hard to build. Shame on you, sir. And shame on your practice. You're a disgrace!"

"Widow Montgomery, I—I meant no offense—"

"Precisely *how* is that meant to be inoffensive, you daft fool? Either I am a supporter who would be scorned by your words of their hero, or I am a dissenter who is still fully aware that you have *stolen* from me. You've cast my husband as a villain and you backtrack only now when you see your vile behavior is chastened. You're a weak-minded, horrible little man, and—and—*I don't like you!*"

Turning on her heel, herbs and oils in hand, she marched from the shop and around the corner. She stomped to where Aurora waited with Faith and the horses, both of them staring at her with wide eyes and incredulity. Aurora was, in a word, awestruck. Faith, even suffering with fever, appeared to have been stunned by some marvelous event.

"*What?*" Kera snapped, fighting with the saddlebags so she could shove her items inside. Action done, she hoisted Aiden up onto the saddle, and then mounted by herself. Her fury pushed her to make it even without a boost.

Damn him, damn him, damn him. She would kneel on rice for a millennium just for the chance to curse him good and proper.

"'I don't like you'?" Aurora quoted.

The tide died an embarrassing death and snapped back to the shoreline where it belonged.

Kera's cheeks burned. *How much did they hear?* It shouldn't matter. It *shouldn't*. She tried to cling to her anger just a little longer. She wanted to hold on to it until they could get onto the road. Then perhaps she could let it out in the privacy of their group. Then, she could feel shame for having shouted at an elderly man over a slight that had no long-term impact on anyone but a memory.

Morpheus was dead. What did it matter if his legacy was mocked? Was she to ride to each dissenter and argue herself blue in the face until they agreed? She didn't have that kind of strength in her. Nor that masochism.

"'Weak-minded, horrible little man'?" Aurora continued, laughter causing her shoulders to shake.

Shouting at one man did nothing. Kera should have known better. She should have. But she didn't want to show Aurora that. "Well he is," she insisted instead, reclaiming her reins and refusing to let her fury be cowed by logic *just* yet.

"I don't think even Morpheus himself could have argued the point better," Aurora teased. It made Faith laugh too, coughing as the giggles overtook her.

Urging her gelding forward, Aurora seemed prepared to leave, but was forced to stop when the apothecary rushed out in front of them. He was out of breath, eyes wild and chest heaving. Kera's lips pressed together, and the man approached her horse with a stumbling gait. He held up his palm full of coins. "Please, my lady, I . . . I acted out of turn and—" He grabbed at her hand.

Aurora slapped him hard with her reins in response, striking him off Kera without the slightest bit of hesitation. She had turned her gelding around, bracketing him between them, and the man cursed and cowered as he looked at Aurora in shock. But Aurora peered down her nose at him, reins held aloft and ready to strike again. Kera's gallant guardian, like in the tales of old.

Seemingly emboldened by Aurora's bravery, Holly stamped her feet and huffed at the man. Her ears pointed forward and she whinnied in protest. "Enough," Kera commanded. The horse snorted unhelpfully, then settled. Aurora merely glanced back at Kera to confirm. "Thank you, my friend," she said soothingly. "But please . . ." Nodding, Aurora shifted so her gelding allowed the man just a little more space to move. As she did, the apothecary approached once more. He placed her coins back into her possession. She felt their weight, and scanned the amount. "You've given me too much."

"Your Grace." He was using the wrong honorific. She was *not* his grace, and never would be. "I've returned all your coin to you."

"I understand that, *sir*. And it is too much." Carefully she counted out two coins and returned them into his possession. "When I leave here, you will be a man whose work was paid for with fair compensation. And I will have been a customer to your store. I will not be the wife of Morpheus Montgomery, who demanded your work for free."

He stared at her. Dumbfounded. But she couldn't bring herself to explain any longer. She tucked her coins back into her purse and released the anger she had longed to hold on to for just a little longer. She adopted the face she'd spent years perfecting, the one that let him know that he would receive no further ill will from her or her party. "Thank you for your honesty, sir. At the end of all things."

He was still staring. Stumbling now, as he tried to formulate words. "Of course, Your Grace, I mean—*Lady*. Widow? Widow Montgomery. Of course. And—and you're going to the griffons, you said?"

"What's it matter to you?" Aurora asked.

"It's only . . . be wary—the nightwalkers between here and Kytesberg are more harsh than they've been in years. All that construction on the capitol is waking them from their graves."

"Thank you for your warning, sir," Kera replied. "We shall be careful. Good day."

"G-good day."

Turning back to Aurora, Kera dismissed the man from her thoughts. She angled her heels down, adjusted her grip on her reins, and nodded at her companion. It was time to move forward; the dead were behind them, but also ahead.

She didn't want to think about the apothecary anymore.

CHAPTER NINE

"**G**- g'day, mi lady," Aurora mocked. She wasn't capable of keeping her amusement to herself. Just kept going on and on and on. Kera thanked the gods that her own skin was dark enough to hide the blush that stained her cheeks. She kept her eyes fixed on the road so Aurora wouldn't see how mortified she'd become with each horrific reenactment. Her saving grace came from the sound of Faith and Aiden giggling at the theatrics. They were both awake enough to enjoy it, even if Kera felt worse with each passing second.

"I don't believe he was quite that bad," Kera tried to excuse. Now that it was over, her mother's voice kept chastising her. She'd been impolite. Rude. Hostile. Ladies didn't shout and Kera knew better than to toss about Mori's name like that. It wasn't fair to him, and it wasn't fair to his legacy.

Having a wife who shouted to defend his honor took away from his image. She shouldn't have involved herself. It was foolish, foolish, fool—

Aurora was laughing again. "We could hear you, you know? All the way round the corner 'n' all. We could hear you clear as day, and I gotta tell you, Lady, there's never been a man given quite the same talking to as that ol' maester."

"Apothecary. 'Maester' is—"

"Oh what's it matter? Maester, *apothecary*," Aurora drew out the word, taking a good long while to say. "'S'all the same thing in the end. Hack physicians who don't know nothing about nothing and can't explain away this plague."

"Ma don' li'e quacks," Faith slurred. She had a pretty voice, even gargled by illness and fever. A sweet sort of dainty soprano that was rather different from the deep alto of her mother. Kera imagined Faith would have a fine singing voice, if she ever had the chance.

"Wassa quack?" Aiden asked.

"It's the sound a duck makes," Kera said.

"Not so." Aurora waggled her brows at Aiden, making him giggle. "It's a doctor who thinks he knows more'n he actually does and makes a right mess of things. Ain't never met a doc who ain't a quack."

"That doesn't mean all doctors are ... quacks, though," Kera tried.

Aiden wriggled a bit in front of her, his left foot swung forward and back, colliding solidly with her shin. She hissed, but he hadn't finished maneuvering, whining as he tried to get comfortable. It took him awhile, but when he finished, he pushed his thumb into his mouth and said around it: "I like ducks." At which Aurora laughed long and hard. She tossed her head back, and her daughter giggled with her, the both taking an inordinate amount of delight in Aiden's claim. She had a lovely laugh, free of the social conventions that Kera's own mother had beaten into her. Aurora neither covered her mouth with her hand, nor tried to silence it. She laughed with no restrictions. Joy for joy's sake.

The sun had started darkening Aurora's already rich skin. Her cheeks carried a warmer tone than just two days prior. Kera's eyes were drawn to a few stray curls that had escaped the wrap, sweat glistening as they sprung about her face. Aurora arched into the light, grinning like she couldn't have asked for anything better or more satisfying. She was beautiful.

As soon as the thought crossed her mind, Kera found herself reeling. She thought back to everything she knew about Aurora. She never thought about the various shades of who Aurora Lawrence was as a person. She didn't know if this was a good look ... or perhaps if there were better looks as of yet unknown.

Aurora smacked her lips and adjusted her own seat. Kissed the back of Faith's head as she shifted her into a better position. "Thing is, unless you've got the money to show for it, you're not getting anyone who's *not* a quack. You see?" Aurora asked Kera with a shrug. "And it's not as though your *physicians* are any better. All of them insist on bleeding us dry and seeing if that'll help. Like that worked well for Lord General Zakaria."

"You know, we're not lords or ladies." The transition from the title had been easy and exciting. She'd enjoyed slipping from the role. Enjoyed asserting herself as Mrs. Montgomery. Some of her peers had wavered and complained that the lack of an official gentry meant that they were no longer superior than those beneath them.

Kera intended to continue that topic, explaining why Mori and the general fought so hard to ensure that there would be no established nobility as there was across the sea in Trent or Ruug. Aurora snorted and cut Kera's thoughts in half with a simple statement: "You all can call yourselves whatever you like, it don't change you into anything different."

She . . . had a point. One that was effortlessly valid. Even after dropping their titles, nothing had changed in Kera's quality of life. She continued to live the same lifestyle as was expected of someone from her status. And Aurora knew it too. She looked at Kera from the corner of her eye, grinning at her with a twist of her lips.

Her garbled and ever-changing accent gave life to new ideas that Kera struggled to argue against. Kera's ear struggled to find the dialect or simple pattern that explained Aurora's cadence, but none came to mind. Perhaps it didn't matter. Instead, she found herself lulled into Aurora's philosophies, leaning closer so as to pick up each and every word, placed all in such precise locations. Grammar and eloquence be damned.

"My family always worked for people like you, rich folk who don't pay us no mind. Not any free labor, mind, but what's a penny a week get you? Not much. But we go and scrub the floors, clean your bed pans, and do what you like. 'N' we got good at filching from your trash to get what all we need."

Kera hated how Aurora said *you* as if she had worked for Kera's family. As if she had served the Leonas or the Montgomerys and had been treated poorly by them on a personal level. But she kept her mouth closed and listened as Aurora went on. "I'd see your physicians and your scholars. Your crystal worshipers"—*occultists*—"and hexers." *Witches*. "You read your books and mind your herbs and you do everything you can to do whatever. And when it comes to us? The poor? Y'all never looked twice. Never cared what we were doing.

"I used to look into your windows and watch you dancing," Aurora continued. "And I'd try to match the steps. Never could get it quite right. But it never stopped me. Always wanted to learn. But you rich folks always seemed to know exactly how to do it. How to move and how to step. Figure you spend hours learning and whatnot. Even saw a few lessons when I was scrubbing some floors once. Watching as the ladies and the gents of the house got together and learned their children."

"Taught their children," Kera corrected; Aurora rolled her eyes.

"*Taught* their children," she amended. "In any case, that's what life is like. You know? You and your fancy dress and your fancy language. Always speaking proper and expecting others to do the same. Even if we don't get the same kinda education as you."

"That's not why—"

"I ain't blaming you, Lady. It's a just a fact. You live your life in your tower and you don't see it from down below. You're a lady, good and proper. And you always will be. You jus' can't understand what life is like from our point of view. And you probably never will."

The road up ahead curved to the left and narrowed along the bend. Holly, the slower horse, fell back in line and let Aurora lead the way. It was a natural break in the conversation, and it gave Kera time to try to formulate a response. She didn't necessarily agree with Aurora, and she certainly didn't know if such a description was fair to impose on *all* persons with money.

But . . . she was right. Growing up in a Leona household meant that she was taught how to dance as soon as she could stand. It went hand in hand with needlepoint and social etiquette. She used to long for her dancing lessons. She'd been eager and excited to show everyone what she learned that day.

Her father was a patient man and he let her perform for their mother. He used to clap his hands and educate her on the proper footwork, while one of her brothers was drafted as her partner. Her mother used to fan herself on the chaise as she practiced. Ciara played the piano with bumbling fingers, and Gale complained. Gale said she never saw a point in dancing lessons, couldn't they go ride ponies instead? But Kera found a sense of comfort in the steps. They were always regimented and understood. She knew her place in the dance.

She knew that at the end of a turn, her partner would be there with his hands at the ready, prepared for the next part of the journey.

Dancing required elegance in every step. It was an entire room filled with tender hearts entwined as one. Kera relished the new dances that came out. She learned each move and brought them home to perform. Her parents never quite understood the newest styles, always complaining that they seemed indecent, but the joy and the inclusivity of the steps were far too alluring for Kera to put off altogether.

"Got asked once if I knew how to dance," Aurora called back over her shoulder. "Was at this old man's house, and he wanted to show his son a thing or two." She paused, as though trying to find the words. "Ma told him 'Yes, o'course, she practices all the time.' Which you know I tried my best, but I never did dance once proper in my life. It don't matter to him. He grabs me and hauls me about expecting me to keep up. And when I couldn't, they all laughed and said something 'bout how the poor don't have no idea how to dance proper. No point in teaching us either. Too stupid to learn."

"That's awful," Kera told her, aghast. Aurora shrugged.

"Happens all the time." The road widened once more, and Aurora guided her horse to walk side by side with Holly as soon as she had room. "I asked your husband to teach me once." Kera bit her lip at the revelation. "When Jacob left us alone, but Mori still needed to stay and neither of us wanted to . . . well. You know." She did. "He was asking what I wanted that night, and said he didn't care. But . . . of all the things we'd done then . . . with Jacob and without . . . that's the one thing he refused to do."

Kera found it harder and harder to control her face, and Aurora caught her struggling.

"I've made you mad again, haven't I?"

Too much! Kera burst. Laughter exploded from up within her. Aiden twisted his neck to look at her face, his flushed baby cheeks squishing against her chest as he tried to see what was so funny. He'd been too young to know offhand, though every other child in the Montgomery household knew Mori's dark secret. "My husband—" Kera giggled "—was a *terrible* dancer."

Aurora's mouth dropped. Her eyes widened. She looked as if she couldn't quite understand what Kera was trying to say, as if the concept had never occurred to her. "Oh, when it came time to teach A—" Kera's mirth came to a halt. She squeezed her arms around Aiden a little more. It had been four years. More than that by now. She needed to force herself not to start counting days. Not to calculate the amount of time that had passed since her first son died.

On her left, Aurora was looking at her with a far more reserved expression. She didn't cast judgment. She kept her thoughts to herself. Kera took a deep breath in. Let it out. *Breathe. Let it out.* "When it came time to teach our firstborn," she continued, struggling to go on. It was like wading through water. Legs struggling to move forward even as her dress dragged her down. The ocean wrapped around her body. Gripped it and held her tight. She tried to press forward, barefoot in the sandy under bottom of the sea, but her toes lost their grip and the wake crested at her hips.

One day she expected the water to pull her down into the depths, where she could never hope to recover nor stand. She would lie on the ocean floor and wait until death claimed her. The grief was unimaginable, and she was so tired of fighting it.

Aiden reached up to her face and touched her mouth. He was all twisted about, big brown eyes staring up at her with strange understanding and awareness for such a tiny little thing. He never knew his namesake. Never knew her first Aiden. His older brother died mere months before his birth. It had been a mistake, perhaps, in naming her youngest son after her oldest. Because now, holding her boy in her arms, she was trapped reliving a horror she never wished to know. She couldn't lose Aiden again.

She pressed into her son's searching fingers and forced herself to keep talking. "I had to teach Mori again so he would not be ashamed in front of his children." She couldn't dwell on the loss right now, and instead tried to remember the joy of the moments she recalled. "He found the beats too difficult to follow, was distracted by the music, and often lost count because he'd be thinking about something else." She kissed Aiden's hand and then encouraged him to sit proper. Bad posture led to sore backs, and he didn't need any more hurts.

Sensing that the conversation needed to be more lighthearted, Aurora offered, "Thinking about politics and not dancing?"

"Oh, thinking about any number of things. He used the most delightful excuses for his poor performance. The first time we danced, he chattered nonstop. Compliments and great tales. He teased and flirted and distracted beautifully. I hardly noticed his performance until my younger sister, Gale, pointed it out. I don't believe he was ever more embarrassed, but Gale always knew how to tease him proper."

"It's hard to imagine him bad at something," Aurora admitted.

"He had his faults," Kera said. "And dancing is not a trait his friends were good at either. You are familiar with the True Lord Amit san Ruug?" Aurora nodded. Of all of Mori's friends, perhaps Amit remained the most famous alongside General Zakaria. Kera always delighted when she saw street signs named in Amit's honor. The man might have been a poised and elegant leader in the army, but he cast a different impression amongst friends. "He once danced so poorly he knocked over Ruug's Noble Lady Aliénor in the midst of a ball!"

Faith and Aurora both shared the same stunned expression. Faith asked a breathy "Is that true?" her eyes wide as could be.

"It most certainly is. His wife wrote to me about his failings, of which she found his abysmal dancing to be quaint. But the good gentleman had no talent for it, and poor Mori never did learn as a boy."

It was a circular argument. One that emphasized Aurora's point to begin with. Mori had grown up in poverty. He'd never learned how to dance, and the fact that anyone thought he *did* know seemed to emphasize the great heights he went to to pretend he belonged with the gentry in the first place.

"Of course, John knew how to dance," Kera continued.

"John?" Aurora's confusion was understandable, the number of *Johns* in the world was astonishing.

"John Sarren, Mori's best friend . . . He died in the war."

The snorting laugh was unexpected, and not the appropriate response that Kera was used to receiving whenever mentioning a fallen soldier. But Aurora laughed nonetheless. "The one with the foot fungus?" she clarified when she caught sight of Kera's discomfort.

Kera could not help but laugh either. Still grinning, she wrapped an arm around Aiden's waist and held the reins with one hand. Stretching her back as much as she could, spine cracking into place as she straightened as much as she could. She twisted a little to the left, a little to her right. Her heels pressed into Holly's sides, but the old war horse ignored it and kept plodding along. She had probably fallen asleep again. Poor girl.

"I never met John." Kera said. "I knew his father of course. Everyone knew his father." Even Aurora nodded. It was hard to ignore the obscenely rich, and the Sarren family *was* obscenely rich. "However, I didn't have the privilege to meet most of Mori's comrades until after the war was over. Even during our wedding he claimed no guests. An embarrassment he apologized for several times over." He had been charming at their wedding though. Nervous and uncertain, but still filled with the same desperate desire for everything to go right. To fall into line just so. "But he danced quite well at the wedding, against all odds. Refusing one misstep. He never danced as well ever again."

Hunger bit at her stomach. Adjusting her hold on the reins once more, she slid her hand into the nearest saddlebag and felt around for something to eat. She found an apple first, and she handed it to Aiden. "Hold that," she commanded, before fishing out some of the salted meat they'd wrapped in linen a few nights prior.

He did as she asked. His small hands cradled the apple to his chest like a relic to be protected. When she finally was sitting properly again, mission complete, he even hesitated before returning it. "Just a moment . . ." she murmured against his head. Using her nails, she clawed out a few decent sized pieces that he could eat on his own. These she handed back to him, smiling when she saw his appetite seemed to allow for it. He ate them without complaint. Chewing and swallowing at a decent speed.

For herself, she finished the core in four solid chomps: swallowing seeds and stem and all. Then she peeled open the linen and separated some of the meat out. She passed over more than enough for both Aurora and Faith, then continued from where she'd left off. "You know, Amit told me afterward that John had Mori dancing for hours, practicing steps and memorizing formations. And apparently John took his duties as teacher quite seriously."

Mori had caught Amit telling the end of *that* particular story and had flushed so dark she had thought he'd asphyxiated. The true lord had laughed at Mori's embarrassment, teasing him far more than was appropriate in mixed company, but finding no shame in doing so. "They had wrapped the arms of Amit's coat about John's waist to provide for the skirt hem, and apparently John would stamp on poor Mori's toes in recompense every time he blundered. He even threatened to find heels to make sure, ah, his . . . *point* sank in."

She had managed to make Faith and Aurora both laugh again, and Kera was surprised by how *good* it felt to be surrounded by laughter. It had been too long since she'd had an occasion to share this story. Her children and family members had heard it already. Multiple times. And she had few other friends or companions to whom she could tell it aside from Najah Zakaria, but they lived too far apart for such casual reminiscences.

"The general happened upon them near midnight. They'd been making such a racket that he'd been beseeched by the young soldiers to please see to his aides' disorderly conduct."

"No!" Aurora gasped, still laughing.

"Yes!" Kera continued. "So there was Isra Zakaria, uniform in perfect placement, hat tucked under his arm, striding into their lodging and being presented with John dancing as a lady, makeshift skirt and all, and Mori stumbling about indecently with toes swollen from repeat chastisements."

"What happened next?"

Swallowing her final bite of meat, Kera wiped her fingertips off on her trousers and fetched her canteen. She drank a swallow, then helped Aiden do the same. "The good general was far too pragmatic to find fault in John's tutelage. He looked at Amit and informed him that if John or Mori ever found which one was leading, to have him report for command promptly in the morning. He then turned around and walked out. The poor boys were quite distressed with embarrassment."

Aurora howled with delight, tears forming at the corners of her eyes.

"Zakaria *did* offer to teach Mori afterward, but he was far too stubborn a man to accept such . . . *patronizing* patronage."

Sometimes her husband's stupidity had been as rampant as his intelligence. Losing Zakaria had been another great blow to their family. And one that had not been easily replaced. Zakaria, then her first son, then her husband . . . all back to back within five years of each other. Mori had received the news with little fanfare. Had thanked the postman for delivering Najah's letter to them, then sat in his study, pen in hand, and failed to write a single word. "His life would have been so much easier if he'd only accepted Zakaria's favor." Kera sighed.

There was a pause, and then Aurora shook her head. "You don't understand."

Irritation bubbled in Kera's chest. She frowned at her companion, disbelieving and disapproving in turns. She understood her husband very well. Of course she understood him.

"He came from nothing, *Lady* Montgomery." Here, the name sounded every bit as vulgar as a curse or a threat. Kera scowled at the sound of it. "Had he accepted the general's patronage, everything he did would be in question."

"It already was; could he not have found some measure of peace in knowing he was loved?" Kera never doubted the general and his wife's love for their family. She had delighted in tea with Najah. She'd penned letters to both parties. She'd sent and received tokens that were always addressed to her, but were also always meant as a gift for them all. Mount Maladh had been a paradise for the children to spend their summers in, and the general had never been shy in offering paternal affection. For all the general's familial kindness toward them, however, Mori responded with stiff formality before both Zakaria and his wife. He was cordial and humorous when required, occasionally he could even be tempted to tease, but he conducted himself in a strictly professional manner more often than not."

"If he found life difficult without Zakaria's patronage, could you imagine how hard it would have been *with it*?"

"The general never would have allowed such talk. It would—"

"Have happened no matter what. His merit would've been all on Zakaria's word. Not his own."

"But what would that have mattered?"

Aurora sighed, long and drawn out. "As I said. You don't understand." Kera wanted to press for more information, to ask what more she needed to know. What else was there to understand? Patronage had been a part of their society for as long as Kera had known. It had always been there. Without a patron, you meant nothing. So why not accept a champion? Older and wiser? More practiced? "Don't you ever feel invisible?"

Kera paused. She needed to analyze and reflect. She had no time to do so.

Aurora continued, "It's never good enough to have someone say *you're the best*. Not for you, not for them. Someone's always doubting. A patron could go up and say 'Morpheus's the best dancer there is,' and folks'll repeat it 'cause that's what the patron says. Don't make it true. Don't change the fact that Morpheus's the worst dancer this side of the city river. And folks *know* that. Know full well that what a patron says don't make things right. They be looking at him like he's gonna mess it all up anyway. And they be right to do it. Patronage means *nothing*. And on top o' being called a loyalist and a traitor. He'd be a *fraud.*"

That wasn't how patronage was supposed to work. Kera brain tingled at the notion. That was not what patronage was meant to be. She could see how it could be perverted to such an extent. But . . . it was love. Trust and belief. Assistance and support. She told Aurora as much, and Aurora rolled her eyes once more.

"No," Aurora argued. "You gotta listen to patrons. Gotta do what they say because they know best. Gotta respect 'em and treat 'em right. And they'll do the same to you in the end. Ain't you ever had someone put words in your mouth you don't mean? That you don't want to say. But you gotta because who *they* are is more important than who *you* are?"

Yes. All the time.

When she sat in her own home and was incapable of speaking for herself because no one listened to her, because she was not the one that mattered in the conversation. Her father, or brothers, or husband knew better. She was the grieving widow in black dress. Her place wasn't in those conversations. It was anywhere else.

"Sometimes you just wanna talk for yourself, you know? Using your own words. Doing your own thing. Being who you are. Without someone else telling you how to talk or how to dress or how to wear your hair. Say all you like about not being lords and ladies, but you've got your patronage horse shit stacked higher than a cathedral. So don't you be blaming him for saying no. I'd've said no too."

It was going to take Kera time to unpack that. She needed to analyze each part of it and come up with an appropriate feeling or assertion. She nodded to show she'd heard Aurora's words, but couldn't otherwise reply. Searching for the right words, she fumbled with an offer. "I . . . can teach you how to dance if you'd still like to learn."

Aurora lips curved upward in a beautiful smile. "Then I can dance proper without anyone speakin' out for me, and no one's going to question what I know, 'cause I'll know it." She nodded, clearly satisfied with her proclamation, drawing herself up so her back was straight. Something stirred in Kera's chest as she watched. "I think I'd like to learn how to dance with you, Lady Montgomery."

And though it was her own idea, Kera couldn't help but blush at the words. She nodded. "Yes . . . me too. It's settled, then." That pretty smile grew, and Kera shifted her position in her saddle as she dreamed idly of exactly which dance they'd learn first.

She thought, maybe, they'd start with a waltz.

CHAPTER TEN

F aith started to fit sometime in the late afternoon just as dark clouds moved into position over the sinking sun. She managed a tiny groan, before her head lolled back onto her mother's shoulder. Her body stiffened and jerked. Unlike Aiden, who Kera could hold with reasonable ability on top of Holly's sturdy back, Faith was far too big to be flailing on Aurora's gelding. The horse startled, head twisting about in an attempt to see what was happening.

Kera snatched the reins from Aurora's hands. She gave them a mighty jerk, shouting "*Whoa!*" as Aurora tried to dismount. The gelding's hooves danced, little hitching hops that threw Aurora and Faith forward. She couldn't dismount. Not like this. Faith thrashed. Moaned. Her voice keened, wet wind smacking harsh against the rocks.

Kera wrapped her own reins around her pommel. "Stay still," she ordered Aiden as she threw herself off. Her son's tiny hands clenched around the swell of the saddle. He stared at her with wide eyes filling with tears, chin quivering. His skin looked bloodless. The gelding stomped his front feet, forcing Kera back. She stumbled between Holly and Aurora's mad beast. It danced worse than her husband, its steps nearly crushing her toes.

Kera pushed the gelding's shoulder, urging it to the left, but he ignored her. She pushed harder. Faith kicked at the same time. Whinnying fury whipped through the horse, and he jumped forward. Kera jerked at his reins. "Woah! *Woah!*" Aurora shouted. Teetered. The gelding bucked and kicked, and both women fell.

Aurora's skull crashed against Kera's cheek. Pain blossomed beneath Kera's skin. She bit her tongue, and copper filled her mouth, hot and sticky. Aurora had managed to hold on to her daughter, but she had just barely gotten her feet under her in time. Still the girl twitched. Aiden whined. "Mama, mama, mama!"

Then Holly was moving. War horse or not, she didn't want to get jostled about. The mare started down the path, ears flicked this way and that. Aurora tried to steady her daughter. Kera reached for Holly's reins again. "Woah, woah, woah, easy, boy—girl! Easy!"

Aiden's lips twisted in a sob. Great tears ran down his cheeks. Dirt smudged under his nose and over his lips. He reached out to her. Grabby hands reaching across a span he would never make. The gelding jerked in Kera's hand, and she snapped the reins again. "No!" she barked.

Aurora cursed—"Great buggering shit!" She dragged her daughter away. She reappeared in a flash and threw her hands out just as Aiden leaned too much. Pitched over.

Aurora caught him before Kera could scream in horror.

She caught him and held him to her chest, cradling Kera's heart close to her own. "Let's not do that again," Aurora told him gently. "You hear?"

He gaped at her as she pulled him from Kera's line of sight. But then Aurora returned empty-handed, fetching supplies without saying a word to Kera about how close she came to losing her son right there on the road, until she said: "Aiden's by the trees, he's all right for a few minutes while you tie them, Lady." Kera realized that *Aurora* was the real lady between them. She hadn't panicked. A lady should never panic.

Kera breathed out. Relief flooded her system. She clicked her tongue twice in her cheek and walked both horses off the road. Holly didn't tend to wander or stray, so Kera dropped her reins and kept her mind on the gelding. Trees were difficult hitching posts, but Kera managed. She did up the knots, proud of how her fumbling fingers didn't bungle too much.

When both horses were secure, she rushed to Aurora and the children. Aiden was sobbing huge tears, and Aurora was doing her best to balance him and ease her daughter's pain at the same time. Kera lifted him from Aurora's hold. His arms encircled her neck and she rocked him. She told him it was all right. They were fine. Faith was fine. They would all be fine.

Faith, was in fact, *not* fine. Her back was arching up off the ground, eyes rolling back in her head; she was gasping for breath, limbs flailing left and right, shaking all the while. Aurora spread the eucalyptus about Faith's body. She drew a line under Faith's nose and around her mouth. She dabbed it along her chest.

They were nearing the quarter hour mark since the fitting started, yet it showed no signs of stopping. If anything, it grew worse. Aurora pled with her daughter to stop. She begged. Each request only encouraged Aiden to cry harder when he realized Faith *wasn't* stopping.

This was it. This was the end. Kera hugged her son and shook. She shivered. Her cheeks felt wet. She rocked Aiden and did the only thing she could think of. She hummed. The tune was meaningless. The words inconsequential. It was a piano piece that she'd learned during technique classes, a small and simple ditty that everyone made up their own words to, with the original lyrics lost to time.

Sitting down next to Aurora, back leaned against a tree, Kera hummed the song as best she could. She rocked Aiden and prayed with each note that Faith would settle. Aiden's arms tightened around her neck. His crying slowed, but his wet cheeks marred her skin with a brand. She half expected him to start fitting too; she continued to hum.

Then Aurora added the words. "Up inside the little house, down along the road. Mrs. Mary little mouse, runs her way back home," she sang, voice cracking with tears of her own. It was a common variation of the tune. Ciara used to sing it to the children as they practiced needlepoint in the parlor. "Winter willow cold and tired, winter swallow flies away. Mrs. Mary in the briars, sings her song each day."

It was a round. One verse meant to roll over the other before culminating in a unison at the end. She stopped humming as Aurora continued, finding her place to join in as Aurora began the next verse. It helped. If nothing else, it kept Kera from thinking too hard on the futility of their situation. It distracted Aiden from his tears.

"Up inside the little house, where spring flowers grow. Mrs. Mary little mouse, find the water flow. Winter willow melts so slowly, summer spring comes near. Mrs. Mary, aren't you lovely, heralds in good cheer."

Call and response. The song started up again. Circled back in and around itself. Minutes passed. The sun shifted out from behind the clouds. Faith's flailing slowed. Her eyes rolled back to where they belonged. Her sweat-stained face no longer seemed to be balancing on the edge of death, and some of the color returned to her lips. Aurora let out a long breath. She hunched over her daughter with her hands bracketed on either side of Faith's head. Leaning down, she kissed Faith's brow and whispered quiet words of thanks to anyone who could be listening.

Aiden's fright abated too. His tears stopped. He still clung to Kera, but she felt his muscles relax. Kera looked back up at the sky. The sun was lower now. They had precious few hours remaining before night fell and they were left outside in the dark.

"Aurora . . ." she whispered, not sure how to discuss the inevitable problems that awaited them.

"I know," Aurora said. "I know." She closed her eyes, then settled back on her heels. She looked up from Faith's still body and met Kera's eyes. She was just as scared as Kera. Perhaps more so after Faith's sudden decline in health. "We're not gonna make it to town before dark."

No. They were not. The map hadn't shown any settlements or outposts in this area. And wandering aimlessly in hopes of finding a hutch would be akin to courting disaster. They could not lose themselves in the wilds. There must be an alternative that they could look for.

Standing up, Kera walked to Holly's bags and felt about inside until she found the books. She pulled out the *Bestiary* and flipped through the pages in hopes of finding something she might have missed in regards to the nightwalkers. She knew there wasn't anything, but desperation was a powerful motivator.

She turned the pages in clumps, often needing to go back and double-check she hadn't missed something. But all she found were pages and pages of documentation on gremlins, gnomes, faeries, selkies, centaurs, and minotaurs, with Mori's shorthand notes filling each corner, and not a damn thing on the dead. All his entertaining commentaries with the other researcher on a few topics were useless. There was no guide in the book for how to manage the night.

Mori must have had such knowledge in his library. She should have planned ahead. Of course there would have been times she would need to spend a night in the dark. Of course she should have prepared for such an eventuality.

Growing up, she had pressed her face against the windows of her home and looked out into the night. She had seen monsters in the shadows and been told one thing: do not open the doors or step outside. Stay within the building until the sun came back up. When it rose, she could as well. The night was no place for the living.

"We need to set up a camp," Aurora told her. "With a fire ring. Get enough wood to last through the night. So long as we got a fire, they can't cross it."

She was right, of course. It was why the towns always lit rings in circles around themselves. Why they always burned candles. So long as there was a fire, the wraiths wouldn't attack them. At least, they shouldn't. Ghosts and specters were far less restricted, but if Rachel was anything to go by . . . so long as you didn't intend them harm, they wouldn't harm you in turn.

Settling Aiden down by Aurora's side, Kera drew herself up to her full height. "Wait here. I will find us some wood." Aurora bit her lip and wished Kera good fortune.

It felt strange, to leave them behind on the side of the road. But the strangeness soon shifted into a need for supplies. She couldn't squander the precious few hours they had left. The sun was fast descending, and they needed to have a camp set up with all the proper protections in place.

Scanning the ground, Kera snatched up twig after twig. She held them in her arms and hummed about Mrs. Mary little mouse as she gathered her first bushel, all the while searching for a better place for them to camp. Right off the road seemed dangerous, as anyone or anything could happen upon them, and they didn't need any more disturbances in their lives.

She managed to locate a flat area that would be serviceable within the first few minutes. There even appeared to be a ring already dug into the ground from a previous traveler's time there. Depositing her collected sticks in a heap, she returned to Aurora and the children and informed them of her discovery. Kera moved the horses first, tying them off to a new post, before returning to fetch Aiden. "I need you to stay here with Holly, all right?" she asked him. Tears started slipping down his fevered cheeks. "Holly's going to take good care of you, but you need to stay here so I can help Aurora with Faith. Do you understand?"

"Uh-huh . . ." She kissed his brow and fetched Mori's book once more. She pressed them both into his hands. He was far too young to read, but he could look at the pictures and feel the rough parchment pages. "I'll be right back," she swore.

Her mind conjured an unpleasant image of Mori scolding her for being so reckless with their youngest son and his favorite horse. Shame warred with reality. Aurora needed her help. She had to help her, propriety be damned. Leaning down, Kera hoisted one of Faith's arms over her shoulders, and Aurora did the same on Faith's other side. They heaved her upward. Her numb legs dragged beneath her as they walked over the misshapen roots and difficult terrain.

Aiden watched them approach with both hands wrapped tight around the books. "Good boy, Aiden," Aurora praised. "So brave." He didn't smile. They settled Faith on the ground next to him, then worked on getting the saddles and saddlebags off the horses. Both animals needed to be tethered inside the ring's outline, and Kera checked and double-checked that there would be no way for them to wander on the opposite side of their perimeter.

With both children more or less settled for the moment, Aurora helped Kera find more wood for the fire. They collected as much as they could, from the smallest twigs to the thickest logs. They stacked their collection in the center of their camp, then hurried out to go find some more. Kera's muscles ached as she bent down for handful after handful. Her back was far too tight. Her legs and arms were cramped. The complaints were never-ending.

"Have you ever seen a wraith?" Kera asked Aurora as they worked.

Her companion took a few moments to answer. Kera was tempted to ask again, in case she hadn't heard, but Aurora opened her mouth before she could try. "I have," Aurora confided. Her lips pursed and her nose scrunched. It was as if she smelled something so rancid she could taste it in the air. "A few times."

"What are they like?" Kera asked.

It was one thing to hear an owl hooting in the forest, but another thing altogether to see the bird in question. Much the same, Kera knew the *sound* that wraiths and spooks made, but aside from a rustle out her window, she had never laid eyes on them. Books attempted to draw them, paintings depicted them from time to time, but the subject matter was not often spoken about. She imagined a living shadow. One that hated and killed. She imagined death.

"They're awful," Aurora told her. "Wicked skeletons floating through the air, still wrapped in the shrouds they've been buried in. No flesh or muscle. No sinew to hold the bones in place. Just them floating about. Shrieking loud and horrid. Fingers reaching out to tear you to the ground. You know how wraiths are made, right?"

She didn't. Children's songs and poems didn't count.

Aurora didn't wait for her to reply. Just kept talking, distracted ramblings as if it would make things easier for her as well. "They're dead who want to live. Who'll trade anything they can for a bit o' life. I've seen 'em when they get their hands on a living being. You know what that looks like?"

"No." Kera's arms were full now, but she waited for Aurora to finish before returning to camp.

"They dig their fingers into the body, and they're like rabid dogs. Scratching and biting. Tearing you completely apart. Probably thinking that if they can get to the heart of you, they'll get your life as their own. Maybe it'll make them real people again."

Kera shivered at the idea. "Has that ever happened?" They walked back to their encampment, quick as can be. Aiden had moved to sit closer to Faith, pressing himself to her side.

"A wraith coming back from the dead? Don't know. Just know that they try to do whatever they can to do just that."

"Not all dead do it though," Kera murmured. "General Zakaria used to keep a lightbringer at camp. He recruited only the highest quality priests, ones with documented records of providing blessings that kept souls from becoming trapped after the body dies. Depending on where they were, the lightbringer would come to the camp and bless each one of the soldiers before battle so they'd never be trapped in a march."

"Well that's mighty kind of him, but it don't change the fact that there were lotsa battles where those lightbringers weren't around chanting prayers or swinging their staffs to blessing folks with."

"Mm-hmm."

"Left a lot of people damned and dead one way or another. And they're still marching about even now."

"He couldn't get everyone . . . but he tried."

"Does trying really matter in cases like this?"

Kera hesitated, biting her lip as she tried to formulate an answer. When one came, it was Aiden who provided it. Nestled against Faith, Aiden spoke sleepily around a thumb in his mouth, fevered cheeks glowing bright. "Mama says that trying matters no matter what."

Aurora smiled at Aiden, expression softening. It lost some of the jagged edges that Kera had become accustomed to. "Your mama is a very determined woman, little one. I don't think she even knows *how* to fail."

"I know how to fail," Kera argued.

"Take the compliment, Lady."

"Was it a compliment?"

"Yes." Dropping their loads, they hurried back to the woods. Kera filled her arms with as much as she could, while glancing over her shoulder at Aurora, back toward the kids, at the horizon. No matter which way she looked, there were thoughts and emotions spiraling uncomfortably out of control.

The woods felt bizarrely claustrophobic. The trees, though not particularly close together, seemed to squeeze all the air out of existence. She sucked in deep breaths, heaving as she gathered more wood. "You know . . . Death marches aren't the same as wraiths."

"Same basic thing. Both come out at night, both can kill you. Both are mean."

"My father said not all death marches are mean. They don't know they're dead, they just act as they would when they were alive."

"People don't generally die violent deaths if they don't have a streak of meanness in them. And even if they weren't mean before, it don't change the fact that the end result of the march is they're going to die. If they get you trapped in their story because you're there too, you'll die with them. Ain't no getting out of that."

"And wraiths?" The trees felt like they were sliding closer together. Dark shadows stretched out across the ground. The leaves plotted against the sun. Kera swallowed thickly, almost seeing the nightwalkers hiding in the gloom up above. The hair on the back of her neck stood on end. She shook her head, trying to get the image loose. Curling her arms around her load, she turned back to camp. Aurora snatched up a few more sticks, then followed.

"Wraiths are worse. I'd take a death march over a wraith any day, and I ain't saying that lightly, but wraiths move around. They're not tied to where they died. Can travel anywhere they want, and do anything they want. And they'll kill anything. My ma said they're always trying to figure out how to come back to life, and they'll do anything to get there. At least you can avoid death marches . . . don't know how you can avoid a wraith."

Kera walked faster, desperate to get their fire started sooner rather than later. Their haul still seemed too small, but it would have to do. She couldn't bring herself to go back out into the woods. Not with the shadows growing longer and their children lying undefended on the ground. Aurora didn't argue as she started to dig the fire ring, she just followed her lead and began arranging the wood in a line.

The ring needed to be wide enough so they didn't choke on the smoke, and deep enough that it didn't catch the rest of the woods on fire. It was a delicate balance they needed to keep, and Kera's hands shook as she dug and stacked and tried to strike the fire into life. She knew what she needed to do. She knew how to do it, had been lighting fires since she was a child. But no matter how many times she struck the metal against stone, she couldn't get a spark.

Aurora came to her side and gently took the materials from her shaking hands. "We're going to be all right," she said. Then she aimed the bit of steel at just the right angle, and sent sparks skittering onto the twisting patch of bark and grass just waiting to burn. Some of the tension left Kera's body. "We're going to make it through," Aurora swore. But as the sun set, the fire line seemed so small and inconsequential in the face of the nightwalkers that screeched through the night.

CHAPTER ELEVEN

Deep in the woods, the dark was moving.

Kera and Aurora sat next to each other, their children on their laps, huddled in close for warmth and security. Though who was securing whom, Kera wasn't quite sure. Both Aiden and Faith were awake. Faith had an arm looped around Aiden even as Aiden snuggled against Kera's shoulder. Aurora supported her daughter's weight and movement without so much as a grimace. A twig snapped in the woods. All four looked toward the noise like rabbits caught in a snare, waiting for the predator to come and finish the job.

Aiden sniffled. He buried his head on Kera's shoulder. "There's a monster out there."

Kera felt the common parental refrain tickling against her tongue. *There's no such thing as monsters.* It was a lie that didn't bear repeating. Monsters *were* real. Lying about it was pointless.

"Fire'll keep us safe," Faith said, voice cracking. She hadn't spoken much since her fit. Even when they'd managed to get something together for dinner, she'd only nibbled on a few bits of salted meat and choked on her water. She couldn't take in much more than that.

They were running out of time.

"You remind me of my Cirri," Kera said, plucking a stray twig from the girl's hair. Her heart hammered. Another creaking noise filtered up from the woods. She needed to swallow twice to make sure her voice came out steady. "She always held her siblings when they were ill."

"I miss Cirri," Aiden said, rubbing at his eyes and sniffling around his sleeve. "And Junior and Auggie."

"I know, love, I know . . . I . . ." Kera glanced toward Aurora, but the woman appeared to have nothing to say. She stared back at Kera with her lips sealed tight, and anxiety coiled about Kera's heart as she looked down at the children. "Would you like to hear a story? It's one of Cirri's favorites."

"A story?" Faith asked, peeking up from behind Aiden's curls.

"Yes, unless you have a preference?"

"Ma doesn't know any stories."

Aurora swatted Faith lightly on the arm like a bad actor in a play. She went through the motions and said her lines: "You're filled with slander you are. I told you all kindsa stories and you know it." But the feeling wasn't there. Her attention was lost. Her eyes kept flicking to the fire, the smoke, the woods.

Faring much better in her role as rebellious child, Faith grumbled out a very firm, but very certain, "Not recently," that left Aurora sputtering. Her cheeks were already flushed in the firelight, but they turned even darker now. She shook her head at Kera as if to convey some secret emotion or thought that Kera was meant to divine by pure movement alone. But all Kera could focus on was how enchanting Aurora looked when flustered. Something in hear heart ached. It was the first sign of something good since the night began. She smiled, blinking back tears that seemed to form all on their own. Anxiety birthing a maelstrom in her head.

Kera took on the role of confident maestro, and showed her smile to Aurora's girl. "This story is my daughter's favorite, and I have it on good authority that it's rather well spun. Would you like to hear?"

"Mm-hmm."

Adjusting her position so she could keep Faith and Aiden comfortable throughout the tale, Aurora slipping in closer to share in their warmth, Kera began.

"Years ago, before the kings of Faron built the empire of Trent, and before Rochendiel faded away into the boundaries of Ruug, before even Absalon was unified under one banner, the gods walked among men."

"A religion lesson," Aurora scoffed. "Truly?"

"Hush. Now. There are three gods of course, Life, Death, and Time—"

"And there was a girl too, right?" Aiden asked. "Sarah."

"Sera, and yes. But Sera wasn't Death or Time. Sera was an Arnocian beauty, a princess of sorts who lived far from her homeland. Back then, the ancient land of Rochendiel had conquered Arnok, and it took its people captive. Sera and her brother Terentheen served the Rochendien King's household, and it was there they met Life. They were just people. Just ordinary people who cooked and cleaned and fought in the service of a king who wasn't theirs. But Life long coveted the life of a human. Life played a game you see, where It would live as a human, age as a human, and then return to live again over and over. Lifetime after lifetime, reinventing Itself on each occurrence.

"Life grew up with young Sera and Terentheen. It played with them in the kitchens, It trained with them in the yards, and of course: It loved them deeply for they were Its and It was theirs."

"Life loved a human?" Faith whispered in the dark.

"Oh yes. Life loved them both fiercely, and even married Sera. Life created a child between them too. She should have been nothing to a god, just a moment in Life's eternal existence. But instead she was Life's world. It was consumed by her. It even swore to give up Its divinity so It could live and die with her as a mortal."

"Life wanted to give up being a *god*?"

"To It, an eternity without Sera was inconceivable. It loved her more than Itself. More than all of existence." Faith tilted her head closer, her wide eyes flickering just as Cirri's had when she'd first heard the tale so many years ago. Kera leaned down and kissed her brow. She traced her fingers through her hair. "But a god cannot die, and though Life wished to stay with her always, Death would not claim Life's soul when It came for hers.

"Death *killed* Sera? Because she loved a god?

"Because Life was preparing to destroy all of reality for her. Death will always reap souls. Death will always in the end come. But without Life to act as a balance, soon there would be nothing left. Nothing except Death and Time locked in a stalemate, neither capable of creation, and both forced to wait for all eternity. Ending Sera's existence seemed to be the only option to them."

"And this is your daughter's favorite tale?" Aurora asked, attention already shifting back toward the fire line.

Not to be dissuaded, Kera pressed on. "But Time took pity on Life's broken heart. Time listened to Life's anguished sobs and Its desperate pleas. Time begged Death to reconsider Its position, and together they created a bargain with Life. Death agreed to return Sera's soul to the world. If Life loved her, Life would find her. And so Life slipped back through Time. It reshaped Itself, rebirthed Itself, remade Itself, over and over, again and again. New mothers and fathers welcomed Life into their home, never knowing that their child was a god after all. Life grows up every day, in every person on this planet and all the infinite lives that exist in our universe. And Sera's always there somewhere, waiting to be found.

"Sometimes they find each other early. They're neighbors who meet and grow up and spend a lifetime of bliss at each other's sides, then one dies and the other soon follows, both to be reborn somewhere else. Then, they might spend decades searching for each other, both shaped by new occurrences and new families." Cupping Faith's cheek in her palm, Kera smiled. "When you find the right person, the one that completes you, it's your *foundling*. Life and Sera rejoined at last. Living out their perfect bliss between you."

"'S'nice story," Faith whispered. She closed her eyes and snuggled closer to her mother, coughing just a little as she settled. Kera adjusted Aiden so he was resting against her, smiling when she noticed he was already asleep. *Finally*. It took only a few minutes more before Faith slipped off as well. A few minutes where Aurora sat perfectly still beside Kera, looking out at the fire with the most peculiar expression wrapped about her face.

Kera thought she might need to pry the thoughts from her, but once Faith was well and truly asleep, Aurora asked, "Is it . . . only boys and girls?"

"What's that?"

"The foundlings, is it only boys and girls? Only, there's a Ruugian boy who says he has a boy at home and . . . and of course there are women who engage in, well, *relations* with other women. Only. I wonder if it's only boys and girls who get their foundlings with each other. Well, the opposite of each other. You understand what I'm saying?" Aurora sighed. "Is it only boys who find their foundlings in girls and the reverse?"

Understanding pierced through Kera quick and sharp. She reached out and placed her hand on Aurora's. It jumped sharply beneath her palm, but then settled, shy as a rabbit in a hunter's gaze. "No, Aurora. It's not only boys who find girls. Life is a *god*, and Sera was a human *soul*. Devoid of a body, there is nothing to differentiate male and female. Their love is simply *love*. Even before Its time in that body faded, Life had loved Terentheen just as It had loved Sera. Some even say that Life hunts for both Sera and Terentheen, and I have known men who have men as their foundlings ... and ... and women who have *women* as theirs. When true love is found, it's merely found. The rest ... the rest is just ... what it is. Gender hardly matters when you find your love."

Aurora nodded, her dark hair falling into her eyes, shielding her expression from view. "You should sleep."

"I don't believe I can," Kera said. She leaned forward, trying to see Aurora's face. She wanted to know what was there, what was being hidden from her. There was a feeling, something nameless yet strong, urging her forward. A kind of intuition that niggled relentlessly at the back of Kera's mind. Her fingers twitched, temptation urging her to move that curtain aside and peak at the dawning emotions on Aurora's face. Just this once. Just to be sure.

But her fingers stayed in her lap.

Dawn couldn't come fast enough, and Aurora's questions about the foundlings continued to echo between Kera's ears long after they'd both fallen quiet.

She thought back to Cirri and the way Junior had teased her about finding someone at university. There hadn't been any time then, but Kera felt the overwhelming need to discuss the topic with her daughter. Who had she found? What were they like? Why hadn't she mentioned finding someone before?

Kera was hyperaware of Aurora's presence at her side. She'd even trembled when the thoughts started to build up into a cacophony.

Aurora responded by shifting closer. "Are you cold?" she asked quietly.

Kera couldn't trust herself to respond. She shook her head, nervously adjusting Aiden where he lay against her chest. Then she reached for her *Herbalism* book, praying daybreak would come sooner rather than later. Then they could separate, and perhaps the burning feeling in Kera's chest would alleviate just enough that she could convince herself she'd never felt this way before.

Even if it was a lie.

Even if she'd felt it exactly once, for a boy who had smiled and wished her all the happiness in the world.

Shivering again, Kera licked her lips. She forced the book open on her lap, searching desperately for anything that could substantiate Aurora's theory. Good will or not, wishes or not, the thought of endangering others set heavy in Kera's heart. But it had been days since they left Ship's Landing, and neither she nor Aurora had fallen victim to the sickness. Their health faded with the sun, growing stronger in waking hours only to seem worse as shadows cast over the land, and as the night persisted, Kera wasn't sure if tonight might be the final tilt that sent both children to oblivion.

More than anything, that was the most frustrating part. The part that made staying calm and not doing anything to stress their children that much harder. She didn't know if she'd wake up one day to her son dead in her arms. She didn't know if she was squandering the last few moments she had with her boy. All she knew was that the stress of the day's riding made the nights worse, and there was no way to make it easier. No way to help, save to rub eucalyptus on his body and pray he made it through another night.

Sharp noises cut through the air, and with each one, Kera flinched. She cast her eyes outward, inspecting the fire circle for breaks. None magically appeared. They were safe, even if Kera did keep seeing something fluttering like a cloak on the edge of her vision. But whenever she tried to focus on it directly, the figure was gone. Vanished in the smoke.

Kera had never been in a fire circle this small before, and the smoke was suffocating. It clung to their skin and their clothes, seeping into their hair, lungs, and eyes. She could breathe, but the air felt thick and threatening. A balm and a poison in one. At least the horses weren't panicking. They seemed to decide that as much as they hated Kera and

Aurora for putting them in this predicament in the first place, they would rather be behind the fire line.

Shivering against a chill that couldn't exist in this environment, Kera trained her eyes on the pages of Mori's book. Her husband's notes curled in and around the texted print of the pages. They were comforting in their own way. A little bit of her brave soldier standing there beside them.

"It's not good for both of us to be awake," Aurora prodded again.

Kera's thumb slid between the pages, marking her spot as she closed the cover. "Holly will follow wherever you lead," she murmured. "You get some sleep now. I'll sleep tomorrow, and she'll lead me along after you."

"Your horse don't follow—she sleepwalks, and having you both sleeping at the same time ain't gonna make it better." Aurora had an outstanding talent for ruining Kera's plans. She moved her hand and placed it on Kera's knee. "It's gonna be all right, all right?"

Kera tried to believe that. She did. She pushed the corners of her lips upward, and leaned a little closer to Aurora's arm. A loud creak cracked through the woods, and Kera flinched. Aiden mumbled against her neck, and she shifted him so he was more secure. Aurora turned her hand over. It was quiet, polite, and timid. Kera could ignore it and no offense would be given. She didn't ignore it. She clung to it. She squeezed her fingers around Aurora's palm and leaned closer. With each screech and strange cackle the woods produced, they squeezed their hands tighter together. Squeeze and release. Squeeze and release.

"Tell me about them other things you got at the quack. Wasn't all you-kah-lip-tus," Aurora took her time on the word, sounding it out even though Kera was certain she had heard her say it right before. It was almost funny how fear made one hypervigilant of their failures. Kera wished she knew how to make things easier for Aurora. She would offer to help Aurora speak better if she wanted, but Kera didn't know if the question would offend her either. *A lady never causes offense.*

Now wasn't the time, in any case. Maybe later. Still, she slowed down to emphasize the pronunciation of her inventory and enunciated each consonant and vowel with care. "Yarrow, peppermint, ginger, and fennel seed," Kera listed.

"Don't do that." Kera flinched at the command. It came harsh and abrasive, and she met Aurora's eyes with apprehension. Aurora's fingers still held hers. They didn't let go. But she scowled at Kera as if she would very much *like* to do more and knew she couldn't. "I'm not stupid. I can understand them just fine. I get it when you read your book."

Her words were flat. Accent-less. They sounded just as normal as anything that Kera would have said herself, even if the diction left something to be desired. Aurora spoke without care, as though she had been waiting until this moment to reveal herself. Hiding the knowledge she could speak quite well enough so she could shame Kera's prejudiced belief. Kera wished she could pull her hand away, but she feared doing just that. Instead, she stayed still. She continued to meet Aurora's eyes, though her heart hurt and her breath felt tight.

"You're doing it 'cause I don't talk as good as you always," Aurora informed her. Some of the tension faded. The accent returned, and settling like it had always belonged on Aurora's voice. *Squeeze and release.* "I get you're trying to help, and that's fine if you wanna speak like you speak. I ain't gonna fault you for that. But I'm me. And I've been me my whole life. And I'm not gonna stop being me because you come along with your books and your practices. So long as you understand me, there's nothing that needs changing."

"I . . . I'm sorry. I'll do better."

"Thank you."

Kera cleared her throat, and started once more from the beginning. "The apothecary gave me yarrow, peppermint, ginger, and fennel seed." Motioning to the book, she flipped it over and with one hand started pulling pages back. Yarrow was easy to find since it was so close to the end.

As with everything else, the page was annotated. *Yellowish white by nature, stalk is of a chartreuse. Bears resemblance to Queen Anne's Lace. Leaves are clustered in alternate arrangement. Note the yellow center of the flower.*

Kera had seen this page in particular before, and recognized the name when the apothecary had offered it to her. When their children fell ill, as children did, Mori had consulted this book with much dedication in hopes of finding a way to ease their ailment. Yarrow had been one of many plants Mori had become quite an authority on over the years. He had made this particular note when she had asked how to find it herself. She was embarrassed that she couldn't tell the difference between it and Queen Anne's Lace. He hadn't mocked her confusion. He'd agreed it was hard.

"That's odd," Aurora mumbled. Startled from her musing, Kera looked to her companion.

"What is?"

Aurora pulled her arm up from around Faith's body. She pointed to a note that had been tucked into the corner of the left page. Kera had been so distracted by the sketch and its reminders, she had failed to notice it. Or, if she'd seen it, she had discounted it as unimportant. The penmanship was poor. Although unquestionably Mori's, there was something hasty to its quality. Something that she couldn't quite put her finger on. There were a few streaks along the page. As though he'd inked his shirt sleeve and not noticed, dragging the mess across parchment as he scribbled in his notes, unaware of his molestation. Even the words he intended to write seemed half-scrawled and fragmented.

She tried to recall his shorthand and what he used for abbreviations. Most of his personal writings had included a barely legible set of stunted letters that meant much to him, though little to anyone else. *Sp. Amit temp only no terminus?*

"He must have spoken to Amit about yarrow at some point." The timing was strange though. Thinking back, Kera was certain that the entry was recent. Perhaps added sometime during the scant few months prior to Mori's death. She had seen this page before without this entry. Its hastiness seemed bizarre and out of place. Mori was far more careful with his books.

All of his other notes were clear and concise. Even if they didn't always understand the teasing jokes he had with his fellow researcher, his words had been insightful. He added clarifications and additional knowledge that aided in greater understanding. But the note here seemed to be unrelated to anything. Yarrow *did* cure fever. And the medicinally trained True Lord Amit san Ruug would have known that.

Further, Mori was persnickety when it came to his books. He avoided damaging them like he avoided damaging his horse. He would have been furious with the streaks he left behind. Kera couldn't remember him ever complaining about the ruined page. "Why's he say it's temporary?" Aurora asked.

Oh! Kera squinted at the word. Perhaps temp *had* meant temporary. So what would only temporarily respond to yarrow? Except for Aiden's current predicament, Kera couldn't recall the last time that someone in their household had need of it. She scowled and shook the thought from her head. Mori was not leaving her messages from beyond the grave in his *Herbalism* book.

Something fluttered just outside her field of vision and she looked up. A black cloak hovered beyond the fire circle. *Squeeze. Squeeze. Squeeze. Squeeze.*

Kera didn't dare breathe. Her throat constricted. The workers went on strike and the manager took a sick day. Her teeth chattered and each individual hair on her head felt electrified. Aurora's fingers squeezed her palm and didn't let up. They stared at the figure and the figure stared back. It reached forward, skeletal hand attempting to breach their ring. It flinched when the smoke and light crackled toward its bony protrusions. It screeched loud enough to rouse both children from their slumber, then disappeared back into the darkness.

Little wonder she was imagining ghosts when ghosts were all around.

"Mama?" Aiden asked. She stared after the creature. The *thing*. It was gone, but it wasn't. It was there. It was there and she was there, and all that kept them from the—the *thing* was a line of fire that could go out at any time.

"It's okay," she lied. "Go back to sleep."

Aiden squinted. Suspicious.

"Ma?" Faith asked Aurora.

"It's fine," Aurora lied too. "Don't worry about it."

The children were smarter than them. Neither went back to sleep. They snuggled close to their parents, pressed in tight. But Kera felt her son's heart against her breast. She could see Faith's eyes staring out into the darkness. Kera shook her head. "I don't know where it's from," she told Aurora. She wanted a distraction from the wraith. She wanted to think about anything else. Please, gods, anything else.

Release. Squeeze and release.

Kera half thought that holding Aurora's hand was the only thing keeping her sane. Aurora dipped her head closer to the page and squinted at it in the flickering light of the fire. Kera watched as Aurora's dark eyes followed the tracks of Mori's shirt sleeve. Watched as Aurora reached out and turned pages.

The spine rested against Kera's knee. Her right hand held one side while Aurora balanced the other. Turning pages with her left, their opposite hands still clasped so tight. She stopped on the page for valerian root. The same streaks were there too. The note just as haphazard. *Temp. works w/ Euc. Not on own.*

"Najah Zakaria used valerian with her daughter Amani," Kera explained. "She had the shaking illness? Najah said that it and eucalyptus would work for her. I recall speaking with her about it on one occasion."

Increasingly it seemed as though Mori's notes were making less sense than they should. Why ask questions he already knew the answers to? Why make notes that contradicted facts they had embraced long before? Aurora kept flipping pages, determined in her search for more strange notes penned in tandem with the absent markings of a man too tired to realize he'd made them. Their answer, it seemed, came in the form of one sentence. One tucked in beside the title for the *usnea* page.

When is a plague not a plague?

There was no answer to his question. Nothing, except for a great dark stain that coated the page like a brand. Kera stared at the blight, imagining how Mori must have knocked his inkwell onto the book. He would have been so upset. But Aurora took the page between two fingers and flipped it backward and forward. Frowning at the book as though it had performed a magic trick.

Perhaps it had.

The dark ink had not seeped through the page to the other side like the rest of Mori's notes had. His frantic annotations had left impressions on the opposite page, but the thick inky darkness of the stain had not seeped through. It stayed as a brand on one side, a haunting specter in its own right, both nonsensical and unreal.

"He was studying the plague before his death," Aurora whispered.

Kera hadn't known that. It wasn't surprising, though. Mori always dedicated himself to learning whatever he could on anything he could manage. But he had never discussed it with her. And while the plague *had* existed prior to his demise, it hadn't been as pervasive as it was after his death.

Even without the extensive devastation that began after his funeral, Mori had tried to help them. Kera eyes prickled with tears. He'd always tried to help others, and the world always found ways to despise him for it. They never understood that he cared too much to stop trying. "He just wanted to help them," Kera managed to get out, dropping her part of the book and rubbing at her eyes. A great gust of wind blew hard through the trees, and Kera lifted her head to watch as the fiery circle flickered, parts almost going out from the strong gust.

The wraith returned.

It was back where it had been before, watching them in its thick cloak, skeletal figure glimmering beyond the flames. Kera could almost see the contours of the nothing of its face. It might have been a man once. Now, scant pieces of fetid flesh dripped from its skull. A hole set just above its left eye socket, cracking out like a spider web from the epicenter. The sockets were empty black divots. Its jaw unhinged and it screeched.

Wind twisted around them. It whooshed over the fire. Kera's hands slapped to her ears. Aiden did the same. He screamed in tandem with the monster; Faith and Aurora echoed it too, and Kera's voice joined the choir. The horses whinnied, their hooves clacking against the ground. They jerked against their posts. The screeching noise never stopped.

Kera's eardrums threatened to burst. Her tongue shriveled in her mouth. She could feel each taste bud resonating with the screeching, screeching, screeching. The noise took her breath away. It choked and strangled. It dug its fingers into her flesh, tearing at each ant that skittered under her skin, squishing them in her muscles and leaving her breathless.

The wind swirled around them. It blew the smoke down at their faces. Kera choked. She coughed and bent over Aiden. She tried to keep him from breathing it in, but there was nothing she could do. It had been hours since the sun dropped. Morning couldn't be that far off. Their kindling was running low. And the wraith. *The wraith* was just on the other side of their fire line, screeching and willing the wind to blow out the only protection they had.

They had to go.

Kera knew it deep in her bones. The fire would flicker out soon. It would die and then *they* would die. Kera dared to pull a hand from her ear. It felt like a nail was being hammered through her skull. Her eyes squeezed shut against the sensation. No complaints to the manager. Every worker was too incapacitated to move.

"Aurora!" she shouted, tears falling from her eyes. She threw a hand out and grabbed Aurora's arm. "We need to go!" Kera couldn't even hear herself. She doubted Aurora could hear her. But Aurora's eyes were fixed on her lips. She nodded. No complaints from her.

Aurora pulled her hands from her ears. She locked in place the moment the sounds assailed her. Tears pressed from her eyes, but she persevered. She kissed her daughter's cheek. Kera pressed Aiden into Faith's care with trembling fingers. Aurora held out her hand for Kera, and together they stood. They gagged on the putrid air, but they stumbled together to the horses.

The wraith screeched louder. Nausea swirled up Kera's throat. She spewed bile on the ground by her husband's saddle, but she never stopped. They had mere moments to spare. With trembling fingers and protesting bodies, she and Aurora saddled their horses. Blankets, bags, tack, the works. Everything went into place. Waves of dizziness shuddered through Kera's body, but she would not submit. The books were tucked back into their pouches.

All at once, the noise stopped.

Kera fell to her knees; the relief was as overwhelming as it was instantaneous. She choked on another mouthful of bile as her muscles trembled. "Get on the horse," she gagged. "Get on the horse." Tilting her head toward her children, she met Faith's eyes. "Get on the horse."

Faith dropped her hands from her head. She pushed herself to her feet. She swayed, but she made it. Her hands reached down for Aiden; together they walked. They walked and Kera rose. On the other side of the fire, the wraith lingered. Watching. Looming. It *knew*. It knew how close they were to walking *to* it, and it waited. Faith tripped, but Kera caught her shoulder. Aurora helped her on the other side. They worked together and hoisted her up. Push here, pull there. Faith was saddled. Aiden next.

The wind began to pick up. The wraith's jaw chewed on air, foul teeth grinding and releasing like a broken mill. It reached toward them one final time. The flames flickered.

Aurora and Kera mounted their brave steeds and the line broke.

Both horses burst forward and flew into the night.

CHAPTER TWELVE

H olly rode like a cloud. Her long legs stretched out in front of her and her head reached forward, neck extended as far as it could go. Her ears aimed precisely where she was looking. Kera kicked her heels into Holly's body. She held her son in one arm, and imagined herself as a soldier in war.

This was how her husband would have sat. One hand holding his reins, one hand around the handle of his sword. Shouting for his men to line up around him. Charging headlong into battle with John Sarren on one side and Amit san Ruug on the other. They were the best of friends and the best of soldiers. Together they rode forth on their great steeds to conquer all foes before them. With guns and swords, whole armies surrounding them, and support on all sides, they would have had no need to fear.

But Kera didn't want to fight the wraith. She just wanted it gone.

Kera kicked her heels into Holly's side, and Holly ran like she was twenty years younger. She stretched out her geriatric legs. She huffed and she galloped through the trees like no other horse had ever galloped before.

Aurora's gelding was struggling to catch up and still Holly flew. There was death on her tail, and she had no interest in letting it catch her. She was a mad creature, every bit as fearless as Mori always described, and Kera could feel his faith in the horse. She could see how her husband had survived the war.

It had been Holly. It had always been Holly. Holly had saved him time and again.

And now, years after she'd survived a war with the most reckless soldier in Absalon riding on her back, she looked death in the eye one last time. She stamped her feet into the dirt, snorting air like a dragon heaving fire and brimstone. *No*, she seemed to say. *Not today.*

Kera was a soldier riding into battle, sword in hand. She was a spy flying through the night, missive pressed to her breast. She was a mother, holding her son to her heart and urging her horse forward with every bit of strength she had in her body. She would not die today, and—gods help her—she would outrun this wraith.

Still, she flew.

Holly burst from the trees. Her hooves dug in, making the transition from grass to road easily. She shifted her stride without so much as a break in her step. Her back rode smooth and even. Kera's seat was hardly altered. She kept her arm locked around Aiden. She slapped the reins against Holly's neck and scanned the horizon.

Even though they had one wraith chasing after them, it was impossible to tell if they were running toward another. Aurora shouted, and Kera turned her head to look. The wind blew her hair askew, and it wrapped around her face, shrouding her in darkness. She couldn't see. Black strands whipped into her eyes. She closed them and twisted forward. With her hands full, she couldn't wipe the locks from her face.

Shaking her head left and right, she grimaced as Holly let out a furious noise. Slowing as Kera provided mixed signals by jerking on the reins even as she kept kicking Holly forward. She clicked her tongue as loud as she could, urging Holly faster, to *go!* She said anything she could think of, but in the end all synonyms devolved into: *Move. Move now. Don't stop.*

Aurora's gelding picked up his pace. They were riding side by side, the night growing loud all around them. Kera opened her eyes and could just make out the bends in the road. Holly never faltered. She guided them forward, pumping her powerful legs with unmatched perseverance. She turned and carried them to safety as if it was the last thing she would ever do. They were her priority, and all Kera could do was beg her to work harder.

A screeching noise sounded far too close to Kera's head, and she twisted. The wraith flew by her shoulder, its skeletal face bright as snow. Its jaw dropped, hideous and laughing. The hole in its head was a mocking divot that proved how immortal it was. It reached out to grab her. She couldn't help the scream of fright that tore itself from her lungs.

Holly pushed herself even further. They were weightless on Holly's back. They were nothing to her proud and triumphant heart. Holly was a force unto herself. She galloped forward, a titan meant for the gods to ride upon. A valiant soldier who had seen battle and knew how to manage it.

Aurora's gelding was terrified. He ran in a panic. She and Faith were falling behind once more as he wore himself out from their combined weight, but Kera could see the whites of his eyes glowing in the moonlight. She chanted under her breath, "Come on, come on, come on, come on." Desperate for him to keep up and not falter under the pressure.

Kera tried to calculate how many hours it had been. How long would it be until sunrise? It couldn't be too much longer, could it? But *too much longer* could still be hours yet, and their horses couldn't manage this pace that long. They needed safety. Shelter. Anything.

Scanning the horizon for the smallest hint of light, Kera saw nothing but the moon casting more shadows in the dark. Trees towered on all sides. The road bent and curved, but there were no signs of anything that could be described as safety.

I don't have time for this.

Kera kicked Holly harder. The trees started to pull back, stepping away from the road. There was a clearing up ahead; the road poured out into a great field. Grass was overgrown on all sides, but the road was patted down. A black cloak flickered in and out of Kera's vision. She turned her head left and right, and could feel the icy chill of the wraith floating too close. Could hear its shrieking laughter as it scratched through the air. Her breath caught in her throat. Cool fingers wrapped about her neck in a tight grip. She did not know if it was the wraith or her imagination. She couldn't draw breath, and the world turned black and inky. She was blind.

"*Mama!*" Aiden screamed. His little voice was so shrill. She remembered the day he was born. Remembered the feel of Mori's hand in her hair. How with each child, he had been reprimanded by women for acting as both midwife and physician, but he stayed with her. He taught himself the science of her body so he could be the one to hold their boy when he first came into the world.

Their relationship was still recovering when Aiden was born. Mori had been terrified to ask if he would be permitted in her birthing chamber for their little Aiden. He had stumbled and collapsed at her feet, begged her for permission to join her. *"Please don't send me away."* She had taken his hand, and they had spent the night together. He at her side, promising her he wouldn't let anything happen to their final son. Their babe was their chance to make it right.

Aiden, part two: an Aiden who wasn't going to die in a boyish duel he had no business being in, an Aiden who would outlive her and be her shining star, an Aiden who would give her a chance to see her boy live past nineteen.

He wasn't supposed to die like this.

She didn't hear the wraith move. Just felt the ability to breathe return to her at the same time that Aurora swung a stick toward Kera's body. Kera had no idea when Aurora got the stick. Maybe before she even got on the horse? Maybe she'd snapped it off a branch as she had ridden by?

She didn't have time to think. Aurora was shouting and yelling obscenities as she slashed her stick through the air. The wraith screamed. Echoing calls seemed to burst all around them. Her Aiden's terrified wails grew louder. He was holding her so tight that she need not worry about the wraith stealing her breath, her son was doing it for it.

The pain, when it came, was indescribable. Everything happened too fast to follow: something pierced the air, screams echoed in her ears, drowning under the *pain* that sliced her from hip to shoulder. She saw the fluttering of a black cloak. The white smear of a skull floating before her face. Images collided together. Hair in her face. Aurora at her side. Faith leaning forward as Aurora tried to get her gelding to *come on. Just hurry up.*

The pain started and it never stopped.

Her skin shred along her back. Her muscles tore beneath the claws—were they claws?—blood burst free from her flesh. Her shirt was a strip of cotton, useless. Her nerves sent shockwaves through her body. Her head was thrown backward as her spine arched, desperate to pull away from the blow. A blur caught in her peripheral, but she couldn't see it clearly.

Aurora was wielding her stick once more, striking at the figure that reached around Kera on all sides. Holly whinnied loudly as the wraith swirled around to their front. She slid to a stop, throwing Aiden and Kera forward into her neck. The wraith darted this way and that just in front of the mare, and with the confidence of more than five years of war, Holly reared up, her hooves kicking forward in rage.

A proper soldier would lean forward, ride out the attack and sit the seat like the paintings in the Overwatch. Brave soldiers on the battlefield. Afraid of nothing at all.

But Kera was afraid.

Each nerve, sense, and receptor on her back flared into focus with all the life the wraith lacked. Her brain filtered images through her mind, each one colored red. Her son. Aurora. Faith. Holly. The air behind her whooshed against her tortured flesh. The saddle shifted. She hadn't secured it properly. *Holly liked holding her breath to avoid the cinch strap being pulled taught—*

—Kera's weight floundered. She released the reins and wrapped her arms around her son. Holly was struck hard by the wraith she'd aimed to kick. It flew through Holly's body, seizing the horse's brave heart as it directed itself at Aiden and Kera.

But they were already gone.

They were falling, falling from Holly's back and down to the ground five feet below. Kera watched as the wraith moved, as Holly let out one final whine. A proud mare losing everything in a final battle she never should have fought.

Kera's shoulders hit the ground. She ducked her head and squeezed Aiden tight. Her back exploded in agony. She couldn't breathe. Aiden's weight was suffocating. Her lungs were crushed. Her ribs were broken. Her head started to spin. Her brain felt like it was buzzing with insects.

Insects like ants.

She had ants in her skin. That was what she'd called it once. Ants in her skin. They were crushed too.

Holly collapsed to the ground, her body pitching opposite Kera and Aiden. That was lucky. She didn't crush them under her weight. But she lay still, and she did not get up.

Hair finally out of her face, Kera stared up at the sky, watching as the wraith began to circle around her. It swooped in low, reaching for her with sickening claws. She rolled to the side, curling over her son, and her backed burned as though it would never heal. She had been stripped raw, and knew that all her prayers were for naught—this was how they would die: with Mori's war horse dead at their sides, their belongings scattered from their bags, and Mori's books tipping out onto the ground. The moon was still high in the sky, but the horizon started to show signs of light. Maybe it was a fantasy. Maybe it was just hope. It mattered little. It wouldn't be fast enough.

Thundering hooves clamored across the earth. The ground tremble beneath her head. Aurora was there, wielding her stick as though it were a sword. Her hair was tied out of her face. Faith was pressed low to the neck of her horse. Aurora screamed out commands, shouting words that Kera could not make out.

She could only stare, broken and in agony, as Aurora slashed her stick through the air. She slammed it into the wraith's skull. Stabbed it through its chest cavity. "Be gone! Be gone! We've had enough of you! Get! Get going!" Aurora's screams were futile, but her actions were vicious.

Brutal.

She was every bit the soldier that Kera had imagined. She was fire and blood. She was a blue coat on a great horse, challenging the foes that they never thought they could defeat. Riding into battle with everything she needed: a dream of tomorrow and a steadfast will to survive.

Kera feared she was going to lead both Aurora and Faith to their deaths. That it would be for naught. All of this would be pointless. None of this would have mattered. They should have run. They should have run and left Aiden and her to die, because at least that way *they* could have survived. And yet, Aurora didn't leave. She hurled expletives Kera's mother would have blushed at. She battered the wraith when it came close, startled it by her refusal to be cowed. She kept it back, back, *back*. The sun rose in the east. Light crossed the grass like a line pulling the world in two. One half living, one half dead.

Kera watched the line travel closer and closer, the wraith grew more confused by the moment. It reached for Kera. She didn't have the strength to move or to flinch away. She lay still on the ground. Her head felt so very heavy. Her limbs ached. It was nothing compared to her back. Her back was a hot pan pressed against her flesh. Her skin was fire consuming her alive. It was death reaching back to the wraith, offering life for life.

It was pain. Pure and simple.

The light shifted closer. The line touched her toes. The wraith vanished as quickly as it came. And Aurora towered over her.

She looked like an angel.

CHAPTER THIRTEEN

K era stared up at the sky and listened. She listened as Aurora tied her gelding off to a tree. She listened as Aurora placed Faith on the ground. She listened as her son cried at her side.

He had wriggled from her grasp at some point. His hands shook her shoulder, but she couldn't respond. She couldn't speak. Her head wouldn't let her, her chest wouldn't breathe. He cried for her, and she looked at the sky. Her consciousness faded.

The world coiled in circles, a snake poised to strike. She couldn't determine if she was the rat caught in its grip, or the mouse in its stomach. Maybe she was the fleck of dirt on its brow, meaningless and easily forgotten, not even worth being swallowed down and used as food for a new world's beginning.

That didn't make sense.

She was tired.

Her eyes struggled to stay open, and her lips trembled as they failed to form words. She felt as though she had been cut in half—a tree chopped down, left as a stump on the ground. Roots held her to the earth, but nothing else could grow. There were no new heights for her. She was going, going, going, *gone*.

Kera's eyes closed.

They opened.

Aiden was no longer at her side. She was no longer lying on her back by Holly's body. Instead, she was lying on her side with her head resting on her left arm. She could hear Aurora heaving something heavy. The younger woman gasped and groaned for a while before exhaling in relief.

Kera squeezed her eyes shut. She breathed in. Her ribs were still broken, but at least her lungs worked.

"There's a crick over there," Aurora said. *Crick*. Not *creek*. *Crick*. Kera opened her eyes. Aurora was crouching by her side. Kera didn't know when that happened. "Faith can bring Aiden. I can bring you and the horse." Faith was a sick child who'd been fitting for half an hour the day before. "She says she's feelin' a bit stronger, c'mon now. While it lasts."

Kera could see Faith behind Aurora, holding Aiden's hand. She was standing. Standing, when Kera could not. Aurora leaned down and wrapped her arms around Kera's body. She hauled Kera up to her feet, and Kera groaned. Her brain issued its complaint to the manager. Then it remembered *it* was the manager and grudgingly returned to work. It let her lean on Aurora, let her feet move so she could walk. It wasn't happy about it.

One foot in front of the other. One step at a time. Kera tripped. She stumbled. Aurora did not let her fall. She kept Kera on her feet, holding her waist to keep from aggravating the wounds. She locked Kera in place and didn't give Kera the chance to falter.

They reached the crick, and Aurora helped her sit. Kera's legs collapsed underneath her. Her head hung low. Her hair was limp around her face. She stared at their ends. They were split and broken. Tears pressed against her eyes.

"We need to take off your blouse," Aurora told her.

Kera knew that.

She lifted her fingers to the strings. Started tugging at the ties, shaking the whole while. Aurora hummed "Mrs. Mary Little Mouse" under her breath. Kera couldn't bring herself to sing it back. It felt like broken glass along her lips and tongue.

Perhaps she always knew. Her mind blocked the reality of the situation from her conscious thoughts until she had half a second to spare. Half a moment to absorb the horror and calamity that had befallen them. Aurora helped ease her shirt over her head. Kera's back screamed at her. Blamed her for her failings.

"Holly's dead," Kera said. The words tasted like ash on her tongue. She'd killed her husband's horse.

Her tears slid over her eyelashes, down her cheeks, and onto her breasts. She raised a hand to wipe at them, and the skin on her back reminded her that she was hurt. The pain was a flash point.

A lightning rod. A beacon. She cried into her fingernails and she told herself, *Don't be stupid. It's just a horse.*

"You and Faith can switch off on Victor when she can manage it." The gelding had a name! "Aiden can ride with whoever's with him. Victor can carry Holly's supplies." Which left Aurora walking. Walking all the way to the Long Lakes. The tears flowed faster from Kera's eyes. She turned her hands over and pressed the palms to her cheeks. The heels covered her chin, the tips hid in the roots of her hair. She sobbed.

The motion pulled at her back, but perhaps it was worth it. Perhaps it was punishment for failing. She listened as Aurora clumped up her shirt and dipped it into the river. After a few moments, she pulled it out, wrung it out, then used it to dab at Kera's back and shoulders.

"How bad?" Kera asked through the shaking and the tears.

"Four long lashes, shoulder to hip." Aurora was tender around the cuts, but there was no stopping Kera from feeling each compression. From hissing and curling forward. She brought her knees to her chest and curled over so the back of her hands touched her thighs while her head continued to hide against her fingers.

Once, when she was younger, her little sister had pushed her down the stairs of their home in Crystal Point. Gale had been furious that she hadn't wanted to go outside and play. She'd tried telling Gale that it wasn't appropriate for them to be running about in their Sunday best, but Gale hadn't listened. She'd retaliated, and Kera had fallen over, her limbs twisted in all directions, and she'd landed on the ground with a broken arm and a split lip.

Kera remembered looking up the stairs at her sister, watching the shock coat Gale's face as she turned and started screaming for help. Kera's arm hurt worse than anything she had ever felt, and until she had given birth, she'd never felt anything as bad. She'd sat at the foot of the stairs, crying until her mother came to see the damage. *Stop crying, it is improper behavior.*

She tried telling herself that now.

It didn't seem to be working. She couldn't get the tears to cease, nor ration her breaths. She couldn't do anything right. She couldn't even keep her husband's horse safe. She couldn't protect his house or save their children. The tears wouldn't stop flowing, but Aurora cleaned her back without comment. She didn't tell her to stop crying or to behave.

Aiden and Faith sat nearby, and Kera knew she should be strong for them. They needed someone to act as a role model. To behave, at all times, as a lady should, in order to establish the proper order. It was her responsibility and obligation to show them how it was proper to act, but she couldn't do it. She was a failure.

The stroking on her back stopped. Aurora shifted around her, and Kera felt Aurora kneeling in front of her. Aurora's hands wrapped around Kera's wrists, dislodged her palms from Kera's face. "You are *not* a *failure*, Lady Montgomery."

Kera stared at Aurora. Her face was blurred somewhat by the tears. "Holly's dead," she reminded. She felt as though she'd already repeated those two words over and over and over again. As if they were the last words remaining in her lexicon. She was exhausted by it. She was exhausted by everything. She had tried so hard. She had done everything she could. And it was never going to be enough. *She* was never going to be enough.

"What you going on about?" Aurora asked her.

Kera stumbled over her next breath. She breathed in and choked on mucus in her throat. She coughed around it, tried to get the feeling to settle. To dissipate. To do something. Anything.

"I don't understand why this is happening," Kera sniffled. Snot was starting to pull from her nose, and she jerked a hand back from Aurora so she could rub it beneath her nostrils, crude and awful. Her mother would give her a beating if she caught her doing that. It was unladylike. It was inappropriate. "I don't understand why any of this is happening."

"The plague?" Aurora hazarded, but it wasn't the plague. It wasn't the sickness that had swept over her son's body, nor her house that was being circled by vultures. Nor her six other children relocated to Crystal Point while she was here on the ground.

The funny thing about emotions was that they all existed on a knife edge of each other. Once one feeling became empowered, all the rest clamored for attention too. They all struggled for attention on the center of the stage, eager for their chance in the spotlight. Each grievance Kera had acquired over the past few years now charged the queue, howling for a chance to be the next prima donna. She felt them clawing into her brain like wraiths in the night. They dug at the gray matter of her mind until she was forced to breathe life into their ethereal bodies and let them step out into the world.

"Why did Mori have to *die?*" she asked her husband's mistress. Aurora's eyes widened and her mouth dropped, obviously taken aback by the sudden vitriol that was streaming from Kera's mouth. Kera couldn't stop it though. She couldn't help but speak these words. She needed to get them out of her head. She needed them off her tongue, wanted to be rid of them now and forever. "Why did he even go to meet Wild that day? He never wanted to *kill* the man. *And even if he did*, what good would it have done? Why was his honor more important than *us?*"

"I don't know," Aurora managed, but it was not the answer Kera wanted.

She doubted she even wanted an answer. She just wanted to shout and to let it out, to thrash against all of the pain and sorrow and demand satisfaction. She deserved it. Had she not been a good wife? Had she not borne eight children, accepted her husband's faults, and done all she could? "He promised me. He promised me he wouldn't leave. He *promised* me forever. He was supposed to be *my* foundling, and he wasn't because no foundling would be so *stupid* as to do what he'd done. He *lied.* He lied and he went to duel a man who should have been his friend. He lied and he died because he was *awful.*

"He was shot just where my son was. Did you know that?" Kera asked Aurora. The younger woman stared at Kera, trembling under the onslaught of Kera's sudden and impassioned fury. The tears had ceased in the face of her anger, and Kera wished she could be grateful, but she wasn't. She didn't have it in her to *feel* one more thing. "He purposefully met with Wild *where our son died.*"

Neither had died there *precisely*, of course. No. They'd both lived long enough to be carted back across the river to their home, so she could kneel at their sides and lament the fact they were dying from duels they had no business fighting. But the thought was the same. He'd taken Wild to the spot her son had lost his duel in. The idiocy was astounding. More than that, it was *not fair*.

"Why would he do this to us?" Mori should have been here. He should have finished his research on the plague, if that was what he'd been researching, and found the cure. He should have been the one to take little Aiden to the Long Lakes. He should have been the one to ride through the night with wraiths at his back. "He left and . . . he was so much better than I am at all of this."

"So what?" Aurora snapped. Kera's mouth shut. She blinked at her companion, and Aurora glared down at her. "He could be the best at everything in the whole gods damned world, but that doesn't matter one bit because *you're* here. You're doing it. That's what you told your boy isn't it? Better to try? Well you're trying, which is more than I can say for him!"

It felt like she'd been slapped. "He tried—"

"People who try don't *piss off* everyone around them so much that they feel compelled to shoot them in the first place." Kera went to argue, but Aurora talked over her, raising her voice and shaking Kera by the wrists. "Your husband never knew when to shut up! He got into arguments with every man he ever met, he screamed and shouted at people till they lost the will to argue back, he had an affair because he never thought about consequences until after he did something stupid. And what about you?" she asked with a furious glare.

Kera shrugged, not sure what she was meant to say.

Aurora plowed onward. "You've never had no help with anything. You've needed to raise a family in the midst of two wars. Needed to move from place to place following his ambition. Never having no chance to settle down or be anywhere comfortable for long. He went and got himself killed and *didn't think* about you or your bairns. He just *died*, leaving you with a house you can't afford and seven children to take care of. And despite all that, you're here. You're here and you're doing it. You're still doing it. What does it matter if he knew how to ride or fight things or not? You're learning ain't you? You're the one *trying*."

"But I'm scared! I'm *scared*—"

"So am I!" Suddenly, her face was being pulled to Aurora's shoulder. Aurora's arms were wrapped so tight around her that her injuries wailed in protest. But Kera didn't care. She hugged Aurora to her as tight as she could. Tears were losing themselves in her hair.

Aurora shook against her as she cried and argued on. "I'm scared too! But it doesn't matter, does it? It doesn't matter."

Kera felt like she couldn't breathe. She choked on each breath, trembling badly as she cried. Each gulping gasp of air left her light-headed to the point of exhaustion. Her head spun dizzily, but Aurora held her still. She didn't sway or tilt over. She let herself be held. Let her body soak in the comfort Aurora was so readily providing.

Something dislodged in her brain, like the shattering of a glass against the stone. The fight drained from her in the tears that streamed down her cheeks. Her anger whipped out of her in a snap. "Why did I never see his or my first son's ghosts? Why do I only see other people's ghosts and not theirs?"

"Why would you want that?" Aurora didn't even sound judgmental. It came out cool and calm. Kera sobbed harder in response.

"I could . . . I could have asked them. I could have asked them why they did it. I could have asked them so many things. I wanted to know, I *deserved to know*." The damper on her wrath was turned off; air blew against the coals and fired it back into a roaring flame. "They were my world and they died, and they left me with this and that's not *fair*."

"They died, Kera."

Tears came fresh and anew. Not from pain. Not from wrath. This time, from sorrow. Long and dark, deep and old. Sorrow that formed the well of her soul. Her life had become an endless march of sorrow, where her requirements included waking up and moving on.

Her happy ending had been stolen a long time ago.

"They died," Aurora repeated, pulling back and cupping Kera's cheeks. "And seeing 'em every day? Seeing 'em over and over? That was never gonna help you. You'd never get out o' the house. Never interact with the living. You'd be trapped there, looking at a dead man who won't grow old with you. Who won't mature with you. Who'll stay trapped like he was when he died, and never let you think o' anything else. He wasted his chance to have a good life with you. He doesn't get a new one. He doesn't get to haunt your chance for happiness."

"*What* happiness? My son is dying, my children . . . I don't even know where my other children are. And Holly—Holly's dead!"

"Yes," Aurora agreed. "But Aiden's not. Not yet. We're halfway there, and we can make it."

"How do you know that?" Kera asked. "How do you know we'll make it? How do you know that the griffons are even there? That we'll even be able to find them?"

"Because if we doubt it," Aurora whispered, "then the doubt will make it true." She took a deep breath. "That's life, Kera. Things go wrong. Plans change. Husbands and children die. But you take what you get and you move forward. One step at a time. And if it's hard to move forward, then I bet you you're doing it right. 'Cause life ain't meant to be easy. Nothing is. So you get up and you go, and you keep going because it's the only thing you can do. You don't just sit down and let it all swallow you. You're better than that. And if nothing else, *I* believe in you."

Kera tipped her head forward. She rested her brow against Aurora's collar. She reached her arms around Aurora's back and embraced a woman she never dreamed of embracing. Aurora was careful about her hands. She hugged Kera, avoiding the wounds that raced across her spine.

"We're gonna make it through," Aurora told Kera. She pressed a kiss to the side of Kera's head. It felt like absolution, wiping the sins away and hiding the doubt. *Give me strength.*

Kera held her even tighter, and commanded herself to reply. "We're going to succeed."

The sun continued rising up above them, filling the world with blessed light.

CHAPTER FOURTEEN

They didn't have many bandages in their bags. They had some, but not enough. Kera sat still as Aurora used what they *did* have to make a wrap. She pulled the cloth around Kera's chest and back, tying it off with a simple knot at the end. It was tight, but not too tight that her ribs couldn't manage the strain.

Faith and Aiden were far too ill to walk, and Kera told Aurora that with no uncertain terms. She found a stick to lean on, pushed herself to her feet, and together—they walked. Victor, Aurora's skittish gelding, was happy to no longer carry two grown women. Even with Aiden and the added weight of the extra saddlebags, he had a lighter step than ever before. He seemed pleased with the slower pace they took as well.

Aurora guided him on the ground with the reins, leaving Faith responsible for holding Aiden as they rode. When Faith dozed, Aurora kept an eye on the children to make sure neither fell. It was more than Kera could do.

Each step forward sent waves of agony through Kera's body. Her ribs squeezed as she walked. Her back twinged on every step. The walking stick was rubbing her hand raw, and it left blisters on her palm. They took breaks and stopped often, managing their time so they never risked sleeping out after dark. It made their journey that much longer.

Generally, during the day, both children appeared to regain strength. Perhaps Rachel was right. Sunshine and fresh air *was* a cure in its own way. Every time the sun set, the children's temperament became far more uneasy. With their poor moods, their bodies writhed and spasmed in the dark, shadows grasping at their limbs, even as they lay safely cocooned in the fire line's warm light. The early dawn was always the hardest, with their eyes still so weary and limbs far too sluggish, as though they'd fought their battles against their demons in the night, beating back the illness with flaming swords of their own, and only able to get their reprieve in the morning. But come midday, they gained their strength and appetite. The timing more than a little unsettling. Mori's question, *When is a plague not a plague?* rotated around Kera's mind, seeming to have only one answer: *when it only comes out at night.* And that made no sense.

It made none at all.

Faith helped Aurora where she could. She held or supported Aiden. She helped him eat, and once even brought him to the woods to relieve himself. At night, things were different. At night, Kera watched despondently as her son jerked and twitched and writhed. He gasped, clawing at his throat like there was something there. Like a great hand was pressing against his skin, choking the life from his small body with everything it had.

When the weather was bad, the children would fit more than usual. Their spines would go rigid. They'd cough and gag, and out of the corner of her eye, sometimes Kera swore she saw Death waiting to reap their souls. It felt like the end was always coming, but whenever hope dwindled, Aurora took Kera's hand and whispered: "We just have to try," into the shell of Kera's ear. She'd kiss Kera's cheek, stroke her arms, and whisper assurances to both Kera and herself. "We just have to keep trying. You said it too. Say it now."

"We just have to keep trying."

"They're not dead yet. Our children aren't dead yet, so don't give up on them. Not yet."

It felt like the chorus of a song. *Not yet, not yet, not yet, not yet.* And so they walked.

Aurora insisted that Kera buy new shoes for herself, and Kera did on the condition that she could buy Aurora some too. If they were both doomed to walk, she couldn't find it in her to not ease Aurora's way too. They would make the money work.

Kera hated how weak she found herself. She needed Aurora's help to clean her back, to dress, and to *stand.* Aurora's hand came up to Kera's brow when she wasn't paying attention. She checked Kera for fever at the same rate she checked the children, and she muttered dark words whenever she felt the heat emanating off Kera's brow. "It's not the plague," Aurora assured Kera ad nauseam. "Ain't nobody getting infected by this damn thing this whole time."

"Are you telling me or yourself that?" Kera asked wearily.

"Both, neither, does it matter? It's not the plague. Your back's a mess. That's all."

"Nothing we can do anyway." The more they walked, the more her wounds refused to heal. It stood to reason she would fall ill from that too. *At least it's easy to fall asleep.* Each night she collapsed onto whatever vaguely horizontal place she could find and slipped off within moments.

Staying asleep was another matter altogether.

Kera flinched awake at each screech of the nightwalkers echoing outside town limits. They never used to bother her. Over forty years of listening to them had given her a kind of ignorance that she could no longer claim. She woke whenever a horrible screech tore through the air. Her heart pounded as she sat upright. Her back howled in agony in response to the wraith's call.

Exhaustion wore Kera down. It clung to her lashes and tried to force her to sleep. Sand formed at the corners of her eyes, and she wanted nothing more than to sleep through the madness, but it was impossible. The comfort of *not knowing* no longer existed. Aurora took to placing Aiden in Faith's care at night. She pulled Kera to her chest and held her head against her heart. She stroked Kera's hair and told her that it was going to be all right. "We're safe here. We're safe, and the wraiths can't come inside the city. We're going to be all right." She kissed Kera's cheek and the burning fire of her touch felt just hot enough to keep the spirits at bay.

In the mornings, Kera found herself lost and unsure. Her mind floated along with her body, disengaged and fractured. Aurora made her drink peppermint tea, and as they walked she reminded Kera that she needed to drink water. Then, she even assisted Kera when she struggled to relieve herself afterward, helping her to pull her trousers up when her back twinged. *Shame!* Kera's mother shouted in her mind. She cried more than once. Aurora hugged her and never said a word. Kera was grateful that her monthly cycles had ceased not long after Aiden's birth. She did not want to deal with *that* on top of *this*. A part of her was tempted to ask Aurora if she needed to handle such things still, but that was more inappropriate than she had the decency to manage at the moment. Aurora hadn't mentioned any discomfort, and that was that as far as Kera was concerned.

Her fever broke by the time they reached the capital, but Kera was still unsteady on her feet. Her balance was made all the more awkward by overcompensating for sore *everything*. She longed for the days of luxury and relaxation once more.

Entering the city had been the last thing Kera wanted on this journey, but she would much rather be here than in a wraith's path again. The construction had started years ago, but it was taking a long time to complete. Every year the rumors circulated as to the new end date. It didn't matter. When Kera laid eyes on the loathsome city, she detested it just as much as she suspected she would. It was short and squat with a horrendous odor wafting through the air. Insects buzzed all around, and the people themselves looked filthy just for living in it.

"It's a swamp," Aurora declared. Muddy roads left thick squelches of crud up and down Victor's legs. His hooves plodded through it under great protest. He snorted and huffed and whinnied at them. *Complaints! Complaints to the manager!*

The manager poked him with her knuckle and said, "Keep moving you lazy lout."

Victor moved. His happiness was not required. As they progressed, Kera squinted up at the sky, hoping that the sun would still be high enough for them to press on. It wasn't. They had no choice but to stay here. She sympathized with Victor. She hated it too.

They walked through the streets and looked for places to rest. Kera wasn't even all that surprised when they discovered that there was no inn or travelers' lodge, just a makeshift fire circle that all the workers clambered into at night instead. Men and women gathered around to laugh and drink, hooting and hollering loud enough that Kera couldn't quite hear the wraiths searching for breaks in the fire line, eager to kill them all.

"It's vulgar," Kera muttered as they found a place in the circle that was tucked away from the worst of the bunch. A collection of women were banded together on one side, all watching a cluster of drunk workers on the other.

"'Appens ev'ry nigh,'" an older woman informed them. She had meandered over when she saw Aurora struggling with Kera's bandages. They wasn't much hope for true privacy here, but some of the other women had formed an impromptu barrier around them. The stranger was frowning when she looked at Kera's back. "Ye've seen a lot, have'n you?" she asked, pitying expression carved deep into the wrinkles of her pale skin. Her gray hair puffed from her scalp, and in the firelight Kera could just make out shocks of red.

"Wraiths, few days back," Aurora replied, and as if on cue, the nightwalkers screeched loud and terrible. Kera saw a flutter of fabric flickering on the other side of the fire line. Her fingers strangled her shirt, squeezing it so tight she feared it might rip beneath her nails. Her sore palm ached in response to her inattention.

The woman sighed and shook her head. "Dey pretty bad down here, specially toward da valley. You been up dere? It's naw quite wut it should be. Awful an such. All from da war we reckon. Only ting dat make sense." The woman's accent was even thicker than Aurora's.

Accents don't mean anything, Kera reminded herself as her mother's firm instruction on proper pronunciation echoed in her ears. She was too tired to argue. She closed her eyes and tried to pretend that her knees and folded shirt could protect her from the roaming eyes of inebriated men. It took time to see to each cut, and more time to wrap the gauze around her body and settle the shirt back into place. The longer it took, the more nervous Kera felt.

"We're going to the Long Lakes," Aurora told the old woman. "Have you ever been?"

"Da Alilaaniwa Long Lakes?" She sounded awed at the very idea of it. "Never in person no. Dey say it's a beautiful place, but ya gotta be careful 'course. Seeing as da place is . . . well . . . *cursed.*"

Everything about their journey had been cursed so far, Kera thought. Why wouldn't the Long Lakes themselves be cursed too? But Aurora was better at social communication these days. Irony of irony. She was better at making friends with strangers on the street while Kera found that she had not the wherewithal or dedication to try. She hurt too much to want to think about propriety and niceties.

"Cursed?" Aurora asked. She finished her ministrations and tugged Kera's shirt back into place. Her hands pushed at Kera like she were raw dough, kneading her into submission. Aurora twisted and turned her and tugged her so she lay with her head against Aurora's shoulder. Slender fingers pet her hair. The message was clear. *Try to rest. Even if it's just for a few minutes.*

"Savage creatures haunt dose trees. Me-tinks dere's a bit o' monsters up in dere."

"Griffons?" Kera wanted to know.

"Aye, yes, lotsa talk 'bout griffons dese days, but dey something awful, don't you tink? Bloodtirsty an' violent. Will kill ya soon as they spot ya. Baddest worst ting out in the wood. Some hunter say dey went out 'n' try ta kill 'em dead, but we ain't heard noting 'bout dem since."

Never mind. Kera *didn't* want know. She didn't want to think about dead griffons. She didn't want to think about this being a great utter waste of their gods damned time. She shoved herself back from Aurora's side, and hissed as her flesh seared in agony. It didn't matter.

She longed for one of the shawls that she or one of her sisters had spent hours warping on their loom. She longed for the warmth and comfort they provided. She even longed for the sound of the loom, and the familiar pattern of pressing the treadles with their feet and throwing the shuttles over and over again. The beater made a *shwunk* as it moved back and forth, pulling the design into place. She had silk thread once, Amit had shipped it over from Ruug after the second war. She had sat down with a sheet of paper and counted out the marks on her page, determining her pattern and then setting it into motion. Once done, she'd held the shawl around her shoulders and settled into its surprising warmth.

Now that she was thinking of comfort . . . she couldn't help herself from thinking of the Ivory Gate. Her mind conjured images of her chairs and carpets and her fireplaces. Kera shivered in the cold. She wanted to go home.

Aurora excused their guest, and Kera listened as the old woman toddled off once more. Kera fumbled through their saddlebags in the meanwhile, searching until she found the *Bestiary*. She turned to the griffon section by memory.

Aurora's hand appeared on her shoulder. "You okay?" she asked.

The notes on the sides of the pages all talked about the family unit of griffons: how griffons cared for their young, how they ate, and what their habits were. Whoever the notetaker was, they'd spent a great deal of time observing the griffons. Far more than the book's writer ever had.

One of the more telling notes spoke to a familiarity with Morpheus too. *Mori, next time you go riding off at midnight, at least try to plot your course less haphazardly.* No doubt in direct response to Morpheus's injury. Unbidden, Kera's mind shifted back to Holly. Sweet Holly, who'd done her very best and was lost on the field.

"Do you think the crows have found her body?" Kera asked.

Aurora's fingers slid through her hair, pushing her bangs back behind her ear where they belonged. Kera's stomach twisted into knots and her head spun. Her skin tingled beneath Aurora's touch. She leaned to it, breathed in and inhaled her scent through the air. After so long at each other's side, it filled her with nothing but a sense of comfort. Relief.

The workers continued dancing around a fire pit they'd created. A fire inside a fire. Like a bull's-eye! Tears pressed against her eyes. She felt like a crazy person. Smoke wafted all around and the noise rose higher. Death lurked just on the other side of the fire line, but Aurora's fingers felt nice in her hair. Kera gave in to the feeling, even as Aurora asked for clarification. "Holly?"

"Yes."

"Likely not long after we left." It was a dead body on the ground. Kera knew that the crows would have been at it soon enough. Vultures too. The scavengers would fight over Holly's corpse and devour strips of meat off her aged bones.

Soon, some travelers would come across the mare. They would find Mori's obnoxious saddle still strapped down on her body. The saddle had been carefully crafted and tended to over the years. It was a relic. One that had survived for so long and had been mended with such careful dedication that Kera had never seen it crumble. Mori had always kept it in such good condition. It would fetch a pretty penny at a market.

If they'd managed to lift the blasted thing up off the ground.

"I should write my sister a letter." The realization sank deep in her bones, and Kera sighed. Her head ached worse than it had mere minutes ago, and Aurora hummed again under her breath. They looked over toward Faith and Aiden.

Both had grown close in their journey. Perhaps suffering made good bedfellows? For Faith held Aiden like she was protecting something precious, and Aiden sought Faith out for hugs and cuddles. He had started doing the same to Aurora as well. All of them falling into an easy pattern. It was a rather hysterical thought.

"I'm not close to my siblings," Aurora told Kera. "They grew up and moved on as fast as they could. And I stayed in Ship's Landing."

"Why?"

Aurora shrugged. "Why does anyone stay in Ship's Landing?"

It was a question that Kera always wanted to know the answer to. She hadn't grown up there. She'd grown up north at Crystal Point in Alexandria. It had been expected she would stay there too, but she'd found a home in Ship's Landing. She'd found love. She'd married and longed to stay right where she was, making her life in a city that always seemed different one day to the next.

She loved the streets, the shops, the commerce, the education. She loved the plays in the theater. She loved the parlors and their gossip. She loved playing the piano and walking with Mori up and down streets that were always safe from the nightwalkers that never crossed the city lines. "The wraiths never scared me before."

Ship's Landing had kept the fear from her mind. It'd kept her from taking note of the horrible things that lived in the night. She had walked the streets with the moon high in the sky and not thought anything of it. She had felt safe in the city, safer than anywhere else in the world.

Aurora encouraged Kera back to her feet, and they returned to sit closer to their children. Faith squinted up at them, brow wet with sweat. She was trying so hard for them. Kera caught her trying to stop her tremors when they came. She even offered to walk not long ago, though Kera wouldn't have anything of it.

Kera was not incapable just yet.

"There aren't any wraiths in Ship's Landing," Aurora agreed as they got into a more comfortable position. Kera encouraged Faith to rest her head on her lap. Aiden was still hugging the girl, but he didn't wake at the change of position. Aurora wrapped her arms around Kera's shoulders and kept her back from touching the wall behind them. It allowed her to relish in the warmth and security Aurora's steady presence provided.

"That wraith ... What you did ..." Kera whispered. Aurora hummed against Kera's hair, encouraging but not prodding. Coaxing without the whip. "You saved our lives." She couldn't remember if she'd thanked Aurora for that, if she'd expressed the feelings that existed within her body. There were words that described her emotions and her hopes, there must be, but she didn't know their names. She didn't know how to tell Aurora that she owed her everything. Or that she would do anything to make it up to her. "I'd never seen anyone more brave or more ..." *Beautiful* was the word that came to mind, but her cheeks burned at the thought of saying it out loud. Her ribs seemed to squeeze down on her lungs, compressing her from the inside. She swallowed thickly. "More selfless," she eventually managed. "I ... Thank you. Thank you for everything."

It still didn't feel like it was enough.

But Aurora said, "You're welcome," and kissed Kera's brow.

Kera stroked her fingers along the pages of the *Bestiary* and tried to imagine what she could do to make it up to Aurora. "When we return to Ship's Landing ... I'd like to introduce you to my sister."

"Why?" It was a fair question.

"Ciara ... she's my best friend. She's always been my best friend. I'd like you to know her. She's wonderful. Truly. She'll teach you anything you'd like to learn. Converse with you about topics that you'd never dream of talking about. She's funny and witty. She charmed every salon in Ship's Landing and beyond."

"That a fact?"

"Yes." Ciara and Aurora would make quite a pairing. Her sharp wit would match Aurora's clever tongue. They could trade barbs and go back and forth. Be the best of friends.

"I don't know what I'll do when we get home," Aurora admitted. "But if you mean to introduce me to your sister, I'm assuming that means we're friends now?"

Yes. They were friends. Kera didn't think she had it in her to retain any pain or discomfort in regards to Aurora. The woman had ridden her horse into battle, with her daughter ill and desperate for aid, all for the sole purpose of saving them. Of course they were friends. "I would be honored if you would take me to be your friend, Lady Aurora," Kera requested.

Aurora laughed, and she didn't stop for some time. Her giggles carried far across their camp, where the men still hooted and hollered, but Aurora's sounds seeming far more genuine and wonderful than them all. Kera smiled when she heard it. It was musical and bright, she could listen to it for hours.

Aurora laughed with her whole body. Her shoulders shook. Her neck bent her head low. Her cheeks turned rosy with warmth, and her lips were pulled back in a wide smile as her eyes squeezed shut. There were crow's-feet in the corners. Aurora kissed her crown again, and Kera cheeks flushed at the familiarity. She twisted her head to press it against Aurora's shoulder. Grateful beyond measure that she was not alone. Her body ached, but her soul felt light. Protected and secured. They were together and they were alive. Grief didn't pull her apart at the seams, nor did it linger too long on her mind. "You could . . . you could stay with us too. If you needed a home. If you needed a place to stay. You could stay with us." A house full of children. Aurora's dry wit. It seemed nice.

Nice . . .

Aurora kissed her brow. "Sleep, Lady," she said. "I've got first watch." Kera closed her eyes, book pressed against her heart.

"Do you think the hunters killed the griffons?"

"No. Fate's not that cruel." She said it with such conviction it must be true. "We're going to find these griffons. Just you wait."

Kera nodded and tried to ignore the sounds of the night. Aurora rested a palm over her ear and stroked her hair until she was lulled to sleep. The nightwalkers still screamed, but they were muffled. Quieted.

"You're safe," Aurora told her. "You're safe."

Kera slept.

CHAPTER FIFTEEN

Kera woke well before dawn. Her watch was easier, though. She told Aurora to get some rest, and shifted their positions so she could hold on to the younger woman instead. She stroked her thumb along Aurora's arm and stared out into the darkness, watching the fire circle flicker for the final few hours of its lifespan.

The workers had quieted down hours ago. She was grateful for it. Even in its quieter state, her body felt tight and nervous. Her anxiety spiked whenever something shrieked too loud. The noise couldn't stop soon enough.

Those who were responsible for keeping the circle lit milled about. Some paced around the line, adding more fuel to burn, others just sat still and drank tea. They all looked out into the darkness and waited for something to look back. For hours there was nothing.

Then it was there.

A wraith.

Just on the other side of the fire ring, staring at them. Its black cloak was swaying in the wind, white face unhinged and unattached. There were sockets where the eyes should be. Its jaw opened and closed as if chewing on air, and there was a hole in its head as though it had been shot. It reached its hand toward them, but this time the fire line held. It couldn't break the perimeter.

One of the men walked by and waved a burning stick toward it, scattering it into the background, forcing it to disappear. Kera couldn't help the tendril of fear that had started to slip through her, though. Especially when the man walked by, muttering to himself, "Those things'll chase prey till the ends of the earth."

It was not a comforting thought.

When the sun rose, she encouraged Aurora to wake. Then they tended to the children and helped them with their morning meal. It was an unmentionable slop that made Kera's stomach start issuing complaints of its own. Aiden threw up after the first bite, and Kera spent another few coins on something that would be easier on his stomach.

He'd lost so much weight already, he couldn't afford to lose much more. His cheeks were hollowed, and there were divots forming beneath his eyes. Even his curls were flatter, and despite his constant exposure to the sun, his skin was far too waxy for comfort. They needed to hurry.

With great effort, they helped Aiden and Faith back on their horse. Kera's feet *burned* as she walked. Blisters bursting almost as soon as they set to the road, she could feel blood filling the soles of her shoes, and she longed for a horse. But each time they'd entered a town, either there were no horses for sale, or her coin was not enough. She couldn't spend all her money on a horse and leave them with nothing for food or supplies.

She hadn't anticipated this particular expense.

Stupid.

"You think the overseer's gonna live there?" Aurora asked her when they passed the phallic monstrosity that was being built in the center of the city.

"I have no idea," Kera said. She hoped the house was never constructed, that Wild must continue to commute to government buildings he didn't care for until the day he died or retired. She had no interest in alleviating any of Wild's discomfort. Let the man rot.

She swung her walking stick forward, spite motivating her to go another few steps, and together they left the capital. Aurora withdrew her map from a fold in her pocket, and she squinted down at it. "There's a settlement we can reach tonight. Something like six or seven hours away I think." Kera hesitated before holding out her hand for the map.

"Mount Maladh . . ." she murmured.

Her friend frowned and leaned closer to see. "That's what that is?" Kera shook her head. She dragged her right pointer finger so that it was just a little ways to the right of the settlement that Aurora had mentioned.

"This is Mount Maladh." There was streak of land that was unmarked there. A small dot, but nothing else. It wasn't unusual, most maps wouldn't have included it. Neither General Zakaria or Najah had desired for such attention made. There was no reason the mass populace needed to know where their private residence was.

"You're sure that it's there?" Aurora asked. Kera was. She had traveled to Mount Maladh on seven separate occasions, and she remembered the exact bend in the road. The exact placement of the trees that lead to the campus.

"Amit's son, Ira, stayed with us for a time when Trent and Ruug were engaged in their own conflicts. When we were able, we brought him to Mount Maladh to stay with the Zakarias. I remember this road." She remembered, in particular, how much Ira had tried not to be afraid. How he hadn't once let her see him cry. How he'd showed off for her children and pretended that the war didn't matter to him. That he was just fine.

"I don' remember," Aiden slurred, grumpy as he wriggled a bit in the saddle.

"Well, you weren't born yet," Kera told him, then looked back to Aurora. "Ira wasn't adjusting well to the transition, and he missed his family. Mori made a game with him and . . . and my first Aiden." She glanced at her son. "Your namesake." Swallowing, she pressed on. "Mori challenged them to find the best route to Mount Maladh, he gave them the map and the markers, and for every day of the journey south, we all examined them together." Mori had even played soldiers with the boys, Ira and Aiden. He'd let them ride about as if they were going into war themselves. He'd let them shoot at him with their very threatening sticks still fresh with leaves.

"I know how to get to Mount Maladh," Kera told Aurora with firm determination. "And they'll let us in. More than that, Najah will have access to a physician who might be able to help ease Faith and Aiden more . . . One whom we can discuss your theory with in full."

"They still call it a theory if it's true?" Aurora muttered under her breath.

"Actually they call it that *because* it's true; it's hypotheses that are unproven."

"Oh . . . well then."

"What I meant to say is that we'll be safe and it's a good place to rest." Mount Maladh was defensible and well-lit at night. The fires that burned never once let out, and spells from witches kept an even tighter barrier from those within the field and those outside. The walls were so thick that the screams were never heard. Ghosts had no place inside the settlement.

Najah had told her long ago that Kera's family would always be welcome. There was no greater time than now, and Kera knew beyond a shadow of a doubt—they would be able to resupply and *rest* at Mount Maladh.

Nodding, Aurora accepted the change of plans. "Lead the way, Lady."

And Kera did just that. She walked the road with intent, scanning for trees and markers that she knew from so long ago.

"It's been almost five years since I last visited Mount Maladh." The last time they were there had been after the general's death. Mori had been silent the whole journey, and when they arrived Najah had looked so old and weary in her black mourning dress.

"*The funny thing is,*" she'd told Kera with her lovely southern drawl, *i*'s and *u*'s turning into *as* and *ahs*. "*They've all made my husband out to be some great hero in their mind. A legend that could never die. And they all forgot that at the end of it all—he was just a man. Same as anyone else. Would that more people remembered he was a man. For a simple man who did what he did is far more meaningful than the fiction they turned him into.*"

Najah Zakaria always knew the right words to say.

With little else to distract them as they walked, Kera told Aurora about the Zakarias. For all her usual lack of interest in anything political or civil-service oriented, even Aurora seemed a touch awestruck by the idea that Kera had known the family well enough to just arrive on their doorstep. She took it upon herself to confirm with Kera no less than three times that it would be all right to go to Mount Maladh. Especially with the children.

"Friends help friends in need," Kera swore. "That's what you do for the ones you love. It's never a burden."

"I'm not exactly a popular figure in your friend group, I wager."

"You will be." Kera's fingers tightened around her walking stick, and she shifted her weight more onto the rod. "You will be."

Noon came about as they started on the long path that led to Mount Maladh's main entrance. Kera was certain they'd crossed into Zakaria's territory at least. She recognized some of the lines and markers from the general's surveying, and she pointed them out to Aurora in hopes of easing her worry that this would all be for naught.

Still, she found herself rambling as the hours slipped by. Uncertainty fed off of Aurora's fears and created a great swell of anxiety within her. She chattered away with clicking teeth; words came in such rapid succession that she half wondered if she'd lost her wits. The constant tide of her emotions had left her with no peace. It wanted to be known. Each moment of silence that stalked their breathless steps was hateful. The tide thrashed, and she kept talking until her thoughts ran in circles and her words slurred together.

Aurora pushed a canteen to her hand and ordered her to drink. She looked at Kera like she couldn't believe what she was seeing. Kera flushed, and tried not to meet Aurora's eyes for fear of seeing the chastisement on her features. "Are you all right?"

Kera didn't know how to answer that. She couldn't explain why she was so nervous, nor why she felt like an actor who had forgotten her lines. Making up the story as she went along, and missing her mark each time.

"Fine," Kera said. Her back twinged and she hissed, hating the sudden surge of total inadequacy that rushed through her body.

A loud crackling sound echoed overhead, and both Kera and Aurora froze. Victor plodded on a few more steps, not realizing they had stopped, but he slowed soon enough. His reins pulled taut in Aurora's firm grip. He looked over his shoulder at them, ears swiveling about.

Kera dared to tilt her head up toward the sky. She hadn't been paying attention, not that her paying attention mattered, but the sky had darkened with thick clouds. A storm was coming. Thunder cracked again in the distance—it sounded closer.

Squinting at the horizon, she could even make out the first signs of rain. Birds were fast taking cover, and the wind had started to pick up. Even the smell of the air had shifted: water, thick and dewy, and earthy pine rushed up from the ground. Ozone wafted around the road, a sharp snap of electricity flashed through the sky.

They still had a few hours to go, but the storm was not going to wait that long. "One step at a time," Aurora counseled. Kera let her eyes stray toward Faith and Aiden. The teenager was holding Aiden tight, but her face was streaked with sweat. Her eyes weren't focusing. She'd been pushing herself far more than any child should in her condition, struggling to stay awake and not drop Aiden.

And Aiden . . . he was shaking and jerking against Faith's chest in small bursts. Kera wondered how long he'd been at it, but the tremors weren't too bad just yet. They might have time, though not much of it. Urging Victor on, Aurora walked with long purposeful strides. Kera struggled to keep up. Her eyes kept trailing to the saddlebags, praying that no drops fell in.

Shifting her weight so she was holding the stick with two hands, Kera hoisted herself forward with all the strength in her body. She heaved air through her teeth and glared at the muddy trail in front of them as huge brown splotches splashed onto their legs. Victor's hooves splattered her and Aurora even more.

When the rain fell, it did so with immediate mockery. No sooner did Kera feel the first drop strike her nose, than did the deluge begin. It was like standing under an upended bucket. Kera's hair was soaked with water. Streams were sliding down her cheeks, her grip felt slick around her stick, and her clothes—

"What in the world?" Aurora stopped walking. She stared down at herself, and Kera couldn't blame her. She was doing the same. Their clothes were *dry*.

Kera watched as the water droplets touched the exterior of the clothing and just slipped right off. The heat that she feared they would lose to the chill seemed to be unaffected. Her bare skin and hair and shoes were sopping wet, but her clothes and body underneath were dry.

The children were the same. Their clothing was dry and impervious to the water that attempted to drench them. Without hesitation, Aurora hurried to the saddlebags. She withdrew one of their spare tops and told Faith to cover her and Aiden's heads with it. She complied, unlacing the shirt and holding over them both like a shawl.

The water didn't go through. "I don't understand," Kera murmured, staring as Aurora thrust a new garment into her hands.

Aurora shrugged. "It's not our place to understand miracles, just to say thank you when they arrive." She tugged a shirt around her head as well, and a grin set upon her features. "If it's not a sign that we're going to succeed, I don't know what is." Kera matched Aurora's pretty smile with one of her own and followed the younger woman. She was the lighthouse keeper, and she kept them safe from harm.

Aurora laughed as they traveled. She was fearless in the face of a storm. Even when lightning flickered up above and the thunder clamored on all sides, Aurora stayed amused. She was scientific in her research of their strange miracle. She hopped about in the mud puddles and watched as the dirt and moisture clung to her trousers, but did not penetrate to her skin. She stayed dry despite it all.

Kera tried to think when the last time their clothes had gotten wet. The weather had held well for the past few weeks, and they had been rather poor on maintaining their laundry—

"Rachel," Kera whispered.

"What was that?" Aurora turned to face Kera with her shirt pulled over her head like a cleric.

Kera snorted. "Rachel was that ghost I met." From the look on Aurora's face, she had no idea what Kera was talking about. "The day I did the wash? I met a ghost. She assisted me in washing the clothes." And now they weren't getting wet. Just like they had dried in their room, quick as can be.

"You washed clothes with a ghost?" Aurora asked, seeming to have a hard time understanding what Kera was telling her.

"Phantom, I think," Kera amended. "I'm fairly certain she was a phantom. That's what the soldiers called her anyway."

From the way Aurora's eyes were still wide and her mouth still hung open, the alteration did not make matters better. "A phantom," she repeated.

"Yes . . . ?"

"How have you not lost your life yet? Between phantoms and ghosts and wraiths, gods above, Kera, you have either no luck or all the luck in the world."

Words shriveled in Kera's mouth and were lost at sea. "That's hardly true," she mumbled.

"Only time I've ever heard of a phantom doing anything *nice* for someone was right before they passed on," Aurora continued. Kera attempted to set the record straight, but Aurora either didn't care or didn't care to hear. It was probably a mix of both.

The rain kept coming down with all the precision of a little drummer boy. Ratta-ta-tatta-ta-tat-tat, ratta-ta-tatta-ta-tat-tat. Thunder crashed like cymbals. She wanted to tell Aurora the analogy, to distract her from disparaging Rachel's good name, but it took three attempts for her to hear Kera over the chaos of the weather. By then Kera was throwing her hands about in an attempt to mime what she meant.

"Can you imagine it?" Aurora shouted back. "A boy on his death march tapping through the night. Pied piper only with a snare instead of a pipe."

Yes. Kera could imagine it. She could also imagine that same boy turning around and shooting them for interrupting his march, killing them for interloping where they did not belong.

So many children had died during the war, it wasn't hard to fathom a little drummer boy still wandering the battlefield with his drum. It was a far more sobering thought than she would like to think of now, made more so by the darkening sky. It felt like the days were growing shorter. Night was already coming.

They hurried just a bit more, wet road slowing them despite their good fortune with their clothes. The wind sprayed their skin with mist, and Victor was far more miserable than they were. Rachel's gift did not apply to horses. He made actual noises of complaint and dragged his feet in protest. Faith even needed to kick him a few times to urge him forward when no amount of jerking on the reins encouraged him to do so.

The sun was just starting to set as they reach the outer wall of Mount Maladh. Someone had set an oil line ablaze already, and the circle was rich and thick. Burning even with the rain coming down as hard as it was. The gates were shut, but Kera wasted no time knocking on the great door. One of the wall patrolmen glanced over the wall at them, squinting at their party in confusion.

"Who's that, then?" he asked, and Kera swiped her wet hair from her face as she tried to make out who was speaking. She didn't recognize him. It would have been far easier if it had been a familiar face. She should have asked Ciara to pen a letter and inform Najah that she was coming. That would have been a smart thing to do.

"Kerryn Montgomery," she said as loud as she could. Her heart beat fast as she listened for the sounds of wraiths. "Please, may you open the door?"

"We're not expectin' any visitors," the man told her. "I've been given strict instructions not to open this door to no one unless I've got permission from the lady."

"Yes, yes, but the *lady* has already given me permission," she countered. "I'm Kerryn Montgomery, Lady Zakaria would be most gratified to know of my presence." She hoped anyway.

The man threw his hands up. "I've not been told of such things."

"Then send someone to find out!" Aurora argued.

The man turned his attention to *her* now. "Who're you, then?"

"It doesn't matter who *she* is," Kera snapped. "Send someone to tell Lady Zakaria that Kerryn Montgomery and her children are here, and that the nightwalkers are almost out."

The man shrugged again. "Can't send anyone, I'm the only one here, and I'm not to leave my post."

It was a circular argument, one that wasn't going to lead them anywhere. Kera glanced over her shoulder. The shadows on the ground seemed so much longer now. The wind in the leaves seemed so much more sinister.

Aurora's hand on her arm steadied her. "It's going to be all right," Aurora swore. "Just wait."

But the faintest sounds of howls had started, and Victor started to prance about. "Shout a message, send a flare, now *tell* her I'm here!" Kera argued. "Good gods, man, do you not see the sun has fallen? Shall you leave us out in the dark?"

"I'm not to open the gates to anyone unless the lady gives permission."

"We've already *got* it, you just need to confirm it. Please confirm it!"

A scream curled about the rain, echoing in tandem with the drum beat on the water. Ratta-ta-tatta-ta-tat-tat. Kera's hands shook, and she squeezed them tight. She gripped the stick with every ounce of energy she had remaining. "My name is *Kerryn* Montgomery, my husband was *Morpheus* Montgomery. I've permission to enter Mount Maladh. And if you do not open this door right now, you'll be disrespecting the very household you serve."

"I'm following the lady's command; you could be the overseer himself and I'd not let you in these gates. I—" His head turned. Someone's voice was calling out to him on the other side of the wall, and he left to answer. His voice was lost on the wind. Kera thought she could hear her name, thought that she might be able to make out the sound of a command being given, but she wasn't certain.

Silence fell on the wall, and it was as pervasive as the rising sounds of the nightwalkers emerging from their slumber. Aurora stepped out and slammed her fist against the door. "Let us in, you brute," she ordered, slamming her fist again.

Kera felt as though she were frozen in place. Terror seized her as the cuts on her back screeched in agony. She turned to face the night.

There was a black cloak flickering down the road. White face bright as the moon. A hole in its head—she recoiled. Stumbled. Aurora started screaming in earnest. Kera's heart hammered and—

The door opened. It was pulled back at a steady pace, but when it was wide enough for a person to step through, Kera was met with the much beloved face of Najah Zakaria.

"Kera, dear." She was as calm and as placid as ever. "I think it'd be best if you came inside." The door opened wider, and they were across the threshold before the wraith could even get close. "Welcome to Mount Maladh."

CHAPTER SIXTEEN

The wraith crashed against the doors of Mount Maladh. Kera flinched badly as it screamed, long and furious as it was repelled by the fire line. She could hear Najah's patrolman shouting in surprise as the doors rattled, as well as the *thwack*ing snap of a bowstring letting loose a fire arrow at the nightwalker.

Quick as it came, the screaming dissipated, the wraith vanishing back into the abyss, but the howl kept echoing between Kera's ears. Her breath stuttered in her chest, and dizziness threatened to overcome her as she swayed on her feet. Aurora's hand snatched at her arm, and she barked out a tight "Kera?" when her vision threatened to fail her.

"'M' all right," Kera mumbled awkwardly. She leaned into the safety of Aurora's body, knowing her friend would help her stand.

"Really now." Najah sighed, taking them all in with a critical eye. "What have you done to yourself?"

For a woman who'd been called such grandiose titles as the True Lady of Absalon to the Mother of Absalon to Najah, the proud owner of Mount Maladh, she was tiny. Yet despite her diminutive figure and advancing age, she always carried herself with enviable grace. As an army wife, Kera had been in awe of her. And despite the many years since their last visit, Kera wasn't surprised to note that her awe remained undwindled.

The rain pelted them from above, and Najah adjusted her shawl so it lay more firmly about her shoulders. She adjusted the ornate cloth she always wore over her hair, patting it into submission. Then she approached Kera and clasped her cheeks. Lips traced across Kera's brow. "What *have* you done to yourself, my dear girl?" Najah asked, southern drawl so warm and welcoming.

Whenever Najah spoke, Kera always imagined that *this* was what home felt like. She'd never lived in the south, had always lived in Ship's Landing or Alexandria. Yet Najah's voice carried quality that made Kera long for fireplaces and hearths. Pianos and parlors. She leaned her head down to rest against Najah's shoulder. It was inappropriate, and she could feel Najah startle beneath her touch, but the woman patted her back anyway.

The gesture would have been far more appreciated had she not struck Kera's wounds. Kera flinched. Her knees buckled; Aurora shot her hands out and caught Kera under her arms when she crumbled.

"Gods above—" Najah gasped. "Horaceon! Horaceon come here at once! See to the Widow Montgomery, *now!*"

The reminder burned. For so long she'd just been Kera. Lady. And yet now it was back. The harsh streak of pain and torment that burned through her like a knife. Just as painful as the gashes that marred her skin and the sickness that held her children hostage. She squeezed her eyes shut.

Your husband is dead, and you're meant to be mourning.

She was not in her mourning clothes. She should be in her mourning clothes. Her hair should be tucked into a bonnet, black should be coating her from shoulders to heels. A shawl, at the very least, should cover her hair if she forsook the bonnet. Tears pressed against her eyes, hidden by the rain. She was so tired of being sad all the time.

Horaceon appeared, and Kera tried to get her feet underneath her. She failed and relied on Aurora's endless strength to keep upright. When Horaceon uttered a brief "Beggin' your pardon, mi'lady," she didn't have a chance to protest before she was hoisted up in the air and held within his arms. She arched her back, hissing as he pressed against her wounds. Aurora snapped for him to move his arm farther up toward her shoulders, and Kera lost time.

She had no memory crossing the beautiful fields of Mount Maladh that separated the gates and the house, only the stunning sensation of burning light once they stepped into the main house's foyer. She squeezed her eyes shut and twisted away, but there was nowhere to go, and Horaceon held her firm.

Panic set in and she tried to wriggle free, but was unable to move. "Hush, Lady," Aurora told her from somewhere over her right shoulder. Kera tried to see her. "It's all right." There! Aurora was standing with Aiden in her arms. Holding her son on her hip, rocking him even as someone else assisted Faith.

Najah hovered around them all, wrapping and rewrapping her shawl around her shoulders. Lips pursed with displeasure. "Up the stairs to the guest rooms please," Najah commanded, authority slipping from her tone with ease. Horaceon hurried to do just that, taking the stairs several at a time while Najah ordered someone else to fetch a physician.

The guest rooms were turned down. A proper guest would have waited for the staff to set them right, but the urgency of their arrival made it impossible. Aurora argued for them all to be in one room, and Kera was lowered down onto a bed almost as soon as it was clear Aurora had won that particular argument. Horaceon apologized for carrying her so roughly, but Kera forgave him. It wasn't his fault.

Still, her back felt as though someone had rubbed it raw with nettles, and her ribs provided equal protest within her torso. Several more people filled the room. Lanterns were lit, and a fire was drawn up in the fireplace in the corner. Kera's head was spinning too quick to try to place names to faces, and searched instead for Aurora.

Her friend was standing not far away, still rocking Aiden, but when she caught Kera's eyes she stepped closer, placing Aiden on the bed and cupping a hand to Kera's cheek. "You all right?"

Kera nodded. "I'm sorry," she started, not sure how else to express the sudden flare of embarrassment that threatened to take her over.

"There is nothing to be sorry for," Najah replied as she bustled into the room. She held fresh clothes in her arms, and towels for them to dry themselves with. She shooed the staff out once the room was made cozy and started to warm. All that remained to be seen to were their injuries and their physical well-being. Horaceon promised to not be far in case Najah needed him, but she flicked her wrist in his direction and closed the door behind him.

Clicking it shut with a gentle press of her palm, Najah drew herself up to an impressive height for such a diminutive figure and placed her fists on her hips. "Kera Montgomery, what *have* you done to yourself?"

Shame flooded Kera's body, and her throat constricted as she tried to explain the events of the past few weeks. Nothing came out. Hot tears pressed against her eyes, and she tried to remind herself that this was her friend, and that Najah was concerned for her.

"Wraiths, Your . . . Grace?" Aurora tried to explain in Kera's stead.

When it came to speaking to Najah, Aurora seemed equally uncomfortable. While she had no trouble arguing with Najah's staff, Aurora was likely too cognizant of Najah's stature as the wife of the former Overseer of Absalon to not have *some* degree of hesitation. Najah didn't even correct her on the title. She'd never been the type to argue over trivialities, though Kera knew she laughed herself hoarse over some of Wild's attempts at honoring Zakaria. Each honorific more absurd than the last, until Kera had been certain Mori had been telling tales when he listed them all.

He hadn't been.

Isra Zakaria had confirmed it himself, shaking his head in abject misery. He'd loathed the spotlight until the day he died. And while Najah was better suited to navigating it, he'd chafed uncomfortably at the attention of his admiring people. "I'm afraid I don't recognize you, miss . . . ?" Najah trailed off, raising a brow as Aurora fumbled over her words.

"Aurora . . . ehm . . . Lawrence. You wouldn't know—"

"You're Aurora Sinclair," Najah interjected.

"—me." Aurora gulped.

Najah's eyes narrowed as they roamed over Aurora's body. She cataloged from head to toe. Najah scanned Aurora's unkempt hair, her dirty cheeks, her filthy (yet dry) clothes, the trail of mud she'd tracked into the house, as well as the calloused and knobby fingers on Aurora's hands. When he had returned from the war, Mori had once mumbled that they didn't need any spies to determine Trent's plans, they only needed Najah Zakaria to sit in a room filled with soldiers. She would find the answers they sought and it wouldn't even take her very long. At the time, Kera had laughed and set the thought aside. Since then, she'd seen Najah unleash her unique gift on the world. Kera had seen her stare down Ira san Ruug when he'd tried to hide his brilliant scheme to return to his homeland and free his parents from the dungeons after they'd been captured during the war. She'd seen her stare down the general himself when he swore he wasn't ill, but he really was.

While she carried neither the unimaginable beauty of some socialites, nor the classic fashion of her peers, Najah Zakaria had a great deal of talent when it came to divining knowledge from those who didn't feel like offering it. But unlike Mori, who couldn't have contained that information to himself, Najah's lips thinned.

Then she straightened her back and smiled. "I've called for a physician," she informed them. "He should be here shortly. I'll have someone fetch some water for washing. Do you need any assistance, dears?"

Dears. Plural. Kera let out a long slow breath of air. She hadn't realized how tense she'd become as she waited for Najah's approval. Aurora was still coiled tight, likely not realizing that Najah had given her acceptance already, and Kera reached a hand out to catch her palm. *Squeeze and release.* Aurora's confused brown eyes turned toward her.

"Could I have something to drink, Najah?" Kera asked, throat croaking. It was rude, but she didn't look back to Najah as she spoke. She kept her eyes on Aurora. *It's safe,* she thought, hoping the feeling was conveyed, *we're going to be all right here.*

"Of course, Kera. I'll send up some food as well," Najah said, ever the good hostess. "Is there anything that should be avoided? Allergies?"

"No." Kera shook her head. She met Najah's gaze. There was something hidden behind the older woman's eyes that was impossible to decipher. Najah knew what parts of the face revealed which hidden secrets, and so she kept her face placid and calm.

Shifting a little, and feeling more than a little rude for not standing while her friend was attending to them, Kera winced once more. Najah's eyes narrowed and she strode closer. "May I?"

Kera nodded, and Aurora helped remove Kera's blouse. As the bandages came into view, Najah offered to assist in the process. Aurora cupped Kera's dark hair and hung it over her breasts, offering her a meager token of modesty that seemed unnecessary after all this time.

It was appreciated all the same. She held on to Aurora's hands as Najah examined her back.

To her great relief, Najah didn't release any crude exhalations. Nor did she turn to prayer. She had served as a wartime wife, staying on battlefields while her husband fought his wars. She had held boys down as their limbs were removed, she had stroked their hair as bullets were extracted from their thighs. She had seen far worse than Kera's back.

Still, she brought her fingers to the gashes and let her hand hover over the wounds. She looked Kera over thoroughly, taking in the bruising on Kera's chest and the red marks that lingered over her broken ribs. "That's not all," she decided.

Kera's trousers were pulled down; her feet slipped from their shoes. Aurora squeezed her hand as she watched Najah's inspection. "Sit down, Ms. Lawrence. You need not stand. I saw how you were walking too, please."

Like a scolded child waiting to be disciplined for poor behavior, Aurora did as she was told. Najah didn't comment. Instead, she assisted in removing the wraps around Kera's feet. She squinted at the blistering flesh and the bloody sores. "You as well, I'm sure?"

"Ehm . . . yes . . . Your Grace . . ."

"Najah, dear, please, or Lady Zakaria if propriety is in your head."

"L-Lady Zakaria." It was strange to see Aurora so subservient after all this time. Strange to see how her head ducked away so she didn't have to make eye contact. How she addressed Najah as if she herself were a part of Najah's staff.

In all the years Kera had known Najah Zakaria, Kera had never felt cowed. She never felt the urge to play supplicant beneath her. She felt the desire to respect and obey, but not wait on each breath for an order to come. Aurora acted as if she were going to be sent to fetch them their wares herself.

She's a laundress for the rich, Kera reminded herself. Her fingers tightened around Aurora's palm. And Najah was as rich as they came. Aurora was acting like she expected to be treated like staff, because she *was* Najah's staff. Perhaps not in reality, but in theory. Aurora had never been friends with the wealthy. She'd never been welcomed into their homes and treated as an equal.

When there was a knock at the door, Najah wrapped her shawl about Kera's body to provide her with modesty, then went opened the door. She accepted a bowl of warm water and the cloth that came with it from one of the members of her staff, sharing words with them briefly before returning. Aurora stared, seemingly gobsmacked, the whole time.

Najah knelt at their feet and reached for Aurora's shoes.

"N-no, ma'am. I can—I can—"

"Hush, child," Najah commanded. "You're exhausted."

She was. She might not have the aches and sores that Kera did, but she'd been slowing down time and again. She'd been stumbling and struggling to keep moving forward. Aurora *was* exhausted. And Najah knew that. She always knew everything.

Najah revealed Aurora's bloodied soles to the world, and Aurora whimpered as the blisters were touched. "I'm sorry," Najah soothed.

"N-no i-it's fine. I—"

"Hush," Kera told Aurora. She reached up and cupped Aurora's cheek. "It'll be all right." Aurora just bit her lip. She almost looked ashamed.

Najah lifted a cloth and sank it into the warm water within her basin. She focused on Aurora's feet first, swiping the dirt and the streaks of blood back. She massaged the tender muscles and the stiff ligaments, and when she finished, she let Aurora sink her feet into the bowl. Let her relax into the soothing heat.

A second bowl arrived moments later, fresh clothing with it. Najah repeated the process with Kera. She was silent as she worked, but her movements were rehearsed. She knew how to do this, and she wasted no time. The soothing strokes alleviated all the tension in Kera's body. The burst of energy she'd felt earlier started to dissipate, and exhaustion now threatened to drag her to the afterlife.

Najah set her cloth aside and stood, joints popping. She helped Aurora and Kera dress. She spared a glance at Faith and Aiden, both sleeping. Neither showed any signs of waking. "We'll let them rest," Najah decided. Then she cupped Kera's face and kissed her brow. "Sleep, dear child." She looked at Aurora; she smiled soft and kind. "All of you need rest."

Gratitude was wordless. It came in so many forms. But in this moment, it was a shapeless void. A well of emotion. A nod of acceptance. A smile and a wish for pleasant dreams. Najah departed as regally as any woman who ever walked the earth, and Kera lay down on a true and proper bed for the first time since she left home. Inns would never amount to the feeling of a real house.

Aurora lay down as well, and Kera wrapped an arm around Aurora's waist, pulling her close enough that she could rest her head on Aurora's spine. She couldn't hear the nightwalkers. She breathed in . . . she breathed out . . . and she fell . . . fell . . .

Fell.

CHAPTER SEVENTEEN

At some point in the night, Aurora had rolled onto her back and Kera had curled in closer with her head on Aurora's chest. Their legs were intertwined, and in the morning, Kera was almost loath to pull away. It was comfortable. But the sun was shining outside, and she felt the distinct need to relieve herself. Sitting up, she forced herself not to hiss as her muscles complained. They were starting their protests early, but she had no interest in listening to them. Besides, at least the pain seemed to have reduced to a dull ache that throbbed rather than stung. She was almost certain that wouldn't last long.

Standing, she stretched as much as she dared. Looking toward the children, she was gratified to see them curled around each other and sleeping still. Their chests rose and fell with perfect breaths. They seemed . . . well. No worse than before at least. For the first time, it seemed as though they'd emerged from the night without being any worse for wear. It seemed like a proper rest had done them both some good. If nothing else came of this detour, at least the children had that.

Rubbing at her eyes, she made her way to a bucket and privacy screen. Her feet stung with each step, but without shoes on, she could apply pressure on the least painful parts of her soles. She felt almost like a child when she gave up all together and hobbled about on her heels.

Voiding inside was far more comfortable than doing so outside. She sighed in relief; they were approaching normalcy at long last. Finishing her business, she set herself to finding clothes to wear. Najah had left them new outfits on a bureau, and Kera let her fingers run over the fabric. Everything was so soft and smooth. There were dresses for her, Faith, and Aurora. A pair of neat trousers and a light shirt for Aiden. It must have belonged to one of Najah's boys, Pasha or Jaavid.

Selecting the pale-green frock, Kera pulled the dress over her body. There was a tie that secured it in the front, and the bodice had several adjustments on the side that ensured there wasn't too much pressure on her back. Once again, she found herself grateful for Najah's thoughtfulness.

Dressed at long last, she found a brush nearby. Her hands wrapped around it, and she treasured the feel of the soft wood against her palms. Sitting before a vanity, she took her long hair in hand and gripped it tight with one fist before setting herself to work.

Each bristle snagged on the army of knots, but Kera found that she didn't care how long it took. She just wanted her hair brushed. She was merciless on the mess. She tore at it with dedicated precision. Her muscles complained whenever she exerted too much pressure, her back reminded her of its injuries, but she was trained to ignore it by now. She pushed the pain to the farthest recess of her mind and focused on her hair.

When the knots at the end came loose, she slid her hand up and repeated the process. Each stroke of the brush was a victory in and of itself. She was familiar with this sensation. It was part of a routine that she'd kept since well before her wedding night. She always brushed her hair, washed her face, cleaned her body for the day, and it always left her feeling empowered and motivated to proceed.

She sighed in pleasure as the brush began to slide through her strands. One by one the knots were conquered, and she let herself relish in the glory of just feeling at ease. She wondered if she could convince Aurora to brush her hair for her. Or if Aurora would think it was demeaning or rude. She meant nothing by it, but she enjoyed the feeling of her hair being touched. Being stroked and tended to. Sometimes Mori would . . .

Kera set the brush back onto the dresser. She was so tired of remembering what Mori would or would not do. Mori was not here. And if she was going to keep moving forward, what he *would* have done didn't matter. What mattered was what she was doing here and now. He had no part to play in her future.

Standing, she looked at herself in the mirror above the vanity. She almost recognized the image she presented. Her hair was perfect. Her dress was beautiful. She straightened her posture and felt how comfortable the new position was. How her body relished returning to the poised picture of being a *lady*! But there was something different about her reflection that she couldn't understand. Something nameless that made her face seem just a touch . . . *off*.

Her eyes were more narrowed, her face more cut in stone. She looked . . . like the boys who went off to war and returned as men. A darkness advancing their age and their minds. "Don't be absurd," Kera whispered. The analogy was very rude. She had not been to war. How could her experiences compare?

She spared a final glance at Aurora and the children as she stepped from the room. They were still at peace, and she wished to leave them that way for a time longer. She had no notion when they would be leaving, but she knew that they would have to continue on soon. They were so close to reaching the lakes. After all this time, they were almost there.

Kera found Najah in her parlor. She had a hoop on her lap and was sliding her needle through the fabric stretched tight between the hoop's compress. In and out, in and out. Najah's needlepoint had always been precise. Although it lacked the flair and imagination of some women, Najah's needlepoint retained a consistency to her patterns. She excelled at flowers. Much of her linens and clothes had neat flowers reaching up along the sides. Kera had at least four different such hand-cloths folded in amongst her drawers at home. The thought of somehow harming the gift always made her hesitate before using them. But once used, she always dedicated careful time and attention to cleaning them.

"You're far too fragile to be standing in the doorway, dear," Najah chided without looking over her shoulder. Chastised, Kera crept inside and found a seat across from Lady Zakaria.

"How did you know it was me?"

"I could hear you walking down the stairs." Najah hadn't looked up yet from her needlepoint. Instead, she focused on the center of what appeared to be a sunflower, looping her black thread in amongst the yellow. "You knew where you were going, even if you took your time about it. I suspect Ms. Lawrence will not be as comfortable wandering about the house." She finished her final stitch and knotted it along the back, snipping the thread loose and sliding her needle free. Securing it in the fabric with a quick tuck, she settled the hoop to the side. With her hands folded in her lap, she looked up to meet Kera's eyes. Kera found herself filled with the strangest desire to go to her, kneel before her like a child and bask in the embrace that she knew Najah would give her. It had been so long since she'd last seen her friend, and after all this time, her care and compassion was one of the few things Kera thought she could crumble for.

"I've missed you," she admitted. Her voice cracked along the words. Watery even though she was not close to tears.

Her borrowed dress felt so strange after so long in breeches and blouse, with free legs and unconstricted hips. The tight confines of her sleeves and the way the bodice clung to her offered a strange form of comfort and peace she hadn't realized she'd missed.

She was grateful she'd taken the time to dress and clean herself up. Just sitting before Najah, fresh and composed, made her feel so much more at ease than only twelve hours ago.

Najah's lips spread into a polite smile, and she reached a hand out. She placed it on Kera's folded ones. "And I as well. I confess . . . I did not think that I'd see you again." Her words carried more melancholy than someone of her age and stature should feel. Kera twisted her wrist and squeezed her palm to Najah's, holding her tender but tight.

"I'm sorry." She should have done more to honor *their* friendship. With their husbands dead and their children growing or grown, there hadn't been much that should have kept them from seeing each other. But neither had put the energy into the journey. Kera should have taken the opportunity beforehand. But— "After Mori . . . one day slipped into another, into another. I found that I did not even speak to my own family, let alone pen letters to dear friends."

Their hands tightened with each passing second, securing and promising that they were both still here. Both were still alive despite everything. They were both widows who had seen the glory their husbands wrought, and who had only memories of legacies to hold on to in the cold of the night.

"I understand, dear." Najah's eyes had sagged some around the corners over the years, her skin seemed to droop more than it used to. She was older than Kera remembered her being, but it did nothing to hide the strength within her bones. "Sometimes," Najah told her, "there are no words."

Kera closed her eyes. She breathed in and let it out, and she felt the memory of Najah's reply turn around and around in her head. She had lived her life not knowing if she had any words to share. Lived it feeling, more often than not, that she would never be able to amount to anything proper, because she didn't have the phrasing right. Because she didn't have the understanding correct. Because she couldn't express the millions of emotions and pains that filled her body.

At the end of it all, though, Najah was right. Sometimes there were no words. Sometimes there was nothing to say. There was nothing that could be done. There were no lives that could be altered by one more person's quiet exhalation, by one more utterance.

Najah held Kera's hands tight, and Kera counseled herself not to cry. She straightened her spine, and she found the words that *did* come sometimes. These ones, she knew how to say. "Aiden is sick."

Najah listened.

She listened with a quiet intensity, eyes sharp and discerning. She nodded her head at certain moments but did not speak. She did not offer her advice or her opinion. She kept her gaze on Kera, and allowed Kera the opportunity to tell her story. Kera told everything she could. She spoke about the bankers that'd come to usher her out of the Ivory Gate (Najah's eyes narrowed at that, though she held her tongue), she spoke about Aiden's sudden illness and the doctor who'd come for him, the decision to leave everything behind in hopes of finding Aiden's salvation.

Aurora.

Kera stumbled a little; she lost her place once, distracted by her feelings of *now*, and having a hard time putting them in perspective of her feelings of a few weeks ago. Before she left, she would have never imagined sleeping in the same bed with Aurora Sinclair. But she found herself longing for the friendship of Aurora Lawrence, and seeking out her warm comfort. Aurora always encouraged Kera and let her know that she was doing well. She always reminded her that even though their struggles were not the battlefields they were used to, they were still triumphing by moving forward every day.

Throughout it all, Najah sat with perfect poise and accepted every word Kera told her. She didn't deviate or offer any words of advice. She didn't lead the story astray with anecdotes or questions. Kera was given the freedom to speak the words she longed to speak and not become sidetracked halfway through.

When she had finished, and had nothing else to say, Kera flicked her tongue out and licked her dry lips. Najah plucked a pitcher of water from the stand near her chaise and poured Kera a glass. Kera swallowed whole mouthfuls, and a dribble slipped out from the cracks of her lips. She swiped at it, flushing the whole while.

But when she attempted to apologize, she was waved off. "Please," Najah told her. "That is hardly my concern, my dear child." Settling the pitcher back on its stand, Najah adjusted herself. She shifted her skirt so it was no longer bunched around her waist, adjusting how her bodice sat. She even pulled her shawl tight around her shoulders, though the morning heat had already started and Kera suspected it would become warmer as the day went on.

"I've come unannounced to your home," Kera murmured, and Najah scoffed at the notion.

"My dear Kera, if I came to you in the middle of the night, cold and sick from rain, terrors behind me and stomach empty, would you leave me on your doorstep too?" It was a rhetorical question, and it didn't make Kera smile.

"Whether I'd let you in or not does not change the matter of the inconvenience it provides. You were out after dark, in the rain, to let us in. And you were up quite late last night tending to us. Summoning doctors for an illness you did not know you were letting into your home, then keeping him in stagnation as we slept."

Her hostess didn't scoff again, but it was obviously a near thing. Najah seemed to be taking personal offense to every word that left Kera's mouth, and Kera grimaced. "Kera, dear, I've let continental soldiers hide on this property while the Trents searched door to door for any who dared challenge them. If you wish to say your thanks, then I will accept them, but you will talk no more of debt or burden. I assure you, I am pleased to have you in my home." Then, before Kera could say anything, she went on. "But if you're insisting on feeling guilty, you'll allow Mr. Burns to examine you all for me. He *has* been waiting."

"I truly wish you hadn't endangered the poor man by summoning him in the middle of the night, and your staff too! There was a wraith out there!"

Najah's lips pursed like Kera's mother's did whenever she was displeased. "I have never endangered anyone doing me a service, and I wouldn't now. You must trust I handled the request with extreme care and that Mr. Burns was never in any danger. Now, you say your children have this plague. Well I say, no one in the south has seen or observed such a thing. Mr. Burns is quite intrigued as to its possibilities, and would like to examine you all for himself. Will you allow this?" There was nothing else to do but accept at this point. Nodding, Kera took a moment to steady herself as Najah stood and summoned a servant to fetch the physician from wherever he'd been staying as they slept. A young Ruugian woman led him over, and Kera hoisted herself to her feet as she shook his hand. Burns was a somewhat young man, close to Aurora's age, and dressed in plain clothes. He carried a cloth bag with him, and Kera could hear glass vials clinking against each other as he walked. Najah led them all back to the guest bedroom, but gave Kera leave to slip inside and wake the others before the examination began. She closed the door behind herself as she entered.

Aurora was already awake. She was sitting upright in bed beside their sleeping children. The borrowed dress was already wrapped around her frame.

"You look *lovely*," Kera said before she could stop herself.

It was true. Aurora was *gorgeous* in the bright candy-orange frock. Her dark skin mixed so well with the subtle hues blending amongst each thread, and her black hair was the *perfect* shade. Kera couldn't help but let her mind wander to that dance she'd promised to teach. As a child, she'd thrilled at the thought of dressing for a ball. She'd found nothing but joy in tying her hair up in the latest fashions, painting her face, and dusting her eyes so she could dazzle with a twirl.

She imagined, suddenly, feeling Aurora's hair between her hands as she set it into spirals. Feeling the heat of her body as she leaned in close to apply the makeup that was only worn at such an event. Smelling the perfume that they'd keep on hand. Dressing her up, and then taking her down to the ballroom, knowing that when everyone looked their way: it was her Aurora was dancing with and no one else.

"I feel strange," Aurora told her. Her lips twisted in an almost grimace, and Kera rushed over, shaking her head. The world seemed to spin dizzily as she smiled.

"No. No. You're perfect." The urge to touch became overwhelming. She stumbled forward and reached a hand out to run her fingers over the sleeve. Aurora lifted her arm to allow her greater access, and Kera found herself wrapping her fingers around it. The fabric was silky and smooth, warmed already by Aurora's skin. "I'm so happy they—they found something so . . . so right."

Aurora had a small streak of gold in her eyes. Gold like the sun on a fall day. Her face seemed darker than usual, but not all of it was blood. The sun had left a burn around her cheeks. Over the bridge of her nose. It didn't detract from anything. *Sun kissed,* she recalled hearing once. Aurora's cheeks had been sun kissed. Her words echoed back in her ears. *Found something so perfect . . .*

Kera licked her lips. She shifted so she was holding Aurora's hand. "The physician is here for Faith and Aiden," she said. Aurora let Kera pull her to her feet. Her hair moved a little around her head, curls shifting to reveal bare ears. "Earrings," Kera mused, mouth moving once more without her express permission. "You need earrings."

"I don't think I'm that kind of lady, Kera."

"That kind of lady?" she asked. But Aurora didn't answer. Just shrugged a little as they walk to the door and announced that it was okay for the physician to come in.

Burns introduced himself to Aurora, not taking *nearly* as much time as Aurora deserved to ogle her beauty, before moving to Faith and Aiden. He frowned deep, then reached over to press his fingers against Faith's wrist. The back of his hand touched her head. He squinted at her face and leaned over her, staring at her chest and he watching her breathe.

Najah encouraged Aurora and Kera to sit, chiding them for remaining on their feet. She motioned to the opposite side of the bed where they both could watch Burns's examination. Faith slept through the whole exchange, not reacting in the slightest when her limbs were poked and prodded. Aiden hadn't risen either, and anxiety squeezed Kera's heart, twisting her intestines tight as she wondered why they wouldn't wake.

Good feelings faded away to nothingness as reality settled back into place.

"Neither of you have been afflicted?" Burns asked.

Aurora's nails dug into the sides of Kera's palm as she answered, "No, we've been fine."

"It's not an illness I've ever seen before," Burns admitted. He leaned over Faith's body and checked on Aiden much the same way. Breathing, heart, skin.

"We've heard of your *plague*, of course," Najah informed them as Burns worked. "But as of yet . . . it hasn't moved south. You've been traveling for several weeks now?" They nodded. "I've not seen nor heard of the plague anywhere except the northeast."

"Ship's Landing," Burns cut in. "The reports I've heard were from Ship's Landing."

"Willowisric too," Aurora added. Burns frowned and motioned for her to go on. "The family I work for . . . the Traverses? They had business in Willowisric over the summer. Lots o' people there got it. When they returned to the city, the mayor had them looked over to make sure they weren't infected."

The physician made a noncommittal noise and returned his attention to the children. But Najah hummed. "The Traverses? I haven't heard that name in years. Didn't your husband offend them in some way, my dear?"

"My husband had a knack for offending anyone with a place in society." Kera sighed and rubbed at the bridge of her nose. "But it seems the family has done well for itself after Travers died in jail."

"Yes," Aurora agreed. "And they've been doing better and better each year; business seems to be going real well . . . even if they are trying to take Kera's house." It was clear she didn't know what to say to Najah. She kept flicking her eyes up and away as though she didn't want to be caught staring.

"Take your house?"

Kera winced at Najah's tone. "They believe I can't pay down the mortgage now that Mori has passed."

"That's absurd."

"Wild won't approve Mori's pension because of the *assassination attempt*; I have no income."

"That's absurd!" She slapped her hand on the hardest surface she could, and the resulting thud echoed about the room.

"Wild won't suffer my audience—"

"He *will* suffer me," Najah hissed. Of that, Kera had no doubt. Wild might have been their duly elected leader, but no one in the country would deny Najah their loyalty. Some might even swear her fealty if she so demanded it. "No, this will not stand. Once the children are settled, I will take the matter to Wild himself. Your house will remain in your custody Kera, you have my word on it."

"Najah, I've been sending petitions to Wild since Mori's death, he won't—"

"He *will*."

Frustration burned beneath Kera's skin. She knew her place was to say that she understood. She was meant to be grateful for her patron's assistance. She met Aurora's eyes, an uncomfortable understanding settling in where she'd never wanted it to. She didn't want Najah's help after how hard she'd worked. She wanted to do it on her own. Aurora winced, as if the thought had been conveyed from Kera's mind to hers without needing to be spoken aloud. She averted her eyes. "Thank you," Kera gritted out.

"Of course dear," Najah said, entirely oblivious to her discontent. The physician cleared his throat. "Oh yes, yes, speaking of the children. Go on Mr. Burns, please."

"Aside from the . . . Traverses . . . there's been no mention of the plague moving any further south. And from what I can see . . ." Burns reached for his bag and withdrew a few vials. "There's nothing *causing* this illness. Nor, as you suspected, is it likely contagious. The symptoms—coughing, vomiting, etcetera, don't appear to have any understandable root. To be frank, though, it will be necessary to study them to devise any kind of cure."

"We're not looking for them to be studied," Kera told him. He frowned at her. "We're traveling to the Long Lakes to find the griffons."

He laughed. It bounced off the walls, and he seemed to believe that she'd made some kind of joke. When he carried on a touch too long, however, Najah cleared her throat. "That's quite enough," she snapped, and he sobered in an instant.

Apologizing, he straightened his cravat. "You've come all this way to find the *griffons*? Why risk your hand at fantasy and myth when a doct—"

"Every doctor in Ship's Landing has done nothing but study this plague," Kera said. "As talented as you are, we do not have the time nor inclination to wait. Our children are dying, sir. And if there truly is no cure, then playing on fantasy at least can soothe a mother's heart."

His expression turned condescending. He was preparing to tell her what she already knew, *Now listen, ma'am, I know you mean well, but*—

"Mr. Burns, I do believe we've tired of your company," Najah intervened. Burns recoiled as though he'd been shot. Najah couldn't have surprised him more than if she'd torn her dress off and pranced about the room. "Horaceon will see you out, thank you for your assistance." She tilted her head a toward the door. "Do please leave the poultices I requested before you go, we'll send your fee along shortly."

"I— Well . . . Yes. Of course, Lady Zakaria." He left as if he expected to be called back. He wasn't.

Instead, Najah shut the door behind him and returned her attention to Aurora and Kera. "I'd very much appreciate it if you spent the night. Get your rest. By the morning I'll have two fresh horses secured for you, and new supplies for your journey. We've some maps available and I've some missives I can give you about the last sightings of the griffons."

"You believe us?" Aurora asked. It was not, perhaps, the question she'd meant to ask. She was missing a polite word or two. But Najah nodded and folded her hands before her body.

"Ms. Lawrence, I've lived in these parts all my life. Griffons and beasts are a part of this land. I know their legends like I know my own family tree. Maybe scientists will find the answer to the plague in a bottle one day, but that doesn't help your children now." Aurora didn't seem to know what to make of that statement. She glanced to Kera for clarification, but Kera had no time to speak. "Faith, Ms. Lawrence. Sometimes all we have is faith. That is, after all, why you named your daughter that, isn't it? I believe in this land. You should too."

CHAPTER EIGHTEEN

Mount Maladh was unlike anywhere else in the world. Even now, with her children sick in the main house, Kera found an indomitable sense of peace and stability within its protected walls. The grass was kept remarkably level, the trees were planted for no other purpose than aesthetics and shade, and even the shrubbery was clipped daily into topiary perfection.

Najah had encouraged Kera and Aurora to rest and relax as much as they could. She told them to eat and bathe, listen to music, and allow Najah's staff time to collect the supplies that they would need. And, for the first few hours, Kera had contented herself with doing just that, but then she saw the tomb in the distance . . . and she needed to go.

Aurora asked if she wanted company, and Kera contemplated it for a long while before quietly saying yes. Najah said she'd make sure the kids were minded while they were gone, then all but shooed them out the door. It wasn't a long walk.

Stonework and masonry held General Zakaria's tomb together with careful mortar and delicate craftsmanship. An iron gate kept visitors from crossing too close. She wondered if fervent patriots made pilgrimages here. Najah would hate it, but she would be too polite to turn them away. At least behind the gate his body could rest in peace.

"The last time we were here, Mori was pretending he wasn't mourning."

"You have that in common with your husband," Aurora told her, blunt as usual. Kera's lips quirked up in a smile that seemed to form whenever Aurora spoke these days. A smile just for her.

"I'm not pretending I'm not in mourning."

"What are you doing, then?"

"I don't know." They stopped right at the edges of the gate. Kera's fingers reached out to touch the twisted iron. There was a split blister on her palm, and it stung, but the contact was worth the pain. "I don't think I've known what I was doing for a while."

"Faith . . ." Aurora cleared her throat, then started again. "When Faith was a kid, well, a smaller kid. When she was younger, she had this toy. I couldn't afford to get her a proper one, but she'd been watching the other girls and their dollies, and I wanted to get her something. So I took up some cloth and got some straw from the stable and made this awful-looking thing that she loved for reasons I never quite understood."

There seemed little point in saying it was because Faith adored her mother. They'd only known each other for a few weeks, but Kera could see the love in Faith's heart every time she looked at her mother. She'd do anything for her, and vice versa. Even if their positions were reversed, Kera imagined Faith would still be right here with her, bringing her mother to the griffons no matter the cost.

"The girls still used to tease her," Aurora said, stepping up so she could hold the iron bars too. "I'd get worried that she'd never have any friends. Then one night I went by her room to see if she was okay, and I heard her talking to the thing. She had it propped up on her pillow and she was sat all cross-legged, blankets up over her shoulders, and I listened for a while as she talked to it."

"What'd she talk about?"

"All her problems with the girls in town. She'd explain each issue, say things like 'Alta wants Jeremiah to walk with her to the river on Thursdays, but Jeremiah can't go because he walks Micah to the river on Thursdays and he can't betray Micah.'" They shared a moment of pleasant commiseration at that. Nothing was more dramatic than the complicated social lives of children, and no amount of explaining how small or petty those social lives were would make any difference to the child in question. If left to their own devices, the youths of the world would have given up on life already, convinced that it ended the moment someone made a social faux pas too grandiose to be ignored. "Anyway, what I'm trying to say, is that the next day, after she'd done her talking to Widget—"

"Her doll?"

"Yes, she'd go to that group of kids and she'd give them the answer and things would get better. Even if the doll never talked back, it was like the mere act of saying it out loud just helped. She said holding it in didn't do anything but give her a headache."

Kera swayed just enough to tap Aurora with her shoulder. "She takes after her mother."

Aurora's left hand was only a few inches from Kera's right. "Bullheaded?" Aurora asked.

But as Kera reached out and placed her palm around Aurora's knuckles, she replied with a firmly sincere "Wise" instead. She squeezed Aurora's hand, and Aurora released the bars. Their fingers tangled around each other until they found a comfortable grip. The grave lay quietly before them, watching without comment.

"There are so many conversations I wished I had with Zakaria before he died. He was Mori's father in every way that mattered save blood, and sometimes I felt like he was the only one who could truly make him do something he didn't want to do. I wish I had that talent."

"Well, if there's one thing I learned from *my* husband, it's that a relationship shouldn't be about trying to get someone to do something they don't want to do. It should be about how to find middle ground between you . . . so that neither one of you is hurt in the process. I never had that relationship, but . . . it's what *I* always wanted."

"Do we meet in the middle?" Kera asked, trying to sound casual as she thought back to their relationship as of late. She couldn't recall the last time they'd argued. It might have been over a week ago.

Aurora's fingers tightened around hers. "More and more." Then, motioning with her joined hands toward the grave, she asked, "What would you say to him? If you could?"

"I'd ask him to forgive my husband for dying in a duel," she admitted, not daring to look up. "He'd have been furious, you know. He was always telling Mori he needed to slow down, plan ahead. Not throw himself into battles he couldn't win."

"And what else?" Aurora pushed.

"What else did Mori do?"

"What else would you say?"

Her free hand fell from the iron bar, and she wrapped her arm around her waist. Her ribs bothered her some, and she straightened her back to alleviate the pressure. The sound of hedges being clipped into submission click-clacked from elsewhere on the property. No one should be close enough to hear, but it didn't stop Kera from lowering her voice anyway. "I'd ask him what he would have done in our situation. If . . . if he'd have left in the first place. If staying here makes more sense now that we actually *are* here. If he would still press on . . . when Faith and Aiden seem to be doing better here . . ."

The clipping went on. Somewhere a bird cawed. Kera waited for Aurora to tell her that she didn't need to rely on anyone but herself. She waited for a chastisement or rebuke, or even some rallying words that helped bolster her inner strength. But when she chanced a glance up at Aurora, she found her companion looking pensive. She was staring at the general's grave, biting her lower lip as if she wanted to say something but didn't know how.

Finally, the younger woman shook her head and twisted so she was half in front of Kera. Their eyes met, and Aurora didn't look away. "After Burns left, when you were helping Aiden eat, Her Grace told me that their daughter had the shaking sickness."

It was surprising; Najah never talked about Amani. "She did," Kera agreed.

"She said the general tried to get help from the griffons." Kera hadn't known that. Despair filled her at once. If Zakaria had gone, but it hadn't been successful, then what hope did *they* have? "He looked for them for days, and when he finally found them, he did get some talons from them. He brought them back, but when he stepped back into the house—she was already in the throes of a fit. She died before he could give them to her."

Pain lanced through Kera's heart. She cupped her free hand to her mouth, tears pressing at her eyes. "Maybe they are doing well now," Aurora said. "And maybe they're just doing well for *right* now. But everyone we know who's gotten this thing has died. And I don't want to stop here, *so close* to those lakes, and not have time to get what we need if they take a turn for the worse. They're underweight, Kera . . . They're . . . Sometimes in the mornings when they just wake up and can't move, I don't know what to do. Aiden's *so small*, and

Faith . . . Faith's always had fits more than him, and all I can think of is being like the general. Holding that cure in my hand, but my daughter's dead on the ground 'cause I didn't go get it fast enough. And I can't . . . I can't take that risk, not for either of them, can you?"

"No." She didn't need to think about that. Not even for a moment. "No, I can't." She swallowed, shaking the sudden image from her mind as her brain conjured it for inspection. She didn't want to see it. She didn't want to imagine it. She wanted it gone from her life, along with all possibility it could occur.

"I just . . . I feel we have to keep going. Especially since we're so close. If nothing else, now they'll be stronger for the journey. Maybe we can even get them to eat a little more while we're here."

"No, no, you're right. I . . . Thank you. Gods, thank you." She huffed, shaking her head again. The image was gone, but when she looked up, she was forced to see the utter belief and sincerity in Aurora's face. It felt too pure to see. "Thank you for not giving up."

"I wouldn't. Not for this."

Forcing a smile, Kera took a deep breath. "In any case, I do wonder what happened to the talons he collected . . . If he'd had them, why didn't he use them when *he* fell ill years later?"

"She said they used them during the war," Aurora replied softly. "When soldiers were dying and loved ones needed aid, they used the talons . . . and when the general fell ill . . . they didn't have any left. He died because he gave his cure away far too soon."

"That's awful."

"Would you have done differently?"

She didn't need to think about that either. The answer came as quick as it had before. Resignation and understanding sighed out around the word no, even as she wished she could claim otherwise. "But being selfless all the time apparently is a good way to get your loved ones killed too."

"Our children aren't dead yet, Kera. And he did a lot of good before he died. Our country is free because of him."

"Just because it's the *right* thing doesn't mean it's the most *painless* thing. I just wish he'd kept some for himself. Then that *ass* wouldn't be the Overseer of Absalon and maybe I could get some peace in my life."

Aurora laughed. It came out harsh and biting at first, then dwindled off into endless chitters that shook down her arm, through their clasped hands, and into Kera's body. Soon Kera found herself laughing as well. "My dear *lady!* I've never heard you use such foul language."

"Brennan Wild *is* an ass," Kera repeated, laughing around the words. "And so is my husband!"

"They really are, both, asses. This is true."

Taking a deep breath, she leaned in close to Aurora, sharing her breath. "I'm going to tell you something, Widget," she said sternly, even as Aurora's lips twitched like she wanted to laugh again, but knew it wasn't the right time. "We're going to do this. We're going to go to those griffons, and we're going to find those talons, and you, me, and our kids are going to live for a *very long time* if only to *spite* my husband for the rest of all time."

Kera looked up at the sky. "So I hope you're well and truly satisfied you self-centered *bastard*. Because none of us are going to be dying anytime soon and you're just going to have to *deal* with that."

Kera waited for several long moments. The tomb, predictably, stayed quiet. Aurora, somewhat unpredictably, did as well. She seemed to be waiting for Kera to say something else, allowing her the chance to speak if she needed to. But when she saw that Kera had finished, she placed a palm on Kera's cheek. Her thumb stroked the skin beneath her eye, and just for a moment, Kera was *certain* Aurora meant to kiss her.

Instead, Aurora just held her cheek and held her eyes in a gaze that seemed to set fire to Kera's body, thawing out parts of her that she'd never thought she'd feel again. "You're going to live forever," Aurora said. "Death's too scared to take you now." Then she leaned in, and instead of kissing Kera's lips, she kissed her brow. "We should get back."

"Thank you," Kera whispered.

"For what?"

"For listening. For letting me talk. For . . . not thinking I was mad. For being here . . . with me . . . even now."

"You're welcome, and thank you for all the same." Warmth flooded Kera's body. She threaded their fingers more securely together and leaned against Aurora's arm as they walked. Her head rested on Aurora's shoulder, and they returned to the house slowly. At their own pace.

She felt strangely lighter, now. Her feet did not ache as much. Her back no longer seared through her mind in agony. She imagined the adrenaline would fade soon enough, and the pain would reignite in all its glory. But for now, she was stronger than she had been in quite some time.

They stepped back inside, and found Najah sitting with Aiden and Faith in their bedroom. Faith was awake, and was eating a bowl of broth with slow jerky movements, and Najah was helping her when she fumbled. She took the spoon in hand and brought it up seamlessly to Faith's lips. "Did you get what you were hoping to receive?" Najah asked.

"Yes." Kera had said what she had wanted to say in any case. "How are things here?"

"They're well enough." Najah sighed. Shaking her head, she tapped her fingers onto the table. "I've already prepared fresh horses for your journey, and I'll see to it your gelding is well taken care of while you're gone."

"You've already done so much for us . . ." Kera hedged.

"And I'll continue to do so. I've terms, you understand." Aurora glanced up at them, lips pressing together, but Kera was not afraid of such terms. She already suspected she knew what they would look like. Kera nodded instead and asked what Najah expected from them. "When this is over, I'd very much like for you to spend some time here proper. The both of you are more than welcome, and your families as well. I have missed the children, and though I am delighted to finally meet your little Aiden, this was not the circumstance I envisioned."

Kera promised easily. "Yes, of course, they would love that."

"I've heard from Ira recently. He and Amit are considering returning to Absalon for a time. I know that Amit will be most gratified to see you well."

"And I him."

"I'd also like for you to pen a letter to your sister to tell her of your progress. I'll send it along for you, but I'd be remiss not to offer you paper and postage to complete the task."

A letter. *Damn*. She'd forgotten. But that, too, was a simple request she was more than happy to accomplish. "And lastly"—Najah sighed—"these items are on loan. I expect to see them, and yourselves, in good health the moment it becomes possible for you to return to me. I will not wait forever, so your timeliness is imperative."

Kera stood and strode to Najah's chair. She wrapped her arms around the woman's shoulders and held her close. "Thank you for all of your assistance," she whispered.

"You are more than welcome, my dear. Both of you. More than welcome."

Kera felt Aurora give her shoulder a squeeze. For the first time in a long while, the reassurances of her allies seemed to actually bolster her resolve. Confidence had slipped in when she hadn't noticed, and standing here beside Aurora, Kera knew they would succeed.

Setting out again after two nights' rest felt strange. The horses that Najah provided were calm and sturdy. Their saddles were lightweight and easier to lift and manage. The saddlebags were easily transferable and packed well. Najah gave them fresh ointment to smear over their wounds, new bandages, and jars of oils for the children. Aiden woke up long enough to blink up at Najah Zakaria. He received a hug from her and a well wish for his travels. Faith, though, was more aware.

While the horses were getting ready and Najah spoke quietly to Aurora and Aiden, Kera steadied the young girl with an arm around her shoulders. "How are you feeling, dear?"

Faith shrugged. Her head twisted this way and that, as if trying to take in all of Mount Maladh at once. "I'm sorry you weren't able to see more during your stay," Kera admitted. "But we'll be back, yes? When you're feeling better? And perhaps we'll even be able to find you a dress so you can look just as lovely as your mother did."

"She did look pretty," Faith whispered, leaning against Kera so her head could tuck under her chin. She felt warm and precious against Kera's side. Right, in a way all of her children had felt from the moment she first had them in her arms. Kissing Faith's crown, Kera smiled against her hair. Hiding it like a secret only they would know.

"Very pretty indeed . . ."

"We—we'll really come back?" A hacking cough rocked the child against her. Kera shifted her feet to take more of the girl's weight.

"I promise. We'll come back, and I'll show you all the wonders of Mount Maladh. My boys insisted that they hid a treasure somewhere out in the fields, but I bet between the four of us we could track it down. Your mother certainly has a knack for ferreting out the truth when she wants to."

"Yeah . . . no good tryin'ta hide anything from her . . ."

"Come, let's get you up on that horse before you fall asleep. We're almost to the Lakes, Faith. You'll see. Just a bit longer now. Soon this will all be over. Come, up you get." It was a well-practiced dance between them at this point. Faith mounted with the last vestiges of her strength, sagging forward on her gelding as Kera held him steady. But she murmured her thank-yous just as polite as polite could be once she'd done it. Kera took the girl's hand in hers, kissing it as a gentleman would. "We're going to make it, Faith. I promise."

"One more thing," Najah announced, stepping up to Kera's side. She held out a small pouch for Kera to take, then gave a matching one to Aurora. Inside there were crystals. "Set them by your fire circle and the wraiths won't be able to see you at all. You should be safe from *them* at the very least."

"There are crystals that keep you invisible to the wraiths?" Aurora asked, holding her pouch like she had just been given the answers to the universe. She had Aiden balanced up on her hip, and the boy was peering down into the pouch as well, one thumb reaching up to press between his lips before he turned and snuggled against Aurora's throat. Aurora's hands tightened around the offering before she shifted to squeeze Aiden close to her side. Aiden was hugging her close, sniffling a little, murmuring words Kera couldn't quite hear. Aurora must have heard them all, though. The more Aiden mumbled, the more tension seemed to radiate through her. Her voice raised with each word she spoke, "We were *attacked*, almost *killed*, how come we never heard of these things before?"

"I thought the stories about Brennan Wild planting crystals around Ship's Landing to defend it from the night were *rumors*," Kera said.

But Najah rolled her eyes with such exasperation that it caught her off guard. "Honestly, child, how do you think Mori managed to ride through the night during the war? It certainly wasn't luck."

"He wasn't a superior rider or soldier?"

"Apologies for breaking the illusion, but Morpheus only attempted such rides twice. His final time, he'd come back nearly collapsing from fright, and the poor horse he'd been on—this was before he received Holly—died of a heart attack the moment after he'd crossed the fire circle." Then, because Najah had a peculiar sense of humor, she said, "It was how Mr. Burns and my staff traveled through the night too."

Kera flushed at the revelation, but Aurora wasn't cowed. "But why haven't we heard of these?" she pressed indignantly, still squeezing Aiden so tight. As if her arms were the fire circle determined to shield him from the world.

"Because they're gifts." It didn't explain anything, and Kera was prepared to ask for clarification when Najah sighed. "Magic, crystals, potions, and hexes? They only truly work when freely given. It's an old-world philosophy, back from when the gods walked the earth. Ruug might be the only place that truly still practices magic properly, but their studies have at least offered us this. Time's a fickle thing, and Death's even more strict. But anytime magic or blessings are involved, there's an exchange of sorts that's wholly based on intent. And an exchange of currency invalidates the purity of the intent. *Intent* is what matters to the undead. Gifts are what matter. If you give the right gift, or you hold the right item close—then that is what feeds the power needed. Those crystals will only work if they've been blessed and tended to, and given without any thoughts of greed or avarice.

"You can't market good intentions, so I fear the crystals fell out of favor for the most part. But cities such as Ship's Landing, Alexandria, even settlements such as Mount Maladh, are all surrounded by buried crystals so no wraiths may enter the property—even without a fire. It was the True Lord Amit who provided many of the crystals around this property. I wouldn't be surprised if he helped Wild with Ship's Landing either."

"But they still burn the circles around the cities," Aurora said.

"It's to make people feel safe. Not everyone believes the crystals will work. After all, if the intent fades, so too does the power. But you needn't worry about the intent here. These are the same crystals I used to give soldiers during the war. They've carried riders through the horrors once before, and they will do so again."

Tears pricked against Kera's eyes, but she ordered herself to stay calm. Focused. She tucked the crystals into her saddlebag, then reached to take Najah's hand. "Thank you . . . for everything."

"Just return safe to me, dear child," Najah requested. And when she looked to Aurora, she smiled still. "And it's been quite my pleasure to meet you, Ms. Lawrence. I do hope to get to know you and your daughter better upon your return. When circumstance are less dire."

"You as well, my lady," Aurora replied. She settled Aiden up on the horse, then went to mount up behind her daughter, Kera steadying both horses with tight hands on their bridles. Najah waited to the side as Aurora got settled, but before Kera could turn to mount as well, she placed a hand on Kera's wrist.

Leaning in close, Najah pressed her face to Kera's hair, whispering in her ear. "It's a fine thing to move on after you've lost someone," she said. "But be certain that you're moving on to the right person, or you may regret it when it's done."

She flinched badly, recoiling from her friend as though struck. Words built up, then died in her mouth. Kera's heart pounded violently, but Najah refused to step back. "I mean this kindly, Kera. You loved your husband, and it isn't fair to anyone if you start down a new journey, and your heart isn't ready to be given away once more."

"Kera?" Aurora called. She jerked around and stared up at Aurora. Watched as her face twisted into something approaching deep concern. Anxiety swirled in Kera's stomach.

"Right," she breathed out quietly. "Right. Thank you." Then she climbed up onto her horse, and settled in around her son. Najah almost looked sad as she stepped away, waving them goodbye with a regal sweep of her hand. But Kera didn't think too much about Najah's feelings. Not when her mind was too busy reanalyzing her own.

CHAPTER NINETEEN

A urora didn't comment on Kera's silence after they left Mount Maladh. She glanced over a few times, but didn't pressure her to reveal anything. It was kind. Mori would have pestered her until she eventually told him what Najah had said, and that in of itself was confusing. She didn't even know if she *wanted* Aurora to ask her what had happened. She wasn't sure if she was *supposed* to want Aurora to ask. All she knew was that it was a relief not being bothered by incessant nettling as they continued to ride south.

Prattling shifted to a strangely companionable silence, interrupted only when one of the kids felt well enough to start a conversation. Faith, in particular, was in good spirits upon their departure. She managed to eat a few more mouthfuls at their mealtimes when they stopped, and she'd taken to humming idly while they rode.

Their new horses were strong and sturdy. They walked with determination and careful steps, and moved forward at a steady pace. Kera found that their procession was covering more ground than before, and that their horses were not exhausted at the end of the day. They minded Kera's and Aurora's commands well, and their placid demeanors were flawless company for the journey.

The crystals they had been given were nothing short of a miracle. Settlements in the south were farther apart than those in the north, and they were forced to sleep outside more than once (despite their careful planning). They set the crystals in the ground, and lit the fires no matter what, but now the nightwalkers didn't approach. There were no screeches or thrashing attempts to cross their barrier. If anything, the woods were silent. It was eerie.

Tonight was no different. Kera rested against Aurora, with their children curled along their sides. They took turns talking to each other and taking watch. Crystals or no, anxious energy wrapped around Kera whenever night fell. She couldn't stop the immediate panic that rose when there was *any* sound in the dark, let alone the howling of the dead.

Talking with Aurora and Faith was lovely. Faith was a quick wit and a clever tease. She was every bit her mother's daughter in terms of inner strength and bravery. Kera longed for the moment when they would reach the end of their quest and the griffons could save her and restore her to her truest form. Kera wanted to talk to her and get to know the young woman that was hidden beneath lethargy and violent tremors.

For now, Kera took what she could get. She ran her fingers through Faith's hair and tried to calm her when her arms shook or legs twitched. "Do you remember when I told you about Cirri? She's just about your age. And . . . and I have a few other children as well. There's Cirri of course, then Mori Junior and August, then John, Marcus, my little Kerryn . . . and Aiden's the youngest."

"'S'alo' o' kids . . ." Faith slurred against Kera's knee.

"It is. They would love to meet you. Especially Cirri. She's been desperate for a friend to spend her time with; so many of the girls around us are interested in frivolities. She wants a true companion."

"Not . . . sure I'd do so well . . ."

"You'd be perfect," Kera told her. "You *are* perfect. She'll love you." Cirri had a heart bigger than anyone Kera knew. She opened her mind and her soul to others with such wonderful acceptance, embracing all of the best parts of her parents.

A twig snapped, and Kera turned her head to peer through the trees. It took her a moment to spot it, but when she did, she gasped. Aurora woke with a start, jerking forward and squinting into the night. Searching for a wraith where there wasn't one.

Instead, a faded blue light shimmered not far away, human-shaped and walking slow. It hadn't noticed them yet, but Kera recognized the hue anyway. She'd seen this before, when her father had been preparing a legal case involving a murder and had the good fortune to observe a death march as part of his trial. He'd brought her and her siblings with him to show them what a death march was. They'd all watched with rapt fascination as the ghosts appeared from beyond and reenacted their final moments.

Death marches were impervious to fire lines, they started wherever they died—circle or no. But with any luck, the crystals should be enough to keep them safe. Either way, unless the living interfered with the dead, the dead wouldn't interfere with the living. Ghosts were meant to replay their deaths, and changes to their schedules were rare. This soldier just kept walking, heading through the trees without looking their way or suspecting that there was anyone watching him back.

"Most of the battles were fought in the north," Aurora murmured. The soldier wore the uniform of the first Absalon army, dark blue made even more ethereal after his death.

"Not all of them," Kera said. "There's every chance we could stumble on one and interfere..."

"Well I got no intentions of interfering, do you?" Aurora whispered back.

"No." They watched as the soldier walked out of sight, still unaware of their presence and not concerned with where they sat. Kera counted seconds in her head, listening as the night continued its standard routine. There was a shout of surprise, cut off like the air was driven from someone's lungs. It echoed through the wood. Then, silence.

"What happens if they don't die?" Faith asked. She yawned wide and shivered. Aurora dragged a light blanket over her shoulders. Najah had given them more than enough supplies to care for their family in what seemed like luxury.

"I don't follow," Aurora admitted.

"If you inter...fere..." Faith paused, gathering her breath. "What happens if they don't die? You stop 'em from dying?"

"They become specters . . ." Aurora said. "Violent and angry. They're aware that they didn't die when they should have, and they know there's no way to the other side now. So they break free of the march and roam the world—attacking or causing trouble wherever they can. Sort of like wraiths."

Kera shivered. She'd never liked any of the nightwalkers, and the fact that they went through so many transitions felt wrong to her. They should have been at peace, but existing as they did . . . felt tragic. She had no desire to live a horrible day over and over again for the rest of time. Why would anyone wish to relieve their final moments? It felt . . . *wrong*.

She thought back to Rachel. As a phantom, she had more leeway. Her violence, if there had even been such a thing, had been a choice she made. Her humanity had stayed intact despite her death. She could change. There was no change with the marches. No time to grow or learn or adapt. They were locked in amber, exactly as they were on that day.

Their dialogue might differ if they were interrupted, but they felt the same emotions as they had in the moments before they died. Happiness, sadness, love, and hate all solidified into one final performance, and the poor souls never realized they were dead. They never knew that they would be fated to relive those deaths over and over.

Of all the nightwalkers . . . Kera felt the worst for them.

Sighing, she mumbled about needing something to distract her. Pulling the *Bestiary* from its spot, she flipped through the pages once more. By now she had nearly memorized the entire book. She'd already learned all there was to know about everything relevant, and yet there was still no answer as to who the writer in the griffon section was. There was still no accounting for the discrepancies between the text and the annotations that surrounded it.

Kera skimmed through the pages. She hoped to find something, *anything* that could help give them more insight. She just needed more information, but the book lacked the knowledge she wished to find. *Someone should write a better book*, she thought. She would pay for it to be written if she had to. More people should have access to this kind of knowledge. It shouldn't just be for clerics and researchers.

Aurora's hand snapped to her arm. She looked up. There was a soldier standing on the outside of their fire pit.

He was watching them with a curious expression, one that made Kera's heart beat rapidly. She licked her lips. She should say something, anything, but she had no idea what she was meant to say to a dead man about to die again. Unlike the first soldier, this one was looking right at them, his death march interrupted because of where they'd set up their camp. Kera wondered if the crystals could protect them from a true and proper ghost, not a wraith ready to tear them apart.

Her hopes were invalidated as the ghost stepped forward, crossing over the fire line as if it were meaningless. Kera's heart hammered. She scrambled to her feet, standing in front of Aurora and the children. Terror wrapped around her.

He didn't seem to mind either way, he just kept *looking* at them. Up and down, up and down, his expression twisted in confusion. It was as if he couldn't quite fathom that they were here either.

"Good morning, mi'ladies," he greeted, unaware of the time or place. He was locked in his mindset of how his life once was. Kera's stomach sank. The sweet southern drawl pulled around the soldier's tone as he asked, "What are you doing out here?"

Kera had no idea what to say.

CHAPTER TWENTY

The soldier was just a boy. They all had been at one point. Though this one seemed *absurdly* young, even if the gold thread on his arm claimed he was a lieutenant colonel. Dark-brown curls were pulled out of his face in a bushy tail at the base of his neck, and brown freckles splattered across his bronzed skin. One thin braid hung down by his chin, colored beads clicking together as he slipped closer.

Kera angled her body to keep between him and her family. He might just be a boy, but he was also a ghost, and ghosts were perfectly capable of killing at a whim.

"I apologize for disturbing you, mi'ladies, but whatever *are* you doing out here?" He held out his hand in greeting. "There's a Trent army not too far away." Kera fixated on the accent. It was unsurprising considering their current location, as it was southern in nature, but there was a slight Ruugian tilt that implied time spent on the other side of the Great Sea. He'd been wealthy then, before his death. He'd gone to school in Ruug and been trained in their customs before returning to Absalon to fight.

Aurora had an arm around Faith's body, her fingers tight on Aiden's shoulder. Weeks ago, she'd warned Kera about death marches. Weeks ago, she'd told her not to talk to any more ghosts, and yet here they were.

Kera was the closest to the soldier, and if she ignored his hand any longer, it would seem rude. Already she was pushing the bounds of social convention by not taking it. They were past the point of being able to avoid interaction, and purposefully infuriating the soldier would only make things worse. Slowly, with Aurora whispering in protest at her back, Kera reached out and cupped his palm to hers.

He was not as cold as she had thought he would be. His skin was as warm as any normal man's, though it continued to gives off the faint blue glow of the undead. She was grateful he wasn't decaying like the wraith, or bleeding like the horror stories her older brothers had told her as a child. The morbidity of such a sight might have made this interaction far less cordial. Still, he didn't seem offended when she released his palm a touch quicker than decency allowed.

If anything, his smile grew as he peered at Aurora and the children. "We're . . . traveling," Kera explained. She swallowed back her tension and tried to summon the least confrontational words in her arsenal. She was not sure what a ghost would find unpleasant, nor what could send one into a rage. But the soldier seemed polite enough for now. "Didn't make it to the inn in time, I'm afraid."

The soldier tilted his head a little, then glanced over his shoulder. Kera followed his gaze, and her breath froze in her chest. More soldiers were walking through the trees, hesitating on the edge of their encampment. The colonel met her eyes, frowning a little. "You need not be afraid, my lady, we're not savages. We'll not harm you or your children."

Kera forced the muscles around her lips to pull her mouth into the best smile she could manage. She felt the corners of her eyes crinkle as she thanked him. The expression must have been less pleasant than she had intended; it made him laugh.

"Oh, don't be like that. I swear on our honor. We've never harmed a lady, and we likely never will. The general would hang us all from the poplars if we did."

"That'd be quite a feat," Kera said. "They're not known for their branches."

The soldier laughed again, a great boisterous sound that was almost musical. Enchanting in the way operas and theatrical productions were on a warm summer night. She heard Aurora hissing her name, and Kera blinked rapidly as she tried to keep focus.

The man was dead. Enchanting or not, *well-meaning* or not, he and his men were a danger to them all. Horror stories of people being pulled into death marches, dying by the spectacle some even purposefully went to see, were not forgotten easily. "Please, my ladies, we'd be serving without honor if we didn't escort you properly. Is there any place we could take you?"

"We'll be fine," Aurora said. "We don't need your assistance." The colonel's face flickered in and out of focus, there and gone in a flash. He frowned, unhappy and discontented.

"Only, you're so busy as it is," Kera hastened to explain. "And your duties are far more important than caretaking us." His expression didn't lift in the slightest. If anything, it became suspicious.

"What were your names, again?" he asked them. *Spies!* Kera's heart jolted as realization struck. He believed them to be spies. Women and children lost in the woods would never turn down such a guard, they should be *thankful* for the soldiers' presence, not wary of their offer for help. More than that, this colonel was a true soldier, not some rascal in a blue coat. With his shiny buttons and well-maintained boots, he was a man (boy) of some importance. He had been well-bred and was loyal to his command. The soldiers that surrounded him, walking closer and closer with each passing second, continued to look to him for leadership and guidance. They trusted him. He wasn't going to ignore the oddities of Kera and Aurora's presence. He wasn't going to be turned away with a few casual words.

"A gentleman would do well to introduce himself first," Kera bargained. She tried to recall every soldier Mori had mentioned. Faces and names blurred. Too many died during the war and the only man she could think of was—

"John Sarren, my lady. And you?"

"Kera," Aurora snapped. "No—"

"I know him!" Kera said, looking back at her partner just for a moment, before focusing back on John.

"Know me?" he asked, too startled to say much else.

"Kera, get away from him; it's not safe!"

But Kera didn't listen. She soaked in the image of John's face. His eyes, his nose, his cheeks. He was handsome. Handsome and boyish, and oh! *They* had been this young once. She and Mori had been this young at some point or another. The dashing young soldier with his lady. She remembered how they'd appeared in the years of her story's prologue. She yanked a memory of Mori at twenty-one years old and slotted him right alongside this dreamlike portrait from their past. They had stood side by side once, grinning and teasing. The best of friends who brought out the worst in each other.

"Madam," John stumbled, blinking so quickly she almost laughed at his shock. "I'm sure I would have recalled meeting such a lovely—"

"My name is Kerryn Montgomery." John's eyes widened. Horror washed across his features before being rapidly replaced by an enthusiastic smile that hinged on the edge of hysteria. He clung to her hand.

"I had known Mori married a lady," John said, sounding perfectly content despite his false start. "But I must confess, he did not impress how tragically *beautiful* his lady was."

The flattery was old and familiar, words misplaced by decades. She'd heard that turn of phrase before, and was struck by a sudden sight of John leaning over Mori's shoulder as Mori penned out her letters. Perhaps he'd even cackled boisterously as Mori grew more excited with his euphemisms. She caught the twinkle in John's eye, the way he shifted his posture from military perfection into something more suave and inviting. A conscious choice to seem less threatening than he was. "And yet you, Lieutenant Colonel," she drawled carefully, "are precisely the scoundrel he described."

Another man might have taken offense, but John laughed again. He threw his body into the motion, delight ringing through the trees. When his guffaws finally ceased, he released Kera's hand. He hurried toward Aiden and looked him over. "Is this . . .?" he asked Kera, eyes growing wide even as his skin seemed to turn more pale. Aurora had pulled Aiden close to her side, her terror obvious for all to see.

But even as Kera was scrambling to find a way to defuse the situation, she heard her husband's voice whispering from a memory long forgotten. *"I wish he could have known our children."* And though it was a memory, she could have sworn she'd heard him speak it aloud, whispering his intentions on the wind. Najah had told her not to give her heart to anyone while she still cared so deeply for her husband, but divorcing herself from those emotions seemed impossible. For all her anger and resentment, she still loved him. Still had shared a lifetime with him. His heartbreak still felt like hers. His wishes still colored her desires. Maybe Najah had been right. Maybe she wasn't ready to move on.

"Yes," she said, opening her eyes and trying not to let the pain show. Trying not to look at Aurora as the pain only seemed to grow worse. "Yes, this is Aiden." John's face was alight with wonder. He leaned down over Aiden and smiled at the boy. He lifted a hand to touch his cheek and was *immediately* slapped for it.

Aurora was shameless. She pulled Aiden away and the colonel recoiled like a scolded dog. His nose scrunched up, and Kera *felt* the temperature of the wood start to drop low. The hazy blue of the dead army brightened.

"Aurora . . ." Kera warned. John was glaring. Disposition inverted in a moment.

"He's sick," Aurora excused. She didn't bother mollifying her tone. She glared without remorse. "We wouldn't want you or your men to . . . become afflicted."

If she thought the words would calm John, she was mistaken. He dismissed her and looked at Kera for permission. It was like seeing Morpheus again, as he used to be. Fiery and vibrant. Emotions in all directions. *The worst of each other . . .*

It was exhausting. All of it was exhausting. Mori and John and all the history of what could have been but what wasn't real. Kera wished, suddenly, that it could all just stop. That things could be simple and easy. That she could just move on without being reminded constantly of the past. A past that was familiar. The safety the past provided was coddling in its embrace. She understood this past. She could negotiate with this past and keep it from causing any undue harm.

Knowing Aurora would hate her for it, Kera slipped around John. She stood between him and Aurora, leaning in close and keeping her voice as low as she could. "He doesn't understand," she said. "He's just . . . a child who wants to meet his best friend's son."

"He's *dead*, Kera. And so is that best friend of his."

"He doesn't know that." Kera reached for her child, not surprised when Aurora struggled to hand him over. "Please . . . I know how to talk to him."

"You were *lucky* with that ghost back in Doleystown . . ."

"It's not that. It's... He's exactly like Mori." Aurora's grip slackened and Kera adjusted it so Aiden was resting up against her own hip.

"Kera..."

"I know," she muttered, energy draining from her like through a sieve. "I know. But... even if they're both dead and it doesn't matter... they deserved this. He deserves this. If only for a little while." Aiden mewled miserably in her arms. He rubbed at his eyes as he looked around them, whining at the sight of the blue man that hovered so very near.

But Kera formed a pretty smile on her face and presented her son for John's inspection, cooing at her boy to keep him calm. Strangely, John hadn't walked any closer as she spoke with Aurora. Instead, he'd stayed back and pretended he wasn't interested. One of his hands rested on the pommel of his gilded sword, the other tucked behind his back. He almost looked aloof, though the display was ruined when his gaze snapped back into focus as she approached. He'd been polite in his patience, but Kera doubted he'd let his attention waver even once. Regardless of his own reasons, Kera was simply pleased he'd given her room to smooth Aurora's rough edges. There was nothing they could do but let this play out, and Kera knew how to handle her husband. She was confident she could handle John.

Holding Aiden close enough for John to see, she said, "He's named after my father." And her first Aiden *had* been. It was something John should have known, and he reacted as expected. A tangible bit of tension left their party like the crack of a whip as John leaned over her son.

He smiled down at her boy and said, "He's a beautiful child," in a warm tone that sent shivers down her spine.

"Thank you." She meant it. "Mori always wanted you to meet him..."

"I was never stationed north enough to have the time to stop by. But with the war ending soon... I'm so glad I had the chance to meet him." Something felt off about the phrasing, but before Kera could think on it, he went on, asking, "You said he was ill?"

"Yes, a sickness that's nigh incurable. We're looking for the griffons in hopes that they can help."

Some of the other soldiers started to talk amongst themselves. But John silenced them with a look. "The griffons live over in the Long Lakes," he told her without pause.

"You know about them?" Faith asked, shifting at her mother's side. Aurora hushed her immediately, squeezing her arm tight around her body, but she seemed just as startled as her daughter.

"Yes," he said, tucking his braid behind his ear. "I know them. The lakes were part of my father's property. I saw them often when I was a child and used to collect their feathers for talismans."

Sloping letters along the margins of the *Bestiary*. Thorough notes on size and mating patterns. Detailed drawings slid in-between pages, glorious in their beauty. "Oh . . . oh!" Kera lowered Aiden so he was on his feet, then hurried toward her husband's book. Snatching it up off the ground, she held it out for John to see. "*You're* the one who wrote the notes in Mori's book!"

It was John's turn to flush, and he tucked his head as if he'd been caught filching sweets. Still, when he took the book his hands were gentle. His touch, reverent. "I'm surprised he managed to keep this in one piece after I left," he said softly. "Has it been of use to you?"

"With all this travel, I admit the *Bestiary* lacks on the nightwalkers more than we'd prefer," Kera said.

John's eyes glimmered when he was amused. Kera wondered if that glimmer had been there before he died. Or perhaps it was new? A strange castoff from the blue glow that wrapped about him like a shroud. John produced a formal bow. "My dear Mrs. Montgomery, you must permit me the honor of escorting you to the Long Lakes." And Kera suppressed the desire to wilt.

He couldn't travel with them to the Long Lakes . . . he wouldn't even be able to leave this wood. John was going to die, just as he'd died the night before. And the night before that. He would relive his steps and his memories for all eternity, and they couldn't break his death march. Not without turning him into something far worse than this.

"No," Aurora answered for her. John's face twisted into something offended. "No, we're not traveling with you."

"And who are you, again?" he asked, a touch of temper flaring across his tone.

Aurora's eyes narrowed. She spat out her first name as if daring him to comment on her lack of patronym, but John didn't so much as blink. He'd never cared that Mori came from nothing and was no one. If he could manage that, he shouldn't care about Aurora's lack of status. He didn't press for details, but instead lathered his voice into a sickly sweet tone that implored in such a distasteful way that Kera's nose began to twitch. "I'm not sure if you've *noticed*, Miss Aurora, but the country is at war. Anyone could happen upon you, and I'd be remiss in my duties if I let you go unattended."

The Travers family bankers came to mind in an instant. *Don't you worry your little head, miss, just trust we know best.* Kera almost chastised John herself, but Aurora was too quick for her.

She mimicked his haughty southern drawl with no small amount of contempt. "I don't know if *you've* noticed, Lieutenant Colonel, but we've traveled from Ship's Landing to Alilaaniwa without your help. We certainly don't need it now."

But, as it turned out, the practicality of their situation *had* gone over John's head. He twisted toward Kera. "You've truly been alone all this time? You're a *lady*! Surely you must have some form of escort?"

"I didn't need one," Kera said, shocking herself with her force. He gaped at her, mouth floundering. "And . . ." She swallowed. "There was quite a lot happening at the time."

"It must have been *quite a lot* indeed if your husband did not take this journey himself. A letter could have been posted to me, and I would have fetched your needs for you had I known."

"There wasn't enough time, good sir. The children fell ill only weeks ago. By the time you received the missive, we feared it would be too late."

Eyes wide with wonder, John looked back at Aiden. "Does Mori not know you are traveling, my lady?" he asked, falling back on conventions even as his imagination took hold.

"Not . . . as such . . ." she admitted. It was as close as the truth as she could manage. If Mori's spirit *did* know what had been occurring, he hadn't made an effort to commune with them.

"Then it is my sworn duty to serve you, Mrs. Montgomery. Mori would not permit me to act otherwise. I'd lose my honor, if not my friend, should I allow you on your own." Any chance they had in convincing John to let them go sans chaperone seemed dashed. He'd been raised to assist women in need, and General Zakaria wouldn't have held him in such esteem if John wasn't capable of good manners.

"We cannot keep you from your war, Colonel," Kera tried one last time. *Words, words, words!* Which ones would work?

"Nonsense, I already told you, the war is almost won!" John grinned, and Kera couldn't tell if he was teasing or if he truly believed that. She let her eyes slide back to his soldiers, all waiting at attention and prepared to follow whatever course of action John set forth.

Reckless, Zakaria had called John. He'd never had any other ill words to say about the man, finding him to be of fine upstanding moral character, but he'd always said that John was *reckless* to the point of distraction.

She raised a brow at him. Adopting an expression she used with her children after she caught them scheming, she asked, "You just want to fight a griffon, don't you?" If possible, his grin became *resplendent* with delight.

"Oh yes, you are the perfect match for Mori. I am so pleased." Closing the *Bestiary*, he waved his hand toward their horses. "Well, if there are no more complaints"—he squinted at Aurora without giving her a chance to voice anything—"then come along! If we leave now, we can reach the edge of the wood by sundown. There's a clearing just on the other side that's very defensible. A good creek for water as well." No need to tell him it was already the dead of night. That they had set up camp and had little notion of whether he would be leading them in the right direction or not.

He believed that he was helping them, but when Kera glanced toward Aurora, it was clear where Aurora stood on this matter. Joining these men on their death march would lead them to one outcome—*violence*. If, by some strange stroke of luck, their presence interrupted the death march and the soldiers who killed John did not appear as they should, then John and all his men would shift and transform into some of the worst nightwalkers imaginable while Aurora, Kera, and the children were right in their midst.

Somehow, even in death, Mori was finding ways to make her life difficult. She wondered faintly which one of them was really struggling to let the other go. "Colonel, I really must protest," she tried again. "And a griffon fight? Truly?"

"One doesn't *fight* with griffons," John told her, lowering his voice as if telling a secret. "One merely bids them hello."

CHAPTER
TWENTY-ONE

C amp was struck faster than Kera could think. Faith swayed as she looked at all the ghosts rushing this way and that to make things ready for them, while her mother scowled at every transition with mounting fury.

"I'm sorry," Kera whispered to Aurora. Aiden squirmed in her arms, blinking wearily at their surroundings without any curiosity at all.

"Sorry isn't going to get us out of this mess," Aurora whispered back. The horses were getting saddled for them, and both of Najah's steeds were whinnying anxiously as the ghosts worked them over.

"I tried—"

"I know you tried, Lady," the title sounded far more gentle than Kera had expected. Aurora even followed it with a hand on her arm, squeezing just enough to show she cared. "But we're still *riding in their march*."

"We are, and we'll have to figure out how to manage that but—"

John barked out an order for his own mount to be brought over, and Aiden kicked Kera's sides as he wriggled about to see. He propped his bony chin on her shoulder, digging in painfully as he wiggled. Kera shook her head and leaned back toward Aurora.

"*But*," she restarted, "he knows about the griffons, I think. Maybe we can—"

"*It's shining*!" Aiden hissed loud enough to hurt Kera's ear. She winced and turned, trying to see what had caught her son's attention, only to find herself staring in shock at the gorgeous stallion walking toward them.

Tall and proud, it glowed with the same ethereal blue that outlined John's body. "Ma," Aiden whisper-shouted again. "Ma, it's *shining*! The horse's shining!" He finished the proclamation with a loud cough that hacked deep from his lungs. He wheezed as his throat croaked around each breath, and Kera swatted his spine sharply in three places before he finally managed to get whatever needed to be dislodged out.

John took hold of his steed with a proud hand at the bridle. He adjusted his reins and showed off a particularly graceful bow. "I see you like my good fellow here; this is Reilly, and Reilly is the best steed you could ask for, I'll have you know." He winked as he brought the horse closer for inspection. Faith peered at it in wonder even as Aiden waggled his fingers toward its sleek hair. "You know," John said conspiratorially. "I'm trying to get Mori to agree to foal Holly when the war's done. Can you imagine the bloodline these two could make?"

Aiden's face contorted, and he rubbed the back of his palm beneath his nose before announcing, "Holly died," in a perfectly clear voice that left no room for argument.

John recoiled as if struck. His gaze snapped from son to mother in a moment. "She *what*? How do you— *When*? I didn't hear this. Is Mori all right?"

"It was recent," Kera hurried to explain, adjusting Aiden so he wasn't quite so close to the horse or John. "Very recent, you wouldn't have known."

"But I . . . I'm so sorry. And Mori, he's all right? He loved that horse . . ."

Aiden whined, "Holly—"

"—died saving her rider's life," Kera interjected, jostling her boy, even though she doubted he had any idea what he was being corrected for. "She was a hero."

"That's . . . that's the important part isn't it?" John sighed wearily. "I had hoped that she'd make it through, though. If only because she seemed so immortal."

"Yes . . ." Kera whispered. "She did."

John shook his head as he told them to get mounted. They did. Slowly, and carefully, trading glances and wordlessly trying to convey every uncertain emotion they felt without letting John know just how desperate they were to not proceed.

After learning about Holly, however, John didn't seem nearly as interested in watching over their every movement. It gave Kera time to give both Faith and Aurora a hug and a kiss. It gave Aurora time to whisper a quiet assurance to Aiden. They mounted as carefully as they could, but Kera checked first to make sure that the cinch was tight enough to handle a quick ride if they needed to escape, and that Aiden was well secured at her front.

"Ah, ready to go, then?" John asked once they'd settled in. "Let's go . . ." He whistled once, sharply, then led the way, posture still slumped despite having the perfect opportunity to rally and hide behind the shield of an aloof soldier's façade.

It felt strangely familiar. And as Kera looked at him, she couldn't help but see precisely what Mori had seen in him. For all his initially perceived arrogance, he was a rather gentle soul. A handsome boy who didn't shy behind his wealth and privilege, and still managed to be sympathetic to those in pain was a rare thing indeed.

Though if she were being honest with herself, she would say that, like Mori, John was very good at playing pretend. His smiles were perhaps too forced. His jokes seemed outdated and rehearsed. He played the game well, acting as a nobleman and gentleman in front of his men, but Kera recognized the pauses. She understood the hesitation. She'd seen all this before.

He spent the good first portion of their ride telling Kera and Aurora about his men. He answered Faith's questions when she was brave enough to ask them, and he delighted in sharing details that made Aurora's nose turn up in disapproval. Kera had heard all of these before, but was startled to find that the teasing she'd enjoyed in Mori's rendition no longer made her smile. Mori had wooed her with the same blue coat, the same boisterous nature, and the same fearless appetite for adventure. But she was no longer the same woman she'd been all those years ago.

At some point, she'd grown up. She'd changed.

And John, trapped forever as a twenty-seven-year-old child, would never do the same.

"Are you all right?" Aurora asked Kera after they'd been riding for almost a mile in silence. She guided her gelding so it nearly bumped sides with hers. John's head tilted just enough to show that he'd heard Aurora's question and was awaiting the answer.

Kera sighed. They'd have no privacy here. "I'm fine, Widget," she said slowly. They'd discuss it later, when she could take the time to analyze her thoughts and put them into words and didn't have anyone else's ears listening in. Aurora hesitated, then nodded.

"You told her about my doll?" Faith whined, blushing so hard she nearly illuminated the night all on her own.

Kera grinned. "It was such a lovely story, Faith; how could I not have enjoyed it?"

Faith groaned miserably, closing her eyes as though she intended to will herself to sleep.

Clearing her throat, Kera called out to their escort, "What are your plans after the war?" She wondered if he'd ever given any thought to anything outside of his present.

John slowed his horse so they were riding side by side. "Well, if you must know, my father has requested that I join him in our new government as a lawyer or representative." It was the kind of delicate response Aurora would never let her get away with anymore. The carefully worded refrain that provided information without insight, and sought no deeper understanding. Kera knew Curtis Sarren's plans for John already. She'd heard them from him as he bemoaned the loss of his son and the great good he thought John could have done for their country.

"But what do *you* want to do?" she asked.

"Oh, if left to my own devices, I'd go home, find a poor beggar, and give them my inheritance," John informed her with a wink, and his sadness near invisible behind a brilliant smile flush with teeth.

"Colonel."

"You don't believe me."

"Nobody would believe you," Aurora said, though her recent contempt and distrust was subdued for the first time since they'd been forced to accompany him.

John had to lean forward to get a good look at Aurora, and he prodded his spectral horse a bit faster to manage it. "Why is that? Have I said something untrustworthy?"

"Your father was Trent's top regional authority before the war, you may as well say what you are: you're a prince, and if you had any sense you would have supported Trent, not Absalon, in this war because you'd have ruled over everything by birthright. And you're talking about just giving it all away."

"Yes." John's smile was gone. His pretending at an end. Somewhere, a director was standing offstage, scratching their head as he abruptly went off his script, changing his story mid-play. "My father *and* I both agree that Trent's involvement in Absalon is a mistake. Father may be trying to salvage his wealth from betraying the king, but I see no justice in that. We have power because our family was meant to be loyal. If we're not loyal, we don't deserve that power. It is as simple as that. I don't want the money, or the title. I just want my wife and daughter to know I did it for the right reasons."

Kera's eyes strayed toward the beaded braid tucked behind John's ear. As a True Lord, Amit had never worn braids or beads, but Ruug was well-known for the tradition. The braids each having a meaning, the beads each telling their own story.

"You have a daughter?" Aurora asked, hugging Faith a bit tighter.

"Suppose I do." He shrugged awkwardly, not seeming to know what to do with his body. "I never met her . . . the war . . ." By now, John's daughter would be around Ira's or her first Aiden's age . . . A young woman embarking on her maturity.

Kera didn't know much about John's daughter, only that Mori had ruminated over whether or not to send her copies of her father's letters after his death. In the end, greed had won out. Mori hadn't wanted to part with a single letter, and he'd kept them closeted away, far out of sight, never to be talked about. "Her name's Circe . . . and if by some divine intervention I survive this war, I've been thinking about bringing them over. Set up a home . . . here or maybe up in Ship's Landing?" It was a shy suggestion. He looked at her from under his lashes, and she told him it sounded like a fine idea. He flushed a little and bit his lip.

"Divine intervention?" Faith asked, no longer pretending to be asleep.

He shrugged again, carelessly rolling his right shoulder and avoiding eye contact. "I've never had much luck, it seems."

He knows something, Kera realized, panic jolting through her body. Aurora whispered her name as quietly as she could. She tilted her head toward a long path off to the right. They should go. Now, before this got worse. Kera's pulse was thrumming far too fast. She swallowed and adjusted her hold on her son.

If they veered off the path, there was no telling what John and his men would do. They were all armed. Their guns still shot bullets. Each soldier had the same number of balls and powder that they had when they died, replenished endlessly for their march.

"You're frightened," John murmured, his voice seeming to echo through the endless rows of trees.

Every part of Kera's body became aware of Aiden in front of her. His small shoulders, his flattening curls, the tremors that she'd started to grow numb to throughout their journey. Her ears fixated on the sound of his strained breathing, the way he sniffled. If she strained hard enough, she could have sworn she heard a heart beating, and all the logic in the world couldn't convince her it was her own.

She held her son close. She looked back toward the path in the trees, watching as they passed it by. They kept moving forward.

"I didn't mean to frighten you," John continued. "I'm sorry."

"You have nothing to be sorry for," Kera said. Aiden's head turned up beneath her chin. His skin burned hot on her flesh.

"My wife . . . well she has a bit of magic, she says our daughter does too, and well . . . she also said I'll not be seeing the end of this war. I'll die here."

Kera's head snapped around even as Aurora gasped, "*Here?*" as if the violence they'd been courting was going to fall upon them now that they knew the truth.

"Oh, probably not *here*," he amended. "But I won't survive the war. I know that."

"She's never been wrong?"

"No. Never. And in any case, it hardly matters. I've made my peace with my end," he said like a man who very much hadn't made peace with his end. The stage was still set for his soliloquy and the director was ready to push him back into position, but there were emotions evolving by the second on his face. Discomfort and uncertainty warring with acceptance and understanding. "There's no point in thinking of after the war. I won't have an *after the war*."

Kera couldn't look at him anymore. She buried her nose in her son's hair, kissing his cheek and trying desperately to pull back on her own emotions that threatened to bubble out en force. In all the stories and tales he'd shared, Mori had never told her about John's wife. He'd never mentioned John's belief that he would die. "You never told my husband this," Kera accused. She didn't look up.

"He'd have worried. We're in a war, my lady . . . he doesn't need to be worrying about something he can't change. And with any luck, when it happens, I'll die alone, and your husband will be nowhere nearby to be caught in the crossfire." She flinched badly at the mere idea of it. An echo of a sob pulled up from her memories. A sob loud enough to draw tears from the sky, as Mori read the note that offered condolences for John Sarren's death in battle. "I would appreciate if you didn't tell him until then."

It was a promise she felt no hesitation in giving. "I won't tell him." The blue light of his outline gleamed ever brighter in gratitude.

They pushed the horses on. And despite the possible escapes they could have attempted, Kera couldn't bring herself to try.

They rode through most of the night. Aurora's discomfort and misery grew by the second. Kera could feel her anxiety like a physical thing. It latched itself to the base of her neck and pulsated up through her brain. Aiden and Faith had fallen asleep some hours back, both too exhausted to be entertained by their circumstances. Faith had started shaking badly at one point, but they hadn't stopped. They'd just kept pressing onward, while Aurora whispered words in her ear and Kera tried convincing herself that she hadn't seen a flutter of a cloak deep in the night.

"Why did you write the notes in Mori's book?" Kera asked after a long period of silence.

"He'd been foolish enough to ride into a griffon nest. I thought it would keep him from doing something like that again." She had suspected as much. From what she had gathered . . . he hadn't been happy with Mori's recklessness at the very least. That was almost endearing, now that she thought about it. Risking life and limb was acceptable if he was the one doing it, but gods forbid one of his loved ones take the chance.

"They're incredibly detailed . . ." It was an invitation to say more on the topic, and for the first time all night, John actually appeared somewhat embarrassed. He kept his eyes in front of him, watching their path as he decided what to say.

"I . . . I used to live by the Long Lakes." His words grew softer and softer until Kera needed to strain to hear them. "I'd go for walks in the woods, and from time to time I'd see them flying. They don't mind children. In fact, I rather think they *liked* having me there. I used to take leaves of parchment up with me and try to sketch them. I was quite bad at it."

"You wouldn't know it from those scribblings," Aurora muttered. "What? I'm just saying, the ones in the book. They seemed decent." It might have been the nicest thing she'd said to John since they met, and it was still only partly true. They'd been more than decent. He had been systematic in his etchings. Each shape and figure had been proportional and particular. He had even added shading around the joints and the feathers to provide a clearer picture. Everything from the talons to the feathers to the beak had been drawn with flawless precision as far as Kera was aware.

Still, despite the subdued compliment, John flushed and fumbled around his thank-you. "Griffons . . . they've earned a reputation for being very difficult to work with and manage. Perhaps because most who encounter them fear that they are mindless beasts. Their very place in the *Bestiary* is still something I'm uncertain about . . . they're not quite the mindless creatures that you might believe them to be."

"You know this for a fact?"

"I do," he said. "They speak, they reason, they have communities and logic. When you reach the griffons, you need only ask for their help. Don't take anything they haven't offered freely, don't try to steal anything you presume is just a castoff. Just trust them. Just ask. That's all you need to do."

"They're *monsters*," Aurora argued. "The hunters—"

"Should never have gone after them to begin with, and they deserve what they got," John snapped back savagely. His temper flared up hot and quick, the blue burning so bright it was nearly blinding.

"Did you speak with them often?" Kera asked, trying desperately to calm him before either one of them could make the situation worse.

It seemed to help. He settled, even though he sent a few irritated glances Aurora's way the whole while. "I used to tell them about home, and they would tell me about their homes. About their society. It's how I know so much about them—they told me, and I listened."

"You must have been a very brave child." Kera had no idea what she would have done to one of her children if she discovered they'd spent their days with beasts. Likely place them in permanent house arrest. That Curtis Sarren had allowed the behavior to continue showed remarkable leniency on his part. Then again . . . "You traveled abroad for your schooling, didn't you?"

John nodded. "I left for Ruug when I was ten . . . There's an academy in their port city: Silex. It's where I met my wife . . ." He shook his head, as if trying to dislodge an image that settled before his eyes that he had no desire to see. "But the griffons, I've seen them more recently than that. I saw them before I left for the war."

"You seem to care a great deal for them. I've never met someone speak so fondly of griffons before."

"My father sent me to Ruug to study law, but if I'd had a choice in the matter, I'd have preferred to study beasts. Our current bestiaries are woefully inadequate."

Kera felt her lips twitch as she shared a fond look with Aurora. In unison, they replied: "We've noticed."

"I wish I could show Circe them . . ."

A shout echoed in the woods, and his head snapped about to listen. His soldiers all came to an abrupt halt, each one of them holding their guns at the ready. John trailed his fingers down to the hilt of his sword. He continued to scan the horizon.

"Is there a problem?" Kera asked, even as her heart beat faster beneath her ribs.

Adrenaline pumped through her body. The roots of her hair prickled as her ears turned outward. Desperate to hear *something*.

Anything.

A bullet cut through the night and John's horse reared. He handled it expertly, not flinching in the slightest as he forced his stallion to back down. There on the horizon was a lone Trent soldier . . . and as they stood clumped together . . . he multiplied. One by one a small contingent began to approach. All flickering blue.

Kera met Aurora's eyes.

The final moment of John's death march had started, and they had waited too long to escape.

CHAPTER
TWENTY-TWO

Bullets flew in all directions. Kera screamed as a soldier fell not far away. Aiden woke up and whined loudly against her. He clutched at the saddle and let out a terrible sound that reminded her far too much of their flight with the wraith. John looked at him, then at Kera. He grit his teeth and pulled his horse around to face his enemy with steely-eyed determination. "Go," he ordered Kera and Aurora. He pulled his sword from its sheath with his right hand. His reins were in his left. He nodded his head toward a perpendicular tree line. "Go, and do not stop running. Not for *anything*."

Despite her recalcitrant behavior prior, Aurora kicked her horse into action and did as he commanded. She raced headlong toward the woods, but Kera stayed. She couldn't help herself; she hesitated and watched as John shouted for his men to form lines. The teasing boy she'd always longed to meet now rallied his troops with single-minded focus. He screamed for his soldiers to prepare for the fight, ducking as a new volley lobbed toward them.

It was different now than in reality. Kera knew that over twenty years ago John had led this fight. Had *started* it, even. He had ordered his troops to attack the Trents, and he had lost badly. They'd counterattacked and slaughtered each member of John's party. But his death march had been interrupted, and the events were perverted. Now the Trents were chasing *them*, brandishing their weapons and preparing for the slaughter.

"Kera!" Aurora screamed. Her voice was fractured porcelain falling through the night, a stained glass window shattering. Colors and lights flickered across Kera's vision even as a gentle trickle of shards struck the earth. Kera looked over her shoulder. Aurora was already on the other side of the field. Kera looked back to John—he was managing as best he could.

He was twenty-seven years old and far too young to be facing death like this, riding his stallion as though it would protect him from all the dangers of the world. He was far too young to be scared of dying alone, heart and mind full of dreams that he'd been trying to pretend he didn't want to achieve. Kera knew, she *knew* that John would find no peace in this place. In this fight. He would wake up tomorrow, then the next day and the day after. He would keep dying over and over, and it was breaking her heart to think about it.

John met her eyes. He froze. His lips trembled. She was staying still when she should be riding as fast as she could go. She should have been setting fire to the earth beneath her horse's hooves as she fled in haste; she should have left with Aurora just after he'd given his first command. But she hadn't been able to kick her horse into action. She sat and stared, and realized, with mounting horror, that unlike Mori, she was going to see John fall and carry the sight with her for the rest of her life.

"Go!" John shouted at her, desperate, eyes wild. "Go! Lady Montgomery, go!"

He's scared. Aiden sobbed in her arms. She squeezed him to her. *Oh gods, he's scared.*

Her breath caught as bullets cut through the air. Soldiers were already starting to die on all sides. Aurora kept screaming her name. She was far too sensible to return for Kera now. With Faith in her arms, it was too dangerous for her to ride back.

"Go!" John shouted again.

Kera could hear the Trent commander ordering his men back into position. John whirled about and raised his sword, shouting, "*Fire!*" as he slashed it down through the air.

Across the field the Trents were falling too. "Fire!" sounded another volley. Riders burst from the undergrowth. John looked like Mori. Like her first Aiden. He looked like both of them in their final moments right before death took them. Eyes wide, face pale. Fear and uncertainty coiling about his body as he attempted to make sense of his life up until that moment.

John begged her one last time. "Please, go!"

She went.

Najah's mare flew across the field. Her legs reached out before her and her hooves dug into the earth. The gallop was a delicate seat. All four hooves left the ground at one point before the back hooves landed and carried them forward. It was a matter of riding out each footfall, of joining body and soul with the creature between her legs and trusting that she knew where to go.

John was shouting orders behind her. The Trents kept advancing. His men wouldn't know where to go. They were going to be flanked. Bullets hailed down upon John's forces. Kera could hear their screams as their souls reenacted deaths long since set in stone. John shouted a command, something about a pincer, and only moments later, he shouted his frustration. The formation never completed itself, and it never would.

"On your right!" Aurora screamed. Kera looked to her side. Two Trent horses were attempting to intercept her. She jerked on her reins, one arm steadying Aiden as she dug her heels into her mare's body. The mare startled and jolted, turning hard to avoid getting cut off, but still struggling to find an opening.

They were not trying to shoot her, not yet, but she could see the guns and the swords. Steel flashed in the moonlight, and she kicked her mare again in an attempt to just get her to go *faster*. Unlike Holly, this mare wasn't used to battle conditions. She was flailing her head in startled terror, and it took everything in Kera's body to keep her steady and on point.

One of the soldiers rode up alongside her, trying to pull her reins from her hand, but Kera removed her foot from her stirrup and kicked the other rider's horse in the rump. It bucked. Kera threw herself forward to avoid getting a hoof in her face, and the other rider sailed from his saddle. Another rider came alongside, but when she went to deliver the same punishment, she stopped. John was already there. He'd slashed his sword through the man's body, disintegrating him into a scatter of blue blood as the long-dead steed galloped riderless into the woods.

Kera was breathing hard, but John was gasping far worse. There was blood splattered on his face, though she couldn't tell whose it was. "Ride!" he shouted at her, and she did. She forced her mare to keep moving, and John abandoned his losing battle just to make sure she and her child survived the melee.

She couldn't hear the rest of his men. *Are they already dead?*

Another shot sounded through the air, a loud volley that had her ducking over Aiden. John cried out, and for a moment, he sounded like Mori. His horse slowed. Another volley cracked through the night.

Twisting about, her heart skipped a beat. John was leaning over his horse's neck, bleeding with one hand pressed to his chest. The other was struggling to maintain a grip on his reins. He looked up to her, tears in his eyes. He was a *child.* He was a child and he was terrified. He was terrified of what was going to happen, even though they both knew it was a fact now. There was no stopping this.

Kera reached Aurora. They could disappear into the night, leaving the death march behind. Another bullet struck John in the back. His horse let out a mighty scream and it collapsed. John was thrown. Long limbs rolled across the ground like a ball of yarn. Curled up to start with, then unraveling faster and faster until it sprawled in a long line of wrinkles in the dirt. Except, even when he landed . . . he didn't stay still. He was trying to push himself up, struggling to draw his knees underneath him. He choked on his air.

"We need to go," Aurora told Kera. She said it gently. Kindly. The most caring she had sounded since they met John hours ago.

But John was shaking now. There was blood streaming down his face. His bushy brown hair was stained black. He stumbled and fell, legs refusing to carry his weight. He tried to rise again, but couldn't manage the task. He crashed back to the ground and lay there trembling.

"Take Aiden," Kera whispered.

"What?"

Kera was already moving. Already dismounting and pushing her reins into Aurora's hand. "No, no— What are you—*Kera!*" Aurora couldn't hold Faith, maintain Kera's mare with Aiden still on her back, and chase Kera at the same time. She was pinned down, only capable of riding forward and nowhere else.

It was cruel to force Aurora's hand, but Kera didn't have time to wait, nor did she consider it an option. If she waited, if she analyzed, if she thought this through, she knew it wouldn't make sense. But it wasn't a matter of making sense. It was a matter of caring, and caring didn't require thought. It only required action.

John had told her to run, and Kera ran. She ran to him. She thought she heard Faith call her name. She thought Aiden screamed, "Mama!" as loud as he could. Still, she ran to John's side and didn't question her choice. She slid to a stop by his crumpled form. She wrapped an arm around his back and pulled his own arm over her shoulder. She lifted him as best she could and he stumbled, legs weak beneath him. She didn't dare count wounds, though she could see them peppered along his body. He was going to die whether she helped him or not, but she refused to leave him to die alone on this field while she rode off.

His last sight would not be her abandoning him.

"Come on," she told John, pulling him with her. "Come on, come on!" John gasped for air. He pressed down on her shoulders and his legs dragged. His weight made her back scream in agony once more, but she pushed it to the side. She couldn't concentrate on it. She needed to get him moving. She dragged him when his feet failed, pulling him as far away from the battlefield as ethereal armies shot guns she couldn't even see. She dragged him to the safety of the wood where Aurora was watching them with horrified eyes. They would be safe in the tree line.

More shots fired.

John screamed. He jerked in her grasp, legs going limp beneath him. He fell, and his weight pulled her down into the dirt. Her muscles howled, but she didn't care. She put her hands on either side of his body and heaved. His blue coat was stained purple, and the white lining was now dark red.

Trent voices called for another volley, and John's hand snatched her around her collar. He jerked her down to the ground, and seemed to find one last burst of strength in order to bracket her beneath his body. She couldn't fathom how many times he'd been struck by now, but pain lined his young face.

Sweat, blood, snot, and tears mixed together and marred the angelic curves of his cheekbones and nose. He was breathing in hitching gasps. His arms gave out and he fell, lying over her in a heavy mass.

Kera struggled to escape his weight and turn him over. She glanced all around for the soldiers that were firing at them, fully intending to kill John—to kill *them*. John was still alive. Awake. Alive. *It didn't matter what he was.* He stared at her, mouth trembling around words he couldn't speak. She cupped his face. "You're going to be all right," she promised him.

He had the audacity to smile, to somehow manage a hitched laugh on his next inhale before his face twisted in agony and he coughed around a mouthful of blood. "No . . .You—you—you need to go," he gasped.

"Soon, soon, I promise. But I can't leave you." She just *couldn't* do it. It was a simple truth. Even knowing he was going to die, even knowing that he'd lost everything that made up who he was, she couldn't leave him.

Her greatest failing in the world was that if someone was in pain, she couldn't leave them to suffer it alone. She couldn't allow them to pass on without knowing they were loved. She hadn't been able to leave her husband and firstborn, despite the anger and hysteria she'd felt surrounding their deaths. She hadn't been able to leave Rachel when she was washing her laundry in Doleystown, a simple ghost that didn't know how to cross over. And she couldn't leave John now.

He was just a frightened boy, who'd only wanted to go home, to study beasts, and live near his friends. He wanted to meet his daughter and share a world he cherished with her. He wanted to live a life he would never live, and this wasn't fair. Nothing about this was fair. And even if she'd known nothing at all about him, she couldn't leave him alone.

"T-tell Mor-Morpheus I'm—I'm sorry?" John asked her. Tears pressing against her eyes.

"Tell him yourself," she whispered. He stared at her, broken face breaking just a little more. He was blurring. Tears fell from her eyes and she lost sight of him for a moment as she squeezed her eyes shut against the pain. "Mori died, John . . . He's waiting for you on the other side."

And he would keep waiting for his loved ones. He would keep waiting for them to join him, because he'd willfully chosen to die in a duel. John Sarren had died wanting to live more than anything else in the world, and Mori had decided it no longer mattered.

Mori was going to be waiting the rest of their lives for them. But . . . he shouldn't have to wait for John. He had already waited long enough. "I'll show your daughter the griffons," Kera promised. There was another command to line up. Kera didn't know where the soldiers were, which way the guns would be fired from. "I'll show her your book." John smiled at her, blood streaming from his lips. It was gruesome and awful. His eyes slid to the left, and then he blinked. Hard. Like he was trying to focus on something important. His mouth opened a bit more. His left hand rose, reaching past her, almost . . . yearning. He whispered one word: "Mor . . . pheus?"

And Kera's breath caught in her throat. "*Kera!*" Aurora shouted. Kera was turning to follow John's line of sight. There was something there, a light just out of view. She was starting to see it take shape when—

"*Fire!*"

Something sharp tore through her throat.

Blood filled her mouth.

Her head snapped back and she crumbled to her side. She couldn't breathe. She couldn't see. Everything was dark around her. Her back pulsated. She was going to die. She knew that more than she had ever known anything else in life.

Cold fingered wrapped around her neck. It was useless. There was no stopping this. There was no—

"You know your own heart. Your choices have always been your own. My beloved Kera, I wish you all the happiness in the world." John's voice echoed like a thought in her head. There but not there. A fantasy that she created out of nothingness. She did not know where it came from or how it entered her body, but she accepted it as truth.

Kera blinked hard and just managed to see his face in eerie incandescent blue. He smiled, bloodstained and covered in gore. His hand tightened on her throat, and the cold palm warmed. Warmed more and more, until it seared like a brand around her flesh.

She didn't notice the pain or anything except what was directly in front of her.

Instead, she stared at John's face. Watching as his eyes fluttered. He smiled as he died. His body slipped from focus, and he flickered out like a light at the end of a wick. Candle shimmering... shimmering... shimmering...

Gone.

Silence fell over the wood. John disappeared, and with him, all of the Trent and Absalonian comrades. There was no sign that they'd even been there to begin with. Kera stared at the place where John had been. Her throat no longer bled. She no longer felt her lungs choking her into oblivion.

She heard Aurora rushing toward her. Hooves echoing like drums in her head. Aurora reached her side. She called her name, but something inside Kera felt certain that Aurora didn't have to rush. Crystals or no, Kera *knew*, for the rest of the night, they would be undisturbed.

CHAPTER
TWENTY-THREE

K era's body didn't hurt. Her back didn't twinge. Her ribs no longer twinged on each breath. Her feet weren't uncomfortable. Her throat—she lifted a hand to the wound she *knew* she'd acquired—had healed and smoothed over. The scar set flush with her skin, barely raised at all. She traced the phantom edges for several moments.

Aurora was there before she could fully take stock. Hand on her shoulder, voice slashing between her ears saying, "I thought you were dead." Kera winced. She sat up slowly, and found that she felt . . . good. Very good. The horses were nearby, and Kera almost suggested leaving now and continuing their journey. She didn't know what else she could say. She stood, fingers still following the line of her scar, and thought.

A bullet *had* gone through her. She could still taste the blood in her mouth. Speaking of . . . she spat, watching as it globbed and settled on the dirt. John's face had been almost unrecognizable beneath her when she washed his skin with her blood.

Then she remembered. He had said *Morpheus*. His eyes had looked past her shoulder. He had reached for something, *someone*, that she'd never gotten a chance to see. He had tried to grasp what she'd never been able to grasp. Her husband had been there. She didn't doubt it. Somehow, in some form, perhaps only as a gatekeeper for those crossing over, her husband had been there. John had seen him.

And John's final act on earth had been to give her the last token of energy he had remaining. He'd healed her in exchange for . . . what? Kera looked back to the field. It was quiet now. But . . . it was a natural quiet. Bugs chirped and fluttered about. Life went on as it had always been.

John wasn't coming back. She knew it like she knew her own name. Even though there were countless reasons why it should have been impossible, she *knew*. He'd found his peace somehow, and taken the whole of the death march with him. The cycle was broken.

And Mori . . . if he had truly been there, if he had truly seen everything and watched John's final moments, if he had *truly* been there to carry John to the other side . . . he'd had his opportunity for her to join him. She would have died in scant few minutes. And yet.

And yet.

John had healed her. Wished her all the happiness in the world. Mori had told her that. The day he'd given her the locket. He'd given her those words, and she'd believed him. Believed that he was going to give her happiness from that moment onward.

Happiness, she discovered, wasn't something her husband was ever capable of giving to her. It wasn't something *anyone* could give her. It was something that she needed to farm and cultivate on her own. Something that she needed to look for within herself in order to bring it out to the surface. And while people could *influence* her happiness, they couldn't provide it to her ready-made. She couldn't place all her dreams in one person and think it would turn out well.

"My beloved Kera, I wish you all the happiness in the world."

"It's what he said when . . ." she trailed off, reaching for her locket. It was cool against her palm. Cool and perfect. John couldn't have known . . . he *couldn't* have known . . . "Moving on . . . it's . . . it's moving on."

"What are you *talking* about? Do you not understand that you could have died? That we thought you were dead? That your *son* just watched—he watched you fall, Kera. He's a child. A baby. And he watched you fall."

Kera turned to look back at the horses. The children were both still on them, but Faith was holding Aiden steady. Hitched sobs were lifting up through the air, waging their own war against the euphoria that was building up within Kera's body. She pressed her hands to her eyes, trying to shake free from the surging rise of emotion, trying to clear her thoughts.

But all she saw, all her mind was willing to accept, was the simple fact that John couldn't have known how to speak those words, nor what they meant to her. Najah's concern had been entirely justified. She'd been worried for Aurora's *and* Kera's sake. That they were falling into something without considering the consequences. And with no one but the children and Aurora to talk to, Kera had had no one else in the world to work through the complexities of the feelings growing within her body. And yet, hearing Mori's words repeated back at her . . . hearing the message he no doubt knew she'd receive and understand . . . it felt like peace.

It felt like permission and acceptance and encouragement all in one. It felt like an apology and a prayer. Be happy, take all the time you need, trust yourself.

Trust yourself.

It had been far too long since anyone had suggested she trust herself. To have *faith* in herself. But when she closed her eyes and thought of what the future would bring, she trusted the peace she'd felt at Zakaria's grave. She trusted the acceptance she'd felt while holding Aurora close. She trusted the strength Aurora made her feel. She felt *powerful*. She felt *free*. The shackle of misery had uncuffed itself from her ankle. The drudging gloom and the hysteria that had been burning her soul for over a year had both been snuffed out by the reminder that she was strong on her own, and that new support structures could be built around the charred remains of her first love.

No more crying, she thought.

She leaned forward and pressed her lips to Aurora's. The younger woman froze, blinking warily the longer the kiss went on. But when Kera pulled back, she leaned forward, as if chasing the feeling that was being taken away.

"I'm sorry I frightened you," Kera said, lifting her hand to cup Aurora's face.

"It's not just me you need to apologize to," Aurora mumbled, flushing deep even as she cupped Kera's hand to her cheek. "It's them too. Your son too."

"I know. I know, I will. I promise."

"You went back to save a *dead man* from *dying*," Aurora accused. She squeezed her fingers around Kera's. She spoke the truth, there was no denying it, and yet Kera couldn't think of John as a dead man.

"He didn't know he was dead," she explained, letting her arm fall and twisting her wrist so she could hold Aurora's hand properly. Emotions bled from Aurora's face and it was *refreshing*. It was so refreshing to see someone's feelings without trying to navigate through a complicated backstory. Aurora's feelings weren't hidden behind a mask, nor obfuscated by pretty words or endless prose. Aurora had always said what she meant, and she always looked as she felt.

It was everything Kera had ever wanted, to *know* what existed in someone's heart. To not be lied to or be led astray. She wanted reality and truth, she wanted consistency and understanding she could depend on. Aurora was worried for her. Worried for *her*! "It was not my intention to hurt you," she said, trying not to sound too elated.

"I don't *care*!" Aurora yelled. "Don't you understand you could have died?"

"Yes." She had known that from the start. But death hadn't frightened her as much as the idea of that boy spending his final moments alive believing he was abandoned. "I trusted you to take care of Aiden—"

"*Kera, your son wants you.* He wants *you*, not me. And what am I going to tell him when you're not there? When you aren't able to help him, to look after him? He's your son." The words struck true, and Kera saw it now.

She'd made a choice and hadn't thought about the consequences. She'd believed in something so much, she'd been willing to give her life for it, even if it *was* an impulsive decision. Perhaps she was more like her husband than she thought. "I just wanted John to be free," she explained. "I wanted him to be at rest. He *deserves* to rest."

"Yes, he does. But doing it like you did? You could have gotten yourself *killed*. And fine, you like talking to ghosts. I can't stop you from talking to ghosts. I have no idea *why* it's something you like doing, but whatever you want. But *think* about *how* you're talking to ghosts, gods above. Don't you understand how dangerous that was?"

Aurora's hand moved to press against Kera's throat. It cupped the scar that had no business being healed, but was nonetheless. Her palm was warm, and Kera closed her eyes so she could lean more into the pleasant touch. Her skin tingled and her heart fluttered. She knew she was supposed to be contrite and feel bad, but she was just too happy to bother.

John was at rest. Mori was with him. And in that final exchange, any doubts Najah's concern had inspired felt like they'd been laid at the wayside. She did love her husband, she always would, but that didn't detract from feeling a wholly different love for someone else. She deserved a life without him. She was allowed to move on, and not even *he* would blame her for it.

She wanted another kiss, and so she took it. Aurora was startled, but looped her arms around Kera's body anyway, holding her gently as Kera apologized once more. "I'm sorry I frightened you."

"Why are you so . . ." Aurora trailed off. From their positions, Kera couldn't tell what expression her face was making, but she had a suspicion.

"When John saved my life—"

"You mean after you got yourself shot going back to sit with a dead man?"

"Yes, *after that.*" Kera sighed, refusing to be cowed. "Have you ever prayed for something? Wanted it so bad that it didn't matter in what form it came, you'd take it?"

Aurora stepped back and turned away. Tension slipped up and down her muscles. Her teeth were grinding hard enough that Kera could hear them pop along the back molars.

Kera waited, letting Aurora search for the words she wanted to use. "My divorce," she said at long last. "I wanted to be free of Jacob."

Aurora's fingers curled into fists. She stood, rigid and straight, tall and imposing like the trees at her back. Kera placed her hand on Aurora's. She cradled Aurora's fist as gently as she could manage, and said: "I wanted to stop hurting." Aurora flinched as though Kera had struck at her, and Kera's hands held her fist even more firm. "Ever since my husband died," Kera continued, "*he* has been my existence. *Him.* My world came to a standstill because of *him.* My name was taken from me, my home, my agency. Everything about my life began and ended with *him.*"

"The Travers family bankers are still taking your home from you," Aurora reminded. "John's death hasn't miraculously fixed that."

No. It hadn't. But— "I will deal with the Traverses soon enough. Ciara is keeping my home safe until I return to manage it on my own."

"You're still the Widow Montgomery."

"Yes," she said simply. "I am."

"And you're . . . okay with this because you went back to hold John Sarren's ghost while he died?"

"I decided this when John Sarren saw Mori on the field, and when he *quoted Mori's vows to me.*" Aurora's eyes widened. "John never attended our wedding. He had no reason to *know* what Mori said, but he said the words anyway. 'My beloved Kera, I wish you all the happiness in the world,' and he said . . . he told me to trust my heart. And no—I never needed his *permission* to feel better, but gods damn it, it doesn't hurt to know that at the end of all this I'm not betraying someone I love when I choose to move on!"

"Did you see him?" She almost seemed scared to ask. She'd gone shaky, nervous in the way ghosts always made her uncertain.

"No," Kera said firmly. "And . . . strangely? I'm glad I didn't. Mori's my past . . . He will always be a part of who I am today. But he's gone. He's gone." She took a deep breath, rallying herself for the end. "I told you at the general's grave I was going to take a long time to die just to spite him, but you know as well as I do how exhausting spite can be. At least with this . . . I can still honor my husband's memory . . . still cherish him as my best friend . . . and still find a way to be happy without him."

Aurora's hand squeezed tight around hers. Her precious face still looked uncertain. But when she'd finished swallowing loud enough for Kera to hear, she said, "Maybe you *should* spend more time with ghosts," with a great deal more strength than Kera could have possibly anticipated.

Kera laughed like John. Free and uncaring. *Good.* She ran a hand through her hair, tucking her bangs out of her eyes. She wanted to get moving. She wanted to reach the griffons. She wanted to prove that she *could* do this. The doubts fell by the wayside and she felt stronger than she had in ages. Her foundation was no longer made of sand. She could do this.

Aurora caught her hand as she went to approach Aiden. Kera never noticed before, but their palms were the perfect size to hold each other with ease. "Just . . ." Aurora took a deep breath. "Just remember that there are people who care about you, Kera. Just remember that when you ride off to face the revelations of your circumstances . . . there are other people in the world who are left behind that aren't just your children."

"I'm sorry," Kera said again.

"I care about you, Lady Montgomery. And at the end of the day . . . it's *you* I want to spend time with. Not the memory of you. Not the dreams of the times we had together. Not the future that I'd face without you. I just want to know *you* more. So . . . if it pleases you . . . try to be a bit more careful next time?"

It was a promise that Kera had every intention on keeping. *Squeeze and release.* She kissed Aurora's cheek. "I promise. Now. Let's go save our children."

There was work to be done.

CHAPTER TWENTY-FOUR

Faith took Kera's apology well. She seemed more than a little shaken by Kera's risk, but when she confirmed for herself that Kera was in good health, she accepted Kera's account and just hugged her in return. Aiden was different.

"I'm sorry, dear. I am. Please, look at me?"

The boy clung to her, sobbing through hitching breaths he couldn't afford to lose, shivering the whole while. "I thought you were gone . . . gone like Daddy and . . ."

"No," Kera swore. "No I'm not going to go like Daddy. I promise." He coughed long and hard against her chest, shaking violently within her grasp. "We're almost done, dear. We're almost done. But I promise . . . I'm not going to leave you like him. Not if I can help it."

After mounting her horse, she squeezed him close.

"You sure you're ready?" Aurora asked.

"More than," Kera said. Aurora's map made it seem like they were almost on top of the first lake, and with each step forward Kera expected to see sparkling brown water. She urged her horse forward, desperate impatience spurring her on.

John had spoken of the griffons as though they were the most majestic and wonderful creatures in existence. He'd been fond enough to continue traveling to visit them and to take the time to edit Mori's book the way he had. He had both praised the beasts and cautioned Mori against future stupidity. Kera couldn't help but wonder what they looked like in reality, and if John's drawings were as accurate as she believed them to be. Would she see one that John had seen as a child? She knew that griffon lifetimes dwarfed those of humans. John's notes made it clear that they could live hundreds of years.

Hundreds of years of life seemed almost impossible to imagine. It was far beyond anything she would ever want for herself. "Imagine what they've seen," she mused.

"The griffons?" Aiden asked, squirming in his seat.

"Four hundred years ago, Trent hadn't invaded Absalon. Our ancestors were free, and now we are again! Things have changed quite a bit since then, I'd say."

"And they'll keep changing," Aurora agreed. "It's the one thing in the world that *doesn't* change, the . . . con-con . . . *idea* that the world will *always* change."

"'Concept'?" Kera offered.

Aurora nodded and thanked her. "Yes, concept."

The arc of a life always follows the same pattern. Seventy years, eighty—it seemed more than enough time to accomplish such goals. And yet . . . griffons lived so much longer than that. They saw the world move about and continue on a mad quest to hurry faster and faster from place to place. They saw humanity racing to the finish line while they took their time. They waited.

Humanity must seem so petty to griffons. So inconsequential.

Kera continued musing even as they drew closer. Letting her mind wander as one arm hugged Aiden to her chest. She stroked his side with her fingers, soothing and calming him as his breath hitched and he mewled in response. His fever burned hotter today than it had all trip. His face was already flushed bright. She'd been trying to get him to drink more water, but he started turning it away, mouth refusing to swallow.

As elated as she'd been since John's death march ended, it didn't overshadow everything. She was aware of her situation, but capable of balancing the feelings that combated one another. Hope, Kera reasoned, was her last stand at the moment.

There was no logic in this journey. There was only hope. Hope and the stubbornness to believe that the griffons could and *would* help. John believed in them, and Najah did too, even if no one else did.

They strode forward, and Kera *felt* it when they crossed into the griffons' territory. Aurora did too. Both horses came to a quick stop, and Kera stared. She half expected the great creatures to land before them just like that.

They didn't.

In fact, nothing changed at all about their surroundings. They still couldn't see the lakes. They still couldn't see any signs of the creatures. There were no scratch marks on trees. No feathers lining the ground. No paw prints offset by bird claws. There was nothing at all except a feeling.

The air *felt* cooler here. The sounds of the woods *seemed* lighter. There was a sparking sensation of nerves crawling about underneath Kera's skin. The ants returned, skittering beneath her flesh. Nipping at her joints. Her hair stood on end, and even Aurora's curls seemed far more frizzy than normal. They sprung from her scalp like a lion's mane, making her all the more courageous in appearance. The summer heat smelt like a lightning storm, even though the sky remained a joyous bright blue and the sun still shone up above.

Kera could *taste* the change on her tongue. Her mouth filled with an almost citrusy sweet flavor. She closed her eyes and imagined suckling on the nectar of a lost fruit, burying herself in the juices and lapping at the folds of its skin. She was burning with desire, and she squeezed her hand around her reins, needing to blink a few times in order to keep her mind moving forward.

She urged her horse forward, and the mare went with ease. The horse seemed almost eager to walk, as if even *her* concern had evaporated. They traveled another hundred yards or so, and then— there was water on the horizon.

Aurora's breath caught. "Kera—"

"I see it." It was a breathless response, and both of them encouraged the horses faster. Hurry, hurry, hurry. They flew through the last of the woods, cutting around the trees and over fallen logs.

Finally, they had reached the first of the Long Lakes.

And they were beautiful.

Though Kera had lived next to the ocean most of her life, she felt overcome by the glittering water and the bright, clear sky above. Unlike the thick murky green of the ocean, this water was crystalline blue. It wasn't what she'd been expecting. It was so much more.

Blue like the fables of the old Mer Sea, where even sailors feared to go, and so clear she could see all the way to the bottom. She could see the fish swimming. There were turtles walking on the shore. A beaver was paddling along toward the center of the lake, unbothered by their appearance. The ground beneath them shifted from a thick forest undergrowth to creamy rich sands. Kera slid off her horse; her feet sank into the soft earth and it felt *wonderful*.

She pulled her son down and held him to her body. She approached the water and knelt by the shore, lowering him so his fevered skin could touch the lapping waves. He shifted in her arms, squirming so he could get a good look at the water. Aiden reached for it and she eased him closer, watching as his fingers sank beneath the surface. He giggled a touch, raising his fever-bright eyes to look at her face. *Perfection.*

Kera tilted her head up, but there was no great flap of wings in the sky. There was no sign of a half-lion, half-eagle creature diving through clouds or soaring over treetops. As far as the woods were concerned, there was nothing here but silence. Silence and the strange, *beautiful* lake. Narrow enough that she could see both sides of it at once, but stretching out so far that she couldn't see its end. It went on for miles. She tried to imagine *miles* of crystal-blue water and picturesque serenity.

"We should keep looking," Aurora said, and Kera agreed. She filled their canteens, then climbed back on her horse with Aiden. They followed the shoreline, looking in every direction for a sign that they had come to the right place.

Hours passed.

There was no sign.

By the time night arrived, Kera couldn't help but wonder if this was how Aurora used to feel when she would stare into windows and watch the wealthy dancing inside. She could see what she wanted, it was right before her, but she couldn't grasp it. She couldn't reach the peace and joy and happiness that were just standing there out of touch.

Maybe we're cursed . . .

They settled for the evening, preparing their circle and pulling their saddles from their horses. Even as darkness descended around them, there were no ghosts here. There were no death marches or wraiths. The woods were silent.

They were quieter, even, than Mount Maladh with all its insulated walls. It felt almost unnatural after so long on the road. Unnatural, but pleasant and safe. Safe enough that Kera managed to convince Aurora to get some rest. She could keep first watch. She wasn't even tired. Tension had taken over her body. Each muscle was locked in and held firm. Breathing was a chore. The children were exhausted and sleeping in moments, but the mere thought of shutting her eyes and missing something sent pinpricks down Kera's spine.

"You've been strange since the march," Aurora said.

"I'm fine." Kera kissed Aurora's brow and tucked the younger woman to her side. It felt natural. Like an extension of herself. "Get some rest."

The griffons had to be here. They had to be. They couldn't have come this far to be let down.

Aurora nodded against her breast, and fell asleep.

The moon cast a pleasant light over them.

It was ghostly white, illuminating the ground so it sparkled. Luminescent insects glowed as they buzzed about the air. They looked like fairies, and Kera rather hoped they *weren't*, because if Aurora hated ghosts, she would hate fairies.

At one point or another, Kera shifted and helped lower Aurora so she was curled up next to Faith on the ground. Then she checked on Aiden. His skin still burned hot beneath her touch. He'd lost even more weight since they'd left Mount Maladh. His cheeks, once coated in a soft layer of baby fat, now had skin stretched tight around his bones. She could feel his ribs on his chest. His flesh was paper thin.

"We're going to find the griffons," Kera told her sleeping child. "They're here somewhere. We're not leaving until we find them, and save you both." They'd come so far. There had to be something here. Even if she hadn't seen it yet, she *knew*. The gods weren't cruel enough to make them fail now.

Gritting her teeth, she wrapped Najah's blankets tighter around him, then checked on Faith at his side. The teenager was twitching in her sleep, kicking like she was trying to run away. Her body was whip thin, her clothes draping over her so much they seemed to sag. Kera ran a hand through Faith's hair, hoping to soothe her, but her fingers snagged as they did. And, to her horror, when she pulled her hand back, a tight clump of hair came with it. Nausea bubbled up Kera's throat. Pushing backward, she threw herself to her feet.

Tears pressed against her eyes, and she walked to the outer rim of their circle, desperately trying to dislodge Faith's curls from her fingers. Faith hadn't even woken when her hair came free. She'd just moaned piteously and jerked and twitched, eyelids fluttering as if she were battling some nightmarish fiend trapped within her mind.

The nausea swam up Kera's throat. She coughed, gagging as anxiety teetered into hysteria. They needed to find the griffons. They *had* to find the griffons. Neither child would last much longer. Faith least of all.

Swallowing again and again, Kera barely managed to keep the sick within her body. She couldn't look back at the kids, too scared that if she did, one would be dead and they really would have been here too late.

Something shuffled in the trees. Kera's head snapped toward it in an instant. She couldn't see anything in the dark, but she cast her ears outward in hopes of picking up the size and location of the creature. The rustling continued, steadily, *rhythmically*. An unnaturally perfect beat that sounded like the soft roll of a drum. Kera walked to the edge of their fire line, and peered out into the gloom.

The rustling continued but her ears identified the sound. Footfalls. There were footfalls in the woods, and each one resonated with a deep bass from the hollow of the earth. Kera's heart sped in response, a snare echoing the bass but driving it faster at the same time. The measure reached the end of its line and it looped about endlessly. There was no rest, no pause to catch a breath, just an endless repeat as the phrase played twenty notes in fast succession, each one louder than the one that came before. It built in a crescendo in her head, but Aurora slept on and the children didn't stir. The woods stayed quiet, and the cacophony was hers alone. But it was impossible to ignore. It drowned the sound of everything else around her. The tide whooshed along in tandem. *Follow it.*

There was a shape in the darkness. Massive. Tall. It walked forward with slow steps. A shadow navigating the underbrush. The bass drum kept on, like a metronome guiding her heart. She counted the beats. One, two, three, four, five, six, one, two, three, four, five, six.

Follow it, follow it, follow it.

It was not a wraith. Something tall spread off the back of the shadow, but it wasn't a shroud. Kera stepped forward. Her toes edged the fire line. She felt it warming her body and licking against her skin. Wings. Those were *wings*.

Kera crossed over the line.

The flames traced up her legs, but she wasn't burnt. She walked without pause, following the figure as it slipped through the trees. Its front was held high and noble; the back swished and swayed with each padding step.

It moved leisurely, emerging from the woods and following the lines of the lake with a kind of grace that Kera had never seen in another animal. John was right. *Beast* seemed like the wrong word. It was too beautiful to be called a *beast*.

Follow it, follow it, follow it.

A massive tail swished from the left to the right with each step forward. Its wings were folded along its spine. Together, she and the griffon walked farther from the camp. The occasional feather slipped from the wings and fluttered to the ground. Kera saw slight bits of hardness left behind on the soft sand beneath her feet. Shavings from the talons? Her heart clenched in her chest. Her fingers twitched at her sides, but she didn't stop. Couldn't. They weren't given freely. Even as castoffs, they weren't hers to take.

She followed it until the griffon stopped. It turned toward the lake and folded its front legs to kneel at the waterside. It lapped a few sips from the lake. Kera's breath caught in her throat, wheezing out a noise she hadn't meant to make. It was an accidental slide of a bow over strings, a squeaking screeching *thing* that couldn't be described as anything except utterly off-key.

The griffon's head rose. Its front legs unfolded and it stood. It turned toward her, great wings spreading and arching so that the whole span could be seen from the crest of the arch down to the end of its primary and secondary feathers. The face was more owl than eagle, with wide piercing eyes, though its body was certainly feline.

The griffon sat, letting its rump plop to the ground with a noisy thud. Its tail curled around its talons, and it looked Kera straight in the eye. "Welcome, Lady Montgomery. We've been waiting for you."

CHAPTER
TWENTY-FIVE

All things considered, Kera was grateful that she *knew* griffons could speak before today. Not that she had *believed* John, but it helped. She managed to bite her tongue in time to keep from proclaiming, *You can talk!* in all its rude and affronting glory. Instead, she stared at the griffon and felt as though the breath was knocked from her lungs, and she wanted nothing more than to organize her mind into compartments that made some semblance of sense, but nothing was working and her mind was a mess and—

"You should breathe," she was advised.

Yes. Breathing was important.

Open mouth. Expand lungs. Hold for at least five seconds. Let it out. She felt dizzy, but the breathing was helping. Good. At least . . . griffons were polite? This one was, in any case. Kera didn't think it was a good practice to make an assumption on an entire species off the representation of one griffon—that was an unrealistic sample. Besides being bad science, it was also rude. Aurora would tell her she was being rude. She would be right too.

Still.

This one was making a good impression.

"You can relax," she was instructed. And just *how* was the griffon speaking? Exactly? Because its—*Hers? The voice sounded feminine?*—beak wasn't moving and it/she was still sitting there and—and— "We can hear your thoughts," the griffon told her.

And John *clearly* missed that in his research, because Kera felt *very* ill-prepared indeed. Also. The griffon was laughing at her now. There were clicking chuckles filling Kera's mind, and the griffon's shoulders were shaking. The wings were fluffing out. Its eyes squinted, feathers puffing as the beak opened just a touch.

"In his defense," the griffon told her. "He *was* a child when we met."

"You're the same one," Kera gasped. She felt dull and dim-witted. Everything was rushing about in her head, and if it was true that the griffon *could* hear her thoughts, then the beast must know how rude she was being. But if this griffon was the same one that John knew—

"We are." Oh. Kera was staring again. "Our name is Raslidor . . . and you may consider us whatever gender you wish. We are not constrained." Kera had no idea what that meant, but she nodded anyway. "Welcome to our home."

"Our . . . we?" Kera looked around, but she saw no other griffons. Raslidor stood. She—no . . . Raslidor kept saying *we* so . . . they?— walked toward Kera, and Kera kept still and did her best not to flinch. She didn't even feel her muscles tightening from fear or stress. The moon shone down around them, and Kera dedicated herself to memorizing the griffon's appearance.

Raslidor's feathers were a tawny brown, dappled with black flecks that grew more pervasive around their face. There was a narrow ring of white feathers around Raslidor's eyes that framed and accented the glowing yellow of their irises with sharp acuity. A lighter brown dipped off from the corners, followed by darker hues that skittered like pepper grains down their body. Their beak curved low in front of their face. It was black, hooked, and savage. Yet Raslidor's face didn't hold even a trace of violence or potential will to attack. Their body language remained neutral.

The tufts of feathers that curved like ears off the top of their head were various shades of brown. The feline hindquarters slid into the avian front with tufts of fluff that seemed to be . . . everywhere. Kera couldn't tell where the feathers ended and the fur began, but the process seemed gradual. Her examination led her eyes toward a curled tail that was far fluffier than Kera had imagined, less *lion* and more . . . house cat. While well-groomed, the tail was perhaps the most surprising part of the whole appearance.

"We are one," Raslidor said. "All of us, all of our kind. We are one. We share one thought. We speak one language. We listen to one voice."

"You mate for life," Kera offered up, flushing as she realized how inappropriate it was to say. But she didn't know what else to add.

She couldn't help but stumble about in a desperate attempt to show she had at least *some* intelligence. She felt so insignificant in front of Raslidor.

But Raslidor didn't seem offended, and instead nodded their great head. "Physically we mate with one of ourselves, but our souls and minds share many partners. We are never alone. We never wish to be alone. We are one. Our children and our families are ourselves."

John had either been too young to understand, or had willfully left such complexities from the book. His drawings had been far more accurate than his reporting of their social structure. "He was a good boy," Raslidor told Kera. "We were sorry to see him go."

"You know he's dead?" Kera asked. She felt as though she were caught in the middle of a song. There was sheet music she could read just fine if the tempo stayed slow, but the metronome kept ticking faster and she wasn't skilled enough to keep up.

"We know everything."

Everything. How could one being know *everything*?

"The same way we know your thoughts. We listen. We think. We analyze and decide." Raslidor lowered their head. They pressed what Kera assumed was their brow against her hand. It took her a moment to respond, but she did. She lifted her fingers up and slid them through the feathers, letting them coil along the tufts and slide across the skull.

Each feather was soft, softer than any bird she'd ever felt. Slight edges of fur lined each feather, so fine that she couldn't see them on the smaller feathers. The larger ones were more obvious. Her fingertip traced an edge. Softer than a baby's skin, more gentle than any fabric. "We've been listening to you for a while," Raslidor continued. "Since you left home."

"How?" Kera asked, still stroking her hand through the down. Some of the feathers were crooked on top of each other. She fixed them, nudging them into place until they lay flat.

When Raslidor responded, their answer was no less vague. "We listened, and we waited." Perhaps there *was* no better explanation. Perhaps it was a paradigm Raslidor had no interest in elaborating on. "Your son and daughter are sick."

Faith was not her daughter. Kera said as much as she finished fixing the feathers. Her hands wanted to travel more, to keep feeling the amazing body beneath her touch. "Blood does not combine a family. We are not blood to many of our kin, but that does not mean we are not kin."

Kera let that thought circulate in her brain for a moment. Then, with a deep breath, she stepped back so she could meet Raslidor's eyes. "Can you help them?" she asked with all the hope in her heart. She trembled as she asked it. Adrenaline flooded her bloodstream and left her dizzy once the words took shape in the air.

"Yes."

It was almost too easy. "*Will* you help them?" Kera clarified, just to be certain. Raslidor's shoulders rose and fell with gentle jitters, their beak opened to make that strange clicking noise. They were laughing.

"Yes."

Too easy. The laughter paused. Raslidor's head tilted to the side, considering.

"Why?" Kera asked. If merely asking was all it took . . . then why did no one believe the griffons would help? Why had each person they'd met tried to turn them away?

It *couldn't* be as simple as asking.

Raslidor stretched out their legs. Their back arched, wings spreading as far as they would go. Sixteen feet? Twenty? Kera had never been good at judging distance before, and it was a greater span than what she imagined they would be.

She was almost disappointed when the wings folded back into their seated position, settling once more. Raslidor lifted their talons next, one by one like fingers rapping on a writing desk. They lifted up and curled down, squeezing sand beneath their claws. "We choose to help because of who you are."

Kera didn't understand. "The . . . Widow Montgomery?" *Lady* Montgomery was how Raslidor had greeted her, but the griffon shook their head and continued curling their talons into the sand.

"That is a name, a title, it is not who *you* are." Raslidor's voice was calming and gentle. It penetrated through Kera's skull with soft reassurances and pervasive intent. "You are many things, but you are not merely a name. You are not a Leona, not a Montgomery, you are you. And who *you* are is infinitely more important than what your name is. Just as *we* are more than our name."

"How do you know who I am?" Kera asked.

This time, when Raslidor sighed it was a whole-body affair. Their wings slid a little from their back. "We listened."

"You keep saying that—"

"You thought of us, in your home. When you held John's book. You thought of us." She didn't know it was *them*, though. She'd been thinking of griffons as a whole. She had done so their whole journey. She'd followed the paths that led her here, but she hadn't imagined Raslidor specifically. "It matters little," they told her. "We are one. And intent, Lady Montgomery, is everything."

Najah had said the same. She'd given them crystals and told them that the intent alone made them work. Only by gifting such an item with the intent to wish well could the gems protect them. "She was not wrong. Intent defines all life. Some thoughts are passing, some are meaningless, but intent . . . that is all that matters."

She wasn't sure what they were talking about any longer. She felt like she was lost at sea, and admitting it made her face burn from shame. "I don't understand," she mumbled, feeling more than a little stupid for not being able to work it out.

"When the humans came, at first they came to ask." Raslidor stepped back and walked toward the lake. Kera followed, each one of the griffon's steps equaling four of her own. She needed to sprint to catch up, feet fumbling in the sand. "They asked for our help. For our knowledge, and we provided. But we listened. We listened as they spoke of taking our gifts. Of selling our gifts. They would ask for our gifts and they would lie. They would not use them for the purposes they indicated. They were greedy. They were wrong."

Lowering their head into the water, Raslidor drank some more. Then they settled down, with their talons dipped into the wet. "When you left home, your thoughts and intent were always clear. You wished to save the life of your son, and later, your daughter."

"I thought I'd steal from you," Kera admitted.

"We know." Raslidor met her eyes, their yellow irises glowing bright under the moon. "But you did not. You followed for miles, watching as we walked. You did not stop to pick up the feathers we dropped. Did not stop to steal the nails we left in the sand. You followed. You may have thought of stealing what is ours, but your intent . . . your intent was different."

Startled, Kera looked back the way they'd come. She barely recognized her surroundings. She hadn't realized they'd gone so far. So curious had she been by Raslidor's demeanor.

Aurora would be furious when she found out. Kera had put herself and all of them at terrible risk, just so she could follow a griffon as it walked. She should have collected the feathers and talons, but instead, she hadn't even considered the danger or the terrible cost of her choice. She had just wanted to see what would happen.

"No . . . you don't think of the danger you're in. You've a remarkable talent for it." It sounded like an insult, but Raslidor laughed as they said it. Their good humor was very infectious. (Perhaps John had learned it from them.) For a creature that had lived hundreds of years, Kera wondered how they could find anything humorous, least of all someone like *Kera*. She flushed, embarrassed by her own poor abilities. Raslidor seemed rather chuffed either way. "Long ago, we decided to no longer involve ourselves with the affairs of the humans. We listened only for their intent, and we did not let them pass. Did not reveal ourselves should they be deemed unworthy.

"But you, Lady Montgomery. You've been strong from the start."

Strong? Kera shook her head. She tried to explain. No, she had been crying. She had been scared. She had made so many mistakes. She kept hurting Aurora time and again. She had become lost and confused. The night terrorized her until she jerked awake each night, body only sleeping when it was too exhausted to do anything else. She feared wraiths yet—

"Why does that not mean you are strong?"

"It doesn't sound brave."

"Yet, you are here, are you not? You have persevered. You have proven yourself. You've made your intent clear."

Raslidor's expression turned fond. It was a strange look for a bird. The beak couldn't change shape, but the eyes lessened in intensity.

The tufts on the top of their head were scooped down. "Rachel," Raslidor explained. "You helped see Rachel to the other side."

"You *know* about that?" Kera asked.

"We listened," Raslidor repeated. "We listened as you met a stranger on the road and you treated them with respect. We listened as you fought the wraiths and as Ms. Aurora showed no fear. We listened as you spoke with John Sarren and you gave our boy peace. Peace that not even his general could provide."

"*Zakaria—*" Kera cut herself off. She was not sure she even knew what she wanted to ask. The question died in her throat, but she stared at Raslidor until the griffon nodded, plucking her intent from her mind.

"Your general, Isra Zakaria, visited our boy often while he was still alive. He spoke to him many times, but never could he find the way to set him free or to give him his peace. You did what no other could do. You helped him go home." Raslidor stretched a wing toward Kera and used it to pull her closer with a slight nudge of their feathers. She let herself fall against Raslidor's body and be enveloped in a comfortable embrace. "You came to us to save your children. And we will save your children, because you have faced every trial, and you have persevered."

The information made her head spin. She tried to come to terms with all of it. Tried to put each moment into perspective, but the waters of her mind splashed onto a shore of nothingness. "I didn't know they were trials."

"Life consists of one trial after another. You will never know what the trials are for or when they will be judged, but each action you take is a trial in and of itself. You are here, and you are succeeding, because of who *you* are. No more. No less."

Tilting their head to the left, Raslidor tapped her with their wing once more. "Sit in front of our wings."

"What?"

"Your children ... Time is of the essence, don't you agree?" They squinted, and the feathers fluffed a little around their beak—like a smile, and Kera reached out. She placed one hand on Raslidor's neck, the other on the space between the wings, and with a careful hoist, she managed to climb up onto Raslidor's back.

Her legs hung over the griffon's shoulders. Her hands clutched against feathers she had just sorted through. She wasn't given time to adjust. Almost as soon as she was in position, Raslidor started to run. Three steps, four, kick! They were airborne and Kera *screamed.*

Wind whipped around her body, her hair flew in all directions. She held on for dear life and gaped at the sights before her. There was a gray sky above her, and ground below. The five lakes stretched out as far as she could see, with no obvious end in sight. The forest was a carpet of green so lush and vibrant she'd never seen anything like it.

Her heart fluttered faster and faster. She was flying. She was *flying*! Kera's mouth widened into a smile. The wind clawed at her face. Tears came to her eyes from the pressure alone, but she felt a sense of unrepentant *glee* bursting out from behind her ribs.

Raslidor landed far too soon for it to be all right. Kera wanted to keep flying. She wanted to stay up in the air and— Oh. Yes. She wanted to stay up in the air and avoid confronting Aurora, who was very much awake and staring at her as if she'd lost her mind. *I left her alone, asleep, and unprotected*, Kera realized as Raslidor landed in the fire ring. She needed to apologize. Again.

But not yet. Not now. Raslidor bent enough for Kera to slide off their back and return to solid ground. "I . . . I found the griffons?" Kera offered, as she met Aurora's dumbfounded expression.

There was a touch of hysteria on Aurora's face as she snatched Kera's arm. "Kera . . . when I told you that 'maybe you should spend some more time with ghosts,' I did *not* mean for you to take that as an active invitation to go riding on *griffons!*"

Raslidor's wings started shaking again, though they didn't produce the laughing sound that Kera had come to recognize. "Aurora, this is Raslidor," Kera introduced. "They said they'd help Aiden and Faith."

"Welcome to our home," Raslidor added politely and Aurora flinched. She stared at the griffon in numbed shock. "We have much to discuss," Raslidor continued. "But first . . . we'd like to see to the little ones."

Without pausing, the griffon lifted up one front leg and slammed it down on the ground. Two strips pulled off one of their longest talons. "Take them and grind them," Raslidor instructed, and Kera scooped them up. There was a rock nearby, not too big and just heavy enough.

Laying the strips out flat, Kera smashed them as hard as she could. It wasn't enough the first time, and so she smashed it again and again and again. She threw all of her energy into the process, eyes keeping track of any stray bits and moving them back into place.

When she had managed to crush them to dust, she looked up at Raslidor.

"Mix it with water, and allow them both to drink their fill."

Aurora fetched their canteen and brought it to Kera. She shook it thoroughly before shoving it back at Aurora.

"Give it to her," Kera told her.

"But Aiden—

"Her *hair* is failing out, Aiden can wait five seconds, *please*."

Tears filled Aurora's eyes as she mumbled out a thank-you before kneeling at her daughter's side and bringing Faith's head up to her lap.

Carefully, Aurora tipped the canteen over and encouraged her daughter to swallow mouthful after mouthful. Faith drank until the canteen was half gone and then Aurora passed the bottle to Kera for her to do the same for Aiden. They held their children while Raslidor watched over them.

Then, just as the sun peaked above the horizon and light began to stretch out across the land, Faith's and Aiden's intermittent shaking stopped, and together, their fevers broke at long last.

CHAPTER
TWENTY-SIX

The fire circle died out, unattended and unimportant. Raslidor lay with their wings folded along their back, as Kera and Aurora sat by their children's sides. Aiden's skin had started to take on a healthy color, a perfect mix of the bronze he inherited from his father and her smoother shades of brown. Kera watched the transition. She traced her fingers along her son's cheek, feeling the heat die beneath her touch. His breathing felt natural. No more hitching gasps. Each inhale long, deep, and *full*. And above all else, his body remained still. His limbs weren't shaking. He no longer mewled in his sleep, coughing and gagging around a lump tight in his throat. He was at peace.

Not far away, Faith was doing just as well. Aurora kept kissing her daughter's face, whispering quiet thank-yous to Raslidor over and over again. She started crying the moment Faith stopped shaking, and showed no signs of stopping anytime soon. Her gratitude was burning hot and bright, and Kera knew she would do anything Raslidor asked of her to show her appreciation. Raslidor told them they had done enough already; their debts had long since been paid.

Faith and Aiden slept now, but this time that sleep felt natural. It felt *healthy*, and no longer sliding down a slippery slope with death waiting for them at the bottom. Kera settled Aiden by Faith's side. He cuddled his head against her in his slumber. *Siblings*, Raslidor would have called them. She supposed after all this time they might as well be.

When she looked up at Aurora, she knew she didn't want to see Aurora leave now that their journey was over. Everything about the other woman was important to her. Even Aurora's accent had carved out a space in Kera's heart, rewriting her past discriminations until she found the sound charming. She wanted them all to go home and live together at the Ivory Gate. She wanted Aurora with her, sharing in her companionship and conversation. She wanted someone to talk to, someone to hold late at night, and someone to be there when the bad dreams threatened to overwhelm the good ones. She had started to become comfortable sleeping in the arms of someone else.

Kera bit her lip when she looked at Aurora, trying to hold back on an urge she knew might very well be inappropriate. She glanced toward Raslidor, knowing the griffon could hear her thoughts and divine her intent. Raslidor observed without comment.

Kera didn't like feeling judged. Of all the feelings in the world, shame in this moment was not the one she wanted. Yet she felt it festering deep within her, starting out as a tingle on the underside of her brain, and growing more and more pervasive with each passing second.

Aurora was beautiful. She was wonderful. She'd helped them and saved them. She had scolded Kera and held her. She wanted Aurora to stay by her side and never leave again.

Kera had no desire to meet for Sunday tea, nor even to spend meal times discussing events of the weeks and then bidding goodbye once they'd finished conversing for the evening. Kera wanted Aurora's hand in her hair and Aurora's arms around her body. She wanted to feel Aurora's smile against her cheek. She wanted to be scolded when she made an error, and to be rewarded when she did well. She wanted to laugh at midnight with the blankets pulled up over their heads. *Listen to what the children did today!* She wanted to wake in the morning and attend to her matters and have Aurora with her on the sofa when the bankers came to barter. She wanted to hold Aurora's hand when she told them to go away, because the Ivory Gate was Kera's and she was not going to let anyone take it from her. She wanted the endless companionship that her husband failed to provide. She wanted the happiness that he'd reached out across the divide of life and death and urged her to seek out. He could never be what she truly wanted. He'd left her, in the end, for nothing.

Kera's lips felt warm. The top and bottom heated up and pulled all her focus to them. She'd rarely paid much attention to her lips in the past, but now she was hyperaware of their presence on her face. Of how they rolled over themselves. How her tongue wet them.

How she needed to stop thinking of it.

How there were other matters to attend to.

How much she wanted to kiss Aurora and hold her close and thank her for everything she did for them.

Kera forced herself to look back at Raslidor. "You said there was much we needed to talk about?"

Raslidor's tail flicked from side to side. Annoyed, though they sighed and responded with little delay. "There is." The disgruntled tone grated Kera's nerves. It set her teeth on edge.

Aurora took Kera's hand—*squeeze and release*—and led her forward until they were standing before Raslidor's face. Even lying down, the griffon's head was massive. It was almost as wide as both of their bodies standing side by side, and at rest it was tall enough that Kera could look them in the eyes.

A bird chirped from a tree nearby, hopping along the branches as it sang its morning song. Raslidor tilted their head to listen for a moment, eyes closed and feathers fluffed in an almost pleasant expression. As the song ended, their eyes opened again. "If you return to your homes now, your children will fall ill again, and you will not be able to return."

Aurora's palm squeezed Kera's like a vise. It crushed her fingers in its grasp. Kera couldn't tell if it was the pain in her hand or the words themselves that caused her to freeze in place. She couldn't tell what the source of the reaction was, only that it was there and it burned her with terror and uncertainty.

"It's temporary?" Aurora asked.

But Raslidor was shaking their head, their feathers ruffling along the sides of their face. Tufts twisted to the left and right before pointing forward once more. "No, they are cured of their current ailment. *This* is not what will kill them. But the next one will."

"I don't understand," Kera whispered.

"Your . . . *plague* . . . is not a sickness at all," the griffon explained.

The words weren't good enough or clear enough for Aurora. Her hand squeezed Kera's even harder. Her voice became harsh and aggressive. "Of *course* it's a *sickness,* that's what you call something when it makes someone die!"

"What we mean to say is that your plague is not an illness of normal means. It's magic," Raslidor told them. "Any other illness would have killed them long before they arrived. But you *did* arrive here. And you did so because you managed the curse."

"*What* curse?" Aurora snapped even as Kera's thoughts spun outward. Of course they were cursed.

When is a plague not a plague? Mori had written, with his page shrouded in black ink. Physicians and learned fellows had told her time and again that there was no cure. Nothing could be done to stop it. No research was provided. Kera's head ached. She pressed her free hand over her nose and squeezed her eyes shut. Breathe in, breathe out. *Think.* The mark on Mori's book didn't seep through the pages. It shrouded the letters and words with black. Shrouded them. *Shrouds.*

The drum beat of Kera's heart began again. She pulled the memory back into focus. Envisioning it before her, she could almost see her hand on the page as it traced the ink splotch. She could see herself flipping the paper back and forth, examining it for its peculiarities before looking up to see . . . to see a wraith.

A wraith who longed to drain the life from the living and use it to become alive again. A wraith powerful enough to summon a storm to blow out their fire. A wraith who had hunted them through the night. A wraith who had followed them to Mount Maladh. Who had only stopped chasing them when they became blind to its eyes. Hidden behind crystals.

She looked to Raslidor, and the griffon nodded. "A wraith's call," Raslidor confirmed, still meeting Kera's eyes.

"That's impossible," Aurora whispered. Her grip around Kera's hand was near bruising. Kera could feel her bones shifting, but she didn't dare pull away. The feeling was grounding. It held her in place and kept her steady and calm. It kept her from crumbling under the weight of the horror that had started to build within her. "They both fell ill within the city, Aiden fell during the *day* even. How could a wraith have affected them at all? How could no one have *seen*?"

"Wraiths hunt in shadows. If there's enough darkness, they can emerge. Wherever the shadows lie, there a wraith can be."

Kera tried to remember the exact moment that Aiden had fallen ill. She'd been in her bedroom, trying not to accept the fact that she was failing in maintaining her home. There had been a scream downstairs, and she'd run to see what was the matter. But the sun had still been up, the light flooding the windows. Aiden had crumpled to the floor and been frothing at the mouth. They had been the only ones in the house. She, her children, sister, father, and the bankers. She hadn't seen anything else. Nothing except the cellar door open. Cracked just a little because the children liked to play down there.

There, where darkness existed all the time and not a hint of light burned through. The children needed candles if they were going to play in the cellar. She didn't remember any candles. Kera was going to be sick. There had been a *wraith* in her house. A wraith close enough to try to steal away her son. *(Something rotting in the floor.)*

Aurora kept shaking her head in disbelief. "There are fires around the city, crystals—Lady Zakaria said."

"Yes, but fire lines can be broken. Crystals . . . temporarily removed. Someone could help. Someone on the other side."

"Who would help a wraith?" Aurora asked.

"Someone who knew who it was," Kera answered. She tried to think. Think about everything Aurora had told her. It wasn't the poor who were getting sick. Not the whole country. Two cities had been affected: Ship's Landing and Willowisric. The rich— No. Not just the rich, but anyone who could prove that it wasn't a normal illness; all the doctors and physicians who'd tried curing it had died.

Kera had walked the streets of the city, seen how houses that had gone to prosperous families after the revolution were now up for sale as frightened residents fled. Many banks had started to take over mortgages but—

"How many people were asked by the banks about their homes *prior* to the plague?" Kera asked Raslidor. The griffon nodded their head.

"All of them."

All of them. Of course. "When they left, the banks received ownership of the houses . . ." Kera told Aurora. "It's what they were trying to do with the Ivory Gate."

Aurora shook her head. "No . . . no, that doesn't make any sense, why would the bankers be working with a wraith?"

"It's not all of the banks," Kera replied. The puzzle was forming itself in her mind. Pieces clicking back into place. Clarity overcoming obscurity. The men who had come to her door over and over had been attempting to convince her to sell the Ivory Gate *prior* to any signs of impending default. Prior to any signs of trouble. While it was true she had a finite amount of money to pay for her home, she had yet to miss a single payment.

Their interference at first could be excused as almost helpful or kind. They were "looking out" for her because she wouldn't be able to continue managing on her own. Everyone acted like they'd been trying to do their best by her, but she found their interest to be contradictory to proper behavior. Especially as she *was* Morpheus Montgomery's widow. He'd created their banking system. They should have given her proper respect for her station.

Instead . . . they had pushed.

"Wraiths aren't known for their planning," Aurora argued as Kera tried to find the next link in the chain. "They seek vengeance. Life. Why would a wraith do any of this?"

"For vengeance," Raslidor replied. "For life."

"Vengeance against *whom*? Who exactly would want to team up with *bankers* to take *revenge* against . . . people who own houses?" Then, seeming to have no end of questions, Aurora asked, "And what would a wraith want with a house anyway?"

Think, Kera commanded herself. *Think*. Who had wanted the houses first? If it was vengeance, then whoever the wraith had been before death, he had wanted the homes and felt slighted by them. He had felt personally affronted that the homes hadn't been his. Who had made enemies of whom? Not only that, but who had access to both Willowisric *and* Ship's Landing?

It struck like lightning. "Henry Travers." Kera breathed out the name with full confidence. Aurora snapped her head about to stare at her. Her mouth closed with an audible click. "Henry Travers died in debtor's prison after speculating with money that didn't exist. He wanted to buy up the real estate in Ship's Landing as fast as he could, but he wasn't managing the inflation properly. He missed his calculations, and Mori needed to step in and stop the financial crisis before it became worse. Mori refused to help him and prosecuted him until he was sent to debtor's prison, where he died in destitution."

"Yes," Raslidor nodded. "He did."

She felt like a ball rolling downhill, starting off slow, then picking up speed, all her thoughts aligning with perfect clarity. "Henry Travers became a wraith, a powerful one at that. He must have materialized at some point. Made contact with his family in Ship's Landing. *They* broke the seal."

"But why take Faith?" Aurora asked. "We'd been working for them for years, before the plague ever got that bad, why take her *now*?"

Why indeed. Kera squeezed her eyes shut, desperate to block out anything that could obfuscate the truth. "How much energy would a wraith need to manifest during the day?"

A wave of pleasure ghosted across Kera's consciousness as Raslidor nodded their great head. "A lot. He would have needed a great deal of energy to remain in that cellar waiting for his prey."

"He attacked Faith so he had the strength to manifest inside our home . . . and as a member of his own household, it would help throw off any suspicion as to why his family wasn't affected."

"But they gave me the map!" Aurora shouted. "They told me to come here!"

"Guilt?" Kera offered. "For having put you in such a position?"

Aurora's expression turned *enraged*, furious and bloodthirsty. Her skin was darkening by the minute, her cheeks flushing purple as her anger grew to an insurmountable level.

"And all this time," Kera spat. "He's been killing people to get back what he thought was his."

"The Ivory Gate was built after his death," Aurora told her, but Kera was already past that.

"But *Morpheus* was the one who let him die. He was the one who turned his back on Travers because the man was a scoundrel and a thief!" Kera's voice rose. She was almost shouting. For weeks she'd watched her children suffer, and it had been because *one* horrible man had decided to make an empire by trying to reclaim life after his flame had flickered out.

There had been a shroud on Mori's page, a hasty flourish as he attempted to find the source of the plague. And Kera couldn't help but ask, "Did he know?" Raslidor cocked their head to the side. "Did he know it was Travers? Or at the very least, a *wraith* causing the plague?"

"He knew when he died," Raslidor replied. They stood up, stretching out their long limbs and arching their back so they could sit in a more comfortable position, towering over Kera and Aurora both. "Your husband requested a meeting with Brennan Wild to show him what he knew. He chose the spot he thought best. The most likely place for the wraith to appear. Outside the city walls, with his intended target in plain sight and no one the wiser. Your husband fired his gun."

"In the sky!" Kera snapped. "He never *shot* Wild. He hadn't even been close!"

"Yes. But the sound of a gun causes a man to fright. And Wild reacted at the noise. *Intent*, Lady Montgomery, is what we listen to. And Wild's intention was not to murder Morpheus Montgomery. He had been startled when your husband drew his weapon, and he shot without realizing he wasn't Morpheus Montgomery's target. Morpheus Montgomery fired his gun when he saw a wraith above Wild's body. With the sun cast in the opposite direction and all eyes on your husband, he was the only one who saw it. A wraith bearing a resemblance to Henry Travers, made whole from the life he'd stolen not long ago. He shot the wraith immediately, and in turn, Wild shot your husband, believing to have been fired upon. The wraith vanished, and your husband suspected that with it—so too would the *plague* end.

"Your husband's bullet did aim true; he grievously wounded Travers, but mortal weapons are not enough to kill a wraith. It only made Travers's appetite stronger. It made it so his need to steal the life of others grew. Your . . . *plague* . . . began in earnest after your husband's death, and it's precisely because of his death it was allowed to happen. Travers lost the ability to appear mostly human . . . and he wanted it back. He wanted his life back."

Kera squeezed her eyes shut. She tried to ration her breaths. She tried to come to terms with the raging hatred she had felt for

Brennan Wild from the moment she discovered he had killed her husband, and redirect it at something else. Anyone else. Henry Travers.

The entire Travers family had been assisting Travers with his scheme to act on those he perceived had wronged him. They had relished the money they felt was owed to them, and had encouraged wanton despair and destruction due to their avarice. Kera squeezed Aurora's hand, and clenched her opposite in a tight fist.

Rage, unbridled and unrestrained, circulated through her bloodstream. "If my husband's bullet could injure him, why didn't it kill him entirely?"

"It injured the vessel, but not the spirit. It made the wraith need to reform itself, but could not release it from its existence . . . something you naturally seem to have quite a talent for already, Lady Montgomery. Spirits can only cross over when you bring them peace or force them to move on. A manmade bullet can injure the physical body of the wraith, but not stop his wrath."

"And while he was haunting those who slighted him, his family and their associates were making a profit off of everyone," Aurora said. Her teeth ground down so loud Kera heard them pop.

"But why didn't he come for us *sooner*?" Kera asked. "My husband's been dead for a year, why only attack my child now?"

"Henry Travers ensured your husband's death, Lady Montgomery," Raslidor said. "For a time that was enough. His greed turned him to other ventures, other avenues. He could regain his strength until you were in a position to fall into the same trap he'd sprung on the others. All he needed was to wait and to grow stronger day by day. He had an eternity to wait for you. It was of no consequence for him not to hurry."

Kera closed her eyes again, desperately drawing out her battle plans. She made lists in her mind, categorized them so everything was in order. She could see now the trajectory she needed to take. The course of action that was going to lead her forward. But first, she was going to need help.

When she opened her eyes, it was to Raslidor bending their head low to the ground once more, almost in a bow. "I will help you, Lady Montgomery. I will take you where you need to go."

"Go?" Aurora asked. She turned to look at Kera. "Go where?"

"To see Overseer Brennan Wild," Kera replied. "At his home in Hame Argyll." Now, more than ever, it was clear that they needed to talk.

CHAPTER
TWENTY-SEVEN

Unlike her husband, who had done nothing but loathe the ground Brennan Wild walked on from the moment they stepped into the political arena together, Kera hadn't hated him until the day she discovered he had killed her husband. Prior to that, she had spent the majority of her time mitigating the potential fallout between every personal encounter Morpheus had with the man. They'd attended Wild's parties, where she'd held her husband in check and kept him from being *too* absurd whenever their tempers started to flare over something meaningless and inconsequential.

It hadn't stopped Mori from ruining his own reputation each time they attended, but it at least kept the peace during those moments. Wild, Kera found, had always been a man of complex ambiguities. He liked playing the pauper farmer, and liked to believe himself a member of "the people" rather than the aristocracy to which he'd been born.

His opinions, though convoluted and often hypocritical, were understandable from his own paradigm. Mori knew why Wild felt the way he did on every issue they argued about; Mori just could never agree with the man. They hated each other, pure and simple. A shame, because had they been able to overcome their obvious grandstanding, they could have done so much more for their country than either of their individual efforts had managed to eke out.

Despite knowing Wild had revealed Mori's affair, Kera hadn't let his actions color her feelings until the moment he tried to paint her husband as an assassin. Her husband's relationship with Wild might have been contentious, but Mori wasn't a *murderer*. Wild had lied, or he hadn't understood, or he'd intended to mislead the people. Perhaps he had even tried to have Mori killed from the beginning. Kera hadn't known, and she hadn't cared. She just knew that he'd *lied*. And he was rewarded by still maintaining control over the Overwatch while she was left to reap the consequences of her husband's action.

Her hatred had grown from there.

"Perhaps speaking to the overseer . . . isn't the best idea?" Aurora offered as they left their children, walking until they were far out of sight, so they could bathe in peace.

Faith and Aiden were both awake now. Faith had walked a few steps too, balancing latent dizziness and a lingering weariness with the sheer determination to move on her own. She smiled so prettily that Kera knew she took after her mother, and she played with Aiden as though they had done so for years. She'd held out her hands and Aiden had toddled to her. She began showing Aiden how to make daisy chains out of the flowers in the woods.

Both children had been amazed at the sight of the griffon, and Aiden had dutifully informed the beast that they were all right even if they really didn't look much like a duck. Kera had hissed for him to apologize, but Raslidor laughed brightly at Aiden's assessment and thanked him for his compliment, strangely worded as it might have been. Both children were sluggish from sleeping for so long, and hungry. Kera and Aurora had watched as their children ate most of the food on hand, and Kera was contended by the thought that they even had appetites to speak of. Faith and Aiden seemed energized the whole while, talking and laughing as normal children should. Kera burned the image into her mind. She didn't want to see their children die because Henry Travers wanted to punish her family over a *financial* dispute. Travers had already lived his life, he didn't get to have theirs.

Raslidor had spoken cheerfully in Kera's mind, ripping it ruthlessly from its pique so as to inform her that they could keep an eye on the children while she and Aurora cleaned up. "You will, of course, be given perfect privacy while you bathe." It was an offer they both accepted, escaping down to the lake with only a few hugs to their children as a goodbye.

"Seeing Wild is *exactly* the best idea," Kera told Aurora, pulling at the strings of her blouse and tugging it off her shoulders. If she was going to talk to the Overseer of Absalon, she was going to look presentable. As much as she wanted to just appear as she was now, she had a firm understanding of propriety. Even if Brennan Wild shouldn't be worth the effort. "And if he doesn't like what I have to say, then I shall *make* him like it."

Aurora nodded her head, tugging her own clothes off, settling them not far away. "Montgomerys and your pig-headedness," she accused.

"You love us for it," Kera said. She dipped a toe into the water. It wasn't *too* cold. It felt refreshing, actually. With her feet sliding through sand, she let herself sink deep into the water. She relaxed into it, relishing the feeling of being surrounded by the lake. It was a cool liquid embrace that settled her to her core. The tide of her mind was at peace.

"I do," Aurora replied after a moment, watching Kera as she drifted back farther in the lake. Kera stayed afloat with a few strokes of her arms, and she tried to work out why Aurora's voice sounded so strange. It was almost dark and husky. But before she could understand it, Aurora joined her in the water. She slipped under and then kicked up off the sandy bottom. Head cresting, damp and beautiful. Her dark hair lay plastered to her cheeks, curls straightening into awkward waves as they were dragged down by the water. Kera bit her lip, treading as she watched Aurora blink droplets from her lashes. Aurora tucked her hair back behind her ears and found her footing.

Words, words, words.

So many to choose from. Infinite in their possibilities. Kera swam closer until she was within arm's reach of Aurora. She knew they should be washing. They didn't have much time. But the children were being cared for, Raslidor would keep them safe, and they had precious few moments to speak to one another without any prying eyes or ears. No one was around, save their eavesdropping griffon who already *knew* everything they could be thinking anyway.

Words were hard, but Kera found two at least. "Thank you."

Her body was warm despite the cool water that rose up to her shoulders. It teased her collarbones with the slightest breath of air. Kera reached her hand toward Aurora. She wanted to touch, but this was far more intimate than anything they'd done before. She waited, hand extended, her heart beating far too fast as she hoped for a positive response.

She had been caught, long ago, like a fish on a line, drawn to Aurora against her will, and now entirely at Aurora's mercy. She would either be taken forever or set back to sea.

Aurora met her eyes. Then she surged. She took her hand, reeled her in. Pulling her until there was no doubting or obfuscation.

Their lips met.

Aurora's hands were in her hair, on her hip, guiding her body close. Kera's eyes fluttered closed. She lost her footing in the sand, but Aurora never let her fall. Aurora embraced her, restraining her with no intentions of letting her go.

Aurora's breasts felt strange and foreign against Kera's. She wasn't used to the feeling, not like this. But she wanted it to go on, wanted to touch them how she knew she liked her own to be touched. Her mouth parted just a little, and Aurora's hand tightened in her hair. Her tongue dove between her lips, and Kera was pulled in closer and closer.

So close that Kera half wondered if she would slip through Aurora's flesh. Join her body and soul, nestle and live in the sacred space around Aurora's heart. She lost her footing again, and Aurora reached down and cupped her under her bottom, urging her upward so her legs stood on nothing at all, but her arms were wrapped around Aurora's shoulders, and her thighs spread around Aurora's waist.

She was weightless in the water. Strangely, it reminded her of the first time she'd ever kissed a boy. Blushing as he stole a kiss she hadn't meant to give and rushing home to tell her sisters what happened. Gale had threatened to show him a thing or two, but Ciara had been sly and curious. *Did you like it?* she had asked. And all Kera could think about was wanting to feel it more.

More, more, more.

Aurora's lips didn't leave hers. They stayed affixed. Moving. Pulsating. The hand in her hair guided Kera's actions. Guiding with an open mouth that encouraged her exploration. Their limbs were intertwined and Kera's body *burned*.

They parted, breathing hard and ragged, brows resting against each other. Kera's hair hung down around them, curtaining them in.

Hiding them from view. Aurora looked up at her, not letting her go. Strong, capable arms managed her weight with expert talent. Kera half wondered if she'd done this before.

"Don't stop," Kera whispered. Aurora adjusted her grip and walked her back to the beach. They stumbled as she needed to let Kera down, but only for a moment. Then, she guided her to the sand. Kera's back pressed against it. Her hair splayed about her head. Water lapped at their legs, but Aurora was at her side. One arm braced her shoulders, and Aurora's other hand was dedicated to stroking Kera's skin. A leg draped over Kera's body, and none of that seemed as important as the kiss Aurora gave her.

She kissed Kera again. Gently this time. Very gently. They traced their lips together and breathed the same air as one. Their noses bumped, but it was nice. It was *sweet*. Kera didn't know what to do with her hands. She didn't know where to put them.

She cupped one around the back of Aurora's neck, and the other . . . the other clung to Aurora's wrist. Traveled with it as her hand stroked along the sides of Kera's body. Feeling as it dipped back into the water to wash the wet sand off her fingers.

Aurora's lips slid from hers. She kissed Kera's cheeks, her lashes, her brow. Her lips mouthed at Kera's throat, and descended lower and lower. Over her breasts and to her nipples, sucking on the one closest to her. Kera's head tilted back. A noise pressed out of her mouth as she gasped on the air. Every part of her was alive in a way she couldn't bear to describe.

Her eyes rolled back in her head, her skin tingled with anticipation as Aurora's fingers traveled downward. They stroked across her inner thigh, moving back up in a curving arc. The tips of her fingers were soft and gentle along her skin.

The wind blew the water up toward them, coating their legs. Aurora kissed her and never seemed to stop: each touch far more sensuous than the last. Her fingertips nestled between Kera's legs, and Kera gasped. Her vision went white and she squeezed Aurora's wrist, desperate for more contact.

Aurora responded immediately. She surged forward and her fingers slid inside. Perfect and wonderful. Their lips met again. It was fast and it was rough, and Kera couldn't remember the last time she'd felt this way about anything. "I found you," Aurora whispered into her ear. Kera's eyes opened wide. She stared up at the sun. Life, death, and the time between the two. She held on to Aurora as tight as she could. "I am found."

She felt like she was flying.

They did wash eventually.

When their bodies stopped singing. When their skin was flushed with the fever pitch they had fallen into. When their lips continued tingling, but their hands were loath to leave each other's hold. When Kera looked at Aurora and knew—she never wanted this to end. When the realization that for so long Kera had felt lost, but here with Aurora: she'd been found.

They washed each other. Aurora was careful with Kera's back, as if the scars John had healed still brought Kera pain. But she kissed them too. She kissed them to make them better, and Kera sighed into the touch. She smiled at the feeling. It was good, *so* good. Latent tension that Kera barely realized she even had fell from her shoulders, replaced by a soothing relaxation she'd long since missed. When it was Aurora's turn, Kera took her time. She kissed her beautiful dark skin and sighed into the curves of Aurora's body. She nosed at parts that were warm and interesting to touch, things she longed to have more time to explore. She looked forward to when they would have that time, when she could lay Aurora down on her bed at the Ivory Gate. There, she could return every favor Aurora gave her, and smile as Aurora lay boneless beneath her.

She wanted Aurora's happiness. She wanted her bliss and her contentment. She settled for washing her and rubbing a loose cloth along Aurora's limbs to help her dry. She settled for helping Aurora re-dress, and checking on her blisters that had long since become calluses. And in the end, she settled for one last perfect kiss before they returned to Raslidor and their children.

They walked back together, hand in hand. Faith was kneeling at Raslidor's side, stroking feathery fur and braiding daisies around the fluffy tail in an endless loop. Aiden was presenting a similar flower crown to Raslidor, who inspected it with the utmost care. Their beak pressed against it, and there must have been excess pollen on the crown, for Raslidor sneezed impressively, wind blowing Aiden's curls away from his face. He stared at Raslidor like they were the most magnificent thing he had ever seen, and he giggled bright and vibrant.

He turned when he heard them approach. And Kera's heart swelled as her son pushed himself to his feet and *ran* to her arms. "Mama!" he called before jumping up to be held. She caught him, hoisting him in the air and holding him to her heart. She breathed him in. He was healthy and safe and well.

Faith stood with far more care, but she was eager as she approached. Aurora wrapped her arms around her daughter and shared a look with Kera. Their families were safe. For now. But, their trials were not yet over.

She and Aurora had already spoken about what came next, and while Aurora wasn't happy with it, she couldn't deny the logic. "Aiden, honey, you're going to stay here with Aurora for a little while, okay?" Kera asked her son. Aiden looked up at her, nose scrunched a little as his lips twisted in a frown. Not quite a tantrum. Not yet. "I've got to take care of something, but Aurora's going to stay with you and you can play with her and Faith as much as you want."

"You'll be back soon?" Aiden asked.

"Yes, I'll be back soon." She kissed his nose and settled him on the ground.

"Our kin will stay with you in the wood," Raslidor told Aurora. "We'll tell them to come. You have nothing to fear during your stay at the Long Lakes."

"Thank you," Aurora said.

Kera adjusted her clothes and met Aurora's eyes. "How do I look?" She was not in a proper dress, nor was she even fully dried. But she didn't have anything except the trousers in the first place, and her hair would dry during the journey. The overseer would *have* to manage.

"Unstoppable," Aurora told her. "Be safe . . ."

Kera nodded. She longed to give Aurora another kiss, even leaned forward to do so, but she hesitated at the last minute and kissed the corner of Aurora's mouth instead, ever cognizant that their children were standing just there. She'd never made a habit of being intimate in front of her children. Her mother would never have allowed such behavior. But Aurora caught her by the hip and returned the kiss properly, and Faith didn't so much as blink. Aiden had already returned to playing with the flowers. Neither cared. "You ladies and your strange thoughts." Aurora kissed her brow, letting her lips linger. "Breathe," she whispered against Kera's skin. "And be safe."

Kera nodded again, mumbling a careful farewell, and then mounted Raslidor. She settled above the wings, just like she had been instructed earlier, and with a few galloping strides, the griffon kicked up off the ground and burst into the sky.

Raslidor's voice echoed between her ears. They would be at Hame Argyll in a matter of hours.

CHAPTER TWENTY-EIGHT

When Kera was fifteen years old, her father attended a ball at the Sarren estate. He had gone for a political excursion, and needed to discuss business with the man. John had already been studying in Trent by that point, and so Kera had never met him. The ball itself hadn't even been an important affair. Not in the grand scheme of life. But her father had wanted to show off his children, and she hadn't been given a choice in attending. Her brothers had disappeared within minutes of the ball starting, leaving Ciara, Gale, and her to their own devices. Those devices namely including Kera listening to Ciara's endless deluge of information regarding potential marital prospects, and Kera keeping an eye on Gale to ensure she wasn't going to set anything on fire.

Their mother had dressed them each in fine Trent-woven clothes. Kera's hair had been braided in tight rows. Her nails had been scrubbed clean. Her face had been caked with clay to hide the blemishes all teenage girls had. Her mother'd lent her a shimmering necklace and slid earrings into her ears, adding a bracelet for effect. She'd been handed a fan and told to behave, and then was dragged in front of the most powerful man in the colonies.

Curtis Sarren had more wealth than Kera ever dared to dream of. He sat in a place of political superiority, and he peered down his nose at Kera. She curtsied low and polite. She held her tongue and kept her face pleasant and cordial. She didn't tell him that the serving staff seemed miserable, or that they seemed flighty and uncertain, as if he struck them or kept them unlawfully indentured. That would have been rude.

The ball itself was quite dull. There were few children her age, and the boys that did attend seemed far more interested in chasing her skirt than engaging in conversation. Ciara decided they were all ninnies, and she took Kera by the arm. They walked the grounds for some time, lamenting how boring it all was.

Around that time, they found Gale chatting with one of the boys. He tried to get handsy with her, and she responded by punching him clear in the nose. Blood splattered everywhere and he recoiled badly enough that he didn't know what to do. Ciara and Kera bracketed their younger sister and snapped at him to leave now. He did so, but not before drawing attention to himself from a neighboring group of partygoers. They all spotted the blood, and for a moment their drama was the focus of the party.

Their father stood on one side of them, while Sarren stood on the other, and they demanded to know what occurred. The boy attempted to say that he'd made a mistake, had fallen and had made a fool of himself, but Gale wouldn't be cowed. "I punched that skirt lifter in the nose because he was a scoundrel who tried to touch me after I said no!"

The boy demanded that she cease announcing the troubling rumor, but Ciara and Kera had stood at their sister's side. They'd seen it, and insisted that she'd spoken the truth. They repeated Gale's declarations. He *was* a scoundrel and Gale deserved recompense. When their father had stood beside them and asked Sarren what kind of hooligans he'd let into his house, Sarren wrought justice upon the boy.

The fight and argument were swept to the side, and the party continued as if it had never been interrupted. The boy's parents dragged him from the venue, and Kera's father told them it was best if they went on up to bed. They didn't offer much protest, and they looped their arms together and waltzed from the room. Once they had been cosseted away, Gale showed them the desserts she'd pilfered into her shawl before they left. She spread out her haul, and they feasted on crumb cake while the adults continued to prance about downstairs.

In the morning, the boy's parents offered their father a formal apology, and it was agreed that the boy's reputation would not be harmed by the event. A lie was made up, he had hurt himself *defending* a woman's honor, not attempting to take it by force himself. Their father had told them the boy had learned a valuable lesson and he was unlikely to repeat his antics again. And they watched as the boy was congratulated for his bravery. Even their brothers had gone along with the ruse, urging Gale to use more restraint in the future.

Kera's first step into public life had been marred by three simple truths that carried her through all her remaining years in *polite* society. One: politicians enjoyed flaunting their wealth, but they never knew what to do with it once they had it. Two: there were rules in public life that must be followed at all times, and if someone broke out of that mold—it startled others into either complacency or violence. Three: To survive in politics, one must know how to lie and do it better than anyone else in the world. More than that, they needed to be able to get away with it, no matter how many bribes they needed to offer in order to make it stick.

Brennan Wild was a master at all three. Hame Argyll sat as a pinnacle of his brilliance. His intensive studies in architecture had provided him a crisply designed compound. A great wall surrounded the grounds and there were no shortage of servants tending the property within. All of them looked up as Raslidor flew over, shouting in terror and running for cover.

Kera actually felt bad about frightening them.

She did *not* feel bad about frightening Wild himself. The pompous and pious Overseer of Absalon had been sprawled out on a chaise in his garden, a fine drink in hand, book on his lap, and meal placed on a low table by his seat. He was dressed in expensive clothes that Kera knew for a fact he would never wear in public as they detracted from his façade of *gentleman farmer*.

He sat up when they landed, one foot sliding off each side of the chaise. His mouth was open and his eyes were saucer wide. He looked like he couldn't quite fathom what he was seeing, and Kera took the opportunity to unseat herself from Raslidor's back and steady her legs on the ground. The Overseer of Absalon took his time noticing she was there.

She couldn't even blame him.

Raslidor was gorgeous.

"Sir," she greeted firmly, forcing Wild's eyes to drop to her face. It took him a moment, a *long* moment, to show some kind of recognition. When he did, he scrambled to his feet and strode to meet her halfway. He loitered before her, hands in the air. He didn't seem to know how to greet her. That was good too. She wanted him unsettled. "Honored Overseer, sir, I'd like to speak with you about a matter of grave importance."

"K— L— *Widow* Montgomery, what is—" The man stopped, shook his head, and then straightened his spine. "Can I offer you something to drink?" he asked, turning on his heel and returned to his chaise. He fetched his bottle of wine and poured himself a glass. She waited as he drank it all in one swallow and then returned to staring at her like he was still trying to convince himself this was all real.

Mori used to complain about the intensity of his smile, muttering on and on about how it was sharklike and awful. Wild was a man both graceful and domineering; one who was comfortable in his skin and *knew* what that confidence could do to someone. He played the perfect host at all times, and despite his hatred of Mori, he'd always invited him to parties. It would have been inappropriate not to. They both were too well-known and well-situated in the Overwatch for Wild to avoid it, and he always had enjoyed baiting Mori by the invitation.

Kera had no intentions of taking the bait for anything. She had no intentions of letting Wild get under her skin. She'd rehearsed what she wanted to say for the entire flight, and discussed her battle plans and tactics with Raslidor until she was certain she knew how to answer each one of Wild's protests or admonishments. She was not a child seeking a parent's approval. She was not a wife begging leniency for her husband.

She was here to make a request of the most powerful man in the country, and she intended to succeed in her quest. Wild had what she needed—legal authority to act. And more than that . . . he had what she needed to save her family from ever struggling with this again. Despite the deep unwavering hatred for this man and all he stood for, she needed him. But that did not mean she would bend for him.

"I do not want a drink," Kera said. "I wish to speak to the overseer of this nation, and I expect him to attend to me as is befitting a man of his station." Wild's eyes narrowed at her sharp words.

"I had not been aware you requested an audience," he demurred, but this was a dance she knew well. One that she had trained for all her life. She might have spent most of her time as the follower rather than the leader, but she knew how to switch her role. She knew how to move forward instead of backward, knew how to walk the room and do so with her head high. Unlike Mori, she did not falter in her steps.

"You would not have been *made* aware," she told him. "It's all been very recent."

Brennan Wild smoothed a hand over his purple coat. He straightened his shirt and nodded. Soldiers appeared at long last, brandishing their weapons as though they intended to fight them off. Raslidor's wings spread wide, and they screeched, stopping the soldiers where they stood, freezing them in open terror.

"Stand down," Wild snapped at his men. "You are not necessary."

Raslidor's wings folded back behind their back, and Wild forced an awkward smile.

Kera hoped that his day continued to be filled with more annoyances. She had no intentions of making this easy for him. "What is it that you wish to speak to me about?" Wild asked once his men no longer seemed ready to open fire.

"The plague."

Wild's posture shifted. His mouth twisted. "I understand that you may be concerned about the—"

"It's not a plague."

The man sighed and ran a hand over his thick hair. He stepped toward her, expressing the perfect placidity of a politician at work. She was uninterested in his lies and excuses, in whatever he thought he could conjure up to make her believe him. He tried to speak, but she cut him off. She didn't want to hear him. "The plague is a wraith call."

At long last, Wild seemed ready to listen. The smile slipped off once more. He examined Kera from head to toe, taking in her poor attire and lack of deference, before returning his gaze to Raslidor. He waved his hand vaguely in her direction and entreated her, "Tell me what you know."

She did.

Kera told him everything. She reminded him about Travers and his death in prison. She told him about their suspicions of just what Travers had become after death, and the evidence that they'd accumulated. She brought up her husband's "assassination" attempt, and gave him Raslidor's testimony as to what *truly* happened that day, and she relished when he flinched just a little at her words. She explained the notes in Mori's book, and the shroud that tried to cover his pages. She listed all the houses that were targeted, and the link to the Travers family's banking connections and the speculations.

She told him everything that had happened on their journey, leaving out only her intimate moments with John Sarren, Rachel the laundress, and Aurora Lawrence. There was no reason to tell him about them, and so her story remained on point, with no scandalous details or fascinating moments he could examine once their business was concluded.

"Gods above," Wild murmured once she'd finished her story. He reached for another glass of wine, and this time he pressed it into Kera's hand. "Please sit," he requested as he signaled for more food and drink to be brought out. One of the soldiers scurried off to do just that. "What is it that you want from me, Widow Montgomery?"

"I want you to send your men to Ship's Landing and Willowisric and arrest all of those responsible for this. For working with and profiting from a *wraith's* desire to seek revenge," Kera requested. Wild nodded but with great consideration. He poured himself another glass of wine and spun the fluid about.

"I'll need physical evidence that this is Travers," he informed her. "I cannot send an army to arrest a family for profiting from tragedy."

This, Kera thought, would be the moment her husband would start screaming. Would stand on a table and shout for all the world to see that Wild was a brainless oaf. Couldn't he tell that time was of the essence? Couldn't he understand that lives were at stake? He and the overseer would devolve into quibbling, never to get anything done. And from the pensive expression on Wild's features, Kera had no trouble believing that he assumed she would react much the same way.

But she was not her husband. And she'd had a three-hour flight from the Long Lakes to discuss this very concern with Raslidor. "I can show you." She took careful sips of her wine, letting the fluid fill her mouth. It was fruity and sweet and she liked the flavor. She couldn't remember the last time she'd drunk something other than water, but she liked it now.

"Show me?" Wild questioned.

"If I can show you Travers's wraith, summon him here and have him before you—will you believe my story and send your men to Ship's Landing and Willowisric?" Aurora would be furious when she found out, but that was fine, at this point it was better to ask forgiveness than permission.

"If it is Travers, then there would be enough reasonable doubt for me to orchestrate such a thing. But summoning a wraith . . . that is no easy task. And I had not known you were a charmer." He was being polite, just barely avoiding calling her a *hexer* or a *witch*.

Kera took another sip of her wine and settled it on the table. "I'm not, but Raslidor has offered to assist us in ridding ourselves from Travers's wraith."

Wild's brow furrowed once more. Kera *almost* felt bad for this, she *almost* felt bad for interrupting his day. She'd been raised to feel perpetually guilty no matter what she did, but after everything he'd done to destroy her and her husband's lives by virtue of his position as the leader of their country, she found she honestly didn't care if he was uncomfortable. If anything, she hoped it hurt.

She stood with her back tall and waited for him to spin an excuse, offer another protest, or attempt to challenge her. He did none of the above. Instead, he bowed his head, and invited her to summon a wraith to Hame Argyll. What did they have to lose? Feeling as though her heart was about to burst, she contained all of her tumultuous anxiety deep within her body. She smiled like a lady, and said, "Excellent. Do you have a smith I could use?"

CHAPTER
TWENTY-NINE

Night fell over Hame Argyll, and Kera stood alone outside the gates. But she also knew that Raslidor was lying in the trees not far away. They watched her, and from the wall, Kera could also feel Wild's eyes on her back. He had petitioned his men to line the wall, burning arrows and muskets at the ready. The measure was absurd. It did *nothing* to make her feel better. The shots would never reach her in time, even if they *did*, they would be just as likely to hit her as they were to hit Travers.

The men insisted on it, however. They told her it was for her own safety. But it was only when Raslidor assured her that they would keep the soldiers from shooting her too that she felt even the slightest taste of relief. In any case, standing out in the open like this, exposed and in more willful danger than she cared to be in, Kera couldn't help but imagine Aurora shouting at her for being stupid again. For rushing back into the thick of things. She really was just as foolish as her husband.

Unlike your husband, Raslidor's voice echoed within her head, despite being well out of sight, *you actually have a plan should things not go your way. Perhaps it's time you stop comparing yourself to him, and realize that you can stand on your own without him? After all . . . he's not the one who actually knows how to defeat this wraith, you are.*

Kera closed her eyes and took a deep breath. *I am*, she thought. *I am.* The sky darkened further, but the night didn't start its howling. Not yet. There was a dull sense of anticipation, one that ratcheted her anxiety tighter and tighter, faster with each passing moment as the darkness grew thicker and any hope of moonlight was overcome by clouds.

She had no crystals, there was nothing to blind her from view. And even though John had healed her scars, they were vestiges of Travers's attack on her body. Raslidor had been very clear, Travers could find her from that alone. Aurora, Faith, and Aiden were safe at the Long Lakes, and so she was the only one that Travers could see.

He will come for you, Raslidor informed her. They did not try to lessen the impact those words would have on her. They already knew. *He wants you dead.*

It was a strange feeling, knowing that someone wanted *her* dead. She used to bring Henry Travers a basket of apples from her garden; she used to dine with his family and offer him her felicitations at the births of his children. They had laughed by the fire and shared stories. They had been friends once. And yet, here they were, standing in the dark at the precipice of a conflict generated solely by greed and misplaced hate.

Something fluttered in front of her. A black cloak flickered into view, the shroud of a dead thing that was torn along the edges. There was a hole in its skull from where her husband had shot him. Henry Travers's wraith was worn and ragged, but he screeched all the same.

Kera took a deep breath. Her hand closed around the hilt of the blade she had requested Wild make for her. Her mind raced with instructions she'd been given time and again. Words she knew she had to say, and more than that—words she *wanted* to say. She wanted to speak to the Henry Travers she knew.

She wanted to see him for who and what he really was. "I know who you are," she told the wraith.

It floated closer to her. It had no body. Just a floating form that hovered in the air and slid above the ground. Closer and closer. Black sockets boring into her soul. She could hear Raslidor whispering in her head. She could feel her breath catch as her fear reminded her it still existed. The manager wanted to leave the premises. She locked all the doors. No. She was staying still.

She would carry this fear with her until the end of her life. No matter the outcome, no matter the joy of winning or the thrill of success, she knew that it would never shake loose the memory of that night in the woods where a wraith tore her apart and killed her horse.

How *dare* he kill her horse.

"I know who you are," she repeated. Travers raised one bony hand and aimed it at her throat. She could almost feel the fingers wrapping about her neck. Coiling along her skin and compressing so tight. There were words she knew a braver person would say. *I am not afraid of you. I am better than this. You will not hurt me.* But those were lies. They were statements that she couldn't make. She found no truth nor comfort in them. Instead, she said what she *did* have faith in. What she knew she could hold on to, because nothing else was right. "I am not letting you kill me."

Her fingers tightened around the handle of her knife, and Travers's wraith-screeches filled the air. He flew toward her, black shroud fluttering in the wind. Her body trembled. Her anxiety pinwheeled into terror. His skull was nearing, and Kera's eyes went to the gaping hole Mori's bullet had left. Her husband always did have good aim.

But not as good as hers.

Wild shouted for his men to be at the ready, but it would be too late. Travers's claws extended toward her body. Kera's heart skipped a beat. She turned sideways and slashed her arm up, pulling her griffon talon knife with her. It slashed clear through the wraith's body, and everything burst into a cloud of black ash.

Kera clung to the knife as hard as she could, turning her head away as the ash coated her skin and the wind blew it away. When she dared to open her eyes, the skeletal figure of the wraith was gone. Instead, lying on the ground, one hand clutching his heart, was the very ghostlike visage of Henry Travers.

Wild yelled over the wall, levying commands she couldn't track. She didn't look back. She didn't dare take her eyes off of Travers. She stared down at him and rationed her breaths. Tried to calm herself. She could allow the anxiety and the hysteria to overcome her later.

Right now, she needed to act. Right now, she held the knife in her hand and felt Raslidor approach her from behind, no longer hiding. They were willing to intervene if he tried anything.

"Griffon talons cure all ailments," Kera recited by rote. "And can even turn a wraith . . . back into a ghost."

"You bitch," Travers hissed. Kera flinched at the word. She squeezed the hilt of her knife so hard her wrist ached. There was a faint smell of sulfur in the air, and she could taste it on her tongue. Bitter and acidic.

"You tried to kill my son," she accused.

Travers rose up. He lunged for her, but she slashed at him again. This time, he screamed in agony. Light streamed from the tear she'd made across his body. He flickered in and out of reality.

When they'd flown to Hame Argyll, Kera had asked Raslidor why they'd never set John's ghost free. If griffons could lay souls to rest, why had they let John continue his death march when they loved him as much as they did? Raslidor had responded, *"We don't put their souls to rest. We give them oblivion. And John Sarren deserved so much more than oblivion."*

Travers didn't.

He screamed and howled, and Kera attacked with one final swipe. She cast Travers's soul into an eternity of nothingness, and ended his wraith's call once and for all. Setting free all those he bound in his attempts to stay alive.

She could feel the shift in the air. The moment he vanished, she *felt* his mark on her disappearing. Her back lost some of its tension, and her chest no longer constricted her breathing. Kera turned and looked up to Wild. The overseer of their nation looked down.

"I want a message sent to Willowisric and Ship's Landing," he announced. The men at his side watched him in rapt fascination, prepared to do anything he said. "Find me every member of the Travers family and their associates."

"Yes, Mr. Overseer," one of them replied.

Kera's hand was still locked around her knife.

We won, Raslidor spoke in her head.

"Not yet," Kera replied. There was still more work to do.

The overseer fetched Kera food and water. He provided her with a blanket and a warm room. She accepted, but only when Raslidor squeezed themselves through the doorway so they could curl up by the fire at her side. Their wings folded along their back, and they rested their great head beside Kera's thighs. With Travers put to rest, Kera found that her legs were quite incapable of keeping her upright. All her energy had been sapped, and she trembled as the startling reality of what she had just done made itself known in her mind.

Aurora was going to kill her.

Wild stopped by to deliver an evening meal himself, deigning to kneel and press a glass of brandy into her hand. "You're a brave woman, Kerryn Montgomery." If he noticed the knife still in her hand, he didn't say anything about it. She, in turn, didn't inform him that she wasn't going to sleep tonight. Too afraid of what might be lurking in the shadows, shivers wracking her body. She didn't feel brave. She just wanted to see her family and make sure that they were all okay.

"By the time you return to Ship's Landing, the Traverses will all have been arrested. We'll have a trial. Find them guilty. The homes they stole will be returned to the ones who lost them." Wild made promises like he had the power to enforce any of it. She supposed he did in a sense. He could influence the courts to put things right, and the people wouldn't stand for the Traverses to be let off easily. He needed to make a show of this.

"Don't let them become wraiths this time," Kera said. "He died in debtor's prison. Someone should have been called to ferry his soul and to provide last rites. This never should have happened to begin with."

Wild winced, but he didn't argue. He agreed, and she found that as long as he kept agreeing, he could be managed. She wished he'd acted a tad more diplomatic in the past. It could have saved them all a great deal of trouble.

"Is there anything else I can do for you, Widow Montgomery?" He was being polite. Polite and perfunctory, and that was fine. It was all fine. Kera drank down the rest of her brandy and met his eyes.

"I want my husband's pension," she told him.

For the second time in twenty-four hours, she'd stunned the man. He stared at her, blinking as he tried to change gears and understand what she was saying. She didn't give him time to pause and ruminate. She stated her case. In small words, lest he pretended to not understand. "He fought for this country during the revolution, and he accepted no pay. He served as the minister for finance, and he rarely took a salary in order to improve the government's revenue.

He fought again when Trent tried to return, not receiving pay at any point. He died a general in the army, and he barely received a single cent for his efforts."

She took a deep breath and straightened her spine so that with him kneeling before her, she was the one who towered above him. "After he died, you refused to allow my husband's pension to be paid. You enabled the conflict with the bankers and nearly put my family on the street. Mori never tried to kill you, sir. He tried to tell you about Travers. And you shot him for it." Wild swallowed, diverting his eyes despite her firm attention on his face. "I want my husband's pension, sir. I want my house to stay in my name. And I never want to see another banker at my door asking me to sell *my* home."

Wild's jaw worked. First to the left and then to the right. He seemed to be rolling his tongue about his mouth. As if the words were a garbled mess and he couldn't work out which he wanted to say first. "There are . . . many challenges in freeing up those funds for such an extended period of time."

"Challenges you saw no trouble overcoming when you ensured that *your* monuments and houses could be constructed for *your* government. When you allotted yourself a salary, and you enjoyed the frivolities that came with it. Challenges that hardly seemed to bother you when it came to freezing them in the first place. Hundreds of people might still be alive today if you hadn't *shot* him, sir. This is truly the least you can do." He opened his mouth, but she still wasn't done. "You told the world that he had an affair with Aurora Sinclair, breaking your attorney-client privilege and turning the public against him so he didn't get elected as overseer after Zakaria stepped down. If your wife were in my shoes, if she were sitting here before my husband, and not the other way around, would you not wish to have your pension paid to her so that she could continue to survive long after your death?"

Wild's expression turned guilty, but she was unmoved by his attempts at placating her. She was indomitable, and stared at him, unblinking. His neck bent. "It's . . . no less than you deserve," Wild agreed, as if the words were killing him to speak.

"It's *far* less than I deserve," Kera corrected. She hadn't asked Wild to fix the narrative. Her husband's story would forever be lost in the annals of history. She knew full well Wild wouldn't admit to his wrongdoings. She didn't expect him to in any case. There was nothing more that could be done on that front. "But I will hold you to your word as a gentleman on this matter, sir. As *my overseer.*"

Wild nodded. "I'll see to it. All of your husband's back pay and finances will be opened up and returned to you." She looked at Raslidor, and the griffon nodded. Wild's intent was clear. He was not lying.

"And you will also see to it that the griffons at the Long Lakes are not disturbed," Kera added, because damn him if he thought she was letting him off this easily.

His face tightened. His nose wrinkled, shoulders turning stiff. "Widow Montgomery—"

She raised a hand in the air and spoke over him. "They helped us because they were given the choice to help. If this happens again, if someone else seeks out their care, and you have made an enemy of the griffons through your own poor management of their territorial grounds, then you've directly done harm to the very people you claim to want to protect. Leave the Long Lakes alone."

At her side, Raslidor shifted to watch as Wild attempted to come up with an appropriate response. He didn't seem interested in making an enemy of a griffon when one sat so close, and he scowled. "I will do my best to keep it off the table, but I have no control over what happens in the future. I will not be overseer forever."

"That's all I can ask of you . . . that's all I *will* ask of you." Standing up, he bid her good night and did the same to Raslidor before hurrying from the room. He almost seemed worried she would ask him for something else.

Still, the moment the door clicked shut, Kera crumbled forward. She squeezed her eyes shut, and Raslidor nudged her legs with their head. "Okay," Kera said. "Okay. I'm done now. I want to go home."

Raslidor didn't say anything in response, but that was the beauty about someone who listened. They didn't have to.

CHAPTER THIRTY

Raslidor flew Kera back to the Long Lakes in the morning. There, Kera met four other griffons who had come to spend time with Aurora, Faith, and Aiden while they waited for her. One was an adult like Raslidor, but the three others were small. One was so tiny they fit in Kera's arms. Aiden could wrap his whole body around them.

Aurora pulled her to her chest the moment she could, cupping Kera's face between her palms and looking her over. It was almost as though she'd expected Kera to come back wounded, and Kera smiled at the open concern. "I'm fine," she promised. "I was perfectly safe."

"You're a rotten liar, Lady," Aurora told her. Then she kissed her the way Kera longed for her to, and held her tight. "Is it done, then?"

"It's done. The overseer will see to everyone's arrests, Travers has been sent away forever, and the wraith's call is over. Anyone still alive who was sick will slowly feel better. They're all going to be all right."

Before Aurora could say anything else, Aiden tugged at Kera's trouser leg. She shifted so she could look at him, and he scaled her like a tree. Aurora rolled her eyes as Kera helped hoist her son up. She settled Aiden on her hip and grinned at her son, relishing his voice as he *chattered* at her. He chattered and flapped his hands as he told her about his day. "I went flying! I went flying on Sarisse and Miss Aurora held me, and we touched the clouds, and I wanna go again, can we please, can we?"

Faith cheerily gave a tale of her own, telling Kera how she and Aiden went swimming and built a sandcastle. Some of the beavers had come over to inspect it, and then she and Aiden had caught fish and eaten them over a fire. The night had been so quiet they hadn't even needed a fire ring; the griffons had watched over and protected them the whole while.

Their enthusiasm was unbelievable, their excitement addicting. Kera let herself enjoy the moment. She set Aiden down and chased him along the lake's sandy beach. She splashed water at her daughter and picked errant leaves from Faith's hair as Aurora straightened Aiden's shirt. She held them both, and loved them both, and wished them all the happiness in the world.

"Are you ready to go home?" she asked Aiden as he pet the baby griffon, giggling as they purred and chirped at once. Their fluffy tail swishing back and forth as tiny talons flexed and bent.

"Yes," he replied. He didn't hesitate, nor let himself get too attached to the pretty creature curled against his body. "I miss everybody." Kera hugged him close. She hadn't dared to think too much about Cirri, Marcus, Junior, Kerri, John, or August. She longed to see each one of her children, missing their precious faces and wanting to hold them all safe in her arms. "Can I still play with Faith?" he asked though.

"Anytime you'd like," Kera promised. There was a lot she and Aurora needed to discuss, but that promise she had every intention on keeping. Aiden seemed more than content with that, and he stood up, holding the baby griffon under their front legs as he went to tell Faith what she said. The baby's back legs dragged along the ground as he walked. Raslidor and the other griffon, Sarisse, were observing the proceedings with interest, grooming each other and clearly relaxing without much concern.

Aurora settled into place at Kera's back once Aiden had gone, pulling Kera so her spine rested against her breasts. Kera melted into the embrace, tilting her head so it leaned on Aurora's collarbone. "I missed you," she admitted softly. It had only been a day of separation, but it felt like too much.

"Me too," Aurora whispered back.

"You're beautiful."

"I'm a mess."

"Still."

Aurora shifted her arms and kissed the top of Kera's head. "Things'll be different when we get back to Ship's Landing." Life was always different in Ship's Landing. There were classes and hierarchy, prejudices and poor judgment, cruelty that had no place in the world, and all of it was centered in a few city blocks.

Kera took Aurora's hand in hers and stroked her thumb over Aurora's knuckles. "I want you to live with us at the Ivory Gate." The arms around Kera's body tightened. The breath against her ear hitched. Kera kept talking, eager to speak her mind. "The Traverses were responsible for your child's pain. You have no home of your own. We have room aplenty. When I spoke with the overseer, he agreed to release Morpheus's pension to me. The Ivory Gate will be mine, and I will have the means to pay for it and our family."

"Our family," Aurora echoed.

"You and Faith and my own children. *Our* family."

Aurora's mouth fell open, her embrace loosened just enough for Kera to turn and meet her eyes. "I want to see you every day. I want to hold you. I *missed* having you by my side at Hame Argyll. I do not want to feel that way again. I do not want to be apart from you. And should this affection die . . . then it ends. But I have no desire to push you away or leave you alone when it is in my capacity to continue to hold you close if that's what you wish for."

"I'm not what your neighbors will want to see. What your family will want to see. I slept with your husband," Aurora reminded her uselessly.

Kera had thought about it for some time. She'd had three hours of flying time to think about it. Three hours of Raslidor eavesdropping on her thoughts and offering occasional bits of advice. Three hours to come to terms with what exactly she even wanted from Aurora. If she had only wanted temporary relief, or if she wanted something far more permanent.

Her sister . . . would need convincing. Ciara had been furious with Mori when the affair had become known, and she'd had nothing nice to say about Aurora in all the days since. They had never met, but reputation alone would mean Ciara had an opinion set in stone. But stone could be eroded. It could be smoothed out. It could be shaped and warped into a new image.

Given enough time, Kera knew full well that her sister would come around and accept their arrangement and their decision. She would support her. Kera wished Gale were still alive too. Gale not only would have supported Aurora, but she would have happily spent her days chatting to her about all of the things they had in common. She would have relished the bravery that Aurora so easily displayed and begged for stories and advice.

"You would have loved my little sister," Kera told Aurora. Aurora's lips twitched. It was not an answer to her concern, but somehow she felt as though Aurora understood. Perhaps, like the griffons, they were starting to understand each other's true thoughts and intentions. "I will manage my family. I will handle the neighbors. I will bear that burden, if you will do me the honor of bearing mine. Please . . . I want you to stay with me."

Aurora flushed again but nodded in response. "Okay," she said slowly, accent thick. "Let's give it a try."

Kera kissed her, and looked forward to doing it every day in the future yet to come.

The next day, Raslidor escorted them to the edge of the Long Lakes, accepting hugs and kisses from the children and nuzzling both Aurora and Kera politely. They sat crouched, happily digging their talons into the ground. The talons Raslidor had freely given during their time at the Long Lakes had already started to regrow. Fresh black claws peeked out amongst fur-coated feathers. It would take time, but soon each claw that was shed would return like they had never lost it.

Kera was allowed to keep her talon knife.

She thanked the griffon, down from the bottom of her heart. There were not enough words to express her gratitude, but Raslidor merely told her that they would like to see her again. That she and her family would always be welcome to join them at the Long Lakes. They were even encouraged to take a handful of feathers with them for good fortune in their lives. Faith and Aiden both promised to return, and Kera imagined they would have many, many adventures when they grew older. She hoped they enjoyed them all.

Riding Najah's horses back to Mount Maladh, Kera found the return journey took more time than they'd anticipated. Faith and Aiden both longed to run about, and neither Kera nor Aurora had the heart to stop them. They watched over their children, instead, as they took turns chasing each other, their laughter and joy worth every delayed moment on the road.

Both children were ecstatic with their health, and they clung to it with the steadfast determination of the formerly ill. They told jokes and teased each other. Faith tickled Aiden's sides, and he called her his sister just as she called him her brother. They were family. At the end of all their travels, they had become a family.

It took almost a week to arrive at Mount Maladh, but once there, Najah very nearly burst with glee. She threw them a party, and they bathed and joined her for the feast. Najah sat at the piano and played beautiful music for them, and Kera took Aurora by the hand and taught her how to dance. She led and Aurora followed. They counted the beats together, one, two, three, one, two, three, one, two, three, and Kera told her she had never seen anyone so beautiful in all her life.

Kera ran her hands over the smooth gown Najah had lent Aurora, grinning when Aurora arched into her touch. No one was looking at them, and Kera took it as all the incentive she needed. She pulled Aurora after her, and found an alcove where they could hide themselves away, giving herself permission to continue feeling the curves of Aurora's hips and the swell of her breasts. They cupped each other's faces and traded tender kisses, stopping only when Najah indelicately informed them that they had a room quite available for them. Aurora blushed furiously, and Kera did too, but she took it as the invitation it was and quickly led her partner up the stairs.

It would take time to reach the Ivory Gate, but they had time. So they spent their evening touching and loving one another. They slept curled in each other's arms, Aurora whispering that there was nothing to fear, the wraith was gone. Kera still kept her knife by her bedside anyway, and they didn't talk about it. They didn't have to. Aurora understood, and Kera loved that about her.

She truly did.

Some days later, Najah made them promise to return as soon as they could, and Kera begged her to visit them at the Ivory Gate. They returned one of her horses, but the other Najah gave them as a gift. Victor was fed, happy, and just as well rested as they were when they prepared him for the journey home. He'd been well taken care of, and he nuzzled them as they saddled him once more.

All of them were ready for consistency to return.

By the time they reached Ship's Landing, news had already spread about the Traverses' arrests. In fact, there was a palpable difference in the air. People recognized Kera. They recognized Aurora. They all stopped and stared, whispering as they watched their party return. Some even started cheering, and it was so absurd and ridiculous, Kera couldn't help but urge her horse on just that much faster.

Crowds started forming soon enough, people thanking them as they went; some women even waved their handkerchiefs obscenely. Aiden scrunched his nose at it all and asked Kera, "Why's everyone acting funny?"

To which Aurora shortly replied, "Because they have nothing better to do."

It made Kera laugh the rest of the way to the Ivory Gate, even though it took far longer than she had hoped and the crowds showed no signs of stopping. Hurriedly, Kera led Aurora to the stable, managed to get the horses into their stalls, and brought the children inside. They locked the door behind them and shared a look of total unabashed humor.

They couldn't enjoy the peace for long.

Kera barely had a chance to catch her breath before she heard her name being called. She looked down the hall and was swept immediately into her older sister's arms. Ciara latched on to her and Kera realized she was crying. She was calling Kera's name and pulling back so she could inspect her face and throat. Exclaiming, "Oh God, what have you done to yourself?" as she fussed.

"I'm quite all right," Kera promised.

"Aunt Ciara!" Aiden cried out, always keen on getting attention of his own. Ciara traded targets immediately, picking up her nephew and tossing him in the air, catching him and snuggling him as he giggled and shrieked in delight. "Oh, Aiden! Aiden! You're all right!"

Aurora and Faith stood awkwardly in the foyer, but Kera took their hands. She led them through to the den, where she set them both on her sofa, only vaguely aware that Ciara was following her. Her sister sat down across from them and smiled so brightly, tears in her eyes. "They're calling you a hero!" she announced. "A hero! The overseer has told everyone what you did! What you've been through! It's remarkable! You saved the city!"

It wasn't how Kera would have phrased it, and she said as much to Ciara. She'd never set out to the Long Lakes to save the city. Her sister didn't care. She always took pride in anything Kera did, no matter what it was. Ciara glanced at Aurora and paused only briefly before returning her attention to Kera. "Please, you must tell me everything," she insisted.

Kera sat with her hands folded neatly in her lap. Aurora, to her left, gave her strength to speak. Her newly proclaimed daughter, on her right, silently offered support where she could. Kera would have preferred to have this conversation with a little less excitement, but there was no stopping hurricane Ciara. She wasn't interested in waiting for later, she wanted to hear it now.

So, with her family piecing itself together and her home finally secure, Kera smiled, and she told the story of how she saved her children, and how she found love.

Dear Reader,

Thank you for reading Lindsey Byrd's *On the Subject of Griffons*!

We know your time is precious and you have many, many entertainment options, so it means a lot that you've chosen to spend your time reading. We really hope you enjoyed it.

We'd be honored if you'd consider posting a review—good or bad—on sites like **Amazon, Barnes & Noble, Kobo, Goodreads, Twitter, Facebook, Tumblr,** and your blog or website. We'd also be honored if you told your friends and family about this book. Word of mouth is a book's lifeblood!

For more information on upcoming releases, author interviews, blog tours, contests, giveaways, and more, please sign up for our weekly, spam-free newsletter and visit us around the web:

    Newsletter: riptidepublishing.com/newsletter
    Twitter: twitter.com/RiptideBooks
    Facebook: facebook.com/RiptidePublishing
    Goodreads: tinyurl.com/RiptideOnGoodreads
    Tumblr: riptidepublishing.tumblr.com

Thank you so much for Reading the Rainbow!

RiptidePublishing.com

ACKNOWLEDGMENTS

There have been endless iterations of this book since I first started writing it, but this version could never have existed if it wasn't for my best friend, Alex, who read and reread this story time and again, listened to me talk about characters for hours, and who was endlessly supportive through every step of this process. Words cannot express how grateful I am for you, your presence in my life, and the friendship you've given me. Thank you, Alex, I couldn't have done it without you.

I also want to thank my husband. Wes, you are the most inspirational person I've ever met. I have rewritten this acknowledgment so many times, trying to figure out how to express on paper exactly what you mean to me. Perhaps the only words that feel right are these: I found you, and with you I am found. I love you more than anyone will ever know, and I can't wait to face our next adventure together. Thank you, mun. I'm with you no matter what.

ABOUT THE
AUTHOR

Lindsey Byrd was brought up in upstate, downstate, and western New York. She is a budding historian of law, medieval, and women's studies and often includes historical anecdotes or references within her works. Lindsey enjoys writing about complex and convoluted issues where finding the moral high ground can be hard to do. She has a particular love for heroic villains and villainous heroes, as well as inverting and subverting tropes.

Twitter: twitter.com/TheLindseyByrd
Tumblr: tumblr.com/blog/lindseybyrd
Email: thelindseybyrd@gmail.com
Goodreads: goodreads.com/LindseyByrd

Enjoy more stories like
On the Subject of Griffons
at RiptidePublishing.com!